THE
NIGHT SHE
DISAPPEARED

Also by Lisa Jewell

Invisible Girl

The Family Upstairs

Watching You

Then She Was Gone

I Found You

The Girls in the Garden

The Third Wife

The House We Grew Up In

Before I Met You

The Making of Us

After the Party

The Truth About Melody Browne

31 Dream Street

A Friend of the Family

Vince & Joy

One-Hit Wonder

Thirtynothing

Ralph's Party

THE
NIGHT SHE
DISAPPEARED

A Novel

LISA JEWELL

ATRIA BOOKS

New York   London   Toronto   Sydney   New Delhi

ATRIA
BOOKS

An Imprint of Simon & Schuster, Inc.
1230 Avenue of the Americas
New York, NY 10020

First Atria Books hardcover edition September 2021

ATRIA B O O K S and colophon are trademarks of Simon & Schuster, Inc.

For information about special discounts for bulk purchases, please contact Simon & Schuster Special Sales at 1-866-506-1949 or business@simonandschuster.com.

The Simon & Schuster Speakers Bureau can bring authors to your live event. For more information or to book an event, contact the Simon & Schuster Speakers Bureau at 1-866-248-3049 or visit our website at www.simonspeakers.com.

Interior design by Erika R. Genova

Manufactured in the United States of America

1 3 5 7 9 10 8 6 4 2

Library of Congress Cataloging-in-Publication Data

Names: Jewell, Lisa, author.
Title: The night she disappeared : a novel / Lisa Jewell.
Description: First Atria Books hardcover edition. | New York : Atria Books, 2021.
Identifiers: LCCN 2021015888 (print) | LCCN 2021015889 (ebook) |
ISBN 9781982137366 (hardcover) | ISBN 9781982137380 (ebook)
Subjects: LCSH: Psychological fiction. | GSAFD: Suspense fiction.
Classification: LCC PR6060.E95 N54 2021 (print) | LCC PR6060.E95 (ebook) | DDC 823/.914—dc23
LC record available at https://lccn.loc.gov/2021015888
LC ebook record available at https://lccn.loc.gov/2021015889

ISBN 978-1-9821-3736-6
ISBN 978-1-9821-3738-0 (ebook)

This book is dedicated to my dad

THE
NIGHT SHE
DISAPPEARED

Arachnophobia

Arachnophobia. It's one of those words that sounds as bad as that which it describes. The hard *ack* at the end of the second syllable suggestive of the repulsive angles of a spider's legs; the soft sweep of the *f* like the awful wave of nausea that washes through your gut at the suggestion of a sudden movement across a wall or floor; the loud *no* at its center the sound of your brain screaming, in disgust, nononono.

Tallulah suffers from arachnophobia.

Tallulah is in the dark.

PART ONE

1

JUNE 2017

The baby is starting to grumble. Kim sits still in her chair and holds her breath. It's taken her all night to get him to sleep. It's Friday, a sultry midsummer night, and normally she'd be out with friends at this time. Eleven o'clock: she'd be at the bar getting in the last round for the road. But tonight she's in joggers and a T-shirt, her dark hair tied up in a bun, contacts out, glasses on, and a glass of lukewarm wine on the coffee table that she poured herself earlier and hasn't had a chance to drink.

She clicks the volume down on the TV using the remote and listens again.

There it is, the very early outposts of crying, a kind of dry, ominous chirruping.

Kim has never really liked babies. She liked her own well enough, but did find the early years testing and ill-suited to her sensibilities. From the first night that both her children slept through the night, Kim has placed a very—possibly disproportionately—high value on an unbroken night. She had her kids young and easily had time enough and room in her heart for another one or two. But she could not face the prospect of sleepless nights again. For years she has protected her sleep vigilantly with the help of eye masks and earplugs and pillow sprays and huge tubs of melatonin that her friend brings back for her from the States.

And then, just over twelve months ago, her teenage daughter, Tallulah, had a baby. And now Kim is a grandmother at the age of thirty-nine and there is a crying baby in her house again, soon, it feels, *so soon*, after her own babies stopped crying.

For the most part, despite it happening ten years before she was ready for it, having a grandson has been blessing after blessing. His name is Noah and he has dark hair like Kim, like both of Kim's children (Kim only really likes babies with dark hair; blond-haired babies freak her out). Noah has eyes that oscillate between brown and amber depending on the light and he has solid legs and solid arms with circlets of fat at the wrists. He's quick to smile and laugh and he's happy to entertain himself, sometimes for as long as half an hour at a time. Kim looks after him when Tallulah goes to college and she occasionally gets a kick of panic in her gut at the realization that she has not heard him make a noise for a few minutes. She rushes to his high chair or to the swing seat or to the corner of the sofa to check that he is still alive and finds him deep in thought whilst turning the pages of a fabric book.

Noah is a dreamy baby. But he does not like to sleep and Kim finds this darkly stressful.

At the moment Tallulah and Noah live here with Kim, alongside Zach, Noah's father. Noah sleeps between them in Tallulah's double bed and Kim puts in her earplugs and plays some white noise on her smartphone and is generally saved from the nighttime cacophony of Noah's sleeplessness.

But tonight Zach has taken Tallulah out on what they're calling a "date night," which sounds strangely middle-aged for a pair of nineteen-year-olds. They've gone to the very pub that Kim would normally be sitting in tonight. She slipped Zach a twenty-pound note as they were leaving and told them to have fun. It's the first time they've been out as a couple since before Noah was born. They split up while Tallulah was pregnant and got back together again about six months ago with Zach pledging to be the best dad in the world. And, so far, he's been true to his word.

Noah's crying has kicked in properly now and Kim sighs and gets to her feet.

As she does so her phone buzzes with a text message. She clicks it and reads.

Mum, there's some ppl here from college, they asked us back to theirs. Just for an hour or so. Is that OK? ☺

Then, as she's typing a reply, another message follows immediately.

Is Noah OK?

Noah is fine, she types. *Good as gold. Go and have fun. Stay as long as you like. Love you.*

Kim goes upstairs to Noah's cot, her heart heavy with the prospect of another hour of rocking and soothing and sighing and whispering in the dark while the moon hangs out there in the balmy midsummer sky, which still holds pale smudges of daylight, and the house creaks emptily and other people sit in pubs. But as she approaches him, the moonlight catches the curve of his cheek and she sees his eyes light up at the sight of her, hears his breath catch with relief that someone has come, and sees his arms reach up to her.

She collects him up and places him against her chest and says, "What's all the fuss now, baby boy, what's all the fuss?" and her heart suddenly expands and contracts with the knowledge that this boy is a part of her and that he loves her, that he is not seeking out his mother, he is content for *her* to come to him in the dark of night to comfort him.

She takes Noah into the living room and sits him on her lap. She gives him the remote control to play with; he loves to press the buttons, but Kim can tell he's too tired to press buttons—he wants to sleep. As he grows heavy on top of her, she knows she should put him back into his cot, good sleep hygiene, good habits, all of that, but now Kim is tired too and her eyes grow heavy and she pulls the throw from the sofa across her lap and adjusts the cushion behind her head and she and Noah fall silently into a peaceful slumber.

Kim awakes suddenly several hours later. The brief midsummer night is almost over and the sky through the living room window is shimmering with the first blades of hot morning sun. She straightens her neck and feels all the muscles shout at her. Noah is still heavy with sleep and she gently adjusts him so that she can reach her phone. It's 4:20 in the morning.

She feels a small blast of annoyance. She knows she told Tallulah to stay out as late as she likes, but this is madness. She brings up Tallulah's number and calls it. It goes straight to voicemail so she brings up Zach's number and calls it. Again it goes to voicemail.

Maybe, she thinks, maybe they came in in the night and saw Noah asleep on top of her and decided that it would be nice to have the bed to themselves. She pictures them peering at her around the door of the living room and taking off their shoes, tiptoeing up the stairs, and jumping into the empty bed in a tangle of arms and legs and playful, drunken kisses.

Slowly, carefully, she tucks Noah into herself and gets off the sofa. She climbs the stairs and goes to the door of Tallulah's room. It's wide-open, just as she left it at eleven o'clock the night before when she came to collect Noah. She lowers him gently into his cot and, miraculously, he does not stir. Then she sits on the side of Tallulah's bed and calls her phone again.

Once more it goes straight to voicemail. She calls Zach. It goes to voicemail. She continues this ping-pong game for another hour. The sun is fully risen now; it is morning, but too early to call anyone else. So Kim makes herself a coffee and cuts herself a slice of bread off the farmhouse loaf she always buys Tallulah for the weekend and eats it with butter, and honey bought from the beekeeper down the road who sells it from his front door, and she waits and waits for the day to begin.

2

"Mr. Gray! Welcome!"

Sophie sees a silver-haired man striding toward them down the wood-paneled corridor. His hand is already extended although he has another ten feet to cover.

He gets to Shaun and grasps his hand warmly, wrapping it inside both of his as if Shaun is a small child with cold hands that need warming up.

Then he turns to Sophie and says, "Mrs. Gray! So lovely to meet you at last!"

"Miss Beck, actually, sorry," says Sophie.

"Ah yes, of course. Stupid of me. I did know that. Miss Beck. Peter Doody. Executive Head."

Peter Doody beams at her. His teeth are unnaturally white for a man in his early sixties. "And I hear you are a novelist?"

Sophie nods.

"What sort of books do you write?"

"Detective novels," she replies.

"Detective novels! Well, well, well! I'm sure you'll find lots to inspire you here at Maypole House. There's never a dull day. Just make sure you change the names!" He laughs loudly at his own joke. "Where have you parked?" he asks Shaun, indicating the driveway beyond the huge doorway.

"Oh," says Shaun, "just there, next to you. I hope that's OK?"

"Perfect, just perfect." He peers over Shaun's shoulder. "And the little ones?"

"With their mother. In London."

"Ah yes, of course."

Sophie and Shaun follow Peter Doody, wheeling their suitcases down one of the three long corridors that branch off the main hallway. They push through double doors and into a glass tunnel that connects the old house to the modern block, and continue wheeling the cases out of a door at the back of the modern block and down a curved path toward a small Victorian cottage that backs directly onto woodland and is surrounded by a ring of rosebushes just coming into late-summer bloom.

Peter takes a bunch of keys from his pocket and removes a pair on a brass ring. Sophie has seen the cottage once before, but only as the home of the previous head teacher, filled with their furnishings and ephemera, their dogs, their photographs. Peter unlocks the door and they follow him into the flagstone back hallway. The Wellington boots have gone, the waxed jackets and dog leads hanging from the hooks. There is a petrolic, smoky smell in here, and a cold draft coming up from between the floorboards, which makes the cottage feel strangely wintery on this dog day of a long, hot summer.

Maypole House is in the picturesque village of Upfield Common in the Surrey Hills. It was once the manor house of the village until twenty years ago, when it was bought up by a company called Magenta that owns schools and colleges all over the world and turned into a private boarding school for sixteen-to-nineteen-year-olds who'd flunked their GCSEs and A levels first time around. So, yes, a school for failures, in essence. And Sophie's boyfriend, Shaun, is now the new head teacher.

"Here." Peter tips the keys into Shaun's hand. "All yours. When is the rest of your stuff arriving?"

"Three o'clock," replies Shaun.

Peter checks the time on his Apple Watch and says, "Well, then, looks like you've got plenty of time for a pub lunch. My treat!"

"Oh." Shaun looks at Sophie. "Erm, we brought lunch with us, actually." He indicates a canvas bag on the floor by his feet. "But thank you, anyway."

Peter seems unperturbed. "Well, just for future reference, the local pub is superb. The Swan and Ducks. Other side of the common. Does a kind of Mediterranean, meze, tapas type of menu. The calamari stew is incredible. And an excellent wine cellar. Manager there will give you a discount when you tell him who you are."

He looks at his watch again and says, "Well, anyway. I'll let you both settle in. All the codes are here. You'll need this one to let the van in when it arrives and this one is for the front door. Your card will operate all the interior doors." He hands them a lanyard each. "And I will be back tomorrow morning for our first day's work. FYI, you may see some strangely dressed folks around; there's been an external residential course running here all week, some kind of *Glee*-type thing. It's the last day today, they'll be leaving tomorrow, and Kerryanne Mulligan, the matron—you met her last week, I believe?"

Shaun nods.

"She's looking after the group so you don't need to worry yourself about them. And that, I think, is that. Except, oh . . ." He strides toward the fridge and opens the door. "A little something, from Magenta to you." A single bottle of cheap champagne sits in the empty fridge. He closes the door, puts his hands into the pockets of his blue chinos, and then takes them out again to shake both their hands.

And then he is gone and Shaun and Sophie are alone in their new home for the very first time. They look at each other and then around and then at each other again. Sophie bends down to the canvas bag and pulls out the two wineglasses she'd packed this morning as they'd prepared to leave Shaun's house in Lewisham. She unwraps them from the tissue paper, rests them on the counter, pulls open the fridge, and grabs the champagne.

Then she takes Shaun's outstretched hand and follows him to the garden. It's west-facing and cast in shade at this time of the day, but it's still just warm enough to sit with bare arms.

While Shaun uncorks the champagne and pours them each a glass, Sophie lets her gaze roam across the view: a wooden gate between the rosebushes that form the boundary of the back garden leads to a velvety green woodland interspersed with patches of lawn onto which the midday sun falls through the treetops into pools of gold. She can hear the sound of birds shimmying in the branches. She can hear the champagne bubbles fizzing in the wineglasses. She can hear her own breath in her lungs, the blood passing through the veins on her temples.

She notices Shaun looking at her.

"Thank you," he says. "Thank you so much."

"What for!"

"You know what for." He takes her hands in his. "How much you're sacrificing to be here with me. I don't deserve you. I really don't."

"You do deserve me. I'm 'sloppy seconds,' remember?"

They smile wryly at each other. This is one of the many unpleasant things that Shaun's ex-wife, Pippa, had found to say about Sophie when she'd first found out about her. Also, "She looks much older than thirty-four," and, "She has a strangely flat backside."

"Well, whatever you are, you're the best. And I love you." He kisses her knuckles hard and then lets her hands go so that she can pick up her glass.

"Pretty, isn't it?" Sophie says dreamily, staring through the back gate and into the woods. "Where do they go?"

"I have no idea," he replies. "Maybe you should go for a wander after lunch?"

"Yes," says Sophie. "Maybe I will."

———————

Shaun and Sophie have only been together for six months. They met when Sophie came to Shaun's school to give a talk about publishing and writing to a group of his A-level English students. He took her for lunch as a "thank you" and at first she felt nervous, as if she'd done something wrong; the association between being alone with an older male teacher and having done something wrong was buried so deep into her psyche she couldn't override it. But then she'd noticed that he had very, very dark brown eyes, almost black, and that his shoulders were broad and that he had a wonderful warm, hearty laugh and a soft mouth and no wedding band and then she realized that he was flirting with her and then there was an email from him in her inbox a day later, sent from his private email address, thanking her for coming in and wondering if she might like to try the new Korean place they'd chatted about at lunch the previous day, maybe on Friday night, and she'd thought, I have never been on a date with a man in his forties, I have never been on a date with a man who wears a tie to work, and I have not, in fact, been on a date for five full years, and I really would like to try the new Korean place, so why not?

It was during their first date that Shaun told her he was leaving the big secondary school in Lewisham where he was head of sixth form at the end of the term to be a head teacher at a private boarding sixth-form college in the Surrey Hills. Not because he wanted to be in the private sector, working in a mahogany-lined office, but because his ex-wife, Pippa, was moving their twins from the perfectly nice state primary they'd both been at for three years to an expensive private school and expected him to contribute half of their school fees.

At first the implications of this development hadn't really hit Sophie. March tumbled into April tumbled into May tumbled into June and she and Shaun became closer and closer and their lives became more and more intertwined and then Sophie met Shaun's twins, who let her put them to bed and read them stories and comb their hair, and then it was the summer holidays and she and Shaun started to spend even more time together, and then one night, drinking cocktails on a roof terrace overlooking the Thames, Shaun said, "Come with me. Come with me to Maypole House."

Sophie's gut reaction had been no. No no no no no. She was a Londoner. She was independent. She had a career of her own. A social life. Her family lived in London. But as July turned to August and Shaun's departure drew ever closer and the fabric of her life started to feel as though it were stretching out of shape, she turned her thinking around. Maybe, she thought, it would be nice to live in the countryside. Maybe she could focus more on work, without all the distractions of city living. Maybe she'd enjoy the status of being the head teacher's partner, the cachet of being the first lady of such an exclusive place. She went with Shaun to visit the school and she walked around the cottage and felt the warm solidity of the terra-cotta tiles beneath her feet, smelled the sensuous fragrance of wild roses, of freshly mowed grass, of sun-warmed jasmine through the back door. She saw a space below a window in the hallway that was just the right size for her writing desk, with a view across the school grounds. She thought, I am thirty-four. Soon I will be thirty-five. I have been alone for a long, long time. Maybe I should do this ridiculous thing.

And so she said yes.

She and Shaun made the most of every minute of their last few weeks in London. They sat on every pavement terrace in South London, ate every kind of obscure ethnic cuisine, watched films in multistory car parks, wandered around pop-up food fairs, picnicked in the park to the background sounds of grime music and sirens and diesel engines. They spent ten days in Majorca in a cool Airbnb in downtown Palma with a balcony overlooking the marina. They spent weekends with Shaun's children and took them to the South Bank to run through the fountains, for al fresco lunches at Giraffe and Wahaca, to the Tate Modern, to the playgrounds in Kensington Gardens.

And then she'd leased her one-bedroom flat in New Cross

to a friend, canceled her gym membership, signed out of her Tuesday-night writers' group, packed some boxes, and joined Shaun here, in the middle of nowhere.

And now, as the sun shines down through the tops of the towering trees, splashing dapples onto the dark fabric of her dress and the ground beneath her feet, Sophie starts to feel the beginning of happiness, a sense that this decision borne of pragmatism might in fact have been some kind of magical act of destiny unfurling, that they were meant to be here, that this will be good for her, good for both of them.

Shaun takes their lunch things through to the kitchen. She hears the tap go on and the clatter of dishes being laid down in the butler's sink.

"I'm going for a wander," she calls to Shaun through the open window.

She turns to put the latch on the gate as she leaves the back garden and as she does so her eye is caught by something nailed to the wooden fence.

A piece of cardboard, a flap torn from a box by the look of it.

Scrawled on it in marker and with an arrow pointing down to the earth are the words "Dig Here."

She stares at it curiously for a moment. Maybe, she thinks, it's left over from a treasure trail, a party game, or a team-building exercise from the *Glee* course that is finishing today. Maybe, she thinks, it's a time capsule.

But then something else flashes through her mind. A jolting déjà vu. A certainty that she has seen this exact thing before: a cardboard sign nailed to a fence. The words "Dig Here" in black marker pen. A downward-pointing arrow. She has seen this before.

But she cannot for the life of her remember where.

3

Zach's mum is older than Kim. Zach is her youngest child; she has another four, all girls, all much older than him. Her name is Megs. She answers the door to Kim in cargo shorts and a voluminous green linen top, sunglasses on her head, a patch of sunburn on the bridge of her nose.

"Kim," she says. Then she turns immediately to Noah and beams at him. "Hello, my beautiful bubba," she says. She chucks him under the chin, and then glances back at Kim. "Everything OK?"

"Have you seen the kids?" Kim says, hitching Noah onto her other hip. She walked here without the pram; it's hot and Noah is heavy.

"Tallulah, you mean? And Zach?"

"Yeah." She shifts Noah again.

"No. I mean, they're at yours, aren't they?"

"No, they went to the pub last night, no sign of them now, and they're not answering their phones. I thought maybe they might have come back to yours to crash."

"No, love, no. Just me and Simon here. Do you want to come in? We're just out in the garden. We can try calling them again?"

In Megs's back garden, Kim lowers Noah down on the grass next to a push-along plastic toy that he attempts to pull himself up onto. Megs takes out her phone and presses in her son's number. Megs's husband, Simon, nods at Kim curtly and then turns back to his newspaper. Kim's always had a horrible feeling that Simon finds her attractive and that his offhand manner is his way of dealing with how uncomfortable this makes him feel.

Megs scowls and ends the call. "Straight through to voicemail," she says. "Let me call Nick."

Kim throws her a questioning look.

"You know, the barman from the Ducks? Hold on." She prods the screen of her phone with blue acrylic nails. "Nick, love, it's Megs. How are you? How's your mum? Good. Good. Listen, were you working last night? You didn't happen to see Zach in there, did you?"

Kim watches Megs nod a lot, listens to her making receptive noises. She pulls a lump of earth from Noah's hand just as he's about to press it into his mouth and waits patiently.

Finally Megs ends the call. "Apparently," she says, "Zach and Tallulah went off after the pub to someone's house, someone Tallulah knows from college."

"Yeah, I know that. But any idea who?"

"Scarlett someone. And a couple of others. Nick seemed to think they were heading out of the village. They went in a car."

"Scarlett?"

"Yes. Nick said she's one of the posh kids from the Maypole."

Kim nods. She's never heard of a Scarlett. But then, Tallulah doesn't really talk much to her about college. Once she's home, Noah is pretty much the only topic of conversation in the house.

"Anything else?" she asks, pulling Noah onto her lap.

"That's all he had, I'm afraid." Megs smiles at Noah and stretches her arms out toward him, but he curls himself closer to Kim and Kim sees Megs's smile falter. "Should we be worried? Do you think?"

Kim shrugs. "I honestly don't know."

"Have you tried calling Tallulah's friends?"

"I don't have any numbers for them. They're all on her phone."

Megs sighs and leans back into her chair. "It's strange," she says. "If it weren't for the baby, I'd just assume they were sleeping something off somewhere, you know, they're so young, and God knows the things I got up to at their age. But they're both so devoted, aren't they, to Noah. It just seems a bit . . ."

"I know." Kim nods. "It does."

Kim wishes that she and Megs were closer, but Megs never seemed to believe in Zach and Tallulah as a couple, and then after Noah was born she backed off completely for a while, barely visiting Noah and acting like a distracted aunt when she did. And now she's missed her moment with Noah, who recognizes her but doesn't know that she's important.

"Anyway," Kim says. "I'll go and do some research into this Scarlett girl. See what I can dig up. But hopefully, I won't need to. Hopefully, they'll be home by the time I get back, looking sheepish."

Megs smiles. "You know what," she says, brightly, in a tone of voice that suggests that really she just wants to get back to relaxing in the garden in the sun, that she really isn't in the mood for worry, "I bet you anything they are."

In Tallulah's room, Kim rifles through the contents of her schoolbag. Tallulah is studying social care; she wants to be a social worker. Most of her coursework is done at home and she has to go into college only three times a week. Kim watches her at the bus stop from the front window sometimes, her fresh-faced baby in her casual college gear, her hair tied back, clutching a folder to her chest. Nobody would ever guess that she has a child of her own at home, she looks so young.

Kim finds a planner in the bag and flicks through it. It's full of Tallulah's dense, somewhat inelegant handwriting—she'd started off left-handed and forced herself to learn to write with her right hand to fit in when she was at primary school. There's no point looking for phone numbers—no one writes down phone numbers anymore—but maybe Scarlett's name will appear on a class list or some such.

And there it is, glued down and folded up on the back inside cover of the planner: "Student Contacts." Kim scans it quickly, her finger coming to rest on the name "Scarlett Jacques: Student Event Planning Committee."

And there's her email address.

Kim immediately starts to type a message:

> Scarlett. This is Tallulah Murray's mum, Kim. Tallulah hasn't come home since going out last night and isn't answering her phone and I wondered if you had any idea where she might be? A friend said she was with someone called Scarlett. Please call me on this number as soon as possible. Many thanks.

She presses send and then exhales and rests the phone on her lap.

Downstairs the front door clicks shut. It's 2:00 p.m. and it'll be her son, Ryan, home from work. He works at the grocer's in the village every Saturday, saving up for his big summer holiday to Rhodes in August, his first without his mum, just with friends.

"Are they back?" he calls up the stairs to her.

"Nope," she calls back down.

She hears him dropping his keys on a surface, throwing his trainers into the pile of shoes by the front door, then bounding up the stairs.

"Seriously?" he says. "Have they called?"

"No. Not a word."

She tells him about Megs calling Nick at the pub and the girl called Scarlett, and as she talks, her phone rings with an unknown number.

"Hello?"

"Oh, hi, is this Lula's mum?"

"Yes, hi, this is Kim."

"Hi. It's Scarlett here. I just got your email."

Kim's heart begins to race painfully, then skitter.

"Oh," she says, "Scarlett. Thank you. I just wondered—"

Scarlett cuts in. "They were at my house," she says. "They left at about three a.m. That's all I can tell you."

Kim blinks; her head rocks back slightly. "And were they . . . did they . . . say where they were going?"

"They said they were going to get a cab home."

Kim doesn't like the tone of Scarlett's voice. She has one of those clipped, chilly voices that tells of four-poster beds and bohemian private schools and gravel on the driveway. But she also sounds disinterested, as though talking to Kim is beneath her somehow.

"And did they seem OK? I mean, had they had a lot to drink?"

"I guess, yeah. Lula was sick. That's why they left."

"She threw up?"

"Yeah."

Kim pictures her slight, kind girl, bent double over a flower bed, and her heart lurches.

"And did you see them? Get into a taxi?"

"No. They just left. And that was that."

"And—sorry—but where do you live, Scarlett? Just so that I can ask around the local cab companies?"

"Dark Place," she replies, "near Upley Fold."

"Street number?"

"No street number. Just that. Dark Place. Near Upley Fold."

"Oh," says Kim, drawing two rings around the words on the paper where she's written them down. "OK. Thank you. And please, if you hear anything from either of them, will you give me a ring? I mean, I don't know how well you know Tallulah . . ."

"Not that well," Scarlett interjects.

"Yes, well, she's not the type just to disappear, not to come home. And she has a baby, you know."

There's a brief pause at the other end of the line. Then, "No. I didn't know that."

Kim gives her head a small shake, tries to imagine how Zach and Tallulah could have spent a whole night with this girl without once mentioning Noah. "Well, yes. She and Zach are parents. They have a son, he's twelve months old. So not coming home is kind of a big deal."

There's another silence at the end of the line and then Scarlett says, "Right, well, yeah."

Kim says, "Call me, please, if you hear anything."

"Yeah," says Scarlett. "Sure. Bye."

And then she ends the call.

Kim stares at her phone for a moment. Then she looks up at Ryan, who has been watching the phone call curiously.

"Weird," says Kim. She relays the detail of the call to her son.

"Shall we drive over there?" he suggests. "To her house?"

"Scarlett's?"

"Yeah," says Ryan. "Let's go to Dark Place."

4

Shaun heads into work early the following morning. Sophie stands at the door of the cottage and watches as he disappears up the glass passageway, toward the main school building. He turns at the double doors and waves at her and then he is gone.

The grounds of the school are full of people wheeling small cases behind them, heading toward the car park at the front of the school. The residential *Glee* course is over, summer is coming to an end, from tomorrow the boarding-school students will start returning. Cleaners wait in the shadows to enter their vacated rooms and prepare them for the new term.

She heads back into the cottage now. It's a pleasant house, functional. The air inside is clammy and cool with small windows grown over with ivy and wisteria branches that don't let in much light. It still smells of other people and there's that odd, damp bonfire smell in the hallway, which seems to emanate from between the floorboards. She's covered the floorboards over with a runner and placed a reed diffuser on the sideboard, but it still lingers. It's going to take a while to make the cottage feel like home, but it will, she knows it will. Shaun's children are coming the weekend after next: that will bring it to life.

Sophie turns to a box that she is halfway through unpacking when there is a knock at the door.

"Hello?"

"Oh, hi! It's Kerryanne! The matron!"

Sophie opens the door and sees a woman with thick golden hair held back with sunglasses, bright blue eyes, and sun-burnished cleavage. She's wearing a maxi dress and bejeweled flip-flops. She does not look like a matron.

"Hi!" says Sophie, reaching out to shake her hand. "Lovely to meet you!"

"You too. You must be Sophie?"

"Correct!"

Kerryanne has a huge set of keys hanging from her hand. "How are you settling in?" she says, passing the keys from one hand to the other. "Got everything you need?"

"Yes!" says Sophie. "Yes. Everything's just fine. Shaun's first day. He headed into work about ten minutes ago."

"Yes, I just saw him. We exchanged pleasantries! Anyway, I wanted you to take my number, in case you need anything. Obviously, my primary function is student welfare, but I'll be keeping my eye out for you as well. I know how weird and new everything must be feeling, so please consider me to be your matron too. And if you're missing home and need a shoulder to cry on . . ."

Sophie blinks, not sure if she's being serious or not, but Kerryanne beams at her and says, "Just joking. But honestly, anything you need—advice about the village, about the staff, the kids, *whatever*. Please just text me. And I'm on the second floor of Alpha block, just"—she crouches slightly to peer beneath an overhanging tree on the periphery of Shaun and Sophie's garden—"that window there. With the balcony. Room number 205." She passes Sophie a piece of paper with her details written on it in neat, schoolteachery script.

"Is it just you?"

"Most of the time, yeah. My daughter comes to stay sometimes, Lexie, she's a travel blogger so she comes and goes. But mostly it's just me. And I hear there'll be some little ones here from time to time?"

"Yes. Jack and Lily. Twins. They're seven."

"Aw. Nice age. Right, well, any questions, anything at all, just ask. I've worked here for twenty years. I've lived in the village for nearly sixty. There's nothing I don't know about Upfield Common. In fact, you and Shaun should come over for a drink tonight, I can chew your ears off over a glass of wine."

"Oh," says Sophie. "That would be lovely. Thank you." She is about to thank her again and head back indoors, when her eye is caught by a pair of magpies taking flight from the treetops in the woodland beyond her garden. "Those woods?" She gestures at them. "Where do they lead?"

"Oh, you don't want to go too far into those woods."

Sophie throws Kerryanne a questioning look.

"They go on for miles. You'll get lost."

"Yes, but where do they come out at?"

"Depends which direction you go in. There's a hamlet about a mile and a half that way." She points to the left. "Upley Fold. Church, village hall, a few houses. It's quite pretty. And if you head straight for a mile or so"—she points ahead—"there's the back end of a big house. 'Dark Place,' it's called. Empty now. It belongs to a hedge-fund manager from the Channel Islands and his very glamorous wife." She rolls her eyes slightly. "Their daughter was a student here for a while, actually. Scarlett. Amazingly talented girl. But I really wouldn't recommend trying to get there. Students head over there sometimes because there's an old swimming pool and a tennis court, but then they can't find their way back and there's no signal in the woods. We even had to get the bloody police involved once." She rolls her eyes again.

Sophie nods. She's feeling a bristle of excitement. In London when she needs writing inspiration, she'll walk up to Dulwich or Blackheath and look at the grand old houses there and imagine the stories that lie within. Now she thinks of her walking stick and her compass and her water bottle and the opportunity to get some proper steps on her fitness app. The sun is hazy, it's about seventy-two degrees, perfect walking weather. The words "old pool" and "tennis court" swim through her imagination. She thinks of the dryness of the air of a house abandoned throughout a long, hot summer, the bleached lawns, the dusty, cracked flagstones, the birds nesting in grimy window casements.

She smiles at Kerryanne. "I'll try to resist the urge," she says.

5

Scarlett Jacques is standing next to Tallulah in the queue at the canteen. She is five foot ten, thin as a stick; her bleached hair is dyed pale blue and gathered on top of her head in a bundle and someone has drawn a tiny rainbow on her cheekbone. She's wearing a man's hoodie, with sleeves that come to her knuckles, and a pair of oversize jersey shorts, with high-top trainers. Her fingers are covered with heavyweight rings and her fingernails are painted green. She hovers over the miniature cereal boxes, her fingers dancing across their spines until they land, decisively, on Rice Krispies. She grabs it and adds it to her tray, next to a carton of chocolate soya milk and an apple.

Tallulah watches her head to the till. Her people are already gravitating toward her, following in her wake, ensuring that they will find space next to her once she has decided where she will sit. Tallulah picks up a ham sandwich and an orange juice and pays for them. She sits at a table close to Scarlett's.

Scarlett sits with her long legs stretched out, her huge high-top trainers resting on the chair opposite her, her shins still boasting a silky summer tan. She opens the chocolate soya milk and pours it onto her Rice Krispies, then lowers her face to the bowl and shovels them into her mouth with a spoon. At one point she spills chocolate milk down her chin and wipes it away with the cuff of her hoodie. She's with the kids she always hangs around with. Tallulah doesn't know their names. Scarlett and her clique all used to go to the posh school in Tallulah's village, Maypole House, which has a reputation for being for thick rich kids or rich kids with behavioral issues or rich kids with ADHD or rich kids with drug-abuse problems. They screech around the village in their convertible Mini Clubmans, stalk into the local pubs with their fake IDs and their loud voices and their rich-kid hair. In the co-op you could hear them before you saw them, calling to each other across the aisles about how there was no fresh mozzarella, then talking across the heads of the village teenagers manning the tills as if they didn't even exist.

Now a small group of them has, for some unknown reason, ended up at the local further education college in Manton, the nearest town. Most of them are in their first year of a fine art diploma. A couple of them are studying fashion. They clearly all come from families that had expected them to end up in good universities and instead had ended up at Manton College of Further Education and consequently there is a defensiveness about them.

Tallulah puts a hand to her belly. The flesh there is still so loose and blubbery. It's been nearly three months since she gave birth, but it feels like half her insides are still made of baby. She just stopped breastfeeding a week ago and her breasts still leak sometimes and she keeps pads inside her bra. She switches on her phone and looks at the photo of Noah on her home screen. Her stomach flips, a mixture of unbearable love and fear. For three months she and Noah have been inseparable; her first day at college last week was the first time she'd left him for longer than a few minutes. Now he is half an hour away from her, a bus ride, six and a half miles away, and her arms feel weightless, her breasts feel heavy. She texts her mum. *All OK?*

Her mum replies immediately. *Just got back from looking at the ducks. All good.*

At the next table, Scarlett has zoned out from talking to her clique and is staring at her phone in a way that suggests she's not really looking at anything. She rolls the apple on the tray around and around with the fingers of her spare hand. Her face, in profile, is interesting; there is a bump in her nose, a slight curve to her chin. Her mouth is a thin line. But still she is somehow pretty, prettier than any other girl at the college, even the ones with perfect noses and pillow lips. She turns and catches Tallulah staring at her. She narrows her eyes, then turns away from her, drops her feet back to the floor, picks up the apple, tucks it in the pocket of her hoodie, and leaves her group of friends without saying goodbye to any of them. As she passes Tallulah she narrows her eyes again, and Tallulah imagines for a split second that she sees a smile pass across her face.

6

Kim buckles Noah into his car seat and gives him one of his fabric books to flick through. Ryan sits in the back with him, while Kim gets into the driver's seat and switches on her phone to put the address into Google.

"Dark Place," she says as she types. "It's only a mile away, I wonder why I've never heard of it before."

She slots her phone into its holder, presses start, and pulls out of the quiet cul-de-sac where she has lived since she was twenty-one years old. She hums distractedly under her breath. She doesn't want Noah to pick up on her anxiety, doesn't want Ryan to have to deal with her mounting feelings of dread and fear.

They drive through the sun-dappled lanes that connect Upfield Common with Manton, the nearest big town. Just before the large roundabout that marks the end of the village, Google tells them to turn right, up a tight dogleg. The signpost is overgrown with buddleia, but Kim can just make out the words UPLEY FOLD ½.

It's a single-lane road and she drives cautiously in case she meets a vehicle coming the other way. It's nearly 4:00 p.m. and the sun is still high in the sky. She peers into the rearview mirror and says to Ryan, "Can you put the screen down on Noah's side? He's in full sun."

Ryan leans across and pulls it down. Noah points at something in his fabric book and attempts to tell Ryan what it is, but he hasn't learned how to talk yet so Ryan just looks at the page and says, "Yes, piggy, that's right. Piggy!"

Google tells her to take the next turning on the right. She cannot believe that there is actually a turning on the right, but there it is, a track with a line of meadow grass running down its center, the hedgerows lower here so Kim can see blinding fields of rape, some cows silhouetted in the distance, a cluster of cottages. And then, after another few minutes, a pair of metal gates, a gravel driveway pointing due south, the name DARK PLACE fashioned out of wrought iron, the suggestion of a turreted house in the distance. Kim turns off the engine and puts her phone into her handbag.

"What are you going to do?" asks Ryan.

Her eyes scan the gate for a doorbell or entry system, but there's nothing. A footpath runs alongside the gravel drive. She gets Noah's pushchair out of the boot and assembles it, batting midges out of her face. "Come on," she says to Ryan, unclipping the fastenings on Noah's seat. "We're going to walk."

Ryan uses his phone to google Dark Place and he gives her a running commentary from its Wiki page as they walk. Kim enjoys the distraction from her thoughts.

"It was built in 1643," he says. "Wow, 1643," he repeats. "But most of it got burned down a few years after it was built. It lay empty for seventy years and that's how it got the name 'Dark Place,' because of the charred wood that surrounded it. The Georgian wing was added in 1721 and the Victorian wing in the late 1800s by a coffee plantation owner called Frederick de Thames. Who . . . God . . ." He pauses and scrolls back. "Who fathered at least thirty-eight children in Colombia, seven in the UK, and died of the Spanish flu when he was only forty-one. The house was left to his last wife, Carolina de Thames, who was only twenty when he died, and who passed it on in turn to her son, Lawrence. In 1931 three of Frederick's older children plotted to have Lawrence assassinated, but the man they hired to kill him got caught in a fox trap in the grounds of Dark Place and wasn't found until five days later when he'd been partially eaten by foxes and had his eyes pecked out by crows. He had the assassination orders on a signed form in the pocket of his coat. The three brothers who'd plotted Lawrence's death were sent to prison and Lawrence lived in the house until he died in 1998. Whereupon, with no living heirs, the house went back on the market and was purchased by an unknown buyer for nearly two million pounds in 2002."

As they walk Kim casts her eyes across the ground, across the horizon, all around her, looking for signs of her daughter. She'd called all three local taxi companies before leaving the house and none of them had collected anyone from Dark Place last night.

They walk for nearly ten minutes until finally she sees the house. It looks just as Kim had expected it to look from Ryan's description. A hodgepodge of disparate architectural styles, blended almost seamlessly together across three wings, set around a central courtyard. The sun sparkles off the diamonds of leaded windows on the left wing and larger Victorian casement and sash windows on the right. It should be a mess, but it is not; it is exquisitely beautiful.

In the driveway are four cars and a golf buggy. Even from here, Kim can hear the sound of people splashing in a swimming pool. Ryan helps her pull Noah's buggy up the steps to the front door and she rings the bell.

A young man answers. A huge Saint Bernard dog follows behind and collapses, panting, at his feet. The man is bare-chested and holding a six-pack of beers in one hand and a tea towel in the other.

He looks from Kim to Noah to Ryan and back to Kim. "Hi!"

"Oh, hi. My name is Kim. I wondered if Scarlett was around? Or her parents?"

"Er, yeah. Yeah, sure. Hold on a sec." He turns and yells out, "Mum! Someone for you at the door!"

Behind him, Kim sees a pale stone staircase, with a striped runner up the middle. She sees modern art and designer light fittings and then a woman in a loose white sundress and white flip-flops appears. The dog stands heavily to greet the woman, who peers at Kim curiously through the door.

The boy smiles at Kim and then disappears.

"Yes?" says the woman.

"Sorry to disturb you like this, on a Saturday."

The woman looks across her shoulder at the gravel sweep and says, "How did you get here?"

"Oh," says Kim, "we parked at the gate, and walked."

"But that's half a mile! You should have rung the bell."

"Well, we looked, but we couldn't see one."

"Urgh, yes, sorry, it's a movement sensor. You need to stand over it. Lots of people miss it. You should have called."

"Well, I didn't have a number. Or at least, I had a number but I didn't realize how far the house was going to be from the gate, but anyway, it's fine. It's just . . . I'm looking for my daughter."

"Oh," she says, "are you Mimi's mum? I think she left this morning . . ."

"No," says Kim. "No. Sorry. I'm not Mimi's mum. I'm Tallulah's mum. She was here last night?"

"Tallulah?" The woman rubs the dog's head absentmindedly with a hand bearing just one wide band on her wedding finger. "Gosh, no, I don't think I know a Tallulah."

"Lula?" she suggests. She hates the name Lula, but her daughter's friends have always tended to shorten her full name; it's something she's learned to accept.

"No." The woman shakes her head. "No. I've never heard of Lula either. Are you sure she was here?"

Kim is hot and anxious. There's no shade where she's standing and the sun is beating down on the back of her neck. She can feel a hot dampness breaking out all over her body and feels a flash of anger at this woman in her crisp white sundress and freshly brushed hair, her cool, dry complexion and the suggestion in her clipped English accent that Kim is somehow mistaken and in the wrong place.

She nods and tries to keep her voice pleasant. "Yes. I spoke to your daughter a couple of hours ago. She said Tallulah was here last night with her boyfriend, Zach, and they left in a minicab at three a.m. But I've called all the minicab numbers and none of them has a record of a pickup from this address or anywhere in the vicinity of this address. And it's nearly four p.m. and my daughter is still not home. And this"—she points behind her at Noah in his buggy—"is Tallulah's son and she would never deliberately leave him. Just never."

Her voice begins to crack dangerously and she breathes in hard to stop herself from crying.

The woman looks unperturbed by this display of emotion. "Sorry," she says after a pause. "What was your name again?"

"Kim. And this is Ryan. My son. And Noah. My grandson."

"Gosh," says the woman. "A grandmother! You look far too young to be a grandmother. Anyway. I'm Joss." She puts out a hand for Kim to shake and then says, "Come on, then. Let's go and see what Scarlett has to say about all of this. Follow me."

She leads them across the courtyard and through a tall wrought-iron gate set in an ancient brick wall grown over with ivy. The huge dog pads heavily behind them. The courtyard is smattered with tiny white stone figures set on Perspex plinths. They follow her down a flagstone path lined with sculptural plants in cobalt-glazed pots and then turn a corner.

In front of them is the pool.

It's set in a cream marble terrace with a curtained pagoda at one end housing a huge cream-cushioned daybed. At angles along its length are teak sunbeds with matching cream cushions. Floating at the pool's center, inside a bright pink inflatable flamingo, is a tall, thin girl with lime-green hair and a black bandeau bikini top. She peers at Kim and her entourage curiously. Then she says, "Oh," as the penny drops.

"Tallulah?" says Joss, shielding her eyes from the sun shining off the pool's surface with her hand. "Apparently, she was here last night. Any idea where she got to?"

Scarlett pushes herself to the pool's edge by paddling her hands through the water; then she dismounts the flamingo and ascends the stone steps. She pulls a black towel around herself and sits down at a teak circular table covered with white candles in glass jars.

Kim sits opposite her. "I know," she begins, "you said that you don't know where they went. I know you said that Tallulah was sick and they got in a minicab. But the cab firms are all saying that they didn't pick anyone up from here. I just wondered if there was anything else that happened last night that might explain where they are."

Scarlett picks at the wax on the top of one of the candles and makes no eye contact with Kim. "Genuinely," she says, "honestly. That's all I know."

"And did you see them getting into a car?"

"No. I was out here, with Mimi. And Zach came and said Lula had been sick and he was going to take her home, that there was a taxi coming."

"He said that? That the taxi was coming? Or did he say he was going to call one?"

Scarlett shrugs. Kim watches crystal beads of pool water coalesce and collapse on her angular shoulders and run down her arms in rivulets. "I'm pretty sure he said one was coming."

Kim can see Ryan hovering in her peripheral view. She pulls out a chair for him and he sits down, bringing Noah's pushchair close to him. "So, is there a chance, do you think, that Zach tried to call a taxi and no one could send one so they ended up walking?"

"Yeah?" says Scarlett. "I guess?"

Kim turns to Scarlett's brother, who is perched on the end of a sunbed across the pool, with a bottle of beer hanging between his knees. "Were you here last night, at the party?" she calls over to him.

He puts out a hand defensively and says, "No. Not me. I just got home this morning."

Kim sighs. "And if they had walked, where might they have ended up?"

Scarlett shrugs again. "It depends, I suppose. On which way they went. If they went up the driveway they could have ended up on the main road, or Upley Fold if they turned the wrong way. If they went the back path, they would have ended up back in Upfield Common."

"The back path?"

"Yes," she replies, waving her hand in a vague arc behind her. "There."

Kim gazes over her shoulder. All she can see are lawns and flower beds and hedges and gravel pathways and pockmarked stone steps and sundials and arbors.

"Where?"

"Beyond," says Scarlett. "Behind. There's a path there that goes through the woods and into the back end of Upfield Common. Near the Maypole. I used to walk that way to go to school sometimes when I was there."

"How far?"

Joss interjects. "A mile, just over. But I wouldn't recommend it. Especially not with a baby. You really need to know where you're going, otherwise you'll get lost."

"Did Tallulah know about the back path?"

Scarlett shrugs. "I don't think so," she said. "She'd never been here before so there's no reason she should have known about it."

"And who else," Kim continues. "Who else was here last night?"

"Just us three," says Scarlett, "and Mimi. Lexie Mulligan was here before they left. She lives at Maypole House. Her mum's the matron there. You know, Kerryanne Mulligan?"

Kim nods. She knows Kerryanne well. Everyone in Upfield Common knows Kerryanne. She's larger-than-life.

"Yeah. Her daughter. She's, like, in her twenties. But she left early. She was driving. And she took my friend Liam with her."

"So, after that, it was just you, Tallulah, Zach, and . . . Mimi?"

"Yup."

"And your mum and dad?"

"Mum was here. She was asleep. Dad's away on business."

Kim turns to Joss, who is sitting on the steps behind her, listening into the conversation. "You don't happen to have security cameras, do you? Anywhere in the grounds?"

Joss nods and says, "Yes, tons of them. But I'm afraid I haven't got the vaguest idea how to use them." She glances across at her son. "Rex? Any idea how to look at the camera footage?"

Rex grimaces. "Not really. I know there's like some kind of centralized panel in Dad's study, but I've never actually used it."

Kim says, "Do you think we might try?" And as she says it she feels the mood change immediately. Until now she's been a minor distraction, entertained on their own terms. Now she's asking people to go indoors, to open doors, work out how to use equipment. She sees the three of them exchange looks. Then Joss gets to her feet and approaches Kim and says, "Tell you what. Save us all traipsing about in Martin's office, why don't I just get Rex to have a look in a bit. I'll get him to give Martin a ring to talk him through it. Scarlett's got your number. We'll call you if we find anything."

Kim still has so many things she wants to ask, so many questions she needs answers to. She's not ready to go. "You said Tallulah hadn't been here before?" she asks, a hint of desperation in her voice. "And on the phone earlier you said you didn't really know her. I mean, you didn't even know she had a child. So what . . . I mean, why was she even here?"

Scarlett pulls her towel over her shoulders like a cloak and rubs at her ears with its corners. "We chat sometimes," she says, "at college. Then I saw her in the pub last night and we had a few drinks and one thing led to another."

Kim's eyes take her in again, this lanky, angular girl with whom her daughter chatted sometimes. She takes in the detail of her; the piercings that catch the light, the tattoo on her shoulder blade, the perfectly painted toenails. And her gaze alights on a black mark on Scarlett's foot, a small tattoo, a pair of letters that she can't at first quite make out. Then she sees that it is the trademark symbol. Scarlett's hand reaches down and covers the tattoo, hard and fast, like swatting a fly. Their eyes meet briefly and Kim sees something defensive and raw pass across Scarlett's face.

She hitches her bag onto her shoulder. "Would it be possible," she says, "to speak to your friend Mimi, do you think? Do you have a number for her?"

"She won't know anything more than I do."

"Please?"

"I'll get her to call you," says Scarlett.

Within a minute they are pushing Noah's buggy back through the wrought-iron gate and onto the front courtyard and Joss is standing under a bower of passionflowers with her gigantic dog, waving them off, and as they walk toward the driveway, Kim hears the splash of bodies hitting the cool, blue surface of the swimming pool, a small squeal of laughter.

7

Sophie comes from an outdoorsy family. They go on walking holidays and sailing holidays and skiing holidays. Her father runs marathons, her mother plays golf and tennis, both her brothers work in the sports industry. Sophie was once a swimmer. She has medals and cups and certificates in a big box in her parents' loft and still has a swimmer's physique although she barely swims at all these days. When they were all small and getting on her mother's nerves, she would zip them into their coats and lock them in the back garden. They would moan for a while and then find something to do. Usually involving climbing very tall trees and swinging off things that weren't designed to be swung off. So Sophie is very comfortable being outdoors and confident in her ability to find her way about and deal with obstacles alone without assistance. And so she sets off into the woods, sensibly dressed and equipped with water, energy bars, a mobile charger for her phone, her compass, some plasters, sun cream, a hat, and a packet of bright red plastic space-marker cones that she can drop on the forest floor at intervals if she needs to find her way back.

Inside the woods, the tree cover is immense and very little of the pale gold August sun gets through. Within a few feet she feels the temperature begin to drop. She holds her compass in her right hand and follows the path alongside the arrow telling her where to go.

After twenty minutes the denseness of the middle of the woods starts to thin out again and there are established footpaths meandering through the trees, signs of humanity, pieces of litter, dog poo in a green plastic bag hanging from a branch. She checks her map again now that she has briefly regained her phone signal and finds that she is about to emerge onto a bridleway. She moves the map across her screen with her fingers and sees the linear representation of a large building to her right.

After a moment she sees a turret and a weathervane. Then she sees the curve of an ancient brick wall and a curtain of bright red Virginia creeper. She squeezes through a parade of trees that abuts the wall and finds herself in front of a rusty metal gate, a broken padlock hanging from its bars, and then she is through the gate and into a clump of woodland; the shimmer of blue sky is visible ahead of her and then she is on a ragged sun-bleached lawn that rolls downward via wide stone steps overgrown with thistles toward a house that looks like something from a Tim Burton movie.

Sophie catches her breath and puts a hand to her throat.

As she runs down the tiered lawns toward the house, she sees the pool appear; it's dark green, a ripped cover half pulled across it, mulchy dead leaves from the previous winter stacked around it. A pagoda at one end of the pool has been covered in boldly colored graffiti.

The terrace between the pool and the house is littered with empty beer cans and cigarette ends, drug paraphernalia and discarded crisp packets and takeaway containers.

How, Sophie wonders, could a house of this magnificence, not to mention market value, have been left like this? Why is it not being cared for, even while it is uninhabited?

She picks her away around the house, trying to peer into windows through gaps in the shutters. At the front of the house is an ornate courtyard and beyond that a long cypress-lined driveway that appears to go on for a mile or more. She turns to look at the front door. Above the fanlight, carved into the dark brickwork, is the date AD 1721.

The air is thick and silent here, and nothing else in sight. This house exists almost on an island. Sophie wonders about the family who lived here, the hedge-fund manager and his glamorous wife and their talented teenage daughter. Where are they now, and what on earth possessed them to leave a place like this to go to seed?

She checks the time on her phone. It's nearly midday.

She stands at the top end of the garden to survey the grandeur of the house one more time. She takes a photograph, then tucks her phone into her rucksack and heads back down the bridleway and into the woods.

8

"Zach called again."

Tallulah glances at her mum.

"About an hour ago. Wondered if I knew where you were, because you weren't answering your phone."

She shrugs and heads to the baby monitor on the kitchen counter and puts her ear to it, listening for the sound of her son's sleeping breath. "How long has he been down?"

"About thirty-five minutes."

She glances at the time. It's four thirty. He'll be hungry any minute. She has a small window of time to get changed, to have a cup of tea, to sort out her college work. She's been at college for four weeks now and has got into a really solid routine.

"Are you going to call him?"

"Who?"

"Zach," her mum replies impatiently. "Are you going to call him? You can't ignore him forever."

Tallulah nods. "I know," she says. "I know." She unknots the laces on her trainers and pulls them off. Then she sighs. Zach asked if they could get back together when he came to visit Noah on Saturday. It was weird because when she was pregnant all she wanted in the whole world was to be back together with Zach. But now she's a mum, now she's at college, it's like she's not that same person anymore and the person she is now doesn't want to be with anyone. She just wants to share her bed, her body, with Noah.

She and Zach had been together for nearly three years when she got pregnant. She hadn't told him she was pregnant until she was four months gone and then he'd freaked out and said he needed time to decide how he felt about it. And now he knows how he feels about it, but Tallulah's no longer sure that she does.

"He's a good boy, you know," her mum continues.

"Yes. I know." She tries to hide her exasperation. She owes her mum everything right now and doesn't want to sound ungrateful. "I just don't know what to say to him."

"You could just say that," her mum suggests.

"Yes, but then he might try to talk me around and I haven't got the energy for it."

Tallulah's so tired all the time. During the summer it had been fine: Noah slept most of the day when he was a newborn, so she had plenty of time to catch up on her sleep. But now he's older and more wakeful and she's at college three mornings a week and has study to do on her days at home and daytime sleeps are a thing of the past.

"If Zach starts crying or something, I'll cave. I know I will."

Her mum passes her a mug of tea, pulls out the chair opposite her, and sits down. "But what is it?" she begins. "That you're not sure about?"

"I just . . . I don't . . ." But she's saved from having to find the words to explain something she cannot explain by the sound of Noah on the baby monitor, rousing from his afternoon sleep. Her mum goes to stand up, but Tallulah wants the bliss and the distraction of scooping her boy from his warm bedsheets and rolling him into her arms, against her chest, the sweet heat of his breath against her collarbone.

"I'll go," she says, "I'll go."

The following day Tallulah has college in the morning.

She leaves the house with the vignette imprinted on her mind of

Noah in her mother's arms, Ryan in his school uniform microwaving Noah's milk for her because she's late and doesn't have time to do it herself, and stands at the bus stop opposite their cul-de-sac. The bus is late. After all her rushing about and not saying goodbye properly to her baby son, she sighs impatiently. She's aware then of a presence beside her and turns to see Scarlett Jacques sliding along the plastic bench.

"Haven't missed it, then?" she says breathlessly.

Tallulah doesn't realize for a split second that Scarlett is talking to her and fails to respond.

"I'll take that as a no," says Scarlett.

"Sorry," says Tallulah. "Yeah. I mean, no. You haven't missed it. It's late."

"Phew," says Scarlett, pulling earbuds from the pocket of her oversize raincoat and starting to put them in her ears. Then she stops and says, "I know you, don't I? You're at Manton College, yes?"

Tallulah nods.

Scarlett nods too and says, "I've seen you around. What course are you on?"

"Social care. First year."

"Ah, so you're new too?"

"Yeah. A few weeks in. How about you?" asks Tallulah, although she knows exactly which course Scarlett's on.

"Fine art. First year."

"That's cool," says Tallulah, and then wishes she hadn't said "cool."

"Well, yeah, it's shit, really. I mean, I *wanted* to go to art school in London but my parents wouldn't let me. Because of all the traveling. And I said, well, then rent me a little flat. And they said no way, and then I didn't get a good enough grade in my art A level to get into any of the good colleges anyway, not because I'm not good at art, but just because I didn't do the work I needed to do, story of my life, and yeah. Here I am."

They both turn at the distinctive rumble of the old-fashioned green bus that services the area as it appears on the far side of the common.

"Do you live around here, then?" asks Tallulah.

"No. Well, kind of. About two miles away. But I spent the night with my boyfriend. He's at the Maypole." She shrugs in the direction of the imposing old manor house across the common.

"Are you allowed to sleep over there?"

"Nope. Most definitely not. But I have a 'special' relationship with the matron there. She loves me. And I'm kind of friends with her daughter too, so she turns a blind eye."

The bus approaches and they get to their feet. Tallulah doesn't know what happens now. Will they sit together? Will they continue to talk?

But the decision is taken from her. Scarlett sees a friend at the back of the bus and strides away from Tallulah, throwing her school bag down on the seat and then herself, her voice traveling loudly, almost gratingly, down the aisle to the front of the bus, where Tallulah sits alone. But when Tallulah turns, just once, to look at Scarlett, she finds Scarlett looking straight back at her.

9

Kim strips off her clothes and gets into the shower, quickly, before the water has run warm. The whole episode at Scarlett's house has left her feeling filthy and exhausted. She pictures Scarlett's mother standing at her front door with her big panting dog, watching them pushing Noah's buggy awkwardly down the gravel pathway and onto the drive.

"I'd offer to drive you," she'd called out. "But I've had a few drinks! So sorry!"

Kim's car was like an oven by the time they returned to it and Noah was now tired and hungry and screamed all the way from the bottom of the driveway to the parking space outside Kim's house, whereupon he immediately fell asleep. Ryan is sitting out in the car with him now.

In the shower she can taste the salt of her own sweat as water passes down her face.

Every few seconds she peers through the gap in the shower curtain at her phone, which she's left perched on the sink, balanced against the toothbrush mug, looking to see if she's missed a call or a message.

After showering she gets into clean shorts and a fresh bra and top. Everything she was wearing earlier is damp and dank and heading for the laundry basket. She glances at her phone again. Still nothing.

Fear grips her gut again; it comes and goes in waves. She sits on the edge of her bed and thinks about the woods behind Scarlett's house. She tries to imagine Zach and Tallulah, waiting in the dark for a taxi that didn't come, giving up after a while and one of them saying, "Those woods take us back to Upfield. We could try cutting through there." It had been a warm night; it might even have sounded appealing, and maybe they thought the fresh air would help clear Tallulah's head.

Kim calls Megs. "Would you mind," she says, "if I dropped Noah with you for a while? I think I know where Zach and Tallulah might be and I'd like to go and have a look?"

There's a pause, then Megs says, "So they're not back yet?"

Kim closes her eyes. It's different with sons, she knows that. But still, she's frustrated by Megs's lack of concern. She pictures her just as she'd left her this morning, stretched out in her back garden with her edgy husband, enjoying not having any responsibilities, any agenda.

"No," she says. "They're not. And none of the local taxi firms has a record of picking them up from their friend's house last night. So I have a theory that they might be lost in the woods behind the college. I want to go and have a look."

"Oh," says Megs. "Right." Then, "Seems unlikely. I mean, it's almost five o'clock. That would mean they'd been in those woods since last night. Surely no one could get lost in there for that long?"

"Well, maybe they had an accident? Fell down a . . . I don't know, an old well or something. Anyway. I'll be over with Noah in a bit. See you soon."

She ends the call without waiting to hear what else Megs might have to say.

———————————

They spend two hours scouring the woods but there is no sign of them. No wells. No holes. No traps. No dropped clues. Nothing. As they pass the accommodation block in the grounds of Maypole

House afterward, Kim glances up at the windows. She remembers Scarlett telling them that Kerryanne Mulligan's daughter had been with them the night before; Lexie, she said her name was. She and Ryan head for the security gate and ring on a buzzer that says RESI-DENCE MANAGER.

A woman replies.

"Oh, hi. Is that Kerryanne?"

"Yes, speaking."

"Hi, this is Kim Knox. I live across the common. I think my mum used to look after your mum when she was at Springdale?"

"Yes, yes. I know you. And I remember your mum. She used to bring Jamaica ginger loaf to my mum's room when I came to visit her for tea. Paula, wasn't it?"

Kim smiles at the sound of her mother's name. "Yes! That's right. And your mum was called Vanda?"

"Yes! That's right. Well remembered. How are you? Do you want to come in?"

"Er, yes, thank you. I've got my son with me."

"Lovely," says Kerryanne. "Second floor, room 205."

There's the smell of cooking in Kerryanne's flat, something steaming on a hob. A younger woman sits on the L-shaped sofa facing a terrace that overlooks the woods that Kim has just been trawling for her daughter and her boyfriend.

"Come in!" says Kerryanne. "Come in. This is my daughter, Lexie, she's staying with me for a few days. Lexie, this is Kim, she's the daughter of one of Nana's carers from Springdale. And your mum. Is she . . . ?"

Kim shakes her head. "No. No, she died two years ago."

"Oh, I'm sorry to hear that. She must have been very young?"

"Sixty-two," she says.

"Oh no. Oh dear. Not that much older than me. I'm so sorry."

"Yes, well. And your mother? Is she . . . ?"

"Four years ago. But she was eighty-eight. So, you know, I can't complain. But she loved your mum. She really did."

They smile sadly at each other for a minute thinking of their poor dead mothers, then Kerryanne rallies and says, "Anyway, what can I do for you?"

"Well," says Kim, "actually, it was Lexie I wanted to talk to."

Lexie turns at the sound of her name and says, "Oh?"

Lexie is a pretty young woman, with mahogany hair cut into a bob with a blunt fringe, large black-framed reading glasses, skinny jeans, and an artfully scruffy T-shirt.

"You were at Scarlett's house last night?"

"Yes!" she answers brightly. "How did you know?"

"Well, because my daughter was there too. Tallulah? And her boyfriend, Zach? And the thing is that Tallulah and Zach haven't come home. And apparently they left there at three a.m. We've just been in the woods at the back." Kim gestures through the glass sliding door. "I thought maybe they'd got lost coming back, but no sign of them. And I know you left early, but I just wondered if you noticed anything. Knew anything. Saw anything. Because I'm running out of ideas here!" She's been trying to keep her voice on an even keel, keep her tone normal, but her words begin to crack apart as she reaches her conclusion, and then she finds that she is crying. Kerryanne rushes to the kitchen to find her a tissue and Lexie looks at her with genuine concern.

"Oh God, I'm so sorry. How horrible. You must be so worried."

Kim nods and takes the tissue from Kerryanne, holds it to her cheeks.

"I mean," she says, "I'm sure it's nothing. I'm sure they just, you know, kids, they just . . ." But she peters off because she's not sure of any such thing. The only thing she's sure of is that Tallulah would never leave Noah deliberately and that something terrible must have happened to her.

Kerryanne leads Kim and Ryan to the large sofa and invites them to sit down.

"Honestly," Lexie begins, "I wish there was something I could tell you. But there really isn't. I was at the pub, the Swan and Ducks, with an old school friend. There was this group in there, a young group, late teens, early twenties, and they were being quite rowdy. I recognized one of them, Scarlett. She used to be a student here. We've always been quite friendly. So I went to say hello and before I knew it I was being dragged into their little group and it felt a bit weird because obviously I'm quite a bit older than them. Plus I was sober. And they were not."

"And was Tallulah there then?"

"Yes, she was there. She was sitting with a boy—her boyfriend, I think?"

Kim nods.

"They seemed a bit quiet at first. I noticed that. And then Scarlett got a load of shots for the table and then another and everyone got even noisier and noisier and then it was closing time and they were all talking about walking back to Scarlett's house through the woods, and I thought that was just an accident waiting to happen. So I offered to drive them there."

"All of them?"

"No, not all of them, just five of them. It was a bit of a squeeze and not entirely legal, but I still thought it was safer than them all walking through the woods off their heads."

"And what happened when you got back there?"

"Well, it was so warm last night, as you know, and the lights were all on in their pool, and they all just stripped off and jumped in."

"Including Tallulah?"

"Yeah. She jumped in in her top and pants. She looked kind of self-conscious."

"Well, yes, she's carrying a little baby weight still."

"She has a baby?" Lexie looks surprised.

"Yes. Noah; he's one."

"Gosh, she looks so young."

"She is." Kim holds down another burst of tears and forces a smile. "So, they all jumped in the pool. And then what?"

"Well, I kind of—at this point I felt like I needed to supervise. I mean, Scarlett's mum was somewhere indoors, sleeping, I think, and I realized I was the only sober person at the party so I needed to keep an eye on everyone. I ended up staying until about one. By that time everyone was out of the pool and there was a bit of"—she looks at Kim quickly from the corner of her eye—"weed. A bit of vodka. Music. But it had calmed down a bit. Tallulah and her boyfriend went indoors. Then Mimi went indoors. So I decided to head back. This guy Liam cadged a lift back with me, because he works here at the school. And that was that."

"Liam?" Kim asks cagily. "Who is Liam?"

"He's a teaching assistant here. He lives in the apartment above us. He used to go out with Scarlett but they're still friends."

"Is he, I mean, is he . . ." Kim can't find the words.

Lexie shakes her head. "Oh," she says, "no. God, no, you don't need to worry about Liam. He's the nicest guy in the world. Honestly."

Kim nods, circumspectly. Then she says, "And was there anything, last night—beneath the surface? Did you get the feeling that there was anything untoward going on?"

Lexie turns out her bottom lip and shakes her head slowly. "No."

"And when you left, who was still there?"

"Tallulah. Her boyfriend. Scarlett and Mimi."

"Well," says Kim, already starting to get to her feet. "Thank you so much, Lexie. I really appreciate your time, and thank you so much for going back with them all last night, for keeping them safe. Drunk kids in swimming pools. Doesn't bear thinking about."

"No," says Lexie. "That's what I thought."

"Well, thank you. And this Liam. Do you think it'd be worth talking to him? Might he have any idea?"

"I doubt it," Lexie replies apologetically. "He wouldn't have seen much more than I did."

Kim looks at the time on her phone. It's nearly six o'clock. She turns to Kerryanne. "Do you think I should call the police?" she asks softly. "It's been fifteen hours. What would you do?"

Kerryanne sighs. "Well, it's different for me, in loco parentis and all that, I'd move quite quickly if someone went missing from school. And in fact they have and I called out search and rescue within a few hours. But as a mother?" She pauses. "I don't know. I mean, Tallulah and Zach are technically adults. They'd been drinking, taking drugs; sounds like they've got responsibilities beyond those of normal teenagers. I'd be tempted to look at the bigger picture. I mean, is it possible they've just run away? In a mad moment of spontaneity?"

Kim closes her eyes and measures her response. "No," she says. "No. Definitely not."

"And between them, as a couple? I mean, was there anything afoot? Maybe they had a row? Maybe something happened?"

And there it is, the thing that's been gnawing away inside Kim's head all day long: the little box she'd found in Zach's jacket pocket the day before when she was looking for the spare door keys she'd lent him. The box with the ring in it with the small but very clear diamond set on a golden band. She'd been expecting them to come back from the pub last night engaged. She wasn't sure how she felt about it; they were so young and she wasn't convinced that Tallulah was entirely committed to Zach. But she'd been ready for it, ready to look amazed and delighted and to hug them both to her and tell them she was thrilled and to take a photo and text it to Tallulah's dad and put it on Facebook and all of that. She'd been ready for it. Even if she thought it was wrong. Because that's what you did. Wasn't it?

When you had a baby. When you had a man who loved you. You got married.

But then Kim thinks of how long it had taken Tallulah to agree to get back together with Zach after Noah was born. She thinks of how Tallulah shrugs Zach's touch from her shoulder, from her arm, the roll of her eyes behind his back sometimes. She's been meaning to start a conversation with Tallulah for a few weeks, just to check in, to make sure she's still happy that she took Zach back. But she hasn't. And then they'd planned this night out together and Kim saw it as a sign that things were getting better between them. And then she'd found the ring.

So what, she wonders, if Zach had asked Tallulah to marry him and Tallulah had said no? Because Zach is a good boy, but he has a temper. She's seen it flare from time to time when he's watching sports on the TV or when he drops something and hurts himself or someone cuts him up when he's driving.

How might a rejection of his marriage proposal have triggered that temper? How might he have responded?

10

Sophie and Shaun arrive at Kerryanne's apartment at eight o'clock that evening, clutching a cold bottle of wine. The apartment has glass sliding doors almost the full width of her living room facing directly toward the setting sun. It's hot and stuffy; a large chrome fan plugged into the wall provides a little relief.

"Sorry," she says to Sophie and Shaun, "it gets so hot in here on a sunny day, the heat gets trapped. Come, we can sit on the terrace."

There's a wickerwork sofa on her terrace and a table set with crisps in bowls and wineglasses and a candle in a jar.

Sophie sits down first, followed by Shaun. The view across the woods is beautiful; the sky is turquoise, streaked with coral, and a half-moon is just emerging from the shadows.

"This is lovely," says Sophie. "Like a different world to the cottage."

"Yes, the cottage is lovely, but you don't get the views. But then again, you don't get the heat either." She pours wine into the three glasses and raises hers to Shaun. "Cheers," she says. "To my fifth head teacher! And to you too, Sophie, my first head teacher's significant other!"

"Are we the first unmarried couple?" Sophie asks.

"You are, yes."

"Is it a scandal?" asks Sophie.

"Oh God, no. Maybe twenty years ago eyebrows would have

been raised. But not now. I don't think anyone cares about these things anymore, do they? And actually, Jacinta Croft—your predecessor, Shaun—she arrived married, but left single. Her husband did a runner. One of those 'popping out for a pint of milk' scenarios. No one ever found out why. That's pretty much why she left, because of the scandal of it. So no, you two will not cause any wagging tongues, I can promise you that."

They chat for a while about Shaun's first day at work, about the school he used to teach at in Lewisham, about the differences between the two areas, the two schools. Then Kerryanne turns to Sophie and says, "Peter Doody tells me that you're a writer, Sophie? Detective novels, he said."

"Yes." Sophie smiles. "Though I doubt you'd have read them. They're quite niche. I'm big in Scandinavia." She laughs the laugh she always laughs when she has to explain to people why they've probably never heard of her.

"I told my daughter about you," Kerryanne says. "She's the reader in the family. Not me. I think she might even have ordered one of your books. What are they called again?"

"The series is called the Little Hither Green Detective Agency. I write under the name P. J. Fox."

"I tell you what," Kerryanne says, "if you want any inspiration for your books, I could tell you some stories about this place. I mean, I could tell you some really, really hair-raising stuff. We had the police here twice last year alone, trawling those woods for missing people."

Sophie thinks of the abandoned mansion beyond the woods. "Wow," she says. "What happened?"

Kerryanne glances across at Shaun and says, "Hm. Probably a bit indiscreet. Maybe not."

But she throws Sophie a sideways glance that tells her there'll be another time.

The following day, Sophie gets up with Shaun at 6:00 a.m. and they breakfast outdoors together, the golden rays of another beautiful late-August day strobing through the trees and across the tablecloth.

"What will you do today?" asks Shaun, collecting the plates and cutlery and piling them together. "Will you go for another epic walk?"

"No," she says. "Not today. I thought I might explore the village today. Maybe get some lunch at the infamous Swan and Ducks."

"I'll try and join you," says Shaun.

"That would be very nice indeed."

After Shaun leaves, Sophie spends some time unpacking boxes in the cottage. Then she makes herself another cup of coffee and takes her laptop to the kitchen table and replies to some emails. She is flying to Denmark in just over a week's time, to attend a crime festival as P. J. Fox, and there are some last-minute additions to her itinerary, including an interview with a TV station, which means she'll want to do something about her hair before she goes. She thinks maybe she'll take a day trip into London, visit her stylist there, maybe have lunch with someone, see if her publishers would like her to visit. She feels herself get quite excited at the prospect.

After a while she switches screens to her latest manuscript. She hasn't looked at it for days. Life has been nothing but packing and unpacking and saying goodbye and saying hello. She hasn't been in the right headspace to get any work done. But now she has no excuse.

The tail end of her last paragraph stares at her blankly, something she wrote in another world when she was a Londoner, when she had a boyfriend who taught at a sprawling Lewisham secondary school, when moving to Surrey was a date in her diary, rather than her reality. She stares back at it for a moment, then scrolls upward through the rest of the chapter, trying to slot herself back into "London Sophie," but just can't do it.

Instead, she flicks screens to her browser and types in "Maypole House" and "missing person." She sets the filter to news and clicks on the first link in the results:

Local Teen Parents Remain Missing After Night Out

Upfield Common resident Kim Knox, 39, has reported the disappearance of her daughter, 19-year-old Tallulah Murray, and her boyfriend, Zach Allister, also 19, who have not been seen since the early hours of Saturday morning. Murray and Allister, who have a one-year-old son together, spent the previous evening at the Swan & Ducks pub, before taking a lift with a local friend to a private home near Upley Fold, where they partied with friends, former students at Maypole House, until three o'clock in the morning. According to the same friends, they left to catch a taxi home but never returned. If anyone has any information about their whereabouts, please contact detectives at Manton Police Station.

Sophie feels a small chill of something ripple up and down her spine. She clicks through the rest of the links, looking for an update, but can't find anything, just varying versions of the same report that the local paper carried.

She then googles "Kim Knox, Upfield Common" and a few hits come up, including a couple of links to a village newsletter called the *Upfield Gazetteer*. One article in the newsletter is about a vigil held in June, marking the one-year anniversary of Tallulah and Zach's disappearance. There is a photograph attached to the article: an attractive woman with dark mid-length hair, wearing a long floral dress with buttons down the front and a pair of black army boots, holding the hand of a very small boy, also dark-haired, clutching a single pink rose. A teenage boy in a dark shirt and cargo trousers stands close to the woman; he bears a strong resemblance to her. Behind them is a sea of faces, a lot of young people.

> Kim Knox, 40, of Gable Close, Upfield Common, led a candlelit procession through the village on Saturday night to mark the first anniversary of the disappearance of her daughter, Tallulah Murray, who would have been 20 in March. Also commemorated during the ceremony was Zach Allister, Tallulah's partner and father of her son, who would also have turned 20 in March. The procession began on the common and concluded at St. Bride's Chapel, where songs of hope and remembrance were sung by a choir from Tallulah's old school, Upfield High, where she was a student until 2016. Tallulah was studying social care at Manton College of Further Education when she disappeared in June of last year after a night at a friend's house.

The other link takes Sophie to an article from three months before that, a rose-tree burial ceremony on the date of Tallulah's twentieth birthday in March.

> The rose tree, an Australian shrub rose called "Tallulah," has been planted behind the bus stop on the common, where Kim Knox used to watch her daughter as she waited for the bus to take her to college.

Sophie turns away from the screen. She feels a chill of raw emotion pass through her at the thought of a woman holding back a curtain, peering across the street, looking for the shadow of her missing child, and seeing roses instead.

11

Tallulah sits at her mother's dressing table. Her mother has a magnifying mirror here, plus things like cotton-wool balls and makeup brushes that Tallulah doesn't own because Tallulah has never really enjoyed wearing makeup. She puts on mascara for special occasions and uses cover-up on her under-eye bags and any breakouts but doesn't bother with the rest of it. The front sections of her dark hair are currently a kind of washed-out navy blue; she'd been hoping for the electric blue of the model on the packaging, but like everything in her life, it didn't turn out how she expected.

She opens up her mother's makeup bag and searches through it for liquid eyeliner, then sweeps the liner across her eyelids, trying to emulate the perfect wings the girls at college always seem to have. It's a disaster. She wipes them away and starts again. Eventually she picks up her phone and texts her mum:

Can you come upstairs and help me with my makeup?

She feels a bit bad. Her mum does enough for her these days. Noah's napping and her mum is enjoying a rare moment of peace on her own.

But a few seconds later her mum replies with a thumbs-up emoji and then she is there, her warmth filling the room immediately. "Right then, what do you need doing?"

"The wings," Tallulah replies, passing the liquid liner to her mother. "I keep mucking them up."

Her mother pulls a stool across the room and straddles it so that she is a few inches from Tallulah's face. Tallulah can smell the perfume on her neck: it's from the Body Shop and has musk in it. Her mum says that musk makes men want to have sex with you. Which strikes Tallulah as unlikely; why would anyone bother doing all the other things you're supposed to do to make men want to have sex with you if you could just wear a particular perfume and be done with it?

The outline of one of her mum's tattoos is just visible over the neckline of her top: the tip of a feather that farther down forms part of a bird. Her mother has six tattoos; she had one done before Tallulah was born, and the rest after she was born. She has Tallulah's baby footprints tattooed in pale pink on the underside of her arm, three inches long, with her initials in a flourish underneath. On the underside of the other arm she has Ryan's baby feet tattooed. On her back she has a Japanese-style fish, on her ankle she has a flock of swallows, and on her ring finger she has a diamond. She says the diamond is to symbolize her marriage to herself; after she split up with Tallulah and Ryan's dad she vowed never to marry again and the tattooed engagement ring would mean she was already taken.

Tallulah closes her eyes and angles her face toward her mother's outstretched hand.

"So," says her mother, applying the brush to the rim of her left eye. "What's with the makeup?"

It's the college Christmas party tonight, a disco in the canteen, famously awful but she knows the cool kids will be there, Scarlett and her lot, because they're on the social planning committee, and she feels very keenly that if she doesn't go, she might miss out on something, but she's not entirely sure what.

She shrugs. "Just felt like it," she says.

Her mother completes the second wing and she turns to see herself in the mirror. The wings are perfect. "Thanks, Mum," she says. "You're the best."

"What are you going to wear?" asks her mum.

"That top," she says, "you know, the one we got when we were at the Belfry last week. With the hearts on it. With my black jeans."

"Oh yes," her mum replies, "that'll look lovely."

Tallulah smiles. It's not the most amazing top in the world but it'll hide her post-baby stomach, which just won't seem to snap back into shape no matter how hard she tries, and that's the important thing.

An hour later she comes downstairs. Her mum has Noah on her lap and they're watching CBeebies together. Ryan is at the dining table with headphones on, doing his homework.

"You look gorgeous," says her mother. "Just gorgeous."

Tallulah leans down to kiss Noah on both cheeks.

"How are you getting there?"

"Chloe's giving me a lift."

Her mother nods.

"Are you sure you'll be all right?" Tallulah asks, touching the crown of her baby's head. "I don't have to go if you'd rather I didn't?"

"Of course we'll be all right. It's bath time in a minute, isn't it, my angel?" Her mother's voice rises an octave or two as she turns to address Noah. "And after that we'll have a lovely story and a lovely long sleep. Yes! Yes we will!"

Noah turns and smiles at her and Tallulah's mum kisses him hard on his cheek. "Off you go," she says. "Have fun. Let me know if you're going to be late."

"I definitely won't be late," she says. "Chloe's mum wants her home by eleven, so that's when I'll be back."

She hears the sound of a car pulling up outside and dashes to the front door. Briefly, she appraises herself in the mirror there.

She looks, she thinks, quite pretty.

The first hour is every bit as crap as Tallulah had expected it to be. Shit sound system playing bad music; the hatch in the wall where the dinner ladies usually serve lunch is open and serving beer in plastic bottles and wine by the glass. She and Chloe sit on a bench with their backs to the wall, each holding a beer, watching the party unfold around them. Chloe went to school with Tallulah, primary and secondary; they were never particularly great friends but have come together out of necessity during this first term at Manton.

Then a buzz passes across the room, and inside the frame of the double doors appear Scarlett Jacques and her gang. They're laughing among themselves and none of them has made any effort to look nice. Scarlett's faded-blue hair is tied back into two short pigtails. She's wearing baggy jeans and a leopard-print vest top and an oversize fake-fur coat. The whole atmosphere of the room changes as they enter.

Chloe tuts. "What the fuck are they doing here?"

Tallulah turns. "Why wouldn't they be here? They helped to plan it."

"I would have thought they were waaaay too edgy and cool for this sort of thing."

Tallulah feels a strange wave of defensiveness pass through her. "They're just people," she counters.

But she knows this isn't true. They're more than just people. They're a mood, a feeling, a vibe, an aspiration. They're like a music video or a trailer for a really cool movie. They're a billboard poster for a hip clothing brand. Within the tiny fishbowl environs of Manton College, they're basically celebrities.

"Want another drink?" she asks, getting to her feet.

Chloe shakes her head. "This is my limit," she says, miming driving a car.

"Coke?"

"Sure," says Chloe. "Diet, if they've got it."

Tallulah tugs down her heart-print shirt so that there's no gap between the waistband of her jeans and the hem of her shirt, no glimpse of the rice pudding mess left behind by her pregnancy.

She heads to the hatch just as Scarlett and her crew arrive. They smell as though they've been drinking already, making a kind of mockery of Tallulah's sober hour in front of a mirror, her quiet farewell to her baby son on her mother's lap, her brother sitting at his laptop, diligently doing his homework. How different their pre-party evenings have been.

Scarlett stares at her phone while someone else queues to get her a drink. Her fur coat hangs off her shoulders, revealing a tattoo on her upper arm and a chiseled collarbone. She takes the beer from her friend's hand and as she does so she catches Tallulah's eye.

"Oh!" she says. "It's Tallulah from the bus."

Tallulah nods. "Yup," she says, "it's me, from the bus."

They'd acknowledged each other a couple of times after their interaction at the bus stop that day a few weeks earlier, but that was as far as it had gone.

"You look nice." She tips her beer bottle toward Tallulah's face, a reference to her makeup, Tallulah assumes.

"Thanks." She almost says, *So do you,* but then thinks better of it.

The guy serving behind the bar looks at her inquisitively and she orders her drinks. She expects, as she turns away from the bar, that Scarlett will have left to join her friends on the dance floor, but she's waiting for her. Tallulah tries to hide her surprise.

"Cheers," says Scarlett, knocking her plastic beer bottle against Tallulah's.

"Cheers," says Tallulah.

"Who are you here with?" Scarlett glances around the room.

"Chloe Minter." She points at her friend, who is sitting scrolling through something on her phone. "She's in my year. She lives in the village. Near me. You know. And she was driving. So . . ." She shrugs, a suggestion that her reasons for being here with Chloe Minter are purely practical. Which, in a way, they are.

The DJ puts on "All I Want For Christmas Is You" by Mariah Carey and there is a huge swell of excitement, arms in the air, a dash to the dance floor.

"Oh! Oh, oh!" says Scarlett. "Come on. We've gotta dance!"

Tallulah blinks. She doesn't like dancing at the best of times. But she doesn't want to sound miserable so she laughs and says, "I'm not drunk enough yet."

Scarlett delves into one of the pockets on her huge fake-fur coat and pulls out a copper hip flask. "Quick," she says, "neck it."

"What is it?"

"Rum," she says. "Really, really good rum. My dad brought it back from Barbados. It's like"—she makes a circle out of her thumb and index finger—"the best."

Tallulah sniffs the rim of the flask.

"Can you smell the spice?" says Scarlett.

Tallulah nods, although really she can only smell the alcohol. She takes a sip and hands it back.

"No, no, no," says Scarlett. "That won't get you dancing! More!"

Tallulah tips the flask to her lips again and takes four huge slugs.

"Drunk enough to dance now?"

She nods and Scarlett pulls her onto the dance floor. They dance toward her friends and she twirls Tallulah in front of her and Tallu-lah is conscious of her new top riding up as she lifts her arms and she tries to lower them but Scarlett keeps pulling them up.

Everyone is singing along and Tallulah can see some tutors join-ing in now, and people she wouldn't expect to be on a dance floor, and the alcohol pumps its way through her blood supply and into her brain and suddenly she doesn't care about her porridge belly or Chloe sitting on the bench, she just wants to dance, dance like she's eighteen years old and doesn't have a care in the world and there's no baby at home, no put-upon mother who should be out at a party herself tonight, no ex-boyfriend loitering in the wings trying to woo her back, just her, eighteen years old, in her first term at college, her whole life ahead of her and the coolest girl in the world holding her hands above her head and grinning at her: Mariah, rum, glitter descending from the ceiling and landing at her feet and in her hair.

The song comes to an end and Scarlett finally lets her hands go.

"Now," she says, "Christmas has officially begun!" She makes a whooping noise and high-fives her friends and then, just as Tallulah assumes she will fade away from her and back into the protective bubble of her little gang, Scarlett turns to her and says, "Come outside with me."

Tallulah looks over her shoulder anxiously at Chloe.

"She'll be fine," says Scarlett. "Come on." She pulls her by the hand, out of the double doors and into the entrance hall, then to the car park. The air is immediately icy cold and while Scarlett is still wearing her huge fur coat, Tallulah is in only her short-sleeved cotton top. "Here," says Scarlett, opening up her coat. "Room in here for two."

Tallulah looks at her uncertainly before shrugging and smiling and nestling herself against Scarlett's bony frame and pulling the other side of her coat around her shoulders.

"Where are we going?"

"A little place I know."

Tallulah blinks at her, starting to feel strangely uneasy.

"Don't look so scared."

"I'm not scared."

"Yeah, you are."

They move as one underneath the carapace of the huge fur coat and end up on a bench. Scarlett goes through the pockets of the big coat and pulls out a packet of cigarettes. She flips it open and offers it to Tallulah.

Tallulah shakes her head. She's never smoked and never wants to.

"Sorry to drag you out of there," says Scarlett, plucking a cigarette from the packet. "Just realized I was too drunk. Way too drunk. Needed fresh air. And fresh company." She rolls her eyes.

Tallulah throws her a look.

"I mean, don't get me wrong, I love them to death, I really, really do. But we've all been hanging out for so long. You know, we were all at Maypole House together and that place is really intense. I mean, really intense."

"What were you doing there?"

"Oh, you know, just A levels. I did the first term of sixth form at a boarding school, but then I got expelled. Nobody else would take me except the Maypole, so my dad bought a house close by, so that I could be a day girl." Scarlett shrugs and lights her cigarette. "What about you? Where did you go to school?"

"Oh, you know, Upfield High, just local."

"Where do you live?"

"In that cul-de-sac, you know, on the other side of the common."

"With your parents?"

"Yeah. Well, with my mum. My dad lives in Glasgow. And my brother."

Her breath catches on the next thing she should say. The thing about her son, Noah. It's there, halfway up her throat. But she can't make it unstick. She doesn't know why. She's pretty sure that a girl like Scarlett would actually think it was quite cool that she had a baby and she was only eighteen. But for some reason, she doesn't want to be that girl tonight, the girl showing remarkable levels of maturity, the girl taking her responsibilities seriously, the girl who wakes with her baby every morning at 6:00 a.m., even at the weekends, who does her college work while her baby sleeps, who remembers to buy her own nappies and sterilize her own milk bottles bought with the allowance that her mother gives her, which other girls would spend on charcoal nose strips and false eyelashes from Superdrug. She's been that girl for six months and she is good at being that girl, but right now she is huddled under a fur coat in the cold with a skinny girl who probably wouldn't have a baby until she was at least thirty-six, who gets expelled from boarding schools and smokes cigarettes and has tattoos and a stud pierced through her tongue, and for now, at least, Tallulah wants to be someone else.

"Yeah," she finishes. "Just us."

"And have you always lived in Upfield?"

"Yes. Born and bred."

"So what's your dad doing in Glasgow?"

"He's Glaswegian. He moved back when he and my mum split up." Scarlett inhales and nods.

"And what about you?" Tallulah asks. "Who do you live with?"

She raises her brow. "Well, ostensibly I live with my mother and father but my mother is kind of two-dimensional and my father is always away. But I have a brother. He's cool. I like him. And we have literally, like, the best dog in the world. He's a Saint Bernard. Like, the size of a fucking pony, but thinks he's a regular dog. He's my best friend. Literally. I'd be lost without him. I'd probably die."

"I'd like a dog," Tallulah says. "But my brother's got allergies."

"Oh God, you have to get a dog. Get a cockapoo! Or anything with poodle in it. They're hypoallergenic. Cavapoos are nice too. You just absolutely must get a dog."

For a moment Tallulah finds herself idly fantasizing about a cavapoo, maybe one of those apricot-colored ones, with huge eyes and soft ears. She pictures herself walking it around the village and putting it in a shoulder bag to take it into shops and then she stops and remembers that she cannot have a cavapoo because she has a baby.

"Maybe," she says. "Maybe."

Scarlett rubs out her cigarette on the ground beneath her heel and pulls the copper flask out of her pocket again. She takes a sip and passes it to Tallulah, who takes a sip and passes it back.

"You're very cute," says Scarlett, eyeing her quite seriously. "Did you know that?"

"Er, no, not really."

"You really are. It's something about your . . ." She tilts Tallulah's face upward with her fingertip under her chin and studies her. "I think it's your nose. The way it sort of tips up, just at the end there. You look like Lana Del Rey."

Tallulah laughs hoarsely. "Don't be mad."

"I think it's the eyeliner, plus the nose." She frames Tallulah's face with her hands. "You should always wear your eyeliner like that," she says, slowly pulling away, but her eyes still taking in the detail of Tallulah's face.

Tallulah feels something flash through her, the kind of adrenaline rush that you get when you nearly miss a step coming downstairs, a sort of thrilling sickness.

And then a flashlight appears from the darkness, and the sound of voices, and there is Scarlett's gang, incapable of surviving without the oxygen of their leader's presence for even ten minutes before hunting her down.

"Oh, there you are," says one, almost cross with her for daring to be elsewhere. "Jayden said he thought you might have gone home."

"Nope. Just out here, chatting with Tallulah from the bus."

The two girls look at Scarlett quizzically, and Tallulah sees them take in the shape of their bodies pressed together underneath Scarlett's coat and sees something like recognition pass across their faces, a small shock of understanding, and she wonders what it is that they've seen.

They nod at her and she nods back, and Scarlett says, "This is Mimi and this is Roo. They're a pair of ho bags I've known for about a hundred years. This is Tallulah. Don't you think she's pretty? Don't you think she looks a bit like Lana Del Rey?"

They look at her blankly, slightly awkwardly.

Scarlett gets to her feet and her coat falls from Tallulah's shoulders and suddenly she is cold, very cold. She looks at the three girls, all of whom are lighting cigarettes and dancing together to the background thump of "8 Days of Christmas" by Destiny's Child emanating from the dining hall and she remembers Chloe sitting alone waiting for her can of Diet Coke and she says, "I'd better get back in. My friend's waiting for me."

Scarlett puts her hands on her hips and narrows her eyes at her in mock annoyance and then smiles and says, "See you around, Tallulah from the bus."

Tallulah gives her an awkward thumbs-up. She doesn't really know what else to say. And then she turns and heads back inside, where Chloe gives her a pained and questioning look.

"I'm really sorry," Tallulah says, sitting down next to her. "I don't really understand what just happened. She just kind of . . . hijacked me."

"Weird," says Chloe, wrinkling her nose slightly.

"Yeah," says Tallulah, caressing the curves of a rather warm plastic beer bottle and staring into the middle distance. "Yeah. It really was."

12

Kim leaves Kerryanne's apartment and walks across the common with Ryan to Megs's house to collect Noah.

He's asleep in his car seat when Megs brings him to the front door. Kim swallows a surge of annoyance. She specifically told Megs that Noah needed to stay awake because otherwise he wouldn't be tired at bedtime and now she'll have to wake him up to get him out of his clothes and ready for bed and he'll be grouchy and miserable and then won't want to sleep when she puts him down at bedtime but Megs just smiles indulgently at him in his car seat, his dark hair damp with sweat, and says, "Bless his little soul, he was exhausted, I couldn't bear to keep him awake."

Kim smiles grimly and takes the handle of the car seat. "Never mind," she says tightly.

"And I take it . . . ?" Megs begins. "Nothing about the kids?"

"No," says Kim. "Nothing about the kids. Although—did Zach happen to say anything to you about what he had planned for last night?"

"No. I mean, I didn't even know they were going to the pub until you told me about it. Haven't really spoken to him the last few days."

"So, you didn't know anything about . . ." Kim pauses, wondering whether to spoil the surprise or not, then decides that, no, getting to the bottom of the whereabouts of Zach and Tallulah is more important than surprises right now. ". . . a ring?" she finishes.

"A ring?"

"Yes. An engagement ring. Did Zach say anything to you about proposing to Tallulah?"

Megs laughs. "God," she says, "no!"

Kim narrows her eyes at her. She has no idea why Megs should find this concept funny.

"Is there anyone else who Zach might have talked it through with? A friend? His dad?"

"His friends, I suppose, but I've already spoken to all of them and none of them knows anything about what happened last night. And no, he wouldn't talk to his dad about it. His dad's not that sort of man. Not much emotional intelligence, you know."

Kim stifles a wry smile. She's rarely met anyone with less emotional intelligence than Megs. She sighs. "Fine," she says, "OK, well, I'd better get this little man home and try and persuade him to wake up and then try and persuade him to go back to sleep again."

Megs smiles at her blankly. She has no clue.

"Please, let me know if you hear anything, won't you?" Kim asks. "I'm going to call the police about Tallulah if she's not back by the time Noah's asleep. You might want to do the same."

Megs shrugs. "Still reckon the two of them have run away somewhere for a break from it all. But yes. Maybe I should be worried. You might be right."

Kim turns then and heads to her car, shaking her head almost imperceptibly as she walks, her eyes closing against the impossibility of understanding how a mother and a grandmother could have so little engagement with their roles.

———————

The first half of the evening passes quickly as she goes through the process of readying a year-old child for bed. Noah, as she predicted, won't settle and it's almost 9:00 p.m. by the time he finally drops off.

Kim craves wine but she needs to remain clear-headed and sober because her evening is far from over. She sits in the living room. There's something on the TV; she doesn't really know what: some loud Saturday-night fare. Ryan sits in the armchair scrolling through his phone, his foot bouncing up and down the only thing betraying his anxiety.

She calls Tallulah's number yet again. It goes through to voicemail, yet again.

She looks at Ryan. "Did Zach say anything to you?" she says. "About proposing to Tallulah?"

She immediately knows that he has by the slight jerk of Ryan's head, the immediate cessation of the foot bouncing. "Why?" he says.

"I just wondered. I found a ring in his coat pocket yesterday. I thought maybe he'd been planning to propose last night. It made sense, you know, given he was taking her out for the night."

"Well, yeah, he did kind of say he was thinking about it. But he didn't say when he was planning on doing it."

"What did he say exactly?"

"Just asked me what I thought. Said, did I think she'd say yes if he asked her."

"And what did you say?"

"I said I didn't have a clue. Because I didn't."

She nods.

Then she looks at the time. It's nine o'clock. It's enough, she thinks, enough. It's time.

With a racing heart and a sickening swirl in the pit of her stomach, she calls the police and she files a missing persons case.

———

A very attractive man is at her door the following morning. He wears a gray suit and a cream open-necked shirt, ID on a lanyard.

He pulls a badge from his jacket pocket and flashes it at her.

"Detective Inspector Dominic McCoy," he says. "You called about some missing persons last night?"

Kim nods, hard. "Yes, yes. God, yes. Please, come in."

She has barely slept. She brought Noah into her bed eventually because he wouldn't settle in his cot after his nighttime wake-up and the two of them had lain there, in the dark, blinking up at the ceiling.

At one point he'd turned to her, grabbed her cheek with one hot hand, and said "umma." He said it three more times before she realized that he was trying to say Mumma. That he was trying to speak his first full word.

"Come through," Kim says now, leading Dominic McCoy into her living room. "Can I get you anything?"

"No. I've just had a coffee so I'm good. Thank you."

They sit facing each other across the coffee table and Kim passes Noah a packet of rice cakes to keep him quiet for a while.

"So, my colleague tells me that your daughter failed to come home on Friday night? Is that correct?"

Kim nods. "My daughter, and her boyfriend—he lives with us. They both failed to come home."

"And they're how old?"

"They're both nineteen. They turned nineteen in March."

DI McCoy looks at her strangely, as if she shouldn't be worried about a couple of nineteen-year-olds.

"But they're parents," she continues. "Noah—he's their son. So it's not as if they're likely to just take off on a whim. They're good parents. Responsible."

He nods thoughtfully. "I see."

She wonders what it is that he thinks he sees. But then she answers his questions about the events of Friday and of Saturday. She gives him Scarlett's address, Lexie's address, Megs's address. She almost mentions the engagement ring, but then decides against it at the last minute; she's not sure why.

Half an hour later he stands to leave.

"So, what do you think, then?" Kim asks. "What do you think might have happened to them?"

"Well, there's no real reason to believe that anything has happened to them. Two youngsters, a lot of responsibility, their first night out in a long time, maybe they just made a break for freedom."

"No," she replies immediately. "Absolutely not. They're devoted to their son. Both of them. Particularly my daughter. Absolutely devoted to him."

He nods thoughtfully. "And the boyfriend, Zach? Was he in any way controlling? Would you say? Were there any signs of abuse going on?"

"No," she replies again, almost too fast, as she tries to override the uncomfortable little doubts she's starting to have. "He adores Tallulah. Dotes on her. Almost too much."

"Too much?"

She realizes what she's said and retreats. "No. Not too much. But, you know, it gets on her nerves sometimes, I guess."

"I wouldn't mind being doted on like that," he says with a smile.

Kim closes her eyes and nods. Men don't know, she thinks, they don't know how having a baby makes you protective of your skin, your body, your space. When you spend all day giving yourself to a baby in every way that it's possible to give yourself to another human being, the last thing you want at the end of the day is a grown man wanting you to give him things too. Men don't know how the touch of a hand against the back of your neck can feel like a request, not a gesture of love, how emotional issues become too cumbersome to deal with, how their love for you is too much sometimes, just too much. Kim sometimes thinks that women practice being mothers on men until they become actual mothers, leaving behind a kind of vacancy.

DI McCoy leaves a minute later. He promises that he will open an investigation. He doesn't say when or how. Kim watches him from her front window, climbing into his unmarked vehicle, adjusting his rearview mirror, adjusting his lanyard and his suit jacket and his hair, turning on the engine, and leaving.

She turns to Noah, who is in his bouncy chair, a mushed-up rice cake in the palm of his hand, and she forces a sad smile designed to distract him from the tears running down the sides of her nose and says, "Where's Umma, Noah? Where is she?"

13

Sophie leans down to read the inscription on a small wooden plaque beneath the rosebush behind the bus stop. It says: "Tallulah Rose, until we meet again."

She stands straight again and glances around herself, looking for the window at which poor Tallulah's mum might have stood, watching her girl waiting for her bus to school. There are no houses directly opposite the bus stop, but there is a small cul-de-sac just off the other side of the common, very close to Maypole House. From here Sophie can see the glint of sunlight off windows.

She crosses the common again and heads toward the cul-de-sac. It consists of about six houses, set in a half-moon around a small patch of green, cars parked half up on the pavements to make room for other cars to squeeze past. The houses themselves are small postwar dwellings, with rendered fronts and wooden porches. She turns and looks back across the common, trying to ascertain which of the houses might have a view of the bus stop. Two of them appear to. One of them seems quite run-down; the other looks bright and modern, with cacti in copper pots in the window and a brown leather sofa covered in brightly colored cushions just visible against the back wall.

The article said that the night they went missing Tallulah and her boyfriend had been drinking at the Swan & Ducks, the local gastropub that had been recommended to Sophie and Shaun by Peter Doody the day they arrived. Sophie carries on circling the common until she finds herself outside the pub. It's very attractive, freshly painted in heritage shades of gray; there's a graveled front area with round wooden tables and chairs, huge cream parasols, and chalk-board signs advertising the menu and the beer selection.

She pushes open the door. It's classic gastropub: tongue and groove, funky abstract art on the walls, designer wallpaper, re-conditioned floorboards, and halogen spots. The woman behind the bar is forty-something, attractive in an unconventional way. She's wearing a fitted black cap-sleeved T-shirt with black trousers and a bartender's apron tied tight around her waist. Her dark hair is pulled back in a ponytail. As she approaches Sophie she rests her hands against the bar, fixes a smile, and says, "What can I get you?"

"Oh, just a cappuccino, please. Thank you."

"Coming right up."

She turns toward the big chrome coffee machine and Sophie notices the tattoos on the undersides of her arms. At first she thinks they might be burns or scars, then she sees that they are baby foot-prints.

"Your tattoos are really cute," she says. "The baby feet."

The woman turns and Sophie sees her smile fade a little. She glances down at one of her arms and touches the image of the foot gently with her other hand. "Oh," she says. "Thanks."

She carries on making the coffee; the hiss and splutter of the ma-chine is deafeningly loud and Sophie doesn't attempt to continue the conversation. Her gaze drops to the woman's feet while she waits. She's delicately built but wearing somewhat incongruous scuffed leather army boots. Something twitches in Sophie's memory. She's seen those army boots before, recently, really recently.

And then she remembers: the pictures in the village newsletter of Tallulah's memorial procession—the mother had been wearing army boots, with the pretty floral dress.

The woman turns, with Sophie's cappuccino in her hand. "Chocolate on top?" she asks, holding aloft the canister.

And Sophie sees that it is her. It's Tallulah's mother. Kim Knox.

For a moment she is silent.

"Yes? No?" says the woman, waving the canister.

"Sorry, yes. Please. Thank you."

The woman sprinkles the chocolate powder over the coffee and slides it to her. Sophie feels inside her handbag for her purse, barely able to make eye contact with Kim Knox, feeling as though she's about to be caught out in her snooping around. She pays using her contactless card and takes the coffee to a small purple velvet armchair set next to a low brass coffee table. From here she watches Kim Knox restocking the shelves with Fever-Tree tonic waters. She has an odd energy about her; she looks as if she weighs no more than one hundred twenty-five pounds, but her movements are those of someone heavier. A young man walks into the pub and heads toward the gap in the bar. "Hi, Nick," she calls after him as he passes through.

He calls out, "Morning, Kim," before disappearing through a door at the back of the bar.

So it's definitely her. Kim Knox.

The man reappears a minute later tying an apron around his waist and then rolling up his shirtsleeves. "Want a hand?" he asks her.

"Sure," she says, scooting along a little to give him space.

Sophie drops her gaze and pretends to be looking at her phone.

She wonders how long Kim's worked here. She wonders if she was working here the night her daughter disappeared. There's so much she wants to know, wants to ask. She feels the tendrils of her fictional South London detective duo, Susie Beets and Tiger Yu, start to thread their way through her psyche.

When she's writing, her brain comes up with mysteries and Susie and Tiger have to solve them for her; that's how it works. And Susie and Tiger would have no qualms about approaching this sad, pretty woman and asking her questions about what happened to her daughter; they would just do it, because it was their job. But it's not Sophie's job. She's not a detective. She's a novelist and she has no right to invade this woman's privacy.

When she leaves a few minutes later, Kim Knox smiles. "Have a good day," she calls out, leaning to collect Sophie's empty coffee cup from the bar where she left it.

"Yes," says Sophie. "You too."

Sophie hauls an old bike out of the shed attached to their cottage, rids it of cobwebs and dead leaves, and cycles out toward Upley Fold.

After a hazy morning the sun is now starting to break through the cloud. The hedgerow smells of cow parsley and dead straw and the air is heavy and warm. She dismounts the bike outside the house and crunches across the gravel driveway toward the front door, where she cups her hands to the glass and peers into the hallway. There's a small fan of mail spread across the front-door mat and a gap under the front door with a brush strip attached to the underside. She delves into her rucksack, her hands searching for the wire coat hanger she'd put in there earlier for this very eventuality. She gets down onto her knees and slides it through the brush strips. It hits something. She gets lower to the floor and manipulates the hanger and the object until she thinks it might be close enough for her finger to locate it and then tugs it gently and there it is: an envelope.

It's a letter addressed to Mr. Martin J. Jacques. She breathes a sigh of relief. *Jacques.* An unusual name. A good name to put into Google. She takes a photograph of the letter and then gently pushes it back under the door.

The time is approaching eleven o'clock. She has another few minutes, she reckons, to snoop about, before heading back to the village for her lunch with Shaun. She circles the house, heading through the pretty wrought-iron gate with the arched top that leads to the back garden and the swimming pool. She peers through windows. She goes into a greenhouse and lifts up featherlight plant pots, watches spiders scuttling into corners. There's a small rusty trowel on the wooden bench and she slips it into the outside pocket of her rucksack. She has an idea.

The arrow on the piece of cardboard nailed to the fence points down and slightly to the left. She has no idea if "Dig Here" is a precise instruction or a general suggestion, but she starts digging as close to the tip of the arrow as she can. She has butterflies as she digs; her blood is filled with the adrenaline of dread.

Fourteen months ago two teenagers went missing somewhere between Dark Place and the village, possibly somewhere in these woods. The sign that appeared so innocuous two days ago, the sign she'd thought a leftover part of a team-building exercise or a treasure trail, the sign that she still feels so strongly she has seen somewhere else, at some other juncture of her life, now carries a shadow of potential horror. Might it be a shred of torn clothing? A tiny shard of bone? A hank of hair tied in faded satin ribbon? She holds her breath as the trowel goes deeper and deeper into the summer-dry earth. Every time it hits a stone she inhales again.

Nine minutes later the tip of her trowel dislodges something small and hard. A dark cube. She pulls it out of the ground with her fingertips and dusts it down. There's a gold logo stamped onto it, impossible to ascertain what it is exactly, and as her fingers feel around it she realizes that it is a ring box.

She pulls it apart with her thumbs.

Inside is a perfect, gleaming, golden engagement ring.

14

JANUARY 2017

College restarts and Tallulah is glad.

Christmas Day was nice, Noah's first.

Her dad, whose name is Jim, came down on Boxing Day, only the second time he'd seen Noah since he was born. He stayed in a room above the Swan & Ducks for two nights, and even paid for them all to have dinner there on the twenty-seventh. He was hugely taken with Noah and sat him on his knee and stared at him in wonder and called him the bonniest baby he'd ever seen. Tallulah's father was normally very self-centered and distant, but becoming a grandfather seemed to have removed a layer of protection from around his heart.

But the Christmas magic soon dissipated and the novelty of seeing Noah in his Christmas elf outfit wore off, and on New Year's Eve she was to stay home alone while her mum went to the pub with a group of friends and Ryan went to a party. It was one of the first moments that Tallulah felt stifled by the responsibilities and limitations of motherhood.

So when Zach offered to come and sit in with her that night, as much as she didn't want him to get the wrong idea and think that they were on again, she also didn't want to spend the night alone with a seven-month-old baby. So she said yes.

He arrived at 9:00 p.m., fresh from a friend's house, smelling slightly of beer and cigarettes, his hood up against a cold wind, his hands stuffed inside his pockets with an off-license carrier bag looped over his wrist.

She held the door ajar so he could come in and he leaned toward her for a quick peck on her cheek. "Happy New Year," he said.

"Not quite," she said.

"Is Noah in bed?" He glanced up the stairs.

Tallulah nodded. "Been down for a while."

"Sorry I'm a bit late. They didn't have what I wanted at the co-op so I had to go into the pub for it. Had to queue for ages. Packed in there."

He opened up the bag and let her peer inside.

Champagne, still cold from the fridge.

She smiled; she couldn't help it. She loved champagne.

"Saw your mum," he said, following her into the kitchen.

"Oh yeah?"

"Looked like she was having fun."

"Good," she said, sliding the champagne into the fridge and pulling out two beers.

"Got crisps as well." He pulled out two bags of tortilla chips and a jar of salsa. "And these, 'cos I know they're your favorites." He presented her with a bag of Cadbury's mini fingers.

She smiled again. "Thank you," she said.

They settled in front of the TV with their beers and the crisps. It was the first time she'd been alone with Zach in weeks, in months. Usually he came over during the day to spend time with Noah when he was awake. She'd thought it might feel a little awkward, but actually it didn't. She and Zach had known each other since they were fourteen years old, when he started at Tallulah's school after moving from a boys' school in the next village where he'd been bullied. She'd befriended him because he looked nice and she'd felt sorry for him and then they'd started dating and that was that. They were one of those teen couples that were part of the furniture, an unsurprising couple, not one to create chatter or intrigue.

So maybe it wasn't so strange that Tallulah should have felt so comfortable in his company that night. They'd been friends, they'd been lovers, they'd been ex-lovers, and now they were parents. There was no reason why they shouldn't be able to be friends again.

They didn't talk much that night, they let the telly entertain them, they looked at their phones and showed each other things that were amusing. At one point Zach snatched the phone from Tallulah's hand and said, "Here, I want to see your camera roll, let me see."

"Get off!" She'd laughed. "Why!"

"Just want to see photos of Noah," he said, and she let him scroll through her phone and it was nearly 100 percent photos of Noah. But then the roll got as far back as the Christmas party at college and Zach slowed down and started looking at the pictures in more detail.

"You look nice," he said, zooming into her face in a selfie she and Chloe had taken just before they went home. "You're wearing makeup."

"Yeah," she said. "Just eyeliner. Mum did it for me."

"Suits you," he said, turning and giving her a strange look. "Not like you to get all dolled up. And who's that?" he asked.

It's a selfie, taken on the dance floor at the Christmas disco when she and Scarlett had been dancing to Mariah Carey. Scarlett must have taken it. The camera was held up high, both of them beaming with all their teeth on show, pieces of glitter just starting to fall from the netting overhead, catching the light.

"That's Scarlett, a girl at college."

"You look really happy," he said, zooming in on their smiles. "I kind of thought you'd forgotten how to smile like that."

She made a dry sound of laughter. There was something accusatory in the tone of his voice, as if she'd somehow let him down by being happy.

"Yeah, well," she said, "they were playing Mariah. You'd have been smiling too."

"Just never think of you as the party type," he continued, and she felt herself starting to tense up. This, she thought, this was why she didn't want to get back together with him. Having a baby had .changed her; it had changed everything about her. Leaving school had changed her again. Being single after three years in a couple had changed her. She wasn't the soft, romantic girl she'd been before she got pregnant, before he'd walked away and left her to cope on her own. And she knew deep down that that version of Tallulah Murray was the only one that Zach was really interested in being with.

"Well," she said, "things change, don't they?"

"I guess," he said, and there was a note of sadness in his voice.

At a few minutes before midnight, they took the champagne out of the fridge and a pair of wineglasses and went into the garden. The next-door neighbor's cat sat on the fence, curled into its haunches, eyeing them curiously before turning to look up into the sky. It was cold and Tallulah shivered slightly. They'd had a couple of beers by then and when Zach put his arm around her shoulders to warm her up she didn't shake him off. They used their phones to count down to midnight and Zach popped the cork and they heard people all around them cheer and cars hoot their horns and fireworks pop and splutter in the blackness of the sky and they held their glasses of champagne aloft and said Happy New Year to each other and hugged and as they pulled away from each other, Zach looked as if he was about to kiss her and she thought, no. No, I don't want to kiss you. I'm not sure I'm ever going to want to kiss you again.

"Oh fuck, Tallulah," Zach said. "I wish I'd never done what I did last year. It's, like, the greatest regret of my life. You know that, don't you?"

She nodded.

"Will you ever forgive me?" He threaded her hands into his.

"I already forgave you," she said. "I forgave you ages ago."

"Then why?" he said. "Why can't we start over?"

"I just . . . I don't know, I just don't feel like I want a relationship right now. Noah, he's enough for me."

She felt his grip tighten around her fingers.

"But Noah," he said, "he's ours, we made him, that makes us a union, a team. It's not just about our relationship anymore, is it? It's about all three of us."

"You get to see him all the time."

"Yeah." He sighed impatiently. "I know that, but it's not the same, not the same as being with him twenty-four-seven. As a family."

"Yes, and that's not what I'm saying. Obviously it would be better for Noah if you were here all the time. But I don't know if . . ." She paused, buying time to find exactly the right words. ". . . if it's right for me."

He laughed, slightly dismissively. "Lula," he said, "for fuck's sake. We've known each other since we were fourteen. We know we're right for each other. Everyone knows we're right for each other. Please. Give me a chance."

"I mean, but where would we even live?"

"Here!" he said. "We could live here. You've got that big bed. Your mum loves me. Ryan loves me. I tell you what, tell you what," he countered quickly, clearly sensing her lack of enthusiasm for the idea. "Let's do a trial run, yeah? Maybe I could stay over one night. Nothing like that," he reassured her. "I'd sleep on the floor. Imagine Noah's face in the morning, waking up and seeing Dad there. And I could do his morning feed and let you have a lie-in. Yeah? Wouldn't that be good?"

He smiled down at her, using her hands to pull her closer to him so that their stomachs just about touched, their faces just an inch or two apart, his eyes boring deep into hers. "Wouldn't it?" he said again, kissing her knuckles, looking at her coquettishly, a lazy half smile on his lips.

And something inside her gave way at that moment, a kind of

sinking feeling in the pit of her stomach paired with a swoon in her groin, a feeling of wanting to be touched by someone, but not by Zach, of wanting to be wanted but wanting to be left alone, all at the same time; and she saw Zach's mouth move toward hers and found herself moving toward him and then they were kissing and all her misgivings fell away in a moment, all her ambivalence crystallized into a single longing for him, for it, for flesh, for limbs and mouths and all of it. Within a moment she was against the back wall, her arms and legs wrapped around him, and it was all over in under a minute and it was what she wanted, it was what she wanted so much, and he carried her afterward, still inside her, her arms and legs still wrapped around him, and twirled her around and around the garden, and she was smiling, properly smiling, the blood pumping through her, the moon shining down from the velvet sky, and when Zach said, "I love you, Lula, I love you so much," she didn't stop for even a second before replying that she loved him too.

Because right then, for that moment in time, she really did.

15

DI McCoy leaves Kim's house at about 10:00 a.m. and at around 11:00 a.m. a call comes through on Kim's phone from a number she doesn't recognize. She assumes that it must be him, that it must be the detective, that there is news, an update, a development of some kind, and her heart immediately begins to gallop and adrenaline pumps hard through her body.

"Yes."

"Oh, hi, is that Kim Knox?"

It's a girl's voice.

"Yes, speaking."

"This is, erm, Mimi? Scarlett's friend? She said you wanted to talk to me?"

"Oh!" Kim pulls out a dining chair and edges onto it. "Mimi. Thank you. Are you able to talk?"

"Yeah. Sure."

"I just wanted to know," Kim begins, "I mean, I've already spoken to Scarlett and her mother. And to Lexie. And none of them has a clue what happened on Friday night. But I just thought that maybe you might have picked up on something? Something that nobody else picked up on, that might explain what happened after Tallulah and Zach left?"

There's a brief silence and she can hear Mimi inhaling, pictures her drawing on a cigarette clutched between the knuckles of skinny fingers with bitten-down nails.

"I mean," Mimi begins, "literally the only thing I can think of is that they might have had a fight?"

Kim's head rolls back slightly. "Fight?"

"Yeah. They seemed a bit, I dunno, like there was something going on between them? A bit of tension?"

Kim swivels toward the dining table and moves the phone to her other ear. "Like what?" she says. "Can you describe it?"

Mimi sighs. "I went indoors, to charge my phone," she says. "Lula and Zach, they were sitting in, like, the little room just behind the kitchen. It's like a snug kind of thing. They didn't hear me go past. But I kind of peered through the gap in the door and I saw he had his hands really tight around her wrists and she was trying to get them free and he just kept them pinned down, like he was trying to stop her hitting him, or maybe trying to stop her leaving . . . I dunno. He looked really angry."

Kim blinks slowly. Mimi's words slot into the space in her head where her own misgivings have been gestating, the place where she wonders how Zach might have reacted to a rejection. As they do so, she feels a jolt of nausea pass through her. The "what if" starts to take shape, and the possibility of Zach having played some part in her daughter's disappearance overwhelms her for a moment.

"Did you hear either of them say anything about a ring? Maybe? Or an engagement?"

There's a solid pause on the line and then, "No. Nothing like that. They were both quite quiet, really. To be honest, I wasn't really sure why they were there. I didn't feel like they even wanted to be. You know?"

Sunday never ends.

Instead of putting him down in his cot, Kim takes Noah for a long walk around the village in his pushchair for his daytime nap, her eyes scanning every hedgerow, every alleyway and crevice between houses. As she passes Maypole House her eyes go to the back of the grounds where the student accommodation is. She thinks of Scarlett's ex-boyfriend Liam, the only person who was there on Friday night whom she has not spoken to. But she's sure, as Lexie had said, that he didn't see or hear anything more than she had, as he left early with her.

A moment later she finds herself outside the Swan & Ducks. The front terrace is heaving, as it always is on a sunny Sunday lunchtime: prosecco on tables in wine coolers, jugs of Pimm's, children in high chairs being fed chopped-up sausage and mash by mums in floaty dresses with sunglasses on their heads, cockapoos curled underneath tables in the shade.

Kim wheels the pushchair through the throng and into the bar, where it is cool and overcast. There are fewer people in here and she goes straight to the bar. She recognizes the young guy behind the bar; it's Nick. He's an out-of-work actor who likes flirting with middle-aged men just to watch them blush.

"Hello, you," he says, "don't normally see you here during the day. What can I get you?"

"Oh," she says, "no. Not here for lunch. Just wondering . . . you were here on Friday night, yes?"

"As it happens, yes, I was. They work me like a dog."

"And Megs told you, about my daughter and her son?"

"Yeah, that's right. Did they get back OK?"

"No," she says, her voice threatening to crack. "No." She draws her breath in hard and regains control. "They're still not back. I've reported it to the police now. I guess they'll want to talk to you at some point, ask you what you saw."

"Oh God, Kim. That's terrible. You must be worried sick."

"Yes," she says, squeezing out a strained smile. "I really am. But I just wondered what you saw exactly?"

"Well, not much really, I'm afraid. They started off over there." He points to a nook at the back of the bar. "All cozy and lovey-dovey. He bought a bottle of champagne. They had the seafood platter. They were so cute. And then there was this other group. A kind of Maypole group, you know? Loud, in your face. And I think they knew your daughter? And sort of infiltrated your daughter's nice romantic evening. I felt really bad for them!"

Noah starts to stir in his pushchair and Kim rocks it a little, absentmindedly.

"Did you see anything strange happen?"

"Strange?" Nick turns and fixes his lighthouse beam of a smile on a customer who has appeared at Kim's side. He takes their order; then he switches back to Kim a moment later and says, "I wouldn't say strange, no. Lots of drinking. And given the amount of cashbacks the Maypole kids were asking for, I suspect maybe a drug delivery of some kind, but I didn't see any evidence of that. And then it was closing time and they all just left. And that was that." He looks at her sadly and says, "Fuck, Kim. I'm sure they'll be home any minute now, they're bound to be. You know what teenagers are like."

She carries on walking. She goes to Tallulah's friend Chloe's house, just outside the village, the last in a row of small flat-fronted cottages with doors opening directly on the main road. Chloe says no, she hasn't spoken to Tallulah in ages. But she also says something interesting. When Kim mentions that Tallulah had last been seen at the house of Scarlett Jacques in Upley Fold, Chloe's eyes narrow and she says, "Weird."

Kim says, "Why?"

Chloe shrugs. "There's just something off about Scarlett and that lot. Something, I dunno, dark, and there was this night, last year, the college Christmas party, when I was sitting with Lula, and Scarlett sort of took her away, kind of rude, and I can't really explain it, but it was like Lula already knew her? Even though she didn't? And they were dancing for a while and then they went outside for like about ten minutes and Lula was all on edge when she came back in. Couldn't really work out what it was about. I mean, as far as I was aware, Scarlett and that lot are just this uberclique, never speak to anyone, yet she spoke to Lula. It was weird. Anyway, Lula and me didn't really talk again after that."

Kim grimaces. "After the Christmas party?"

"Yeah. I mean, we say hi if we see each other, but we don't hang out."

"But what about in February? When you were . . . going through the thing you were going through?"

Chloe gives her a blank look.

"You were feeling really low and Tallulah came and spent the night with you?"

"Are you sure you mean me?"

"Yes, back in February, Tallulah told me you were really low and she needed to spend the night with you in case you did anything stupid."

Chloe shakes her head. "God, no. No, that definitely never happened. I did not feel low and she did not stay the night. I promise you, Lula and I have barely said a word to each other this year. We've barely seen each other. It sounds like she might have been lying to you, to be honest."

16

The grounds at Maypole House fill slowly but surely during the weekend before term begins. The empty buildings come alive with the movement of people, the sounds of voices and music, of doors opening and shutting, ringtones and car engines, laughter and shouting.

Sophie feels strange, less like she's in the middle of nowhere, as she'd feared, and more like she's actually in the middle of everything. From the garden outside the kitchen she can sit and watch the students leave their rooms and head into the main building for breakfast. Some of them take morning jogs around the grounds. She starts to recognize certain faces, certain groups of friends, and she can tell even from a distance who is new to the college and who is a returner by the confidence with which they traverse the school grounds.

On the Sunday night before term officially starts, there is what is called the Registration Day Dinner. Registration Day is the busiest day in the run-up to the new term, when the majority of students arrive from home to board and sign up for their classes. In reality, most of this is done online before the students ever set foot on campus, but it's an old tradition and it's a good way for students to set eyes on their classmates before they hit the classroom. And then there is the dinner, which, according to Shaun, is what it is really all about.

In days gone by, it was a sit-down affair, but since the new accommodation block was built ten years earlier, doubling the size of the student population, the dinner has morphed into a party with a buffet and a DJ.

Sophie, for some reason, wants to look stunning for the party. Not just nice, but knockout, drop-dead amazing so that the students will all talk about her behind her back—so they'll say, "Wow, Mr. Gray's girlfriend is really pretty, isn't she?" She wants, for some reason, to win the approval of some of the handsome-looking boys she's seen jogging around campus. Not the young ones, obviously, but the nineteen-year-olds, the nearly men with their summer tans and their thick hair and their swaggers.

She pulls on a black satin camisole top with lace trim and a lace-paneled back. She teams it with fitted black trousers and high-heeled black sandals and she fixes her hair into a side ponytail that sits on her shoulder. She blobs her face with things that promise to *illuminate* and *shimmer*.

Shaun does a double take as she walks into the hallway. He says, "God, wow, Soph, you look lovely." And she can tell he means it.

The noise from the main hall is deafening. It has a barreled, wood-lined ceiling and windows set up so high they only let in light, no view. But there are three pairs of huge double doors open onto the lawn, where there is a marquee, and tables and chairs laid out in the early-evening sun. She and Shaun wander across the lawn together, her arm linked through his, throwing smiles at people and stopping to say hello. They find an empty table and Shaun leaves Sophie to go and get them drinks. Her gaze travels across the scene as she waits for him to return, to the clusters of lovely young things curled around one another in little pockets, impenetrable, slightly terrifying, the power and yet the patheticness of them, the know-all- and know-nothing-ness. It's not just their youth that glitters, she ponders as she watches them, it's their backgrounds, their innate privilege, the suggestion in the way they touch their hair, the way they hold their drinks, the way they scroll so nonchalantly through their phones. They come from places that aren't like the places most people come from and they have the high-gloss veneer of money that shines through the scruffiest of exteriors.

Sophie comes from modest houses and cars that drive till they die and state schools and weekly Tesco shops and biscuits off plates at her grandma's flat every Saturday. She hadn't missed out on anything: there was always food and holidays abroad and shopping trips to Oxford Street and takeaways on Friday nights; there was always enough of everything. Her life was perfect. But it was matte, not gloss.

She thinks about Dark Place, about the Jacques family, about the swimming pool that must once have sparkled icy blue in the summer sun, the art that must once have sat on the Perspex plinths, the music that must once have tumbled out of double doors and across the manicured lawns, the especial laughter of people with numerous cars and horses and chalets in the Alps. Their daughter, Scarlett, had once been a student here, according to Kerryanne Mulligan.

Shaun reappears with two glasses of wine and takes his seat next to Sophie. "Sorry I took so long," he says. "Got waylaid."

"Let's drink these," she says, "and then we can mingle."

"Urgh, God, do we have to?" he says, dropping his forehead against her bare shoulder.

She ruffles the back of his neck and laughs. "I kind of think we do have to, yes. You're basically the king. You have to get out there."

"I know." He lifts his head and puts a hand on her knee. "I know."

They drink their wine and within a minute or two are joined at their table by a couple called Fleur and Robin who are the geography teacher and the photography teacher respectively and who live in a cottage just outside the village and have a Border terrier called Oscar and a rabbit called Bafta and are both very talkative indeed. Halfway through this conversation they are joined by a middle-aged man called Troy, who has a magnificent beard. He is the philosophy and theology teacher and he lives on campus and has a lot of recommendations for local delicatessens, wine shops, and butchers. Someone whisks Shaun away and for a while it is Sophie and Troy, and that is fine, Troy is very easy to talk to, and then they are joined by someone with a French accent and someone with a Spanish accent and soon her table is overrun with people whose names she barely has time to catch, let alone their jobs or roles at the school, and then she notices a younger man, standing at the periphery of the group that has gathered around her table: he's holding a beer in one hand; his other hand is in the pocket of a pair of navy chino shorts. His brown hair is short and wavy; he's wearing a white shirt with the sleeves rolled up to just above his elbows and white trainers, without socks. He has a nice physique. He looks a bit like a film star, one of the ones called Chris, Sophie can never remember which is which.

He's talking to an older woman; Sophie can tell he doesn't know her all that well, that he's making an effort to be charming and polite. She sees him turn very vaguely in her direction, as though he can feel her eyes upon him, and she looks away. The next time she glances over she sees that the older woman has turned to talk to someone else and left him adrift. He lifts his beer bottle to his lips and takes a thoughtful slug. He sees her looking at him and smiles. "You must be Mr. Gray's partner," he says, approaching her.

"Yes," she says brightly. "My name's Sophie. Lovely to meet you."

He passes his beer bottle to his other hand and offers her his hand to shake. "Great to meet you too. I'm Liam. I'm a classroom assistant here. I work with some of the kids with special needs, you know, dyslexia, dyspraxia, that kind of thing."

He's well-spoken, but there's a kind of rough Gloucester undercurrent to his accent.

"Oh, that sounds really interesting."

He nods effusively. "Yeah, it's amazing. I mean, it's not, like, my life's ambition or anything, it's just temporary, but for now it's really, really satisfying."

"So, what is your life's ambition, then?"

"Oh, yeah, right." He passes his hand around the back of his neck and screws his face up. "Haven't quite worked that one out yet. Still trying to find one, I reckon." He smiles. "Twenty-one going on fifteen. Failure to launch."

He sounds apologetic and Sophie finds herself reassuring him.

"No," she says, "you're working, you have a really important job, that's more than a lot of young men your age these days."

"Yeah," he says. "Maybe." Then he says, "So, what do you think of Maypole House?"

She glances around and nods. "Yes," she says. "I like it. It's not what I'm used to. I mean, I'm a Londoner, born and bred, I've never lived outside London before, so country living is a bit of a shock to the system."

"Oh, this isn't country," says Liam. "This is not country, believe me. I was brought up on a cattle farm in Gloucestershire. That was country. This is just a nice place for people to live who don't want to live in cities."

Sophie smiles. "Fair enough, I guess." Then she says, "How long have you been teaching here?"

"Well . . ." He smiles sheepishly. "I actually used to be a student here, believe it or not. I was sent here by my parents when I was fifteen to do my GCSEs because I was getting too, er, distracted by other things at my old school. And then I liked it here so I stayed on to do my A levels. Failed them all. Retook them. Failed one. Thought about retaking it . . . So yeah, I was a student here for . . ." He narrows his eyes as he makes the mental calculation. ". . . four and a bit years? It might possibly be an all-time record for the Maypole. Most students aren't here for much longer than a couple of years. And now they can't get rid of me."

He laughs and Sophie laughs too.

Then she says, "So, you must know a lot about the place, about its history?"

"I am the world expert in Maypole House, yes, that's about right."

"So if Shaun needs to know anything, you're the man to talk to?"

"Yeah, I guess so. Just send him my way. I'm his man."

"So . . . you were here last summer," she begins carefully. "When those teenagers went missing?"

A shadow passes across his face. "Yeah," he says. "I was here then. Not only that, but I was there."

Sophie starts. "There?"

"Yes. At the house. The night they disappeared. I mean. I was friends with Scarlett, the girl who lived there. I didn't see anything, obviously. I didn't know anything. But yeah. Shocking times, really. Shocking times." He changes tack, swiftly, to Sophie's frustration. "And what about you? What do you do for a living? If you were in London, did you have to leave your job, or . . . ?"

She shakes her head. "No," she says. "No. I mean, I was once a classroom assistant, like yourself, in fact. At a primary school in London. But now I'm self-employed, I can work from home, so nothing much has changed for me in that way. You know. Though, to be perfectly honest, I haven't quite managed to get back into any kind of discipline yet. I keep getting distracted by things." She laughs, lightly, but actually she is worried by how, after nearly a week at Maypole House, she hasn't written a word of her latest book. Every time she opens it up and begins to type, she starts thinking about Tallulah Murray and Dark Place and Scarlett Jacques and the rosebush across the common and the pink baby feet tattooed on the underside of Kim Knox's arm and the engagement ring in the dusty black box hidden inside her makeup drawer. She thinks of Martin Jacques, whom she googled after snooping on his mail, thinks of the man she saw online, tall and haggard with a quiff of thinning steel hair and a stern expression, the man who is described on LinkedIn as the CEO of a Guernsey-based hedge fund and is currently, according to another Google result, living alone in Dubai, having separated from his wife.

She'd found no mention of his ex-wife or grown-up children on any page of the internet but the separation seemed the obvious explanation to Sophie of why Dark Place had been abandoned and left to rot.

"Oh well," says Liam, "I'm sure once the college gets into a routine, you will too."

She smiles gratefully. "That's a very good way of thinking about it," she says. "Thank you. You're very wise."

As she says this, she sees Shaun appear over Liam's shoulder. She's struck for a second by the contrast between them: the twenty years that divide them. Shaun looks, for all his handsomeness and charisma, old enough to be Liam's father.

"Hi," he says, putting a hand out to Liam, "Liam, isn't it?"

"Yeah, that's right. Good to see you again."

They conclude that they've already met and the conversation becomes diluted with other people and other topics and soon Sophie is no longer talking to Liam at all; he's been absorbed into another group. She finds herself alone and walks across the lawn toward the bar inside the marquee. Here she gets herself a second glass of wine and carries it back outdoors. She can just see Shaun across the lawn, deep in conversation with Peter Doody and Kerryanne Mulligan.

Then she sees Liam walking across the lawn toward the main hall and, on a whim, she follows him. He carries on walking though the hall and out the doors on the other side. Then he crosses the back courtyard and heads toward the accommodation block. She sees him tapping the security code into the panel and, with a buzz and a click, he's gone. She sits on a bench in the courtyard, glad of a moment to herself before going back into the fray. The wine is warm but she drinks it anyway. The evening sun is strobing through ribbons of purple cloud and she turns her face into it, her eyes closed, listening to the distant din of chatter and laughter.

She shudders slightly to right herself, and then she opens her eyes and, as she does so, she sees a pair of tanned feet overhanging the bars of a balcony on the third floor of the residential block, the edge of a paperback book, a cold beer sitting on a table.

It's Liam.

For a moment she toys with the idea of calling up to him, of inviting herself in, of drinking a cold beer with him and asking him what he thinks really happened at Dark Place that night.

She shakes her head to herself; then she heads back through the cloisters to the party.

17

Zach spends the night with Tallulah on New Year's Eve and never goes home. When Tallulah wakes up for her first day back at college five days later, she awakes in a bed shared with her baby and her baby's father. She and Zach haven't had sex again since New Year's Eve, but they sit side by side on the sofa at night and they kiss each other goodbye and hello and they hug and they touch.

Tallulah's mum is pleased. Tallulah knows that she's always felt guilty for marrying a man who wasn't cut out for the hurly-burly of family life, who ran back home to his mum the minute she said she needed him and left them all behind without a glimmer of remorse. And Tallulah can tell that she is pleased that Tallulah and Zach are going to make a go of being a proper family and that Zach is going to relieve some of the pressure on Tallulah as a single parent.

Tallulah kisses her mum goodbye on her first day back at college. In the front garden she looks up and sees Zach and Noah at her bedroom window, Zach holding Noah's tiny hand up and waving it for him. She sees him mouthing, "Bye-bye, Mummy. Bye-bye, Mummy." She blows them kisses and then walks away.

At the bus stop she finds herself looking for Scarlett. Scarlett never appeared at the bus stop again after that first time and Tallulah didn't see her to talk to after the Christmas party but for some reason Scarlett has left an imprint on Tallulah's psyche. Their two interludes feel important to Tallulah, and she feels like something is meant to happen now, a third act, a conclusion of some sort. The bus arrives; she takes one last look across the common, toward Maypole House, sighs, and gets on board.

After lunch that day Tallulah decides to visit the art block. She's never been in the art block before; it's a squat square building in the middle of campus, kind of ugly. The corridors inside are decorated with rows of slightly alarming self-portraits. She finds a door toward the end of the corridor that says YEAR ONE FINE ARTS and peers through the window. The room is empty but locked. She passes through more corridors lined with more art and then finds one that is labeled as SCARLETT JACQUES YI.

Tallulah stops. It's a portrait of Scarlett in a crop T-shirt and oversize shorts draped inside a huge red velvet throne-like chair, wearing a tiara at an angle, high-top trainers, her hair scraped back, and hoop earrings, wrists layered with rubber bands. At her feet sits a gigantic brown dog, almost the same size as Scarlett, also wearing a crown. Both of them stare directly at the viewer, the dog looking proud, Scarlett looking challenging.

It's an arresting image; it draws the eye first to Scarlett and then to every other detail: a pile of silver cream chargers on the floor catching the light, a small window behind with the suggestion of a face, staring as though watching her. There's a gun on a table, an Apple phone, a dish with a fresh red heart in it that looks as if it's still beating. On another table there's a cake with a slice missing and the knife used to cut it has a drop of blood on it.

Tallulah has no idea what any of it means, but it's beautifully painted, all in sun-bleached shades of pink and green and pale gray with shocking slashes and spots of red. She finds herself mouthing "Wow" to herself.

"Amazing, isn't she?"

She turns at the voice behind her. She'd thought she was alone. It's one of Scarlett's gang; she can't remember her name.

"Yes, I mean, I haven't seen her work before, but this painting is incredible."

"You know she left?"

Tallulah blinks, feels a kind of tightness in her stomach. "What?"

"Scar's gone. She's not coming back." The girl makes a kind of popping noise with her mouth, as though Scarlett were a bubble that had burst.

"But why?"

"No one really knows. I keep messaging her and she keeps saying she'll tell me when she can, but she can't tell me right now, so, yeah . . ."

Tallulah turns back to the painting. "What a waste," she says.

"Yeah," the girl agrees. "She's a fucking idiot. All that work and all that talent and she's just walked away from it. But there you go. That's Scar. An enigma. Wrapped in a blanket." She smiles. "You're Tallulah from the bus, aren't you?"

Tallulah nods.

"Mimi. We met at the Christmas party."

"Oh, yeah. Hi."

Mimi cocks her head at Tallulah and says, "Are you doing art?"

Tallulah shakes her head. "No, just fancied looking at the art. Someone said it was really good."

Mimi looks at her curiously for a moment. Then she pulls her heels together, straightens up, and says, "Anyway, time to get on. And if you see Scarlett around your neck of the woods, tell her to stop being a fucking dick and get in touch. Will you?"

Tallulah smiles. "I will," she says. "I promise."

———

After that, Tallulah looks for Scarlett every time she leaves the house. She knows that Scarlett's boyfriend, Liam, is a student at Maypole House, so it's more than possible that Scarlett would be in the village from time to time. Every now and then Tallulah flicks through her photo roll to get to the picture of her and Scarlett at the Christmas party and tries to remember the way she'd felt that night, the person she was when she was under the red-hot glow of Scarlett's attention. She googles Scarlett's name from time to time too, idly, just in case she's ended up in the newspapers somehow. She doesn't know where Scarlett lives, just that it's somewhere walking distance from the village, which could be anywhere; there are at least three hamlets near Upfield Common and the roads between are peppered with private driveways leading to the sorts of big houses that Tallulah imagines Scarlett to live in.

And then one day, during the last week of January, Tallulah sees Scarlett getting out of the passenger seat of a Smart car parked outside the co-op on the high street of the village.

She's wearing what look like pajamas, with her fake fur coat over the top. Her hair is straggly and she's wearing beaten-up trainers over fluffy socks. In the driver's seat of the car, Tallulah sees a young man. He's staring at his phone and there's the dull thud of music emanating from the car. A moment later Scarlett emerges with a carrier bag and jumps back into the Smart car. The boy in the driver's seat looks at her briefly, turns his phone off, and drives the car toward the road that goes to Manton.

Tallulah stands, watching it disappear as though it might carry some clue as to its final destination. Then she remembers something. Her mum had mentioned a few days ago that she'd seen Keziah, one of Tallulah's best friends from primary school, working at the co-op. Tallulah hasn't seen Keziah for months; last time was when she was just starting to show in her pregnancy and Keziah had put her hand to Tallulah's bump and made a sound as if she were about to faint because she was so overawed by it.

Keziah's behind one of the tills when Tallulah walks in a moment later. Her face lights up when she sees her. "Lula!" she says. "Where've you been hiding?"

Tallulah smiles and shrugs. "Tend to do big shops now," she says, "with the car. Easier with all the nappies and formula, you know."

Keziah smiles warmly at her. "How's the bubba?"

"Oh. He's amazing," she replies.

"Into everything, I bet."

"Not yet. He's too young for that. But he's mellow anyway, you know. He's a little Buddha."

"At home with your mum?"

"Well, yeah, my mum. And Zach."

"Oh," says Keziah. "I thought you two had . . . ?"

"Yeah, we did. And then we got back together again. Around New Year."

Keziah beams at her. "Oh," she says, "that's amazing! I'm so pleased. You two were made for each other."

Tallulah smiles tightly. "It's nice," she says, "nice for Noah. And nice to have another pair of hands. You know."

"You look really different," says Keziah.

"Do I?"

"Yeah, you look, kind of, I dunno, really grown up. Really pretty."

"Oh," says Tallulah. "Thank you."

"You should come out one night. With me and the girls."

"Yes. I'd like that." She's not sure she would like it. She's always thought there was a reason why she hadn't stayed in touch with her friends from primary school but has never been quite sure what that reason might be—something deep-seated and subconscious, something that even now makes her feel strange when contemplating the idea of a reunion.

"That girl," she says, "who just came in wearing pajamas? Do you know who she is?"

"The skanky one, you mean?"

Tallulah shakes her head slightly, trying to align the way she sees Scarlett with the way someone else might see her, and then she says, "Yeah. The one with the furry coat."

"Yeah. That's the girl who lives in Dark Place."

"Dark Place?"

"Yeah, you know, that big old house in Upley Fold?"

She shakes her head.

"You must know it," Keziah says. "It's like the biggest house in the area."

Tallulah shakes her head again and then says, "What did she buy?"

Keziah scoffs a little. "Why d'you want to know that?"

"I dunno. She's just . . . I kind of know her from college and she left really mysteriously, no one knows why, and I'm just being nosy, I guess."

"She bought rum, rolling tobacco, and tampons." Keziah rolls her eyes. "Such a skank," she says.

"Did she say anything?"

"You're kidding me, right? As if someone like *her* would make conversation with the checkout girl at the co-op." She tuts and then her eyes drift across Tallulah's shoulder to a customer waiting to be served. "Better go," she says. "Love to the bubba. Bring him in next time, so I can see him. Yeah?"

Tallulah smiles. "I will. Promise."

She walks home slowly, googling Dark Place on her phone with one thumb as she goes. A Wiki page comes up for what looks like a house out of a fairy tale or a ghost story; her eyes scan the text and she catches fragments of a story about coffee plantations and Spanish flu and assassination attempts and people having their eyes pecked out by crows. She wonders why the house isn't famous or open to the public, how a place like that could just be a family home, the place that Scarlett lives, where she is headed right now with her tobacco and her rum and her packet of tampons.

Curiosity suddenly swamps her and she crouches down to feel through her rucksack for her college planner. She flicks it open to the back page and scans the contacts listed there until her finger hits Scarlett's name. Before she can change her mind she words an email:

> Hi, Scarlett, this is Tallulah from the bus, just checking in, hope you're OK. See you around, luv T.

She presses send before she changes her mind, puts her planner back in her bag, and heads home to her baby.

18

Kim calls DI McCoy at eight o'clock on Monday morning. He answers within a few rings.

"DI McCoy."

"Oh. Hi. Sorry to call so early. It's Kim Knox. From Upfield Common? I wondered if you had an update about my daughter, Tallulah Murray?"

"Ah, yes, hi, Kim." She can hear him flipping through papers in the background. "Sorry. We've not got anything to report right now, I'm afraid. We've been over to the house in Upley Fold; we've spoken to the family there. But there were no leads as a result of that. We're heading into the village right now, a couple of my officers are going into the pub, the, er"—more paperwork being flipped—"Swan and Ducks, to talk to the manager there, see if they can shed any light."

"But the woods," says Kim, "are you going to send anyone into the woods, because, you know, it's still possible they're in there somewhere. That they decided to walk back when they couldn't get a taxi, and that something . . . they might have fallen into an old well or something or . . ." She draws in her breath. She can hardly bear to bring herself to say what she's about to say, but she has to, because it's relevant, it's important. "Maybe they had a fight," she says. The words all tumble out on top of one another. "Scarlett's friend Mimi, she told me she saw them having an argument, at Scarlett's house. Apparently, Zach was being a bit physical with Tallulah. Had her by the—by the wrists."

She hears DI McCoy fall still. The papers stop ruffling. "Right," he says. "And that sort of physical aspect? Was there a lot of evidence of that between them? From what you could see at home? I got the impression from our chat on Sunday that they were quite lovey-dovey."

There it is again. *Lovey-dovey.* The same expression Nick at the pub had used yesterday to describe them.

She sighs. "Well, the thing is, he is. Zach is lovey-dovey. He's the romantic one. Tallulah, I often felt, was just putting up with it. That she'd rather be left alone. But no, I never saw anything physical between them."

"Never heard anything behind closed doors?"

"Nope. Nothing like that. I mean, Zach has a quick temper sometimes. But never with Tallulah. Never with the baby."

"So what . . ." DI McCoy begins, and Kim can hear the creak of a chair as he moves position, "what do you think might have brought about the row Tallulah's friend said she saw them having on Friday night?"

Kim's mind goes back to the engagement ring in Zach's jacket pocket, the conversation Ryan recalls having with Zach about the idea of him proposing to Tallulah. It feels like such an intimate thing to share with a stranger, as though she's giving away a bit of Zach's heart. But she has to tell the detective—it might, as she can't stop thinking, be the key to everything.

"On Friday morning," she begins hesitatingly, "I found something in Zach's jacket pocket. A ring. Looked like an engagement ring. A diamond in a gold band. And my son, Ryan, says that Zach had mentioned something vague about proposing to Tallulah. And yesterday I was talking to the barman at the Swan and Ducks and he said that Zach and Tallulah had been drinking champagne that night before they hooked up with Scarlett and her gang. And it's possible, you know, that he asked her. And she might have . . ." She swallows. "She might have said no."

There's a slight pause and then DI McCoy says, "And you think Zach might have responded negatively to this?"

"I don't . . ." Kim draws in her breath. "I don't know what I think. But it is just *possible*," she says, "that they got into a row on their way home from Scarlett's house and Zach lost his temper and . . . something happened and now he's hiding somewhere. It's possible, that's all."

But even as the words leave her mouth she knows it's not just possible, it's likely. What's the aphorism? *It's always the husband.*

"Right," says DI McCoy, "well, I think we now have enough to go on to launch a search party. Leave it with me, Mrs. Knox."

"Ms."

"Sorry. Ms. Leave it with me. And I will be in touch with exact timings. Et cetera."

"We searched a bit already," she says. "On Saturday. A few of us. In the woods."

"Oh."

"I mean, we didn't find anything, we didn't, at least I think we didn't touch anything or disturb anything. I think it's—"

"It's fine," he cuts in. "I'm sure it's fine. Anyway. I'll be in touch with details as soon as I have them. And, just before I go, I'd like to talk to Zach's family? Do you happen to have a phone number or an address?"

"Yes, of course." She reels off Megs's address and then says, "You won't say anything to them, will you? About what I said, about Zach? I mean, we have a grandchild in common, I can't have something like that between us. It would be incredibly difficult. It would—"

He cuts in again. "Absolutely not," he says. "Please don't worry about that. We'll be very discreet."

"Thank you. Thank you so much."

She looks at Noah as she ends the call. He's in his high chair eating dry Cheerios off the tray top. He looks back at her and he smiles.

"Seeyos," he says, his eyes blazing with pride, his finger pointing at the cereal hoops. "Seeyos."

Kim closes her eyes.

"Yes!" she says, mustering some spirit. "Yes! Cheerios! Well done! Clever boy! You are such a clever boy!"

Her voices catches and she turns away.

Noah's second word. And Tallulah has missed them both.

The search of the woods begins in Upley Fold that lunchtime. It's what Kim wanted but it's also terrifying. The sudden burst of energy and people, when for so many hours it's just been her alone, rattles her.

She sees Megs and Simon standing at the edge of the woods as she approaches. Megs turns and looks at her and Kim sees something like fear pass across her implacable face. She says something to Simon and Simon glances up.

"This is mad," Megs says to Kim as she nears her. "I mean, I know it's odd that they've not been home, I get that, but still, this . . ." She spreads her hand out in an arc to describe the squad of police officers in high-vis attire, the sniffer dogs. "It's all a bit OTT, isn't it?"

Kim doesn't reply immediately; she's not sure what to say.

"Did they come and talk to you?" she asks finally. "The police?"

"Yeah. Bloody ridiculous. They were there for ages. Asking all these questions about Zach, about what sort of boy he was, about how he got on at school, about his job. I was just, like, what on earth are you asking me all this for? It's almost like they think he's done something wrong."

She says this glibly, but Kim catches a glint of something hard in her eye as she glances up at her.

Ryan is at home with Noah and the police have asked family not to join in the search yet. So for now it is just Kim, Megs, and Simon standing together, while the detectives loiter together in a huddle a few meters away and the search team and their dogs arrange themselves to head into the woods.

It's warm again today and Kim feels clammy and anxious.

"How long do you think this will take?" Megs calls out starkly to the group of plainclothes detectives. DI McCoy turns at the question, gives his colleagues a look before walking over to join them.

"Well," he says, "there's no way of knowing. Luckily at this time of year we have daylight on our side, so we can just keep going until it gets dark. And then it depends on what we find. We're sending one party through from the back of the Jacques property, assuming that's the way they went, and another party through from this entrance"— he gestures toward the wooden stile that forms the public entrance to the woods—"in case they'd already left the Jacques property before deciding to head back through the woods. So we'll have two teams in there and they'll splinter as they get deeper into the woods to cover as much territory as possible."

"And what are you looking for exactly?" Megs asks chippily.

"Your children, Mrs. Allister. We're looking for your children."

"There's no way they're in there. Kim's already looked, and if there was anything, she'd have found it."

"Well then, we're looking for proof that your children *were* there. That they were there and that something befell them and then we'll use that evidence to try and put together a picture of what happened on Friday night and where your children might now be."

"You'd be better off talking to those cab companies again. I bet half the time they don't even write things down. The woman who runs the one in Manton is asleep half the time, literally facedown on the desk, fast asleep. I've seen her. I reckon she runs so many jobs that she never actually goes to bed. You should talk to her again. She'll have sent them a taxi but forgotten to write it down."

DCI McCoy smiles patiently at Megs. "I think you mean Carole

Dodds? At Taxis First? Yes, we've spoken to her twice. She wasn't working on Friday night, she was unwell, so her husband took her shift and he told us that every booking goes straight into the computer system, that they can't actually send a car without it going through their system."

"Oh, well, you know computers. You can't trust them as far as you can throw them."

"So you still think they did get a taxi, Mrs. Allister?"

"They must have."

"And where did that taxi take them?"

"They're kids," she replies loudly. "Who knows?"

DI McCoy stifles a sigh. "Anyway," he says, "we're about ready to go in, I'd say. You're welcome to stay here and wait for developments, or we could meet you back at the village? Whichever you'd prefer."

Kim glances at Megs. Megs shrugs. Kim says, "Well, I'd like to stay here while you're at this end, and then head into the village when the search teams are getting closer. If that's OK?"

"Absolutely."

Megs and Simon exchange a look. Megs says, "Yeah, I think we'll just head back to Upfield and wait at that end. Maybe at the Ducks." She touches Kim's arm, making her jump slightly. "See you there," she says, and then they all head back to the road where their car is parked in a passing place, just in front of Kim's.

From her car Kim watches Megs and Simon's car doing a slow eight-point turn in the narrow lane, before heading back toward Upfield. Megs issues a slow wave from the passenger window as they pass by and Kim returns the gesture.

She is chilled by Megs's response to this crisis. It makes no sense to her whatsoever. She knows that boys are less terrifying to parent than girls—she's done both and she knows that she feels less anxious when Ryan is out after dark than Tallulah. But still, it's been nearly three days. The disappearance of anyone for that amount of time is just fundamentally worrying. Yet Megs is not worried in the least. For a moment, it crosses Kim's mind that maybe Megs is not worried because she knows something, because she knows her son is safe but she cannot, for whatever reason, tell anyone. But no, she immediately corrects this train of thought. If Megs was lying to protect her son or the person responsible for her son's disappearance, she would surely at least *pretend* to be worried. But her reaction to this is too authentic, too real, too Megs.

Kim turns and watches the high-vis-clad police officers and their dogs as they finally head into the woods. The plainclothes detectives stay where they are for a while before heading back to their vehicles.

It's strangely quiet. A car drives past after a few moments; the elderly couple inside look curiously at the lineup of police vehicles parked on the verge and then slow down.

"What's going on?" the old man asks an officer.

"Just a local police investigation," the officer replies.

"Another break-in?" asks the lady.

"No," he replies. "We're just looking for a missing person."

"From Upley Fold?" says the man.

"No, from Upfield Common."

"Oh," says the woman. "Well, good luck. Hope you find them," and they drive on.

Kim looks at her phone. It's one forty-five. She texts Ryan.

Everything all right?

All good, he replies. *You?*

So far so good, she replies, adding a smiley face and a heart to reassure him.

The minutes pass horrifically slowly. Every time she sees one of the detectives put a phone to their ear, her blood turns to ice. Her imagination fabricates a dozen scenarios, all involving Zach somehow snuffing the life from her beautiful baby girl in the woods; she sees him throttling her on the ground, pinning down her limbs with his. She sees him producing a knife from somewhere, who knows where, maybe he picked one up in Scarlett's kitchen, a premeditated move, approaching her from behind and slicing through the soft white of her throat, her blood turning black and sticky on the dry earth. Or just beating her, beating her and beating her until there was nothing left to beat, her beautiful face mashed into a pulp, he staggering breathlessly through the woods afterward with bruised, bloodied fists.

Eventually one of those detectives will take a call from one of the searchers and something will etch itself onto his or her face and they will come to her car, to her window, and she will wind it down and they will say, "They've found something," and then she will know. She will know what has befallen her beautiful girl.

But for now, she sits, she looks, she watches, and she waits.

19

The first day of the new term has arrived at Maypole House. Shaun has been at work for days already, of course, but there's something new and shiny about the day as she watches Shaun readying himself this sunny Monday.

The day will start with an assembly and Shaun has been writing his first-day speech for days now. He'd practiced it in front of Sophie last night standing at the foot of their bed in just his boxer shorts and socks, while she lay on the bed, playing the role of his audience.

"Wonderful," she'd said, giving a round of applause. "Really wonderful. Warm, relatable, inspiring."

"Not too short?"

"Not too short," she'd reassured, "perfect length. Perfect pitch. And judging by the way people reacted to you at the dinner tonight, they all love you already."

"You think?"

"The affection was tangible," she'd said. "Truly."

And it was true. She'd felt it everywhere Shaun went the night before, the feeling of genuine engagement he left in his wake, the sense that people had been uplifted by him, flattered by his attention, that he'd created a kind of buzz about the new term to come merely by being present, before he'd so much as held an assembly or read a speech.

Now Shaun has gone and Sophie is alone. The cottage is cool and quiet, her laptop is open on the kitchen table, her novel is blinking at her from the screen, her email inbox is full of work-related things that she should really be attending to, the dishwasher needs emptying, and she still has boxes left to unpack, but she doesn't do any of those things. She switches screens, opens her browser, and googles "Liam Bailey."

As she'd expected, the search term brings up a hundred people who are not the correct Liam Bailey. She adds "Maypole House" to the search. The school's website appears.

She deletes "Maypole House" and adds "Scarlett Jacques."

No results found.

She adds the name "Zach Allister" to her search for Liam.

No results found.

She sighs and leans back into her chair. How can two people go to the pub on a Friday night and never come back and nobody know what happened to them? The mystery consumes her, whole. She can feel it whispering to her through the branches of the trees in the woods, down the corridors of the college, from Liam's balcony, across the surface of the duck pond on the common, from Kim Knox's window facing the bus stop and the ring in its box in the back corner of her drawer.

At this thought she gets abruptly to her feet and runs up the stairs to her bedroom, wrenches open the drawer in the dressing table, and pulls the box out. She brushes the dirt off the lid again with her fingertips but it's still impossible to make out the writing printed on the top. She takes the box to the bathroom and rubs it with the wetted corner of a towel. As she does so, the blackness shifts and gold block lettering begins to appear. She rubs harder, dampens the towel again, rubs more. And there, distinctly, are the words MASON & SON FINE JEWELLERY, MANTON, SURREY.

Her heart skips a beat.

Manton.

That's the big town six miles from Upfield Common. The town

where Tallulah went to college. Sophie wants to go there. She wants to go now. But she can't drive. And she has no idea how one would summon a taxi to come to Upfield Common and maybe the receptionist here could tell her but she feels strangely like she doesn't want anyone to know she's going to Manton. And then she thinks of the bus stop, by Tallulah's rosebush. She grabs her bag, drops the ring box into it, strides through the school grounds and across the common toward the stop.

———————————

The bus comes half an hour later.

She takes a seat halfway down. There are only two other people on board. As the bus trundles through the country lanes and then out onto the A road toward the big roundabout, Sophie imagines Tallulah sitting here, as she is, her rucksack perched on her lap, her delicate features set pensively, the sun glittering off her nose ring, her dark hair covering half her face.

The ride into Manton takes twenty minutes. The stop on the high street is the end of the route for the bus and the driver flashes the lights on and off to encourage everyone to disembark.

Sophie puts the name of the jewelry shop into Google Maps and follows the directions to a small turning just off the main street.

It's a tiny, ancient shop, with low-set windows that are designed to be gazed down upon. Sophie stops and admires the display for a moment before pushing open the door. Her breath catches a little; it's exactly the type of shop she would use for one of her Little Hither Green Detective Agency books, replete with a slightly comical-looking owner behind the glass-topped display cabinet, sitting on a tall stool, reading a hardback book. He's terribly small, with close-cropped white hair and red-framed glasses, and when he glances up at her his face breaks into a smile of pure joy. "Good morning, madam," he says, "and how are you today?"

"I'm very well, thank you."

"And how can I help you?"

"I have a strange request actually," she says, putting her hand into her bag.

The man jumps off his chair and put his hands up in the air. "Don't shoot!" he says. "Don't shoot! Just take what you want!"

Sophie stares at him blankly for a moment. "I, er . . ."

The man laughs overloudly. "Just kidding," he says, and Sophie thinks, There you go, you should never take a man wearing red glasses seriously.

"Oh," she says. "Good." Then she takes the ring box out of her bag and puts it on the counter between them. "I found this," she says, "buried at the end of my garden. I wondered if you had any idea who it might belong to? I mean, I don't know if you keep records anywhere?"

"Well, yes, I most certainly do!" He pats the cover of a large leather-bound ledger on the desk to his left. "Everything is in there from the day I got the keys to this shop back in 1979. So, let's have a look here, shall we?"

He opens up the small box and takes out the ring between his thumb and his index finger; then he holds it under a bright light on a bendy post, using a small eyeglass to examine it.

"Well," he says, "I'd like to say I remember this ring immediately—I do tend to pride myself on committing everything I sell to memory—but obviously some pieces carry more resonance than others and this carries little resonance. But I can tell you it's contemporary, not antique; the hallmark says 2011. It's nine-karat gold and while that is a very nice sparkly little diamond indeed it is not of great value. But," he says, flashing her a wicked look, "thankfully, I am a man who values the importance of good systems. And one of the things I do to everything that passes through this shop is to assign it a number. In case of robbery, or theft. Insurance claims.

You know. So . . ." He pulls the ring box toward himself and hooks his fingers under the blue velvet–covered filling. He levers it out and turns it over, and there, stuck to the underside, is a tiny sticker. "There," he says, lowering the eyeglass and beaming at Sophie. "Number 8877. So, now all I need to do is cross-reference with my bible here."

He's thoroughly enjoying himself, Sophie can tell. She smiles blandly as he slowly flips through the pages of his ledger, running his finger down lines of text, humming quietly under his breath as he does so, and then suddenly he stops, stabs the page with his fingertip, and says, "Eureka! There it is. This ring was bought in June 2017 by a man called Zach Allister. He paid three hundred and fifty pounds for it."

A chill goes up and down Sophie's spine so fast it almost winds her.

"Zach Allister?"

"Yes. Of Upfield Common. Name rings a bell actually, come to think of it. Do you know him?"

"No," she says, "no. Not really. I mean, no, not at all. Do you happen to have an address for him? So I can return this to him?"

"I . . ." He pauses. "Well, I suppose I could give you the address. I probably shouldn't, but you look trustworthy enough. Here." He turns the ledger around and Sophie quickly takes her phone from her bag to photograph the entry. As she lets the lens focus on the text she recognizes the address; it's Kim Knox's cul-de-sac. Of course it is. It must be where Zach was living when he and Tallulah went missing.

"What a very strange thing," says the shopkeeper. "Burying a nice little ring like that in your back garden. I can only assume," he continues, "that the lady in question must have turned down his proposal." He looks sad for a minute, before rallying. "Are you going to reunite the ring with its owner?" he asks.

"Er, yes," Sophie replies brightly. "Yes, I know this address. I can definitely return it."

"I wonder what kind of applecart *that* might upset?" he says in a tone that suggests he'd love to be a fly on the wall.

"I'll let you know!"

"Oh yes, please do. I'd love to find out what happens."

"I'll be back, I promise," she says, tucking the ring into her bag and heading for the tiny shop doorway. "Thank you so much."

———————

The bus brings Sophie back to Upfield Common an hour later. She glances at the time. It's nearly midday. She crosses the common and heads toward the cul-de-sac. It looks as if someone's at home; the front window is open a crack and she can hear the sounds of a child's laughter and a TV on somewhere.

She presses the doorbell and takes a step back, clears her throat, wonders what she's doing for a moment, almost changes her mind, but then sets her jaw and reminds herself that when someone's child is missing, what they crave more than anything else is information and the ring in her handbag might provide some kind of answer. And then the door is opened and there is Kim. She's wearing a denim miniskirt and a black cap-sleeved T-shirt. Her feet are bare and her hair is tied back in a ponytail. She looks at Sophie through trendy black-framed reading glasses and says, "Hi."

"Hi," says Sophie. "Er, my name's Sophie. I just moved into the cottage in the grounds of Maypole House. A week ago. And there's a gate in the garden that leads out into the woods, and I know this sounds weird, but there was a sign, nailed to the fence, saying 'Dig Here,' so I got a trowel and dug and I found something. A ring. And according to this guy at the jeweler's it was bought by someone called Zach Allister, who lived at this address. Here." She takes the ring box from her handbag and offers it to Kim.

Kim blinks at her and her gaze goes slowly to the box in Sophie's hand. She picks it up and opens it. The diamond catches the light immediately, sending spots of light across Kim's face. She shuts it quickly and then says, "Sorry, where did you say you found this?"

Sophie tells her again. "I just took it into Manton. To see if I could find out who it belonged to. The guy there kept records. He said this ring was bought by someone called Zach Allister. In June 2017. From this address. Look." She turns her phone to show Kim the picture of the handwritten entry in the ledger. She can't say anything else. To say anything else would be to suggest that she knows more than she feels she should know.

Kim's face has lost some of its color. The TV in the background is suddenly loud. "Turn it down, Noah," she calls out over her shoulder.

"No," comes a firm response.

Kim rolls her eyes. She looks as though she's considering escalating the episode of intransigence but instead shakes her head slightly and pulls the door to behind her. Sophie follows her to the garden wall, where they both sit.

"This ring," says Kim, snapping the box open again. "My daughter's boyfriend, he bought it for her. To propose to her. And then the night he was going to propose to her, they both disappeared. And all this time," she says, "I wondered about the ring and then you find it, buried in the grounds of Maypole House just next to the woods where we searched and searched and searched for those kids. And there was an arrow, you say?"

"Yes." Sophie nods. "I took a photo, actually, because it was so strange. Look."

She scrolls through her phone to the photo she took before she started digging.

Kim studies it in fascination. "The cardboard," she says. "It looks new. It doesn't look like it's been sitting there for long."

"I know," says Sophie. "That's what I thought when I saw it. At first I thought maybe it was something left over from a treasure hunt, maybe from one of the residential courses that were held at the Maypole over the summer. I sort of ignored it. But now, I don't know. I can't help thinking that someone might have left it there deliberately, for me to find."

Kim throws her a look. "Why would they do that?"

"I don't know," she says. "Just that it was our first day and my partner, Shaun, he's the new head teacher at the school, and it was attached to our garden fence and I thought . . ." Sophie realizes she needs to backpedal a bit to avoid sounding like she knows too much. "Well. I don't know what I thought."

"I'll have to take this to the police," Kim says, somewhat absently. "They'll need to come back. They'll need to search again. And the sign," she says, pointing at Sophie's phone. "The cardboard sign. Is it still there? Did you leave it?"

"Yes." Sophie nods. "Yes, I left it there. I didn't even touch it."

"Good. That's good. That's . . ." And then Kim starts to cry and Sophie unthinkingly throws an arm around her.

"I'm sorry," she says. "I didn't mean to throw you such a curveball. I had no idea . . ."

"No." Kim sniffs loudly. "It's not your fault. Please don't worry. And this. This is great. Honestly. The police. They've done nothing for months. Ran out of avenues. Ran out of resources. Basically gave up. So this is amazing." She sniffs again. "Thank you so much," she says. "Thank you for taking the time to find this, to find us. To give it back."

From indoors a child's voice calls out, urgently, "Nana! Nana! Now!"

Kim rolls her eyes again. "My grandson," she says, getting to her feet. "Noah. Well into the thick of the terrible twos. Honestly, I love him to death but I'm looking forward to him going back to nursery school next week."

She goes to the front door, the ring held in her fist. She looks back at Sophie and says, "I feel like I know you. Have we met?"

"You served me a cappuccino in the pub the other day."

"Oh," she says, "yes, that's right." She waves the ring box at her and smiles. "Thanks so much. I can't tell you how grateful I am to you, truly."

Kim lets herself back into her house, and from the open window, Sophie hears her talking to her grandson. "Look," she's saying, "look what a kind lady found. It's a ring that your daddy bought to give your mummy, but he never had the chance. What do you think? Isn't it pretty?"

20

Each day that term, Tallulah arrives at college, scanning every corner of campus for Scarlett's furry coat, listening out for the lackadaisical drawl of her voice, feeling for the energy that always spins in hoops around her. But there's nothing; the intense buzz of Scarlett is gone, taking everything else with it in its wake. Days that had once felt piquant with possibility now feel flat and muffled and Tallulah becomes once again the studious teen mum with a weight on her shoulders.

But the weight on her shoulders isn't Noah.

The weight on her shoulders is Zach.

He is good, he is *so good*, with Noah. He doesn't resent nighttime wake-ups, sharing a bed with a wriggling baby, changing nappies, endless walks around the common with the buggy. He's happy to sit and peel through the same fabric books time after time after time, repeating the same words again and again. He bathes Noah, towel dries Noah, buttons Noah into pajamas, mashes up food for him, spoons it into his mouth, cleans up after him, carries him when he doesn't want to be put down, sits for ages at the side of his cot when he goes down for his daytime naps, sings to him, tickles him, loves him, loves him, loves him.

But the same intensity of love he uses to coddle his baby boy, he also shows to Tallulah. And Tallulah doesn't want it. She loves Zach, but she loves him more as the father of her child than as a man in his own right. She wants him for help with the baby, to slowly circle supermarkets with her, push the trolley, put his debit card to the contactless machine as the total goes through. But she doesn't want him for cuddles or companionship or emotional intimacy. She doesn't want him to always be *there*. And he is always so *there*. If she goes to the kitchen, he goes to the kitchen. If she decides to have a lie-down when Noah's napping, he'll lie down with her. If she's at the desk in her room doing college work, he'll be lying on the bed texting his mates. Sometimes she hides in the garden, just to escape him, just for a few minutes, and she'll hear his plaintive voice coming from indoors: "Lules. Lules! Where are ya?"

And she'll roll her eyes and say, "I'm just out here."

And he'll appear and he'll say, "What you doing out here, then? Aren't you cold?" And then hustle her back indoors and make her a mug of tea and sit with her to drink it and ask her about things she doesn't want to talk about, or say, "Come here," and bring her into an embrace she doesn't want, and she tries not to let him feel it in the sinews of her body, the need she has just to push him away, just to say *please please can you not just leave me alone for five minutes*.

On Sundays though, Zach plays football with his friends on the common and Tallulah has the house to herself. She and her mum eat toast and play with Noah and it just feels nice and easy.

On the first Sunday of February, Tallulah waits until Zach has left the house and then she heads down to the kitchen.

"Morning, beautiful," says her mum, taking her head in her hands and kissing her on the crown.

"Morning," she says, hugging her mum briefly and then leaning down to kiss Noah, who sits in his high chair. "How are you?"

"I'm fine, sweetie. How are you?"

She nods. "Good," she says, but even she can hear the doubt in her own voice.

"You look tired," says her mum. "Bad night?"

"No," she says. "No. He slept well. Only one little wake-up and Zach did his baby whisperer on him, got him back to sleep."

She sees her mum smile indulgently. She knows that her mum sees Zach living here as kind of an experiment and that she's watching it with optimistic interest from the sidelines.

Tallulah feels a sudden longing to open her mouth and talk, to say everything that she's been keeping locked up inside these past few weeks. She wants to tell her mum that she's feeling suffocated, controlled, that Zach has suggested she switches to home learning, that Zach always gives her a strange look when she gets home: his head cocks slightly to one side; he narrows his eyes, as though he suspects her of something, as though there's something he wants to ask her but he can't. She wants to tell her mum that Zach doesn't like her locking the bathroom door when she's having a bath, that he sits on the toilet by her side sometimes, playing with his phone, tapping his foot impatiently as though she's taking too long. She wants to tell her mum that sometimes she feels like she can't breathe, she simply *cannot breathe.*

But if she starts telling her mum these things, then what happens next? Her mum will take her side, the atmosphere in the house will curdle, the experiment will be a failure, Noah will grow up not living with his dad. It is only her mother's belief in the experiment that is keeping it alive.

"Why don't you go and watch Zach playing football?" her mother asks. "It's a nice morning. I can take care of Noah. Go on," she says. "Think how happy it would make him if you showed up. Maybe you could even go and have a drink together after, at the Ducks?"

Tallulah smiles tightly and shakes her head. "Oh," she says, "no. Thanks. I'm happy just hanging out here with you."

Her mother gives her a questioning look. "Really?"

"Yeah." She smiles. "I miss just the two of us spending time together."

"Since Zach moved in, you mean?"

"Yeah. I guess."

"You're not . . . ?"

She shakes her head. "No. No, it's fine. He's just a bit clingy, isn't he?"

Her mother narrows her eyes at her. She says, "I suppose he is a bit. I guess with his family situation, it must be such a change for him to be here with you two, with so much love around. Maybe he's just getting used to it?"

"I guess," Tallulah says again, cutting another slice off the farm-house loaf.

"Do you need some space?" her mother asks.

"No," she says, dropping the bread into the toaster. "No. It's fine. Just getting used to it, like you say. And he's amazing with Noah." She turns to her baby and beams. "Isn't he?" she says in a high-pitched voice. "Isn't your daddy amazing? Isn't he just the best daddy in the world?" And Noah smiles and bangs his hands down on the high-chair tray, and for a moment it is just the three of them, in the kitchen, smiling, as the sun shines on them through the window, and, for a moment, Tallulah feels like all is well, all is good.

———————————

Zach is there when Tallulah walks out of college the following lunchtime. He's waiting in the shadows of the small copse opposite the main entrance. Tallulah looks briefly at him and then at the time on her phone. It's one fifteen. Zach should be at work now. He does midday-to-8:00 p.m. shifts on Mondays at the building supplies yard just outside Manton where he works.

He stands straight when he sees Tallulah approach and gestures at her with his head. As she walks she can see him casing the environment, his eyes behind her, around her, as if he's expecting her to be with somebody else.

"Surprise," he says as she crosses the street.

"What are you doing here?" she asks, briefly allowing him to pull her to him and hug her.

"Pulled a sickie," he says. "Well, being honest, I did actually feel a bit ill. Thought I was coming down with something. But now I feel fine. Thought I'd come and escort you home." He smiles and Tallulah looks into his eyes, the same eyes she's been looking into since she was virtually a child: the gray eyes with dark lashes, the soft skin, the small dimple just next to the left-hand corner of his mouth. He's not the best-looking boy in the world, but he's nice-looking, his face is good and kind. But there's something there now, something that's set in since they were apart last year, a hard, metallic glint in his eye. He looks like a soldier back from war, a prisoner back from solitary, as though he's seen things he can't talk about and they're trapped inside his skull.

"That's nice," she says, "thanks."

"Thought I might see you coming out with friends," he says, his gaze going back to the college entrance, to the streams of students leaving for their lunch.

She shakes her head.

"What about that girl?" he says. "You know, the one in the picture with you?"

"What girl?" She knows what girl and hears her own voice catch slightly on the lie.

"The one with her arm around you. At the Christmas disco."

"Oh, Scarlett," she says. "Yeah. She left."

He nods, but his eyes stay on hers, as though waiting for her to betray some kind of deceit.

A group of social science students leaves at that moment. Tallulah barely knows them, but they glance over at her curiously. One of them raises a hand tentatively. She raises a hand back.

"Who are they?"

"Just people from my course," she says. Then she looks at her phone. "Bus comes in six minutes. We should go."

He looks for a moment as if he's not going to follow her, his eyes still resting on the group of students across the road.

"Come on," she says.

He slowly takes his gaze from them and catches up with her.

"I wish you didn't have to do this," he says after a slightly ponderous silence.

"What?"

"College. I wish I earned enough money so that I could just take care of you and Noah, so you wouldn't need to get a job."

She inhales and then breathes out slowly. "I want to take care of Noah too," she says. "I want to help pay for him. I want a career."

"Yeah, but, Lules—a social worker. Do you know how draining that will be? How hard? The hours you'll have to work? The stuff you'll bring home with you? Wouldn't you rather just get, like, a shop job or something? Something easy? Something local?"

She stops and turns and looks at him. "Zach," she says, "I've got three A levels. Why would I want to get a shop job?"

"It would just be easier," he says. "And you'd be closer to home."

"Manton's not exactly the other side of the world," she says.

"No, but I hate it when we're both so far away from Noah during the week. It's not good for him."

"But he's got my mum!" she says with exasperation.

"I know. But it would be better for him to be with us. Wouldn't it?"

"He loves my mum."

Zach stops walking then and pulls Tallulah toward him, his hands tight around her forearms. She glances at him and sees that cold metallic look in his gray eyes. "I just . . ." The glint in his eyes fades. "I just want it to be us, the three of us, always. That's all."

She pulls her arms from his grip and starts walking faster. "Come on," she says. "I can hear the bus coming, quick, we need to run."

They jump on the bus just as it's about to close its doors and sit for a moment, breathing heavily. Tallulah stares from the window, rubbing the soft skin on her forearms, still smarting from Zach's grip.

The following Sunday, when Zach goes to play football, Tallulah asks her mum if it's OK if she goes out for a while.

"Of course, baby. Of course. Going to watch Zach play?"

"No." She shrugs. "No, just fancy some fresh air, might pop by Chloe's."

She won't pop by Chloe's. She and Chloe have barely spoken since the night of the Christmas party, when she abandoned her to hang out with Scarlett.

"Can I borrow your bike?"

"Of course you can," says her mum. "But be careful, won't you? And wear a helmet."

Tallulah kisses Noah and her mother goodbye, then lugs her mother's bike out of the side return and onto the road. Tallulah hasn't ridden a bike since she was about thirteen. She's not altogether comfortable on two wheels, but she has no alternative.

After a slightly wobbly start, she sets off toward the common and then onto the road out to Manton. Just before she gets to the roundabout, she turns right, up a tiny one-track turning, toward the hamlet of Upley Fold, toward Dark Place.

21

The police search party emerges from the other side of the woods three and a half hours later. Kim jumps off the bench on the common and runs toward the small lane opposite that leads down the side of Maypole House. The detectives let themselves out of their car and Megs and Simon appear lugubriously from the other side of the common, where they've been sitting nursing drinks outside the Swan & Ducks.

Kim pulls back at first, letting the detectives convene with the search party. She watches, her breath held. They point behind them, they shrug, they shake their heads. She moves closer, trying to hear what's being said, catching only parts of words she's too scared to hear.

"What's going on?" says Megs, appearing at her side, breathing wine all over her. "Any news?"

Kim shakes her head and puts her finger to her lips. "I'm trying to listen," she whispers.

"Why don't you just go and ask?" Megs tuts and strides toward the police. "Anything?" she asks loudly.

Kim turns and glances sideways at Simon, who looks at her from the corner of his eye. She feels a plume of discomfort pass through her and walks quickly away from him to join Megs.

"Nothing," Megs says, almost triumphantly. "They found nothing. Literally." She stares at Kim scathingly, as if this somehow proves that Kim is wrong to think their children have come to some harm.

Kim looks at DI McCoy. "So sorry," he says. "Not a trace. The dogs didn't pick up anything either."

"But did they cover every part? What about the part that backs onto the school? There's another entrance there. They might have come that way?"

"I promise you, Ms. Knox. Every inch has been covered and it doesn't appear that Tallulah or Zach have been anywhere near those woods. I'm really sorry."

Kim feels her heart drop into the pit of her stomach. "So," she says numbly, "what now?"

"Well, we've still got the investigation ongoing of course. We're going to take the dogs around the village now, for a while, across the common, even though, as we know, nothing came up on any of the CCTV. We've taken some evidence from around Dark Place and Upley Fold, some tire tracks that we're following up. We're going to talk to the kids again, the ones who were at the house on Friday night. We're trying to get a warrant to search the Jacques place, to look at their home security footage, but I'm not sure we'll get it. We're looking at all the CCTV from here to the boundaries of the county for sightings of your children. And we'll be talking to Tallulah's teachers and Zach's employers tomorrow. There are still dozens of avenues left to go down and lots of things to follow up on." He gives Kim a cautiously encouraging smile. "We're very much on the case, Ms. Knox. Just keep the faith."

Kim smiles tightly. Her stomach clenches with anger and fear and dread. Anger that no one can tell her where her child is, fear that no one ever will, and dread of what it would feel like to find out that Zach had hurt Tallulah.

"Well," says Megs, sighing loudly. "I guess that's as much as we can hope for for now. So we can all just, you know, get on with our days."

The knot in Kim's stomach hardens and she turns to Megs and

she says, "What the fuck is the matter with you? Huh? I mean, what the fuck is the fucking matter with you? Our kids have been missing for *three days*. Three days! And all you can do is moan and tut and sigh and act like this is all some kind of massive inconvenience. Well, I'm *so sorry* to drag you out of the pub, out of your back garden, so sorry to keep you from *getting on with your day*. And what even *is* your day, Megs, eh? What do you even do? Because I tell you one thing you don't do, and that's give a shit about any of your fucking children. Not to mention your only fucking *grandchild*."

Kim reels as she feels her tirade come to an end. She closes her eyes hard and then opens them again. She feels DI McCoy's hand on her arm and she shakes it off. "I'm fine," she says in a dark whisper. "I'm fine. I'm going home." She straightens up and says, "Thank you, Detective. Please keep me up-to-date with things."

Then she strides away from the police and the dogs and the nosy neighbors, and Megs with her jaw hanging open and Simon with his creepy half stare, and she gets into her car and she drives it around the common and into her cul-de-sac and then she sits, as the engine dies, with her face flat against her steering wheel, tears rolling down her face, saying, *"Tallulah, Tallulah, Tallulah,"* again and again and again.

22

Sophie finds herself aimlessly circling the school grounds when she gets back from Kim Knox's house. In theory, she is meant to be clearing her head, rebooting her thoughts, trying to get back into work mode. In reality, as her gaze alights hopefully upon each person she sees, she finds she is looking for Liam.

She justifies her search for a handsome young man in the grounds of the building where her partner works with the fact that if she can just off-load the mystery of Tallulah Murray and Zach Allister and Scarlett Jacques then she might have enough headspace left to focus on her work. But then her breath catches when she sees a figure leaving the main building who looks like Liam, and as she draws closer to him and sees that it is in fact him, her heart begins to pound and color floods her cheeks and she has to breathe consciously, properly, to bring herself back to some semblance of calm before she can greet him with a breezy "Liam! Hello! Nice to see you."

He recognizes her immediately and says, "Sophie. Yeah?" pointing at her with a hand made into a gun.

"That's right. How's it going?"

"Yeah," he says, "not bad. I'm just heading back to my room, fetching a book for a student."

He says this as though trying to explain himself, as though she might be trying to catch him out in some way, and she suddenly remembers that she is the head teacher's "wife" and thus might be seen as a figure of authority by some.

3

34

LISA JEWELL

"Oh," she says, waving away his explanation, "of course. Whatever. I'm just doodling about trying to avoid work."

"Yes," he says. "I remember you said you were struggling with focus. What is it you do, exactly?"

"I'm a novelist," she says.

She sees his face light up.

"Oh," he says, "wow. That's amazing. Are you published? I mean, I guess you must be, otherwise you wouldn't say 'novelist,' you'd just say 'I'm writing a novel.'"

She laughs. "Well, you say that, but you'd be surprised by how many people still ask me if I'm published when I tell them I'm a novelist. But yes, I am published. And no, you won't have heard of me, unless you're Danish or Swedish or Norwegian. Oh, or, for some reason, Vietnamese. I sell a lot in Vietnam."

He shakes his head at her in awe. "That's incredible," he says. "Wow. That must be just amazing, thinking of your work out there in all those languages, all those people in other countries reading your work. What sort of novels are they?"

"They're what's called in the trade 'cozy crime.'"

He nods. "Yeah," he says. "I think I've heard of that. Like crimes without violence, kind of thing?"

"Yes." She smiles. "That kind of thing."

"Oh God," says Liam, "I'd love to read one. Do you write under your own name?"

"No, I have a pseudonym. P. J. Fox."

"And what's it called? Your book?"

"It's a series, actually, called the Little Hither Green Detective Agency. I'm not sure it would really be your—"

"Wait," he says, pulling a phone from his trouser pocket, "wait. I want to write this down. What was it again?"

She repeats it and watches as he painstakingly types it into his phone. He jabs at the screen with one fingertip, not with two fast-moving thumbs like most people his age. She swallows down a smile.

"There," he says. "I'm going to order myself a couple."

She smiles and then notices that he looks as though he needs to be on his way.

"Listen," she says, "before you go. Remember when we were talking last night? And you said that you were the world expert on Maypole House?"

Liam smiles, but then narrows his eyes and says, "Why do I feel like I'm walking into a trap?"

Sophie laughs. "No trap, I promise. But I just wondered what you knew about the woods?" She gestures toward them with a tip of her head.

"The woods?"

"Yes. I know it might sound strange, but I found something near the woods. Just behind the head teacher's cottage. Something really interesting, to do with the missing teenagers. And I'm starting to think that maybe it had been left there on purpose, for me to find. Or for Shaun maybe. I just wondered if you had any ideas."

He looks at her and then toward the woods and she sees something shadowy pass over his face. "Yeah," he says, "sure. Maybe later? I could, I dunno, I could meet you? I finish work at four. Shall I come to the cottage?"

"Yes," says Sophie, knowing that Shaun won't be back until at least six, if not later. "Come at four. I'll see you then."

Sophie has discovered more about Dark Place over the past day or two. As well as the Wikipedia entry, the house appears in many online documents about buildings of architectural note and historical interest. She finds an article from a local historian based just outside Manton. He describes the house as "a hodgepodge of styles and eras, soldered together like a broken cake, but somehow appearing all the more glorious for it." He retells the various stories attached to the house in much more colorful language than that used in the Wiki post, bringing the characters vividly to life. The moment when the assassin is brought down by the animal trap is described in painful, agonizing detail. It was high summer apparently, the trap was laid in an unshaded area, the man lay scorching, toasting, his skin blistered and looking like "the hide of a spit roast pig" when his body was found six days later.

Toward the end of the article, the historian makes brief mention of the most recent inhabitants:

> Currently, Dark Place is under private ownership, the main home of a family originally from the Channel Islands. Planning applications show that they have added a glass extension to the rear of the central Georgian wing and installed a swimming pool at the back, with a separate pool house, designed to echo the surrounding architecture and bounded by a sweep of reclaimed Palladian-style pillars, said to have once belonged to a mansion just outside York burned to the ground by a vengeful lover. A suitable addition to a house that has never stopped evolving and never stopped finding tales to tell about itself and its inhabitants.

There was one section in particular that had really grabbed Sophie's attention. About halfway through the article, the historian casually tosses in the lines:

> There has long been a rumor of an escape tunnel linking Dark Place to the woods that abut it, dug during the English Civil War, but evidence of either an entrance or an exit to this tunnel has never been found, despite concerted efforts from inhabitants over the years.

A shiver had run down Sophie's spine as she read the lines.

She checks the time now and sees that it's nearly four. She turns her phone camera to selfie mode and inspects her face. Feeling she looks a little lackluster, she applies an extra coat of mascara and some tinted lip balm. A moment later there's a knock at the front door.

"It's me, Liam."

She pulls the fronts of her cardigan together over her summer dress, which is slightly too low-cut for a doorstep greeting.

"Hi," she says. "Thank you. So nice of you to spare the time."

He smiles nervously. "I strongly suspect I won't be of much use, to be honest, but I'm happy to try. Shall I . . . ?" He indicates the hallway behind her.

He follows her through the kitchen and into the back garden.

She holds the back gate open for him and turns to face the sign.

Liam stares at the sign for a moment, mutely. "Weird," he says eventually. "Did you?" He mimes a digging action.

"Yes. I did. And I found . . ." She scrolls through the photos on her phone. "This." She turns the camera to face him and shows him the photo of the ring.

She watches his face for some kind of visceral response, but there's nothing there. "It's a ring," he says after a moment.

"Yes, I know. And I found out who it belonged to."

"You did?"

Again there is nothing in Liam's reaction to suggest that he knows anything about this ring, its provenance or its backstory.

"Yes. I went to the jewelry shop and apparently it was bought in June 2017 by someone called Zach Allister?"

She sees a small charge pass through him.

"The shop owner gave me his address," she continues. "I went there yesterday and gave it to the woman who lives there. Kim Knox. Tallulah's mum." She waits a beat before framing her next question.

She doesn't want to say the wrong thing and put him off talking. "What . . . what happened?" she begins. "I mean, that night? What's your take on it?"

He sighs and looks at his feet. Then he looks up at her and says, "How long have you got?"

PART TWO

23

Liam had been at Maypole House for more than two years already when Scarlett Jacques turned up halfway through the school year. She wasn't a boarder like him, she was a day girl, a local, just arrived in the area from Guernsey.

She appeared in the refectory on the first morning of that spring term wearing earmuffs and a miniskirt; she still dressed like a girl at that time. Her hair was dark and worn in two plaits with a blunt fringe. She had a piercing in her eyebrow and peered out of a huge green scarf wrapped high up her neck like a viper appearing from a basket, shivering lightly in a thin lambswool sweater even though it was warm in the school hall.

Liam watched her grabbing food from the display: bread rolls, ham, a bowl of cornflakes, hot chocolate, a boiled egg. You could always tell the new kids by how high they stacked their breakfast trays. She stood for a moment then, her tray held in front of her, elbows out like baby bird wings, looking around over the top of her huge scarf. Liam saw her shiver again before heading toward an empty table next to a radiator. He watched her for a moment, peeling her egg with pink-painted fingernails.

Liam didn't see her again for a few days. The next time he did, she was surrounded by people, a different proposition entirely, a queen bee, no shivering, no anxious eyes over the top of a scarf that covered half her face. In less than a week she'd gone from being adorable to unapproachable.

Liam pursued Scarlett quite openly during those dark January days; he was a farmer, a country boy: if you liked a girl there was no point sitting about hoping she'd get the message. At first she seemed resistant to his charms: clearly he wasn't her usual type, he was too wholesome, too clean-cut, not clever enough, not weird enough. "You know what the issue is, Liam Bailey?" she said to him in the student bar one night. "You're too good-looking. I can't deal with how good-looking you are."

And he'd punched the air and said, "Yes!" because being too good-looking was a hurdle they could clear.

They finally kissed during the February half-term break when the school was almost empty and most of Scarlett's friends had gone home. She invited him to the local riding school and they took some horses out for the day; she wore a navy jumper and a navy quilted coat that he suspected belonged to her mother and with her riding helmet on she suddenly looked like one of the girls from home. She had rosy cheeks when they kissed, the air around them full of the glitter of their breath, and Liam knew then that he was, for the first time in his life, madly, properly, just like his mum and dad-ly, in love.

When half-term finished and her friends returned to the Maypole, Liam had expected to be sidelined, but instead he was welcomed into the inner sanctum of Scarlett's clique.

Mimi. Jayden. Rocky. Roo.

They were all studying arty subjects, and were colorful, intense characters, very different from Liam. They treated him like a mascot, like a pet bear; they teased him and called him "Boobs" because they thought he looked like Michael Bublé although he didn't, not even slightly. They copied his faint West Country burr and made jokes about shagging sheep and marrying cousins, and Liam didn't mind in the least because that was his sense of humor too; he loved teasing people and getting a rise out of them. He called Scarlett's gang "the groupies" because they only hung out together when Scarlett was around. They never hung out without her and often you'd see one of them alone, just sort of loitering about campus, staring at their phone, and Liam would say, "What you doing?"

"Waiting for Scarlett," they'd reply.

Scarlett changed over that first year, went from the sort of girl who liked riding horses occasionally and plaited her hair to the sort of girl who used a fake ID to get tattoos in Soho and experimented with Class A drugs. She cut off her dark hair and bleached it. She pierced her lip, her nose, her tongue (Liam hated the tongue piercing, every time he saw a flash of it his gut clenched with discomfort). She stopped wearing feminine clothes and started dressing like a twelve-year-old boy from the Bronx. Liam didn't mind. When they were alone together, she was just Scarlett, plain and simple, the girl he'd loved since the very first time he'd seen her peeling an egg.

They were together for the whole of her eighteen months at Maypole House. Liam was easygoing and uncomplicated, a good foil for Scarlett and her moods and her weird friends, and for a while he had virtually lived at Scarlett's house in the next village along—Dark Place. Words could barely describe the splendor of Scarlett's home. Liam had seen a lot of stunning country homes in his life, but none as beautiful as Scarlett's place. It was in a constant state of improvement during those years, builders' vans on the driveway, drilling, banging, squares of dusky hues painted onto walls and painted over again, wallpaper samples everywhere, boxes of expensive tiles.

Doing the house up was Scarlett's mother's job. Joss was exactly what you'd imagine Scarlett's mum to be like: loud, bossy, something of a narcissist. Liam met Scarlett's father only once or twice during the eighteen months that they were together. Martin Jacques worked in the City and had a pied-à-terre in Bloomsbury. He was very thin and distant, with a plume of silvery hair and an almost constant twitch in his cheek.

And then there was Scarlett's older brother, Rex, closer in age to Liam, awesome guy, right up Liam's street, if a bit full of himself and loud on occasion, very much his mother's son.

The Jacqueses loved Liam. He was made to feel one of the family, a part of the furniture. Joss always had a little job for him to do; a leaky U-bend that needed tightening, a kettle that needed rewiring, a car that needed to be taken to a garage for a service. And he was always happy to be that guy, the practical guy, the one who could be relied on to know how to reboot a treadmill or keep foxes off your lawn.

And then it all changed. Scarlett finished her A levels in June 2016, after which she and her family went sailing for most of the summer—Liam was invited to go with them but was needed at home because his dad's back had gone. By the time Scarlett was back from her travels and Liam was back from the Cotswolds, there was barely a moment for them to spend together before Scarlett started her fine art course at Manton College. Liam, meanwhile, was still at Maypole House, retaking one last A level. Without their regular lunches together, without the times when they had free periods between lessons and sneaked into Liam's room in the residential block to have sex or watch TV, without the sheer proximity of each other, the whole thing seemed to slide away from them, the easiness and the closeness, and toward the end of that first term, just before Christmas 2016, Scarlett took Liam to the Swan & Ducks and bought him beer and fish and chips and told him that it was probably best if they were just to be friends. And Liam shrugged and said, "Yeah, I kind of knew this was coming."

"Are you sad?" she asked, her eyes wide, her bottom lip pinned down on one side by her teeth.

"Yes," he said. "I'm sad."

"I'm sorry," she said, grabbing his hand.

"You don't need to be sorry. You're young. Life moves on. I get it."

"Am I allowed to change my mind?"

He laughed. "Only if you change it in the next fifteen minutes. After that, forget it."

She dropped her head onto his shoulder and then looked up at him again and said, "I might just go AWOL without you, you know. I might lose the plot. I might . . . I don't know, I might do some terrible things."

"Don't be daft."

"No," she said. "I mean it. You're the thing that keeps me on the straight and narrow. You're the rock. And I'm hacking myself off you. And I don't know what happens after that."

"I'm not going anywhere," he said lightly. "I'm going to be right there." He pointed through the window of the pub, across the common, to Maypole House.

"Yes, but . . ." She trailed off and he saw something dark pass across her face.

"What?" he said. "What's the matter?"

"Nothing," she said. "Nothing's the matter." She forced an unconvincing smile and then they embraced for a while and Liam breathed in the smell of her and tried his hardest not to cry, not to show her that she was killing him.

———

Liam went home for Christmas. He was quiet, but nobody noticed because that wasn't what it was like in his house. He had three brothers and a sister and now there were nephews and nieces and there were cows to be calved, fences to be fixed, and bales to be shifted, and by the time Liam got back to Maypole House in January he was almost over Scarlett.

Almost, but not quite.

After a few days back at school he decided to ditch his final retake. He'd signed up for it only so that he could be close to Scarlett and without Scarlett he was adrift in a school full of people younger than him. He had the grades he needed for his degree at the agricultural college. He didn't need to be there anymore. He planned to leave Maypole House and go home to help his dad with the farm for a few months, but the day he was meant to be leaving, he got a call from Scarlett.

"I need you, Boobs," she said.

She didn't sound like Scarlett. She sounded different. She sounded hollow and scared.

"What?" he said. "What's the matter?"

"I can't tell you on the phone. Can you come here? To the house? Please?"

Liam looked around his room, at the bags half-packed, the empty bookshelves, the closing down of this chapter of his life, ready to begin the next. He'd intended to hit the road by 6:00 p.m. and it was already nearly three. He sighed and he let his shoulders slump and he said, "Sure thing. Of course. I'll be there in, like, a couple of hours."

"No, come now. Please. Come now!"

He sighed again.

"No problem," he said. "I'll be there in ten."

"And what was it?" Sophie asks now. "What did Scarlett want?"

"Some kind of breakdown, I think," Liam replies. "She was shaking, fetal. Her mother sort of made out she was attention-seeking." He shrugs. "Maybe she was. I don't know. But I knew I couldn't leave her. I knew she still needed me. Told my dad I wasn't coming home yet and moved in with her for a while. Then a vacancy for a classroom assistant turned up here at the school and I thought I could just do it for a few weeks, just to stay close to Scarlett." He sighs. "And, yeah, here I still am, more than a year later."

"Why?" asks Sophie. "Why didn't you go home when Scarlett left?"

"I just . . ." He grimaces. "I didn't know she wasn't coming back. I thought they'd just gone away for the summer. And then it was September again and they didn't come back. And then I thought they'd be back for Christmas, and they weren't. Then it was 2018 and Scarlett stopped replying to my messages and my phone calls completely and I thought, well, she's moved on. It's over. But I liked it here. So I stayed."

"And the pool party," she asks gently, not wanting to push too hard. "What happened that night?"

He lifts his eyes to hers and sighs. "Christ. Who knows. All I know is that I have no idea why those kids were even there. The guy, Zach, I'd say he was kind of dark. I kept picking up on a weird vibe between him and the girl. At the pub, it felt like the girl really didn't want to come back to the house; he really had to persuade her. And then, once they were there, at Scarlett's place, they just felt kind of out of place. They didn't really want to join in. You could tell the guy was brooding about something or other. Jealous, probably."

"Jealous? Of what?"

Liam blinks and she sees him hold his breath. "Oh God, I don't know. The size of the house, the privilege, all of that kind of thing, I suppose. Anyway, the atmosphere was awkward. And then my friend Lexie—she lives here too, she's Kerryanne's daughter?"

Sophie nods.

"She was driving back to the school and I'd had enough by then and we offered the couple a lift back to the village, and she was like, yes, that'd be great. But he said no, we're staying. I saw him sort of tug her back into her chair and I felt really sorry for her. And I told all this to the police at the time, obviously, and I think the girl's mother,

Kim, I think she thought there was something a bit off with him. That it might have had something to do with him. That he offed her. Then disappeared somehow. But you know, how could there be no evidence? That's what's always confused me. They were there, and then they weren't. Not a drop of blood, not a sniff of death. Two whole people, just gone. It doesn't make any sense. Does it?"

He drops his eyes to Sophie's phone and looks again at the photo of the ring.

"And now," he says, making the image larger with his fingers, "it's starting all over again."

24

Tallulah stares down the long driveway, through the elaborate metal gates toward Scarlett's house where it emerges from a crown of trees at the top of a small hillock. It looks like it could still be another mile away. She squeezes her bike through the narrow pedestrian gap to the side of the gates and then remounts and cycles onward.

She doesn't know what she's doing or why she's doing it. She just feels like the walls of her life are closing in on her and she needs to find a gap just for a minute, just so she can breathe.

As she draws closer to the house she gasps quietly to herself. It's magical, the sort of house that you have a really intense dream about and then wake up the next morning feeling sad that it's not real.

She leans her bike against a wall and crunches across white gravel toward the front door.

For a moment she considers calling Scarlett, giving her a chance to pretend to be out or to hide. But then she looks at the time and sees it's only an hour until Zach gets back from football and she's made it all the way and she just really, really wants to see her. She presses the doorbell and clears her throat and touches her hair and clears her throat again and a moment later she hears a female voice calling, "*Coming!*" And it's her, it's Scarlett, and she's getting closer to the door and she's opening the door and Tallulah realizes she has been holding her breath and as the door opens and Scarlett's gaze takes her in there is a tiny fraction of a moment where someone should say something but nobody does and Tallulah almost says, *I should go.* But before the words leave her mouth Scarlett gives her head a small shake, blinks, and says, "Oh my God. It's Tallulah from the bus."

A large dog ambles into view. It's the dog from Scarlett's self-portrait in the art block at college. It's gigantic.

"Hi," says Tallulah. "I'm sorry to just turn up, but I was chatting with Mimi and she said if I saw you in the village I was to say hello and tell you to get in touch and then I did see you in the village but you drove off before I could say anything and the girl in the shop, I kind of know her and she told me where you lived and I just kind of thought . . . I could come and pass on the message in person. Kind of."

"You emailed me, didn't you?"

"Yeah, after I saw you in the village."

"And I didn't reply."

"No. But that's fine. Totally fine, I wasn't expecting you to."

"How did you get here?"

Tallulah turns her head toward the bike. "I, er, cycled."

The dog has walked past Scarlett and is now standing right next to Tallulah, panting loudly. "Can I . . . ?" she asks. "Can I stroke him?"

"Of course you can. My God. Yes. He lives for being stroked by strangers. He's a total whore."

Tallulah presses her hand into the dog's thick fur and smiles.

"I remember," says Scarlett. "You like dogs. You said you wanted one. Did you get one?"

Tallulah shakes her head and crouches down to be face-to-face with the dog. "What's his name?" she says, scratching under his huge jowls.

"Toby."

"Yeah, he looks like a Toby."

For a moment it feels like there's nothing left to be said. Tallulah straightens up and says, "Anyway. That was all really. Just Mimi says to stop being a fucking dick and to let everyone know how you are because they're worried about you."

She glances at Scarlett, assessing her response to the message. She sees that Scarlett looks thinner than ever, that her hair has grown out into surprisingly dark roots, that she's dressed less theatrically than she used to dress for college, in plain-cut jeans and an old sweatshirt with the words GUERNSEY YACHT CLUB and a little red-and-white flag printed on it. "Wanna come in?" she says.

"Er, yeah. Sure. If that's OK with you?"

"It's OK with me."

"I can't stay long, I need to be home by two. So . . ."

"Let's have a cup of tea," says Scarlett. "Everyone's out so it's nice and quiet."

Tallulah follows Scarlett through the hallway and into an extraordinary kitchen, which looks like a glass box stuck onto the back of the house. Even on this overcast day it is dazzlingly bright, a dozen halogen lights sparkling off the glossy work surfaces and cabinets. A delicate wooden table surrounded by gray velvet dining chairs sits by a set of huge sliding doors that open out onto a sun terrace and, just beyond, what looks like a swimming pool with the cover drawn over it. Overhead is a Perspex chandelier dripping with red beads. The walls are white-painted brickwork hung with abstract canvases. At the other end of the glass box is a seating area with an electric-blue L-shaped sofa and the biggest plasma screen Tallulah has ever seen.

The dog follows closely behind Tallulah and then collapses at her feet when she sits down.

"He loves visitors more than he loves his own family. It's pathetic, really," says Scarlett, filling up the kettle and switching it on.

Tallulah smiles and says, "He's lovely. You're really lucky." There's a beat of silence. "So," she says. "Have you got a message for me to send back to Mimi and that lot?"

Scarlett, who has her back toward her, sighs. "I don't want any-thing to do with Mimi. Or Roo. Or any of them. So no. Just don't tell them you've seen me."

"Oh," says Tallulah. "Did you fall out?"

"Well, no. I just . . ." She pulls open the fridge door and takes out a bottle of milk and says, "Milk?"

Tallulah nods.

"It's complicated," Scarlett continues. "I'd rather not talk about it."

She finishes making their tea and brings the mugs over to the table.

"So, how are things at college?" she asks Tallulah.

Tallulah shrugs. "Boring."

"What is it you're studying again?"

"Social science and social work."

"So, you want to go into social work, then?"

"Yeah." She nods and picks up her tea. "That's the plan."

"Well, that's very worthy. You're clearly a very nice person."

Tallulah laughs nervously. "What about you? What do you want to be?"

"Dead, mainly," Scarlett replies darkly. "Yeah. Dead would be good." Then she rallies quickly and says, "Do you want to see some-thing amazing?"

"Er, yeah? Sure?" Tallulah replies uncertainly. She puts down her tea and gets to her feet. The dog lumbers up onto his feet too.

"Now," says Scarlett, "seriously, you cannot tell a soul about this, OK? I mean, this is literally mind-blowing and I am literally the only person in the whole world who knows about it and in a minute you will be literally the second person in the world to know about it. Can I trust you?"

Tallulah nods. "Yes," she says. "Of course."

Scarlett's eyes stay on her for a moment, assessing her. Then she smiles and says, "Come on. This way."

They wend their way through the house, through snugs and piano rooms and boot rooms and hallways and studies and dining rooms and sitting rooms and drawing rooms until they reach a small door set into the corner of what Scarlett refers to as the "Tudor wing." The room is small and contains just a black lacquered desk, a brass standard lamp with a red velvet shade, and a piece of modern art hanging from an ancient timbered wall. The door is wooden and has a latch opening.

"So," says Scarlett, opening up the door and peering upward. "This is the staircase to the turret room." She moves out of the way so that Tallulah can see. It's a set of spiral stone stairs, very small, very narrow. They look like the sort of stairs tourists queue to go up in cathedrals and such.

"Oh," she says, "wow."

"Well, yeah, but that's not the amazing thing. The amazing thing is this."

Scarlett falls to her knees and pulls a strange tool from the back pocket of her jeans. It's ancient-looking, slightly rusted, has a long handle with a kind of flat foot on the bottom, which she inserts into the underside of the first step and then uses to lever away the stone from its setting. She carefully removes the piece of stone and sets it behind her. A cold draft blows through the hole and Tallulah shivers slightly.

"I found this book," Scarlett is saying as she slides her hand into the open hole in the staircase. "A history of this house. And there was something in there about a secret tunnel. Like an escape tunnel. This wing was built during the English Civil War in 1643 and the architect was asked to include a secret tunnel in case the inhabitants needed to hide or run away. And"—her face contorts as she tries to get hold of something inside the hole—"the plans were destroyed in a fire that burned down half of the building. In fact, that's why it became called Dark Place, because of the black circle that surrounded it after the fire, all the charred wood.

"So the house was abandoned and empty for nearly seventy years until a really cool young couple from London bought it, probably equivalent to hipsters of today, wanted a doer-upper, something with a bit of character. And they were the ones who attached the Georgian wing. It was seen as super super modern at the time, no one could quite believe their eyes; it was the talk of the village. Anyway, this couple had no idea where the tunnel was and spent years trying to find it and moved back to London when they were old without ever finding it and by the eighteen hundreds everyone just thought it was a myth. That it had never existed.

"And then early in 2017, a young woman called Scarlett Jacques, who had nothing to do all day because she'd left college under a cloud and was depressed and incredibly bored, decided to make it her mission to find the tunnel. And finally, after many, many days, she had a brain wave. What if?" She pants slightly as she pulls hard at something in the hole, suddenly lifting the entire stone panel, removing it, and putting it next to the first piece of stone. "What if," she continues, "the architect decided that the best place for an underground staircase was at the base of an overground staircase? And what if that weird metal thing that's been hanging off a hook in the woodstore since the day we moved in, what if that might be the key to open the base." She leans back and brushes some hair from her face. "And lo and behold," she says to Tallulah, waving her arm across the opening, "she was fucking right."

Tallulah's mouth is hanging open. She stares into the hole and then up at Scarlett. "Oh my God," she whispers. The dog has been snuffling at the pieces of stone and now passes Tallulah to peer down the hole, sniffing the air loudly.

"Want to come and have a look inside?" says Scarlett, turning on the flashlight on her phone.

"Erm, I'm not sure. I really need to get back. And I'm arachnophobic. Like, seriously. Full-blown panic attacks."

"Just come and see the room at the bottom of the steps. There're no spiders there, I promise. It's really cool. Come."

An image passes through her subconscious, an image of her in a spider-filled tunnel, looking up at Scarlett, who cackles maniacally whilst pulling the stone cover back into place.

Tallulah told no one she was coming here. There's nobody else in the house. All that's here is her mother's bike, which Scarlett could easily dispose of. She could seal Tallulah up down there and no one would ever hear her and no one would ever know.

She thinks of Scarlett's self-portrait in the art block at Manton, the cake knife with the blood on it, the handgun, the fresh beating heart on the plate, and she wonders about this girl whom she barely knows. Who is Scarlett Jacques? *What* is she?

But then she looks at Scarlett and sees the cool girl from college, the girl who everyone wants to be, and she's looking back at Tallulah with a playful smile, saying, "Come on. I'm not going to eat you," and she follows her into the hole, her hands grasping onto damp brick walls as the steps lead downward.

25

June turns to July. Noah turns from twelve to thirteen months. Kim gives up her part-time job at the estate agency up the road. Ryan cancels his first parentless holiday to Rhodes. On the calendar on the kitchen wall, Kim sees her handwriting in the square for 17 July: "Last day term, Tallulah." She weeps.

The police had finally gotten permission to search the Jacques house but they found nothing untoward and it turned out that the Jacqueses' security system hadn't been armed that night, that all the cameras were off. "My fault entirely," Joss Jacques said. "I never follow instructions properly. Drives Martin insane."

Shortly afterward, Scarlett and her family flew out to their house in the Channel Islands and never came back.

Toward the end of July, Kim cancels her August holiday to Portugal, to the cute little family-friendly resort with the crèche that she and Tallulah had pored over pictures of, imagining Noah there, making new friends, maybe toddling by then, splashing in the baby pool with inflatable arm bands, a zip-up swimming costume, and a sun hat. The lady on the phone is incredibly understanding when Kim explains her circumstances and grants her a full refund. Kim cries for half an hour afterward.

Kim's ex-husband, Jim, comes and goes; he stays for a few nights, as long as he can get off work, as long as his mother will let him leave her, and then he goes back to Glasgow again. In a way Kim would prefer it if he didn't come at all. He brings nothing to the situation, no reassurance, no practical assistance, just extra food to buy and cups of tea to make and bedsheets to wash.

In early August he comes again and the moment he walks into the house, Kim knows that something's up with him. He looks washed-out and tense.

"I just saw that woman," he says, dropping his jacket and his bag onto the floor in the hallway. "The mother."

"Megs?"

"Yeah. Whatever her name is. Do you know what she said to me?"

Kim lowers her eyes. She has tried her hardest to avoid Megs and Simon ever since the day of the police search. She crosses streets when she sees them, turns and walks out of shops. "Oh God," she says. "No, tell me."

"She said that she thinks Tallulah and Zach have eloped. Gone off for a nice extended honeymoon. She said, 'It was all too much for them, having that baby so young. I can't say I'm surprised.' "

Kim sighs and shakes her head. "And what did you say?"

"I said she was mad. I said she needed her head tested."

"Was Simon there?"

"Yeah."

"What did he say?"

"Not a lot."

"Did you remind her that neither of them has used their bank accounts since the night they went missing?"

"Yup. She said they were probably using cash."

"Right," says Kim, rolling her eyes. "Course they are. They're probably rolling around in banknotes in the bridal suite at the Ritz fucking Carlton right now."

"I'm so angry," says Jim. "So angry that they can take it so lightly. When their son might have . . . you know . . ." And then he starts to cry.

And finally, for the first time since Tallulah disappeared, Kim feels like she and Jim are in the same place, a place of shared horror and fury and rage, and she opens her arms and he comes into them and they hold on to each other for a long time and it's the first time they've touched like that in more than ten years and, for a moment, Kim is glad he's there, glad to have someone to share this with, to stand in this corner of hell with her and hold on to her. But then she feels his cheek pass across her cheek and his groin a little too close to her thigh and his lips are suddenly on hers and she gasps and pushes him away, hard, so hard he almost loses his footing. He stares at her for a moment and she stares at him, her breath coming hard, and then she watches as he picks up his jacket and his bag, opens the front door, and then closes it quietly behind him.

———————

Soon it is September and Kim sees the square on the calendar in her kitchen in which she has written the words "Tallulah back to college." She feels too numb to weep.

Noah turns fifteen months and can walk and talk. Ryan gets a girlfriend called Rosie with whom he spends all his time in his room. Kim runs out of money and has to take out a bank loan.

DI McCoy calls occasionally with that which seem much more like they should be called downdates. Each time he speaks to her it becomes clearer and clearer that they have nothing to go on. The tire prints on the driveway outside Dark Place belong to Lexie Mulligan's car. CCTV footage of the main roads in and out of Upfield Common and environs show nothing. Zach's employers say he was a good lad. Tallulah's college says she was a great girl. A sea of blank faces, shaken heads. Nobody has an explanation for what might have befallen them.

Kim is haunted constantly by the image of Zach gripping Tallulah's arms in the snug at Scarlett's house that midsummer night and the sparkly ring in the pocket of his jacket. She goes to Tallulah's room sometimes, to search again and again for the thing that will open up the mystery to her, dislodge the logjam. But she finds nothing and months pass.

Soon it is June again and Noah turns two and has his first haircut. On the anniversary of Tallulah's disappearance Kim leads a candlelight procession through the village in an attempt to get some more publicity for her missing girl, in an attempt to get people to care again. Megs and Simon leave the village to live closer to two of their adult daughters, who have both recently had babies. They don't say goodbye. Kim gets a place for Noah at the nursery school in the church hall at St. Bride's for four days a week and she gets a job at the Swan & Ducks doing the lunchtime shifts. She pays off her bank loan. Ryan and Rosie split up and Ryan gets a new girlfriend called Mabel who has a flat in Manton and he moves in with her. And this is now Kim's life: dropping Noah at nursery, shifts at the pub, collecting Noah from nursery, shopping, cooking, eating. She doesn't go out now on Friday nights because she has no one to sit with Noah. She drinks wine alone and watches programs about plastic surgery gone wrong and dogs having hip-replacement operations.

And still nothing changes.

Nothing happens.

Until one morning in early September, fifteen months after Tallulah disappeared, a woman appears at her door, a strikingly attractive woman with soft blond hair and a pretty summer dress, and this woman, her name is Sophie, has found a ring in the grounds of Maypole House and it's Zach's ring and it had, apparently, an arrow next to it suggesting that someone dig for it, that someone find it.

And there it is. At long last. A sign that someone out there knows something. A sign that Tallulah's story is not yet over.

When the woman leaves, Kim picks up her phone and she

scrolls through her contacts to one she has not used for months and months.

"Hello, Dom, it's Kim." (She stopped calling him DI McCoy some time ago, and he stopped calling her Ms. Knox.) "There's been a development."

26

"Erm, Soph. There's a Detective Inspector McCoy here to see you? In reception?"

It's Shaun on the phone, sounding rather confused and distracted.

"Oh," she replies. "Yes. That's probably right."

There's a beat of silence during which Sophie realizes she's meant to say something. "I dug that thing up," she says. "In the woods. Turns out it's connected to a missing-person case."

"The thing?"

"You know. That sign I told you about on our garden fence that said 'Dig Here'? I dug. It was an engagement ring."

"Oh," says Shaun. "Right. You didn't tell me."

"Well, no, I only found out who it belonged to yesterday and you were at work and—"

"Well, anyway," he cuts in. "What should I . . . ?"

"Shall I come over?" she asks, slightly breathlessly.

"I suppose. Yes. I'll get someone to find a room for you."

And then he hangs up, rather abruptly, and Sophie thinks it's the first time he's ever spoken to her impatiently.

DI McCoy is disarmingly attractive: a deep summer tan, sun-burnished brown hair, a crisp baby-blue shirt under a dark blue suit.

He's sitting in a small meeting room just behind the reception office. There's a pane of glass in the door through which Sophie is aware of a head bobbing just out of sight. The presence of a police officer in the school is causing frissons of warped energy. The fact that he is here to talk to the new head teacher's girlfriend is adding even more controversy to the situation.

DI McCoy gets to his feet as she enters and shakes her hand.

"Thank you," he says. "I'm sorry to interrupt you in the middle of the school day."

"Oh, no, honestly, that's fine. I don't work here. So it's, you know . . ."

"Well." He sits down again. "I assume you know what I'm here to talk to you about?"

"The ring?"

DI McCoy checks his notes. "Yes. The ring. Found in the school grounds? By you?"

"Correct."

"And this was when, exactly?"

"A few days ago. I put it away at first, in a drawer, because I didn't know what to make of it. Then it kept playing on my mind. So I got it out of the drawer and cleaned the box and found the name of the jewelry shop. I took it there yesterday and then took it straight around to the owner. But he doesn't live there anymore. Apparently, well, the woman who lives there, Kim, she told me that he's a missing person?"

"That's right. He disappeared on the sixteenth of June 2017, with his girlfriend. And there was a theory that he might have taken his girlfriend out that night to propose to her. So the ring suddenly reappearing after all this time is quite a big development. Essentially, it reopens the case."

Sophie nods, somewhat fervently, trying not to betray her excitement. "I suppose it does," she says.

"So, Ms. Knox tells me that you found this ring after following the directions written on a note?"

"Kind of. There was a sign, nailed to our garden fence. With an arrow. I can show you if you like? It's still there. I didn't touch it."

"Yes. Yes, please." The detective puts his pen and notepad back into his jacket pocket and gets to his feet.

She leads him through the grounds of the college and through the cottage. "I saw it the first day we were here," she says, opening up the back door. "I just assumed it was left over from a treasure hunt or something." She unclips the back gate and gestures at the fence with her left hand. "I didn't really think anything of it at all at first."

DI McCoy looks down at the fence, and then looks up at Sophie questioningly.

Sophie looks down.

The sign is gone.

27

Tallulah gets home thirty seconds after Zach.

He's sitting on the bottom step, unlacing his trainers, a towel draped around his neck, his hair shiny with sweat. He looks at her strangely.

"Hi," says Tallulah casually.

"Where've you been?"

"Just for a cycle," she replies.

He narrows his eyes at her. "On a bike?"

She laughs drily. "Yes. Of course on a bike. What else?"

"You haven't got a bike."

"Borrowed Mum's."

"But what about Noah?"

"What about Noah?"

"You left him?"

"Yeah. I left him with Mum. She told me to go out and get some exercise. I had a headache."

He pulls off his second trainer and lays it next to the first. "Where'd you go?"

"Just around," she says, unzipping her coat and taking it off. She hangs it up then calls out for her mum.

"In here."

She follows her mum's voice into the living room, where she's sitting on the sofa with Noah on her lap.

She takes Noah from her mum and spins him around, then kisses him noisily on his cheek and hugs him to her. "How's my gorgeous boy?" she says. "How's my gorgeous, gorgeous boy?" The feel of him in her arms after her time at Scarlett's house is indescribably relieving. Her skin still crawls with the damp memory of the walls of the tunnel underneath Scarlett's house and she's been rubbing imaginary cobwebs off her face, out of her hair, ever since she climbed out of the hole and back into the daylight.

"Isn't it the coolest thing ever?" Scarlett had said, her eyes shining in the light from her phone.

Tallulah had smiled nervously and rubbed at the bare skin on her forearms and said, "It's so spooky."

"Yes, but just think," Scarlett had continued, "we might be the first people to have been down there for, like, three hundred, four hundred years. The last people who set foot down there would have been wearing, like, wimples. Talking Shakespearean."

"Have you walked to the other end?"

"Fuck. No." Scarlett shook her head hard. "God knows what's up there. A fucking Demogorgon!" She shuddered and pulled the sleeves of her sweatshirt down over her hands.

Tallulah shuddered too and put her hands into the soft coat of Toby, who stood panting lightly beside her.

Then Scarlett put her hand into Toby's fur and her fingers found Tallulah's and laced themselves around them and Tallulah's breath caught at the sensation. She glanced up and saw Scarlett staring at her, a soft smile playing at the corners of her mouth.

Tallulah had left a few moments later and cycled hard all the way home, trying to purge the darkness of the tunnel, the feel of Scarlett's fingers entwined around hers, and the slightly nauseating jolt of energy she'd felt pass between them that suggested something so far beyond herself or the person she perceived herself to be that it felt almost like a wound.

Now she sits Noah on her knee and rests her lips against the crown of his head, relishing the smell of his scalp, the feeling of being home. Her mum says, "Did you have a nice ride?"

"Yeah," she says. "It was good to get out."

Zach walks in.

"How was the football?" Tallulah asks, wanting to move away from the topic of her bicycle ride.

"Great," he says, sitting down heavily next to her and placing his hand around the back of her neck. "We thrashed them. Four-nil." He smells of the pitch, of men, of fresh sweat. She's suddenly repulsed by his proximity, the feel of his hand against her skin, his very precise male odors.

"Aren't you going to shower?"

"Do I smell?" He lifts his arm and sniffs his own armpit.

She forces a smile and says, "Of course you don't. You're covered in other people's sweat, though."

He returns her smile and gives the back of her neck a small squeeze before getting to his feet. "Message received and understood," he says.

As he leaves the room and they listen to the sound of his bare feet heading up the stairs, Tallulah's mum turns to Tallulah and says, "He's a good boy. He really is. I'm so glad you've let him back into your life."

Tallulah smiles tightly. She thinks, You didn't see the look he gave me just now on the stairs. You don't know how he looks at me when you're not in the room; the way his voice sets hard like stone, his eyes bore through me like lasers. You really don't know.

Scarlett is waiting at the bus stop on Monday morning.

"Morning T from the B," she says, sliding along the bench a little to make room for her. "Happy Monday. You look tired."

"What are you doing here?" Tallulah replies. "Are you going back to college?"

"Hell no," says Scarlett. "I'm here to see you."

Tallulah's eyes widen. "Why?"

Scarlett loops her arm through Tallulah's and rests her head against her shoulder. "Because I missed you."

Tallulah laughs drily. "Right," she says, casting her eyes across the street, toward her house, imagining eyes upon her and this blue-haired girl with her head on her shoulder.

Scarlett lifts her head and pulls her arm back, stuffing her hand into the pocket of her furry coat. She narrows her eyes at Tallulah and says, "Do you like me?"

Tallulah laughs again. "Of course I like you."

"But do you, you know, *like* like me."

"I don't know what you mean."

Scarlett sighs and blows out her cheeks. "Never mind," she says. "I'm just so fucking bored. So fucking bored."

"Why don't you come back to college?"

"Never," she replies.

"But why? I've seen your work. You're so talented. What happened? Why did you leave?"

Scarlett sighs, drops her head, and then raises it again. "Oh, you know, just *stuff.*"

They both turn at the sound of the bus approaching from the other side of the village.

"I'll come with you," Scarlett says, getting to her feet. "Keep you company."

Tallulah glances across the common again, toward her house. She feels very strongly that she's being watched.

———

On the bus, they take the back seat. Scarlett squeezes close to Tallulah, who has the window seat. She keeps up a running, slightly hyperactive commentary about the scenery, about a smell on the bus (toenail cheese), about how much she likes Tallulah's trainers (they were £19.99 from New Look), about how bored she is, how she misses her brother, hates her mother, wishes she had bigger breasts, wishes she had bigger teeth, a bigger nose, wishes she lived in London, hates her voice, misses making art, wants a puppy, wants a Sunday roast with all the trimmings. And Tallulah nods and smiles and thinks, Why are you telling me all this? Why are you sitting so close?

Finally, as they cross the roundabout and draw closer to town, Scarlett stops talking and turns to look from the window on the other side of the bus. Tallulah waits a few beats before saying anything. Scarlett's like a cat, the sort that lets you tickle their stomach for quite some time before suddenly scratching you and running away.

She gently touches her arm and she says, "Are you OK?"

Scarlett shrugs and Tallulah notices a film of tears come to her eyes.

"Oh, you know," she says, her voice cracking slightly. "Just your typical level-two fucked-up rich girl having a stupid crisis. Just ignore me. It's best."

"What happened with your boyfriend?" Tallulah asks, wondering if maybe Scarlett has a broken heart. "The one who's at the Maypole?"

Scarlett shakes her head. "We finished," she said. "Just before Christmas."

"Oh. I'm sorry."

"No. Really. It was fine. I ended it. It had been going on for too long. I wasn't in love with him. But, you know, in so many ways he made me happy. He kept me safe. And now it's just me. And it's all a bit of a car crash really. I'm a bit ADHD, so I kind of need someone calm around me. Someone to remind me how to behave. Liam was really good like that." She sighs. "I miss him."

"Can't you get back together?"

Scarlett shakes her head. "No. I did the right thing. I cut him free." She pauses. "What about you?"

Tallulah looks at her questioningly.

"Do you have a boyfriend?"

"Oh," she says, "yeah. Kind of. We split up a year ago but we got back together. Just after New Year."

"What made you decide to get back together with him?"

Tallulah starts to speak and then stops. Words to describe her son, her motherhood, her real life, sit on the tip of her tongue, waiting to be spilled. But she cannot bring herself to do it. Once those words are out of her mouth, she will be Tallulah the teenage mum, not Tallulah from the bus.

"I don't know," she replies after a moment. "I'm starting to think maybe it was a mistake."

Scarlett raises an eyebrow. "Oh shit."

"Yeah. I know. He's changed since we were last together. He's more . . ." She scrolls through a dozen adjectives in her mind before finding the right one. "Controlling."

Scarlett draws in her breath, audibly, and shakes her head. "Oh," she says. "Oh no. No, no, no. Controlling men. They're the worst. You need to get out of that. You need to get out of that fast."

Tallulah turns to the window, not saying what she should be saying, that it's not that simple, that he lives with her, that they have a baby together.

"Yes," she murmurs. "You're right."

"Who was that girl? At the bus stop this morning?"

Zach is lying on their double bed in his work clothes. He's still supposed to be at work and makes her jump.

"God, Zach." She puts her hand to her heart. "What are you doing here?"

"Had a headache," he says. "Asked to leave early."

She squints at him. "Couldn't you have just taken some pills?"

"Didn't have any on me." He sits up and wraps his arms around his knees. "Was it the girl?" he says. "The one in the photo on your phone. From the Christmas party?"

"Yes. She lives near here."

"Thought you said she'd left college."

She blinks. How did he remember her telling him that? "Yes," she says. "She left. She was just going into town."

He nods. "She seemed quite touchy-feely."

She shrugs.

"Seems strange," he continues. "A girl you barely know, yet you have selfies with her on your phone and then she's cuddling up to you at the bus stop like she's your best friend."

"She's just that sort of person," Tallulah says, unzipping her rucksack and taking out her assignment folder. Noah's napping in her mum's room and she'd planned to use the quiet hour to get some homework done. "A bit intense, you know?"

"Where does she live then? This intense girl?"

"No idea," she replies. The last syllable catches on a gulp. "Somewhere around here. That's all I know."

He nods, then slowly pulls himself off the bed. He takes a couple of steps toward her and then draws himself up tall. He looks down into her eyes and hooks a finger under her chin, tipping her face up toward him. His eyes trace circles across all of her. "You're different," he says.

She pushes his finger away from her chin and turns away. "No I'm not."

He pulls her back hard, by her arm. "Don't walk away from me. I'm trying to talk to you."

Her head rocks back slightly at the force of his words. "I've got college work to do. I haven't got time for this."

"This?" he says. "You mean *us*. You haven't got time for *us*."

"No," she says, feeling her heart pump hard, "I haven't got time for us. I've got time for Noah. I've got time for college. And that's it. I don't have time for us. You're right."

There is an immediate and profound silence. Zach shifts from one foot to the other. "What are you trying to say, Lula?"

"I'm not trying to say anything. You said I don't have time for us and I'm agreeing with you. I don't have time. There's never time."

"But—if you really wanted this to work, you'd find the time. So what's the deal? Do you want this to work? Or not? Because I've got a job, Lula. I actually work to bring money into this family. Every day. And I'm hands-on with Noah, twenty-four-seven. But yeah, funny thing, I've still got time for you. For us. So why haven't you?"

"I don't know," she replies. "I don't know."

There's a beat of silence and then Zach sighs and pulls her toward him, pulls her so hard that she feels her rib cage bend under the pressure, her lungs contract, her breath stop halfway up her throat.

28

The police have cordoned off the woods again. The sight of the plastic ribbon fluttering in the late-summer breeze sends Kim back in time to the hazy, burning heat of that June afternoon last year, the weight of Noah in her arms, the sweat running down her back, the blinding white glamour of the Jacqueses' house in Upley Fold, the cobalt blue of the swimming pool, the empty eyes of Megs and Simon, the stale smell of lunchtime rosé on their breath, the eager rustle of the sniffer dogs as they headed into the darkness of the woods. She shivers at the sight of it, but then straightens up and smiles when she sees DI Dom McCoy climbing out of his unmarked car.

"Hi," she says.

"Nice to see you, Kim," he replies. "Here we go again."

She rolls her eyes and says, "Indeed we do."

He leads her to a spot away from the cars, in the shade of a large tree. "The sign has gone. I went to view it with Miss Beck this morning and it's been taken down. The nail is still embedded in the fence, but the sign has gone. However, thankfully, Miss Beck did think to take a photograph of the sign, so we have that to send out for analysis. She writes detective novels, apparently, so I guess her mind works like that."

Kim raises an eyebrow. "Does she, really?"

"Yes. I know. She doesn't look the type—not exactly Agatha Christie, is she?"

Kim smiles. "No, not exactly."

"Anyway, we've sent the photo for handwriting analysis. Et cetera. But it definitely looks to me like someone is actively trying to draw us back to the case. Someone who knew that a new head teacher was arriving. Someone who wanted the engagement ring to be uncovered. Someone, it feels like, who wants to play games with us."

"But why would someone want to do that?"

Dom sighs. "People want to do all manner of things, Kim. If it wasn't for people doing things that the likes of you and I would never do, I'd be out of a job. My theory, currently, is that this is someone who has known something all along whilst remaining in the shadows. Someone who knows what happened to Tallulah and Zach. And for whatever reason they've grown bored of the silence. Grown bored of nobody being caught."

Kim flinches at his use of the word "caught." "Caught" suggests that someone has done something to her child. It suggests that her child is dead. And not once, not in all of the nearly fifteen months that have passed since she watched her daughter leave the house in cut-off denim shorts and a smock top, an uncertain smile on her face as she kissed her baby son goodbye and headed out into the soft warmth of a sunny midsummer night, not once has Kim imagined that possibility to be anything other than a sliver of a bad dream that she could easily chase away with the power of her own thoughts.

"Annoyingly the school's CCTV doesn't extend this far. It cuts off just on the boundary of the residential area. Miss Beck and Mr. Gray have CCTV on the front of their cottage, but not at the back. We're going through footage now, but unless we have a picture of someone flagrantly walking across the campus holding a cardboard sign, a nail, and a hammer, it'll be a little bit of a needle in a haystack. But"—he shrugs and smiles hopefully—"you never know."

Kim closes her eyes briefly and musters a smile.

"Are you OK?"

"No," she says. "I feel sick."

"I'm not surprised," says Dom. He reaches out and touches her arm. "But maybe this is it, Kim," he says. "Maybe this is the turning point. A little flame of hope."

"Yes," she says. "Maybe it is."

She calls Ryan when she gets home and fills him in on the police activity in the woods. It's lunchtime, but she's not hungry. She puts her hand into a bag of Noah's favorite cereal and eats the nuggets from the palm of her hand, like a pony eating sugar cubes. She checks the time. Three hours until she collects Noah from nursery. Dom told her that he'd have an update for her in the early evening. Her next shift at the Swan & Ducks is not until tomorrow. She'd been pleased when she'd seen the gap between shifts on her rota the previous week, she'd been looking forward to the time off, but now she wishes she was at work, her mind taken off the painful events unfolding behind Maypole House.

She opens up her laptop and types, not for the first time, the name "Scarlett Jacques" into the search box. And once again, the internet shows her nothing. A defunct Instagram account. A defunct Facebook page. A defunct Twitter account.

She types in the name "Joss Jacques" and gets nothing at all. She cannot for the life of her remember the name of Scarlett's brother, the handsome boy who'd opened the front door to her all those months ago with a beer in his hand.

As she's done at intervals over the past year, she tries calling Mimi on the number that remained on her phone after their conversation when Tallulah and Zach had disappeared. And as happens every time, it hits a dead tone. She sighs and runs her hands through her hair. The key players, all the people who were there that night, the people who might know what happened, have vanished. The only ones who remain are the nice boy Liam, Scarlett's ex, and Lexie Mulligan, who comes and goes from the village for long intervals.

It can't be a coincidence, she thinks now; it can't be a coincidence that they've all gone, that they've abandoned houses, social media platforms, college places, friends. And now this: the deliberate presentation of the previously missing ring to the world, someone purposely restarting the engines of the investigation. But why? Why now? And who?

And as she thinks this, she thinks again of the nice boy called Liam, the big bearlike boy with the gentle West Country burr. She thinks of the fact that he is still here, he who had the most reason to leave. He's still in the village, still at Maypole House, where he works as a teaching assistant. He would have known that there was a new head teacher arriving. He would have known about the entrance to the woods at the back door of the head teacher's cottage. He was there the night that Zach and Tallulah disappeared. Maybe he found the ring? Maybe Zach dropped it and Liam found it and kept it for some reason?

Or maybe . . . ? No. She shakes her head against the thought. Such a nice boy. There's no reason why he would want to harm Zach or Tallulah. None whatsoever. But maybe he knows who did and maybe he's tired of keeping the secret.

She switches on her phone and types in a message to Dom:

You should talk to Liam Bailey again.

A moment later Dom replies.

Good idea.

29

The police are busy at the entrance to the woods. From the kitchen window Sophie can see a police officer in a high-vis gilet holding the lead of a silver-and-white springer spaniel, also wearing a high-vis gilet. She turns at the sound of the front door opening and closing and calls out, "Hello?"

Shaun walks into the kitchen, looking tired and concerned.

"Bloody hell, Soph," he says, taking off his lanyard and putting it on the kitchen counter. "What have you started?"

"That ring," she says. "It belonged to the boy who went missing. You know, that couple I told you about who disappeared from the village last year. He bought the ring from a shop in Manton and was going to propose to his girlfriend with it that night. And then they disappeared and so did the ring and now . . ." Her words spill out in a rush; she feels guilty for some strange reason.

"Someone wanted us to find it?"

She blinks at him, surprised that he has worked this out so quickly. "Yes," she says. "At least, that's what it looks like."

He opens the fridge, pulls out a packet of ham, and starts to make himself a sandwich. "Do you want one?" he says, waving the packet at her.

"No," she says. "I'll probably have something a bit later. When the police have gone."

"God," he says, "this is the last thing I need. New job, new school year, dead fucking teenagers in the woods." He sighs.

Her breath catches. "You think they're going to find bodies?"

"No. I doubt it. Apparently, they did a full search of the woods twice when they disappeared. But still, even if they don't find anything, the press are going to jump on it, aren't they? And I'll be overseeing a media circus." He sighs again.

"Do you hate me?" she asks him.

"Of course I don't hate you. But I am wondering why you didn't tell me about the ring? Why you didn't mention to me that you'd found it? That you were going to take it to the woman, to the mother?"

He spreads butter onto fat white bread. She sees the muscles of his face straining under his skin, his knuckles white and pronounced. She thinks of the suntanned man in T-shirts and shorts she'd spent her last few London summer weeks with, the guy with the ready smile and the look in his eye of a man who couldn't quite believe his luck. She wonders where he's gone, a week into this new life.

"I suppose I thought you had more important things to worry about," she says. "I was bored, I guess, and I thought it would be fun to follow up a mystery. It just went a bit further than I thought it would. I'm sorry it's landed on you, I really am. Hopefully it'll all fizzle out."

"Hm," he says, snapping the lid onto the butter tub and putting it back in the fridge. "Unlikely. They just asked to speak to a member of staff."

Sophie's heart jumps slightly. "Which . . . ? I mean, who?"

"Liam Bailey?" he says. "He's a special ed assistant. I think you met him at the Registration Day Dinner? Apparently, he was around the night those kids disappeared." He closes up his sandwich and cuts it in half. "So, yeah. I suspect this might run on a bit."

"But if they find out what happened to the teenagers, then it'll be worth it, yes?"

He bites into his sandwich and leans up against the kitchen

counter, his legs crossed at the ankle, his gaze fixed hard on the floor at his feet. She watches him wipe a smudge of butter from the corner of his mouth, hears his jaw grinding down on his food.

"I'm sorry," she says.

He lifts his gaze from the floor and his eyes meet hers and his face relaxes. He smiles at her. "Don't be," he says. "It's not your fault. And you're right. If they find out what happened to those teenagers, you'll have done a good thing. I just wish you'd involved me, that's all. Remember, we're a team now. You and me. We work together. Yes?"

She smiles, grateful for the softening of his mood. "Yes," she says. "I know that. I love you."

He gazes at her for a moment and then, after a beat, says, "I love you too."

"Let me know," she says a moment later as he places his plate in the dishwasher and collects his lanyard, "let me know what happens with the teaching assistant. With Liam. Won't you?"

———————

Sophie spends the afternoon wandering around campus, trying to pick up developments via osmosis. The school grounds manager and Kerryanne Mulligan are overseeing the search of the woods; students going between lessons slow down as they glimpse the activity. She feels the bubble of her pulse as the drama ripples through the grounds. She thinks of her hand on the rough wood of the trowel from the Jacqueses' greenhouse, her fingers scrabbling in the soil, the feeling of dread that she might be about to find something gruesome; she remembers how alone she was then, how small a moment it was in the scheme of her life and how weird it is that that tiny, lonely moment has somehow blown up into this: detectives, dogs, a potential media circus.

At around three o'clock, Sophie finally feels hungry, decides she doesn't like the look of any of the healthy stuff in their fridge, and heads to the vending machine outside the school refectory. She finds some coins in the bottom of her purse and slots them in, presses the buttons that correlate to the salt-and-vinegar crisps and the Dairy Milk bar, which is all she can face, collects them, and walks to the cloisters at the back of the hall. Here she sits on the same bench where she'd sat on the evening of the Registration Day party, looking at Liam Bailey's feet.

The sun appears suddenly from behind a cloud and she closes her eyes against the rays. When she opens them, Liam is standing in front of her. She jumps.

"Sorry," he said. "I thought you'd seen me coming."

She laughs to hide her embarrassment at being caught with her eyes closed in public. "No, it's fine. How are you?"

He shrugs and says, "Bit wrung out. Just had the third degree from the cops. They seem to think that ring being buried there is something to do with me." He shakes his head in bafflement.

Sophie moves up the bench and gestures to him to sit down. He looks up at the windows of the college and then back to her. "I should go back to class, really, I've already missed a whole lesson."

"Just quickly, what were they asking you about?" she asks.

"Just, you know, more of the same about the night those kids went missing. Who was there. What time did I leave. What did I see. What didn't I see. The same questions I answered a hundred times after it happened. They showed me the ring, asked if I'd ever seen it before. I told them you'd shown me the photo of it."

Sophie starts. "You did?"

"Yeah. I mean, I just wanted to answer all their questions one hundred percent truthfully, and when they said, 'Have you ever seen this ring before?' I had to tell them that I had. I mean, it's OK, they didn't seem to make anything of it. And anyway, hopefully that's that. Hopefully they won't be back asking me any more questions, because I can tell you for nothing, they'd be totally wasting their time." He puffs his cheeks and then exhales. "Well," he says, "I really should get back to it. Enjoy your lunch," he says, eyeing her crisps and chocolate bar.

"Liam," she says quickly. "Before you go. The Jacques family. Did you ever think it might have been them? You know, that they might have had something to do with those kids' disappearance?"

"Of course I thought that," he replies. "It's the only theory that makes any sense."

"But why would they have wanted to hurt them? And how did they get away with it? And the ring? What about the ring? Who would have put it there? And why?"

He shakes his head slowly. "I really need to get on now," he says. "But maybe we could meet up, another time?"

"Yes," she says, "yes. Please."

He tips his head at her, throws her a smile, and heads away. But then he turns back and he says, "Oh, I meant to say! I ordered your books, the whole series; they arrived this morning. I started reading the first one straightaway."

"That's so lovely of you. You really didn't have to."

"I know," he says. "But I wanted to."

By the time Shaun gets home from work at eight o'clock that night, the police have gone and the school feels restored to equilibrium.

The sun has already set, the summery day turned instantly to autumn, and Sophie is on her knees in the spare bedroom, finally unpacking some of the movers' boxes, almost, she suspects, as a silent apology to Shaun for making his first few days in his new job more stressful than they needed to be.

His children are coming at the weekend and it's time to make the place look like a home for them. He calls up the stairs to her and she calls back: "In the kids' bedroom! I'll be down in a minute."

But she hears his steps coming up the stairs and then he is there. He sees that she has dressed the beds in fresh sheets, the same bedding that had adorned their beds in his spare bedroom in Lewisham. He sees that she has hung the prints on the wall, that she has folded towels onto the feet of the beds, plugged in bedside lamps, and thrown down sheepskin rugs. His demeanor softens at the sight of it.

"Oh God, Soph, thank you so much. This has been hanging over my head. I was going to do it . . . I was going to . . . *I don't know.* I don't know when I was going to do it. I'm so grateful to you. You really didn't need to."

"It's nothing," she says. "I'm all over the place right now and I can't get into work so it's good to have something mindless to focus on." She rises to her feet and surveys the room. It looks lovely.

"Shall we go to the pub?" he says, pulling her to him. "For dinner?"

She thinks of the crisps and chocolate she had for lunch and realizes that she would love a proper meal, a glass of wine, some time away from this place, just her and Shaun.

"Give me a minute," she says. "I'll put something warmer on."

"This is where they were," she says to Shaun as they settle themselves at a table in the small lounge area just to the left of the bar. "Zach and Tallulah. They were in here, with the kids from Maypole House. They all ended up back at a girl's house just outside the village. Liam Bailey was with them. Kerryanne's daughter too."

Shaun nods. "I'm starting to get the full picture. It's all a bit unsettling."

"Have you spoken to Peter Doody about it?"

"Yeah, I called him earlier when the police were here. He was very dismissive. Very blasé. It's clearly not a topic he wants to give any oxygen to."

"But was he involved with the school? At the time? Did he know about the connection?"

"Yes, was very much part of it at the time. He dealt with the press, the PR side of things, kept the parents happy. I mean, really it's nothing to do with the school or our children or their families. The students involved had already left the school by the time the couple disappeared, and Liam and Lexie had returned to the school that night way before anything untoward happened. The woods aren't technically school property and as far as Peter's concerned it's nothing to do with us. And he'd like it to stay that way."

"And what about the previous head, Jacinta What's-her-name? Was she here when this was all going on?"

"Yes, she was right in the thick of it. It was a nightmare, by all accounts."

A waiter appears then; it's the same guy who'd been behind the bar with Kim when Sophie came in earlier in the week for a coffee. He smiles a brilliant white smile and says, "Hi, guys! How are you both doing tonight?"

Sophie returns his smile and says, "We're great, thank you. How are you?"

"Knackered," he replies. "They work me like a dog in here." He rolls his eyes. "Have you had a chance to look at the menu yet?"

"No," they both reply apologetically.

"Could we order some wine?" Shaun asks.

"Absolutely. And who would blame you? The day it's been today. Police all over the place. Again."

"Oh," says Sophie. "Were they in here?"

"Yes. You know those two kids who disappeared from the village last summer? Looks like it's all being raked up again. On the plus side, the hot detective is back." He flashes his white teeth at them again. "Sorry. Anyway. Wine, you say?"

They order the wine and then wait until the waiter is back behind the bar before Shaun looks at Sophie and says, "Well, there you go, the cat is well and truly amongst the pigeons. What would Tiger and Susie do?"

She smiles at Shaun's joke and shrugs. But inside she's thinking, she knows what Tiger and Susie would do. They would talk to the woman who was running the school when Zach and Tallulah disappeared.

They would talk to Jacinta Croft.

30

Scarlett messages Tallulah later that night. The phone chirrups in her hand as she sits next to Zach on the sofa and she feels his eyes search out the screen of her phone. She switches it off quickly when she sees Scarlett's name.

"Who was that?"

"No one," she says. "Just Chloe."

"What does Chloe want?"

"I dunno. Probably just wants to talk shit about people."

She feels him bristling with questions he wants to ask, but her mum is there and Zach is always sweetness and light when her mum is around.

She has to wait twenty minutes for Zach to leave the room before she can check the message. She puts the phone on the sofa and switches it on there so that she can easily tuck it out of sight if Zach comes back.

Yo T from the B. Can u come round after college on Friday? My mum's out of town for the night. You cld sleep over maybe?

She switches it off, feeling her heart racing beneath her ribs. Scarlett believes Tallulah to be your average eighteen-year-old girl, the type who can come and go at her own pace, the kind with no commitments. And now Tallulah thinks of this other version of herself, the one with no commitments, and she imagines that other Tallulah thinking, Well, I don't have college the next day, I could go over to Scarlett's, we could have a few drinks, stay up late, eat cereal with hangovers the next morning in her big glossy kitchen. Suddenly, she wants this other Tallulah's life more than anything in the world. She turns her head to the door of the living room, checking for Zach, but there's no sign of him, so she taps the screen of her phone, as quicky as she can:

Maybe. Yeh. I'll c what I can do.

For the rest of that week, Tallulah builds a story about Chloe. Chloe, she tells her mother, is being bullied by a group of kids from college. Chloe can't tell her mother what's happening because Chloe's mother would just make things worse. Chloe is feeling suicidal. Chloe has been talking about slitting her wrists.

Her mother tells her that she really should tell someone, someone at the college, maybe. Tallulah says no, Chloe would definitely not want her to talk to the college, that she doesn't want anyone to talk to the college.

And then, at about four o'clock on Friday afternoon, Tallulah tells her mother that Chloe has just called and that she is in crisis and that she needs her and that she is going to her house. "Can you look after Noah," she asks her mum, "just until Zach gets back from work? Is that OK?"

Her mother nods fervently. "Of course, yes, of course. But please stay in touch. Let me know if you need me to do anything. Call me, please, if it looks like she's going to do anything stupid."

She touches Tallulah's cheek and says, "You're such a kind person, such a good friend. I'm so proud of you."

Tallulah feels so guilty she almost wants to throw up. She leaves before she betrays herself in any way, leaves without even saying goodbye to Noah. She passes Chloe's cottage on the way out of the village and stops, just for a moment, just in case someone is watching, just so they could say, Oh yes, I saw Tallulah outside Chloe's house. In the pockets of her jacket are a spare pair of underwear, a toothbrush, and her debit card.

She waits for a minute or two and then carries on cycling. Zach will be on the bus heading back along this road on his way home from work in just over an hour, so she keeps her hood up and sticks to the shadows and the pavements where they veer off the edge of the road between avenues of trees. She turns off the main road with a sigh of relief; then she cycles to the gates of Dark Place and messages Scarlett.

I'm here, she types. *I'm outside.*

"You look pretty," says Scarlett, wheeling her bike away for her and tucking it out of sight behind the garage.

"Er, no," Tallulah replies. "I do not look pretty. I literally came straight here and haven't even looked in a mirror."

"Well, I have two good eyes in my head and they both see pretty."

Tallulah smiles and follows Scarlett into the house.

Toby greets them in the hallway and joins them in the seating area in the big kitchen extension.

"How was college?" asks Scarlett.

"I didn't go today. I only go three times a week."

"Oh," says Scarlett. "How come?"

"Just the way the course works," Tallulah replies, not mentioning that she'd worked closely with the course director to construct a timetable that fit around her other role as a parent.

"So you study at home the rest of the time?"

"Yeah."

"That's cool," Scarlett replies. "Do you have your own room?"

"Yeah," she says again. Technically it's not a lie. Technically it is her own room. She just happens to be sharing it with her boyfriend and an eight-month-old baby.

"What's your house like?"

"It's . . . I dunno. It's just, like, a house. You know. A door, some windows, a staircase, some rooms. It's not like . . ." She spreads her arm in an arc across the extraordinary glass structure they're sitting within.

"Yeah, well, not much is like this place, I guess."

"What was it like, your old house? In Guernsey?"

"Oh, you know. Pretty spectacular too. Right on a cliff's edge. Overlooking the sea. We still own it."

"Wow," says Tallulah, shaking her head slowly at the concept of owning not one but two properties as incredible as this.

"Plus there's my dad's apartment in Bloomsbury."

"He has an apartment in London?"

"Yeah. A penthouse with views over the British Museum. It's really cool."

Tallulah shakes her head again. "What's it like to be so rich?" she asks.

Scarlett smiles and rises to her feet. "It's nice, I suppose. But, you know, it would also be nice to have a father who wants to live with you and a mother who likes you and a brother who doesn't always have something better to be doing. It would be nice just to be a normal family. Like the ones on *Gogglebox*. You know." She points at the drinks cabinet behind her and says, "Rum? Or is it too early?"

Tallulah looks at the time on the oversize clock hanging on the wall beside her. It's five o'clock. Zach will be leaving work now. In about forty-five minutes or thereabouts he'll get home and Tallulah's mum will explain to him where Tallulah is and he will try calling her and she will have to ignore his call and then send him a lie in a text message. She doesn't want to be drunk then. She needs to keep a clear head.

"Six o'clock would be better," she says.

Scarlett smiles. "You," she says, turning away from the drinks cabinet, "are a good influence. I had a feeling you might be. Cup of tea?"

"Cup of tea would be lovely."

The sky is starting to darken. Tallulah sees it growing bruises across the top of the trees behind the house, feels the night start to close down her options.

"Will you stay over?" asks Scarlett, as if reading her thoughts.

"I don't know yet. Maybe."

"Maybe?" she responds teasingly.

"Yes, maybe." Tallulah smiles and realizes she's doing something she's never done before in her life. She's flirting. She wonders at this for a moment, as she stares at the outline of Scarlett's body, the jutting angles of it, the long stretch of off-white wrist visible below the turned-up cuff of her scruffy sweatshirt, the tight lines of cartilage and bone pressing at the skin. She looks at the bobbles on Scarlett's sports socks, the patches of dog hair on the knees of her joggers. She looks at the way her hair is hanging halfway out of a scrunchie. She looks at the large zit on her jawline and notes that her lips look dry and she needs to put some balm on them. She looks at a girl who is too thin and too scruffy and might not have had a shower this morning and maybe not even this week. She sees a girl who drinks rum when she's alone and cuts off friendships when they threaten to overwhelm her and boyfriends when they're too good for her. She sees a girl who's on the edge of oblivion, maybe looking for something to hold on to, and she knows somehow that that thing is her.

"Well," says Scarlett, topping up the kettle from the tap. "I'll have to see what I can do to persuade you, then."

"Where's your mum?"

"Date night with Dad in London. She drops in on him unannounced whenever she suspects there might be someone hanging around. You know."

"You mean, having an affair?"

"Yes. That sort of thing."

"And is he?"

"Having an affair?" She shrugs. "Fuck knows. Probably. He's rich and old. Rich old men get mega muff." She sniffs and puts the kettle back on its base. "Whatever. I don't care. It's just old-people stuff."

They sit with their mugs of tea and Scarlett puts a playlist through the Sonos speaker system and they chat for a while about their lives, their parents, their plans. At some point it gets entirely dark and Tallulah is quietly surprised when her phone buzzes.

She turns it over, glances at the screen, sees Zach's name, turns it off, turns it over.

"Who was that?"

"No one," she replies.

A few seconds later her phone buzzes again. This time she picks it up and says, "Sorry, I should probably get this."

Zach's message says:

Chloe isn't yr problem. Tell her to call the Samaritans. I need you. Noah needs you.

She pauses for a moment before replying.

I'll be here as long as it takes. Might stay the night. Please don't message me again.

Her phone starts to ring the moment she switches it off. She ends the call and puts the phone on silent. Adrenaline pumps through her, sickeningly. She breathes in hard to bring her heart back to normal.

"Trouble?" Scarlett asks.

"No," she replies. "It's nothing."

She glances up at the huge clock on the wall again. It says 5:51.

"Rum o'clock?" she says, tipping an eyebrow at Scarlett.

"Hell yeah," says Scarlett, leaping to her feet and heading to the cabinet. "Hell yeah."

Tallulah wakes the following day in the custard-yellow light of the early-morning sun filtered through thick cream curtains. Her phone tells her that it is seven fifteen. On the pillow to her left is one of Scarlett's feet; soft white skin, perfect toenails painted black, done by a professional, belying the rough-and-ready image she tries so hard to portray. Tallulah stares at the toenails, imagines her at the fancy nail place near Manton Station with the pink walls and the glittery cushions, her phone in her hand, her feet extended in a leather chair toward a masked woman, on minimum wage.

Tallulah has never had a manicure or a pedicure. She would feel too embarrassed.

Her hangover starts to leak into her system as she pulls herself up to sitting. She checks the messages on her phone. Thirteen from Zach. She doesn't bother reading them. One from her mum, sent at 2:00 a.m.

Just checking in. Hope all's OK with Chloe. Zach told me you were sleeping over. All good with Noah, Love you, Mum.

She slowly unpeels herself from the heavy down of Scarlett's duvet and slides off her huge king-size bed, her feet landing on soft sheepskin. Scarlett's head is buried under the bottom end of the duvet, just a small tuft of blue hair visible. A memory blasts through Tallulah's head, her fingers in that mop of blue, her lips on those lips, Scarlett's hand . . .

She shakes her head, hard. Really hard.

No, she thinks. No, no, no.

That hadn't happened.

Her mind is playing tricks on her.

She glances at Scarlett again, at the shape of her, upside down, under the duvet. Why is she upside down?

Then she remembers, she remembers pushing Scarlett's hand away last night, pulling away from her lips, taking her hand from her hair, saying the words, "No, that's not who I am."

Scarlett had pulled back and looked her hard in the eye and said, "Well, then, who the hell are you, Tallulah from the bus?"

And Tallulah had shaken her head and said, "I'm just me."

Scarlett had put a finger against her narrow lips, run it across the place where Tallulah's own lips had just rested, sighed, and said, "Ah, well. There you go. Timing is everything."

Tallulah didn't know what she'd meant by that. But she knew that she'd asked Scarlett to call her a taxi, that she wanted to go home, and that Scarlett had said, "Don't be stupid, it's two in the morning, stay." She'd pressed her hand against her heart and said, "We'll sleep top to toe. OK?"

Now Tallulah sighs and tiptoes from the room, picking up her jeans and her phone.

In the white marble bathroom, she messages her mum.

Just woken up. All good. I'll be home in half an hour. How's Noah?

Her mother replies immediately.

He's fine. He's just had his breakfast. No rush. Stay as long as you need to stay. Come back when you're ready.

She replies with three love-heart emojis in a row, and then, with a heavy heart, she opens Zach's messages:

This is bullshit.

You don't have time for me, but you have time for her?

Noah is crying for you.

Call yourself a mum?

You don't get to do this!

Fuck's sake, fucking get fucking home, I'm serious.

What the fuck are you playing at?

Fuck you, Tallulah, fuck you . . .

In between are brief voice recordings of Noah crying. Behind the sound of her son's tears are the sounds of Zach soothing him in whispers, *It's OK, little man, it's OK. Mum's with someone she cares about more than you, but don't you worry, little man, Dad's here for you and Dad loves you, don't you ever forget that . . .*

She glances up at the sound of a creaking floorboard outside the bathroom and quickly locks her phone.

"Lula?"

"Yeah."

"You OK?"

"I'm good. Just on the toilet."

"Thought I heard a baby crying."

"Weird," Tallulah says quietly.

There's a beat of silence and she hears the floorboard creaking again. Then Scarlett says, "Yeah. Weird."

They eat their breakfast together, just as Tallulah had imagined they would. Bare legs, oversize T-shirts, smudged eyeliner, thick breath. The sky outside is dirty gray, full of snow about to fall. The big glass box at the back of the house feels chilly. Scarlett tosses her a fake-fur throw when she sees her shivering.

This is where Scarlett had kissed her the night before. Right here. Tallulah puts a hand out to touch the square of leather she'd been sitting on when Scarlett had slid toward her last night, put a hand to her face, and said, "Don't you know how beautiful you are?"

She remembers the shiver of energy that had passed through her as she realized what was happening.

"I'm not . . ." she'd said quietly, the words almost a gasp.

"Not what?"

She didn't reply because she couldn't. She didn't know what she was. All she knew was that when she was with Scarlett she felt as though she could be anyone she wanted to be.

Now Scarlett smiles at her indulgently. "God," she says. "You are such a cutie."

Tallulah smiles and says, "You're so weird." Then she drops her smile and says, "Have you ever . . . I mean, are you, like, gay?"

"Labels," says Scarlett, faux-theatrically. "Boring, idiotic labels."

"Well, then, am I the first girl . . . ?"

"Yes. You are the first girl. Oh," she says suddenly, putting her hand to her cheek, "apart from all the other girls."

"Really?"

"Yes. Really. But you're the first girl for a long time. A long, long time."

Tallulah's phone buzzes. She looks at it vaguely. It's another message from Zach.

What the fuck, Tallulah?

It buzzes again. This time it's a photo. It's Noah. Zach's face is pressed close to his and he looks angry.

For a moment Tallulah feels scared. Zach looks like he could hurt Noah. She gets to her feet and then sits down again. No, she thinks, no. Zach would never hurt Noah. Never. He's just using Noah to control her.

"You OK?"

"Yeah. I'm just . . . my boyfriend."

"Is he giving you grief?"

"Yeah. A bit."

"Can't cope with you having your own life away from him?"

"That kind of thing."

Scarlett rolls her eyes. "Men," she says. "They're such losers." She leans forward toward Tallulah and fixes her with her pale gray eyes. "Whatever you do," she says, "don't let him play you. OK? Stick to your guns. Stay strong."

Tallulah nods. She'd already decided that that was what she would do.

"You go to him now, and he's won, and the next time it'll be just that bit easier for him to control you. Yeah?"

She nods again.

Scarlett leans back again. "Good girl," she says. "Good girl."

And as she says these words, Tallulah feels something bubble up inside her, something hot and liquid and raw and red and it rushes from her groin through her heart to her limbs and she jumps to her feet and she strides toward Scarlett and she straddles her with her bare legs against hers, and she kisses her.

31

The following morning, Sophie calls her hairdresser in Deptford and makes an appointment for later that day.

"I'm going into London today," she tells Shaun, "to get my hair done for the Denmark trip."

"Denmark trip?"

"Yes. I told you. Remember? Next Monday? It's only for one night."

He nods distractedly. "Can you not use the hairdresser in the village?"

"No," she says, "definitely not. And besides, I'd like to go to London. I might meet someone for lunch. Make a day of it."

He nods again. "That's nice."

She suspects that if she asks him again in thirty minutes to tell her what she just told him, he will have no idea.

"What's going on with the police today?" she asks, watching him thread his tie through the back of his shirt collar. "Are they coming back?"

"No idea. I guess I'll find out once I get to my desk."

He flattens his collar down against the loop of his tie and straightens it in the mirror. It had thrilled her at first, the sight of Shaun in a suit and tie, the flecks of gray in his chest hair, the smart leather shoes, small people calling him Daddy. She'd go for drinks with her friends and say, "It's so nice to finally be with a grown-up, you know, a real man." And they'd nod enthusiastically and tell her how lucky she was. But now that reassuring maturity has started to solidify into something else; into a kind of rigidness. The tie seems to sit straighter and tighter. His jawline is harder. His hugs are briefer, almost abrupt.

She approaches him and kisses him on the cheek. He looks at her in surprise.

"We'll have a lovely weekend," she says. "With the kids. Yes?"

"I hope so," he says, "I really hope so."

Jacinta Croft, the previous head teacher at Maypole House, had been easy to find. She's now the head of a large private girls' school in Pimlico. Her face smiled out at Sophie from the screen of her laptop, at the top of a press release about her new position. An ageless blonde in a cream blouse with a gold chain around her neck.

Sophie leaves her hair appointment at midday, takes the train from Deptford to London Bridge, and then gets on the tube.

The warm thrum of the London Underground envelops her, the familiar smell of oiled metal and recycled breath, the copies of *Metro* strewn over the seats, the gentle rocking back and forth. She closes her eyes and breathes it in.

At Pimlico she follows the directions on Google Maps to Jacinta's school. It's housed in a Jacobean building with curved mirror-image steps that meet up at the front door.

She hasn't written to Jacinta. She knows that an email would have gone through an assistant or secretary and she'd have received a polite response suggesting that it might be best to leave the case in the hands of the police. Instead, she rings the bell and tells the young woman on the desk inside that she wants to pick up a prospectus.

Inside she engages the young woman in a very detailed conversation about her stepdaughter, Pixie, who's coming to London next month from New York to live with her and her father. Pixie is very bright, very creative, excellent at languages, wants to be a lawyer. She asks the young woman lots of questions about the school and then she asks her about the new head teacher and the young woman's face lights up and she says that Jacinta is an incredible woman, she's totally transformed the place, all the girls love her, she's inspiring and nurturing, and Sophie says, "Gosh, she sounds amazing. I don't suppose there's any chance I could meet her, is there?"

"Oh," she says. "No, I'm afraid not. She's in meetings all afternoon."

"I understand. My brother's a head teacher too, at a school out in Upfield Common. He's always so busy."

"Upfield Common?" says the young woman.

"Yes. Surrey Hills. Do you know it?"

"Well, no, not really, but I'm pretty sure that's where Jacinta used to be, before she came here. What's the name of the school?"

"It's called Maypole House. I think."

The young woman claps her hands together and says, "Yes! Maypole House. That's where she used to teach. Well, what a coincidence. And you said your brother works there?"

"Yes, he just started there. Wow, well, that really is a coincidence."

Sophie has no idea where she is going with her subterfuge, but at the very moment that her unplanned narrative starts to unravel in her head, the young woman glances keenly over her shoulder, gets halfway to her feet, and calls out, "Oh! Jacinta!"

Sophie turns and sees a tiny woman striding across the entrance hall behind her in a black polo-neck jumper and red tartan trousers. Her blond hair is tied into a sculpted bunch at the base of her neck and she's wearing incredibly high heels, in an obvious attempt to add height to her build. She smiles questioningly at the woman behind the desk. "Alice!" she says. "What can I do for you?"

"Sorry, I can see you're busy, but this lady was in asking for a prospectus for her stepdaughter and we were chatting and it turns out that her brother is the head teacher at your old place."

Jacinta's eyes narrow and she glances curiously at Sophie. She touches the chain around her neck and says, "Old place . . . ? Sorry, what was your name? I'm afraid I didn't catch it."

"Susie," Sophie replies hastily. "Susie Beets."

"Jacinta Croft." She offers her a tiny porcelain hand. "Lovely to meet you, Susie. And your brother's at Maypole House, you say?"

"Yes, he just started this term, but oh my goodness, he's gone in at the deep end. Only a couple of days into term and the police are already all over the school, apparently."

She watches Jacinta's reaction closely and sees her eyelids twitch, a muscle spasm slightly under her cheekbone. "Really," she says, guiding Sophie gently away from the desk and into an alcove lined with wooden panels carved with the names of former head girls.

"Yes," Sophie continues disingenuously. "Apparently, some children went missing near the school last year and now it looks like they've found some new evidence, in the grounds. I mean, actually, if you were there last year, maybe you know about it?"

She drops this last humdinger of a question with wide eyes. She is channeling Susie Beets so entirely that there is barely an iota of Sophie left.

Jacinta's small-boned face twitches again. "The teenage couple, you mean?"

"Yes," Sophie replies. "I think that's right. My brother didn't really tell me that much."

"They were very young. They had a baby. It was horrible." She shakes her head. "They never found a trace of them, as far as I'm aware. But, God, the rumors afterward." She shakes her head again and puts a hand to her neck. "So much gossip, so many conspiracy theories. Because, unfortunately, and I don't know if your brother is aware of this, but the girl whose house the couple had been at before they went missing was a former pupil at Maypole House. And they were with another former pupil of the school, plus a teaching assistant and the matron's daughter. So it all got very messy for a while, from the school's point of view, even though none of those children was under our care at the time. It was one of the things that made me want to leave." She sighs. "Your poor brother, having it all raked up all over again. What was it they found, exactly?"

"Oh," Sophie says. "Something in the woods, just behind the cottage, he said? A ring?"

"A ring?" Jacinta arches an eyebrow. "How strange. I thought you were going to say—" She stops.

Sophie looks at her questioningly.

"Nothing," she continues. "I'm just not sure why a ring would bring the whole case back up to the surface." Her eyes go to the clock on the wall behind Sophie. "I'm really sorry," she says. "I do have to go. But please wish your brother all the luck in the world with the new job."

Sophie smiles and thanks Jacinta again.

Then she turns to leave and waves at the girl called Alice at the desk.

As she heads toward the sliding glass door, Alice calls out, "Mrs. Beets. Don't forget your prospectus. For Pixie."

Sophie turns back and takes the shiny brochure from the woman's hand. "Thank you," she says brightly. "I can't believe I nearly forgot!"

———————

Sophie breathes out hard as she turns the corner back onto Vauxhall Bridge Road. She finds a recycling bin and tosses the prospectus into it. Then she looks at the time and realizes it is still early and that she is in no hurry whatsoever to head back to Upfield Common, so she texts her friend Molly, who works in Victoria, and asks if she's free for lunch. Molly replies immediately that she is.

As she slides into the soft leather banquette of the buzzy, pistachio-hued brasserie a few minutes later, she feels it all start to fall away from her: the remoteness of her existence, the silence at night under the sloped ceiling of their bedroom in the cottage by the woods, the little rosebush behind the bus stop, the sad face of Kim Knox polishing glasses behind the bar of the Swan & Ducks, Shaun's brittleness, the preciseness of his necktie, the smile she hasn't seen for days. Suddenly it is as if she never left, as if none of it exists; it is just her and Molly and a glass of wine and the three businessmen across the way eyeing them, hungrily, and it almost comes as a shock to Sophie when the lunch comes to an end that she is not to return to her flat in Deptford, that she is instead to get on a lumbering, creaking train out of Victoria and sit on it for forty-five minutes watching London fade into the distance.

"You know," she says to Molly as they pull on their jackets and prepare to leave, "I miss London so much."

"The grass is always greener," says Molly. "I'd give anything to go and live in the country. With a handsome head teacher. And *no rent*."

Sophie smiles a tight smile. "I know," she says. "I know. I just . . . I feel a bit lost."

"You'll find your way," says Molly. "It's not even been two weeks. You'll find your feet. You're such a flexible person, Soph. You always have been."

———

It's nearly two thirty by the time Sophie and Molly part ways outside the restaurant. For a moment, Sophie stands on the spot, her feet strangely glued in place. She looks across the street at the dark shape of Victoria Station. She doesn't feel ready to head back. Not yet. She takes a tube to Oxford Circus and spends an hour trawling up and down its infuriating pavements full of people walking either too slowly or too fast. She wanders blindly around a branch of Zara, a branch of Gap; she goes in one side of Selfridges and out the other without really looking at anything. Her head churns with everything and nothing. She doesn't want to go back to Upfield Common and the thought chills her.

She keeps walking and she keeps walking. She sits in a Starbucks and drinks strong tea from a paper cup. She looks at books in a bookshop, checks the spines in the Fiction D–F section, finds only one copy of one P. J. Fox book, and sighs. No wonder she doesn't sell if the shops don't stock any. She spirals through the huge Primark at Marble Arch and comes out with three pairs of lacy underpants for seven pounds.

It's four thirty. She still doesn't want to go home.

Her thoughts go back to Jacinta Croft as she threads through Mayfair backstreets and on to Park Lane. She'd stopped, hadn't she, at one point during their conversation. Stopped at the moment that Sophie had told her about the ring. What was it she'd said? Something to do with expecting there to be something else dug up in the woods?

Sophie finds the number for Jacinta's school on Google and calls it. To her surprise she is put straight through and a moment later Jacinta's warm but professional voice is greeting her.

"I had a feeling I'd be hearing from you again," she says.

32

Kim's phone rings. She picks it up from where it was balanced on the edge of the kitchen sink and sees the name *Megs*. At first she thinks, Why on earth is Megs calling me? And then she remembers.

She hits the answer button and says hello.

"Kim. It's Megs."

"Yes," she says. "I assume you've spoken to Dom?"

"Yes, he called yesterday. What's going on?"

"He told you about the ring?"

"Yes. He told me about the ring. He told me they've searched those blessed woods, yet again. And that's about it. Any more developments?"

Kim sighs. "Nothing. They talked to Liam again, they've talked to Kerryanne's girl. And they've got a handwriting analyst looking at the writing on the sign that was next to the ring."

"Fingerprints?" says Megs. "On the ring? Have they found any?"

"The police have it. I'm sure they'll be looking for prints. But the woman who found it, she had to clean the box to find the name of the jeweler so it's unlikely any prints will still be on it."

Megs murmurs down the phone. Then she says, "Anyway, how are you?"

Kim starts slightly. She was not expecting any small talk. "I'm OK. You know, a bit freaked-out."

"Yeah," says Megs. "It is a bit weird, isn't it?"

There's a pause that Kim leaves empty, deliberately, to give Megs the opportunity to ask after her grandson. But she doesn't.

"Anyway," Megs says instead. "Keep me posted. I can't quite believe that we might finally find out what actually happened."

"Me neither," says Kim. Then, sensing a hint of softness in Megs's tone, she says, "How are you doing? Are you coping OK?"

She hears Megs draw in her breath. "No," she says eventually. "No. Not really. But it is what it is, isn't it? You just have to pull on your big-girl pants and get on with it."

"Have you had any thoughts," asks Kim, "any theories? About what happened? Because you always thought they'd just run away together. Didn't you?"

She asks this question gently, as if it is a tiny egg that she doesn't want to crack.

"Well, yes. I did think that. And, to be honest, a part of me still does. It's the only thing that makes any sense, really."

"I can see that," Kim continues carefully. "I can see that some people might think that a mother and father would just abandon their son in order to walk off into the sunset together, and yes, I agree it could happen. Some people might do that. But Tallulah wouldn't. And neither would Zach. He worshipped Noah. He was going to propose to Tallulah. He was saving up for a deposit on a flat for the three of them. So I know, Megs, that it's easier to think of them living somewhere happily together, not wanting to be found, but that doesn't mean it makes any sense. Because it really doesn't."

"I do sometimes wonder . . ." Megs begins, then stops. "I don't know," she says. "Did you ever wonder if the baby was really Zach's?"

Kim feels something crash inside her head. She says nothing because she can't find any words.

"I mean, it's just a theory. But it might explain it."

"Explain what?"

"You know, whatever it was that happened that night. Maybe

Zach found out he wasn't the father and there was a fight. Maybe he was just so humiliated that he stormed off, too ashamed to come home. And maybe something happened to Tallulah out there in the dark. Or maybe she couldn't face the shame of it either. You know."

Kim opens her mouth to say something and then closes it again.

Megs continues: "Because I never really thought that Noah looked much like Zach and usually babies look just like their dads, don't they? And Noah, he just never did. I never felt that sense of connection with him, like I have my other grandbabies. I—"

Kim stabs the screen of her phone with her finger to end the call and drops it onto the kitchen counter as though it is burning her. She rocks backward slightly against the edge of the kitchen counter.

There, she thinks, there it is. Finally. Megs doesn't believe Noah is Zach's son. She thinks that Tallulah slept with another boy and got pregnant and then pretended to Zach that the baby was his so that he would look after them. Even though Zach virtually had to beg for six months to be allowed to be part of the family. And not only that, but Megs thinks that somehow Zach's disappearance and Tallulah's were separate events. That poor, emasculated, cuckolded Zach walked off, leaving Tallulah either to be murdered in the dark or to run away from her child in shame.

Kim looks around her kitchen. She sees the ghosts of the moments that have now passed into unimaginable history. Tiny Noah in his high chair, his cheeks high with color, thumping his fist against the tray with the joy of discovering that he could blow a raspberry. Tallulah filming him on her phone and laughing so hard her eyes streamed. The pure white-hot love that connected the three of them. The way it filled Kim's tiny kitchen to the farthest corners of the room. And now Tallulah is gone and Noah is a trying, screen-obsessed two-year-old who spends his days either away from home at nursery or here pushing Kim's buttons as hard as he possibly can, who blows raspberries not because he can but because he wants to express his disgust with the world that Kim has carved for him out of what was left over when his mother disappeared in the night. And Kim is so alone and her world feels so small. And she wants it all back, all of it.

She drops her head into her chest and she weeps until she runs out of tears.

33

Scarlett returns to Manton College at the beginning of March. Tallulah watches her mother dropping her off in a black Tesla, sees the suggestion in the driver's seat of black sunglasses on top of dark shiny hair, gems glinting on clawed fingers gripping a leather steering wheel, and then the unmistakable outline of Scarlett emerging from the passenger seat, her hood up, her shoulders slumped. The door slams, the Tesla pulls away, and Scarlett's eyes meet Tallulah's.

"Hello, you."

Tallulah feels her stomach churn at the sight of her. It's been ten days since their sleepover and she's been avoiding Scarlett's calls, her text messages, her Snapchats, her voicemails, the slightly unhinged sequences of GIFs of people dancing, begging, kissing, jumping, spinning, hugging that make no sense whatsoever. She's ignored the sad-face selfies, the photos of Toby the dog accompanied by the words *Where do go nice hooman?* She keeps her phone on silent at all times so that Zach doesn't wonder what on earth is going on.

"Er," she begins, "hi?"

"It's my mum," Scarlett begins. "She said if I didn't come back she was going to send me to live with my grandma. So she made a call and here I am."

Tallulah shuffles slightly on the spot. It's a bitterly cold morning and there are spots of freezing rain in the air that sting where they hit the skin on the backs of her hands. She shoves them into the pockets of her coat and says, "Sorry I didn't reply to anything."

Scarlett shrugs but doesn't respond.

"It's Zach. You know. He's always there."

"You could have come on Sunday. When he does his football."

Scarlett sounds brittle, less of her usual bluster and volume.

"He's still cross about that Friday night." Tallulah hates the sound of the words on her lips. They make her sound so pathetic.

"Who cares?" Scarlett responds. "Who cares what Zach thinks? You're eighteen, Tallulah. You're not an old married woman. Just tell him that you don't care. Tell him to fuck himself."

"I can't."

"Why not? What do you think would happen?"

"Nothing," she says, thinking of the feel of his fists around her wrists, the way he tugs on her hair just a little too hard sometimes. "Nothing."

They walk together toward the college grounds and for a while they are silent. Then Scarlett says, "So, what's the deal with you and me?"

Tallulah glances around, making sure that they are not within earshot of anyone.

"I don't know. I—" She stops and turns to face Scarlett and talks to her in a hushed whisper. "I don't know how I feel about it. I don't know what to think."

"Well, running away from it isn't going to help you work it out."

"I know. I just . . . I need time. It's all new to me."

Scarlett's face softens. "I was lying about my mum, by the way. She didn't make me come back to college. I asked to come back."

Tallulah looks at her curiously.

"I just thought, this way we could hang out. Without, you know, Zach the Ballsack telling you what you can and can't do."

Tallulah stifles a laugh. *Zach the Ballsack.* Then she says, more seriously, "I have to go now. I'm already late."

"I'll see you at lunchtime, then, maybe, in the canteen? Yeah?"

Tallulah feels the resolve she's spent the past week building up start to crack and crumble under Scarlett's bright-eyed assumption that they are going to meet for lunch, that they are going to become something.

"Scarlett," she says as Scarlett turns to go.

"Yes."

Tallulah lowers her voice to a whisper. "This," she says. Gesturing between the two of them with a hand. "This is secret, yes? Just us? Nobody else?"

Scarlett nods and puts two fingers to her cheek side by side. "Scout's honor," she whispers. "You and me. Nobody else." Then she moves the fingers down to her mouth and kisses them, before turning them toward Tallulah and blowing on them. She mouths the words "See you later," and goes.

For the next few weeks, Tallulah and Scarlett develop a routine of sorts. On Mondays Scarlett's mum brings her into college on her way to her yoga class at the leisure center and she and Tallulah meet outside college and walk in together. On Wednesdays and Thursdays Scarlett meets Tallulah at the bus stop in Upfield Common and they take the back seat and they talk and they talk and they talk. At lunchtime sometimes they sit in the canteen, where Tallulah plays the role of Scarlett's quiet new friend. The others, Mimi, Roo, Jayden, and Rocky, talk over her and act as if she isn't there. She doesn't blame them as she is trying so very hard not to be noticed or thought of in any way as significant in Scarlett's life.

On Monday afternoons, when Tallulah and Scarlett both finish early and Zach works late, they meet on the corner of the next road down after classes and go to the funny little tea shop on the high street where all the old ladies go but none of the kids from college, and they order slices of homemade carrot cake and mugs of tea and they sit in a booth right at the back where they can stare into each other's eyes and fiddle with each other's hands and grab each other's legs underneath the table and no one can see, and even if they could see they wouldn't have anyone to share it with because nobody in the tea shop knows who they are.

And then on Sundays, while Zach is playing football and Scarlett's mum is at the leisure center in Manton meeting a friend to go swimming, Tallulah borrows her mum's bike and cycles through the country lanes with her heart full of anticipation and nerves and excitement and glee, and Scarlett meets her at the door of Dark Place and they stumble upward, quickly, hotly, madly, to Scarlett's bedroom and fall onto her bed and Tallulah feels all the things that anchor her down all week long melt away into the golden places where they meet in the middle. They say things into each other's ears with warm breath and soft lips, they fold themselves together, and they block out the world with each other, and afterward Tallulah doesn't want to shower, doesn't want to wash the beautiful stain of Scarlett's touch off her flesh, so she goes home to her boyfriend and her baby, still smelling of Scarlett's mouth, Scarlett's bedding, Scarlett's old-fashioned French perfume that her aunt gives her every year for her birthday because she once told her she liked it when she was five years old. And nobody notices. Not even Zach, who now accepts Tallulah's new hobby: her Sunday-morning cycle around country lanes, to get fit, to help her lose her baby belly. He thinks what he can smell is the smell of Tallulah's exercise. He thinks the flush in her cheeks is down to country air.

———————

Tallulah can feel herself begin to blossom and grow during these weeks, as winter turns to spring. Her life now brings her two sources of joy. Her baby boy. Her secret girlfriend. The days grow longer, the nights grow warmer, Noah gets bigger and learns how to hug,

Scarlett dyes her hair lilac and has Tallulah's initials tattooed on the side of her foot.

"If anyone asks," she says, "I'll say it stands for trademark."

tm

But Zach is still in Tallulah's life and Zach is not a source of joy.

He's working extra hours at the builders' depot, desperate to grow a nest egg of money so that they can get their own place together. He has a spreadsheet and demands that Tallulah sit down every evening to look at it with him.

"Look," he says, pointing at figures, scrolling up and down. "If I can get the promotion to assistant aisle manager next month, that'd be an extra sixty-eight a week. Plus overtime. Plus my mum says she can lend us a couple of thousand, so I reckon by the summer, look . . . we'd have 13,559 pounds. In the bank. And obviously we'd end up in a shared ownership, most likely, but there are some really nice ones, just outside Reigate. Look." And then he switches screens to a new tab where he has the details of some tiny, boxy flats with no outside space for Noah, miles and miles away from here, from her mum, from Manton, from Scarlett, and Tallulah nods and makes a smile and says, "They look really cute," and all the while she is thinking, No, no, no. No, I do not want to live there with you.

Instead, she is thinking of a world without Zach in it, trying to imagine the contours of that world, how smooth and perfect it would be just to exist for Noah and for Scarlett, not to have to exist for anyone else.

At the beginning of April, when she is nineteen years and old and Zach is nineteen years old and they have had their joint party—a subdued affair at an American-themed restaurant in Manton, just family, not friends, saving money for the flat that Tallulah has no intention of ever moving into, for the life that she has no intention of ever living—Zach books a viewing at one of the flats on his shortlist for Saturday morning.

He's buzzing with it all that morning as he showers and dresses.

"Nineteen years old," he says. "Nineteen years old and about to buy his first property. Ha!"

Tallulah's mum drives them to the development and they all peer through the windows at the half-built blocks of flats lined up alongside the A25. They are constructed from a kind of off-black brick, with areas of dark gray plastic cladding designed to look like wood. Each block is built around a courtyard lined with tiny saplings encircled with wooden fencing and new baby grass covered in netting. A woman in a glass office greets them effusively and expresses wonder at their young age, at the cuteness of Noah, and excitement at the concept of *their very first home*.

She takes them to see three units. They're all icy cold and smell of paint and laminate glue and their voices echo when they speak. One has views across the A25, the next has views across the central courtyard, and the last across the scrappy edges of Reigate's suburbs. The kitchens are shiny and white, designed to emulate the huge glossy kitchens of rich people's mansions, but a tenth of the size. Around the bathtub there are metro tiles in shiny dark gray to match the cladding on the outside of the building. It's all very smart. It's all very modern. It's all so very not what Tallulah wants. But her mum makes all sorts of positive noises and a conversation buzzes around her head between Zach, the saleswoman, and her mum about the layouts, the potential, which would be Noah's room, what color you could paint the walls, the local area, the new supermarket about to open in the retail development across the way, and Tallulah feels numb and scared that she is letting this happen to her; angry that she is nineteen years old and in love with Scarlett Jacques, but looking at flats in a cold block with a man she wishes were dead.

In the car on the way home she sits in the back and holds Noah's hand as he sleeps. In the front Zach and her mother are chatting. After a moment her mother turns to Tallulah and says, "What did you think, sweetie?"

"They were nice."

"Which one did you like best?"

"The one facing the courtyard," she replies dutifully, as she knows that's the one Zach likes the best and it will draw the conversation away from her.

In bed that night, in the warm, airless space between Noah's and Zach's sleeping bodies, Tallulah decides that when she sees Scarlett the next day she is going to tell her about Noah. She is going to tell Scarlett that she is a mother, that she has had a baby, that the stretch marks Scarlett has run her fingertips over are not because she "used to be fat" but because she once grew an eight-pound, two-ounce baby inside her. And then she is going to ask her to stop being her secret girlfriend, and be her real girlfriend, and she is going to tell her mother, and she is going to tell Zach, and she is going to stop her life veering off into this place of flats on A roads and controlling boyfriends and secrets. She is going to own her destiny, own her identity; she is going to be true and real and honest, her best, most authentic and pure self.

The following day she watches Zach leave with his football kit bag over his shoulder from her bedroom window and she throws her things into her bag, runs down to the kitchen, kisses Noah and her mother, grabs the bike from the side return, straps on her helmet, and cycles as she never cycled before to Dark Place.

But at the front door she sees another bike, leaning up against the place where she normally leaves hers. She glances around herself but can see no sign of anyone. Maybe, she thinks, it's the gardener, maybe it's a cleaner or someone come to skim leaves off their swimming pool. She rings the doorbell, her heart pattering under her rib cage with the exertion of cycling so fast, the anticipation of seeing Scarlett, and the door opens and there is Scarlett, still in her pajamas, her hair scraped back into a spiky bun, and there is a young man, in jeans and an old-fashioned navy-blue jumper with a high zipped neck.

Scarlett looks at Tallulah and then at the man, and then she says, "Lules. This is Liam. Liam, this is Tallulah."

Tallulah throws Scarlett a questioning look. She sees Scarlett's hand go to her neck to cover a mark. She sees that under her pajama top she is braless. She looks at Liam, who eyes her strangely before saying, "Nice to meet you."

He has bare feet and his shoes are nowhere to be seen.

"Liam came over last night," Scarlett says, her hand still clutching her neck. "I was having a freak-out and my mum was out. He decided—well, *we*—"

"It was me, really," Liam chips in. "I decided to stay over because we had a bit to drink—"

"Yes. It was safer. So, he stayed."

"Yes. I stayed. And now," he says, "I'm going, if only I could remember where I put my shoes." He starts to wander about the hallway, hunting for his shoes, and Tallulah looks at Scarlett.

"What the hell?" Tallulah whispers.

Scarlett shrugs. "I'm not allowed to call you. So I called him."

Tallulah peels Scarlett's fingers away from her neck and sees the telltale gray-red graze of a love bite.

Scarlett's fingers snap straight back to the spot. "It was a messy night," she says. "We didn't have sex. We just . . . you know . . ."

Tallulah opens her mouth to say something, but seeing Liam reappear clutching a pair of brown leather hiking boots, she closes it again. She feels tears pulsing through her sinuses. She wants to cry and she wants to be sick. They stand in silence until Liam has laced up his boots and is ready to leave. She watches him lean in to kiss Scarlett briefly on her cheek. Scarlett clears her throat and smiles tightly and says, "Thanks for coming. You're a star."

"Bye, Tallulah," he says, "lovely to meet you."

"Yes," she says in a tight, high voice, "you too."

And then he is gone and it is just her and Scarlett in the hallway. Scarlett comes toward her to touch her and Tallulah flinches.

Scarlett tuts. "I swear," she says, "it was nothing. It was just, you know, he's *Liam*. Me and him. We've got a history. And we drank far too much and it was just silly, you know, mucking about."

Tallulah can't think of any words. She stands with her arms folded and she glares at the floor.

"I mean, come on, Tallulah. You aren't really in a position to judge. You live with your fucking boyfriend. And don't tell me you don't have sex with him, because I know you do."

Tallulah thinks of the snatched moments she offers up to Zach because she knows that if they can get it out of the way he won't ask her at a moment that's even worse. She'll say, "Come on, Mum's taking Noah to the pond, we've got five minutes. But be quick." And then he would be quick and she could buy herself another two weeks of him not pestering her, of not having to think about it. So yes, they have sex, but no, it is nothing compared to the Sunday mornings that she and Scarlett spend in Scarlett's king-size bed on her 800-thread-count cotton sheets. Nothing whatsoever.

"That's not the same," she says.

"Of course it's the same. It's comfort. It's habit. It's a way to keep them onside. Because we need to keep them onside."

"Whoa."

"Whoa, what? Come on, Lules. You know it's true. Your Zach, what is he for? What is it he gives to you that means that you won't

end your relationship with him, that you still sleep with him? There
has to be something."

"There's nothing," she says. "Zach doesn't give me anything."

"So why do you want to stay with him?"

"I don't want to," Tallulah says. "I want to leave him. But we've
been together since we were children. He's the only man I've
ever . . ." She stops briefly as tears come to her eyes. "I sleep with him
because I *have* to. For reasons you could never begin to imagine. But
what about you? You didn't have to do whatever you did last night
with Liam. You're not in a relationship with him. He knows you
don't love him, that it's over. So why?"

Scarlett sighs and throws Tallulah an infuriatingly gentle look.
"Just . . . because?"

"Because?"

"Look, I'm not really . . . I mean, I can prioritize people but never
entirely *limit* them."

"Limit them?"

"Yes, so, like, you're my priority. You are one hundred percent
the most important person in my life, like, ever, probably. But that
doesn't mean there won't be other people in my life. Who aren't as
important as you. Who I don't *feel* about the way I feel about you.
But who are there, and who I am not going to get rid of."

"You mean, you don't do monogamy?"

"I guess, if you want to put it that way. But honestly. Please. Just
forget about that." She gestures at the front door. "Let's start over.
Come on. There're pecan Danishes in the kitchen. They're from
yesterday but they're still really, really good. Please. I've missed you
so much . . ."

The thought of sitting on the blue sofa in Scarlett's huge glass
kitchen and licking the icing off a pecan Danish under a furry blanket
and then finding the angles of Scarlett's body in her bedroom and
sitting together with the dog afterward discussing which bits of him

they like the best feels like all she wants in the whole world. But that's not what she came here to do. She'd come to hand herself to Scarlett, all 100 percent of herself. And now she knows that she will never be 100 percent of Scarlett, that Scarlett will always have intimate gaps and spaces where other people fit in, and that is not what she wants for herself, or for Noah, or for her future. And she realizes that she has never been more than an experience for Scarlett, just as Liam had been. An experiment. A thing to do to try and decide if she likes it or not, so that one day she can tell whoever she decides she wants to spend her life with that when she was young she tried out a posh farmer boy with a penchant for zip-neck jumpers, and then when she tired of that she tried out a village girl from a cul-de-sac who was training to be a social worker. And that after her there would be someone or something else.

So she looks at Scarlett with tear-filled eyes and says, "No. I'm going home. Forget it. Forget this. I'm worth more."

She slams Scarlett's door behind her and mounts her bike, cycles hard all the way home, her eyes blinded with tears, thinking of her last words to Scarlett and wondering if they were even true.

34

Sophie meets Jacinta Croft in a small wine bar around the corner from Victoria Station at 6:00 p.m. She has messages from Shaun on her phone, asking where she is. She's about to reply to them when she looks up and sees Jacinta approaching.

"I can't stay long," Jacinta says, detaching a huge leather bag from her shoulder and resting it on the table in front of her.

"Me neither," says Sophie. "My train goes in thirty minutes."

"Good, well, then, let's get some wine, pronto."

She calls over a waitress and orders two small glasses of something French without asking Sophie if that's what she'd like and then she turns to face her and says, "So, Susie Beets, I googled you after you left. Something about you didn't quite stack up."

"Oh."

"I take it you're not really a fictional detective in a popular series of books written by someone called P. J. Fox. I assume you are in fact P. J. Fox herself, otherwise known as Sophie Beck, born in Hither Green in southeast London in 1984." She says this with a wry smile.

"Yes. Sorry. I—"

"Look. I work in private education. There's nothing I haven't seen or encountered. But why did you lie?"

"I didn't want to cause any more ripples, I suppose," Sophie says. "It's actually my boyfriend who's the new head teacher, not my brother. And it was me who found the ring in the grounds."

Their wine arrives and Jacinta picks it up immediately and takes a large sip, eyeing Sophie curiously over the rim. "Well, listen, I don't get to chat with detective novelists turned amateur sleuths every day and sadly I can't tell you much you don't already know, but when you said they'd found something in the woods behind the college, I did assume that you were going to say something else."

"Yes?"

"Apparently, there's a tunnel," Jacinta continues, "that runs from the big house where Scarlett Jacques used to live."

"I read something about that. It was dug out during the civil war?"

"Correct," says Jacinta. "And I always wondered, when this was all going on, I wondered about that tunnel. I told the police about it and they looked into it, but Scarlett's family had never found the entrance and neither had the family who lived there before them and before that the house had lain empty for quite some time. They even got a house historian in to search for it, but nothing. And that was that. But I still think, to this day . . . I mean, that family, the Jacqueses, they were, I don't know, they were quite the gang of narcissists. All of them."

"In what way?"

"Well, the girl, Scarlett, she wasn't a student at the Maypole at the time of the disappearance, but she was there for the two years before that and she was such a pretty girl. But such a damaged girl, I always thought. She had this way of managing people, by making them think that she needed them, making them think she was a hopeless mess and that only they could keep her together. But underneath it all I always felt she knew exactly what she was doing. And the mother—awful woman. All image, no substance. The father I only met once, at Scarlett's initial interview. He disappeared halfway through the interview to take a call. He was very distant. Cold. The whole family felt like this group of ice floes, just sort of drifting about, never touching. And so, when this couple went missing, and

I heard they'd last been seen at the Jacques house, I suppose I wasn't surprised at all."

"But there was no connection, was there? I mean, according to what I've read, the couple only met the Maypole kids that night."

"Well, not quite. Remember, Scarlett and the girl were at Manton College together."

"Yes, but according to the other kids, they didn't know each other all that well."

"Well, that's not entirely true. There was a girl called Ruby, also a former Maypole girl. She wasn't at the pool party that night but she told the police that she thought there might have been something more going on between the girl—I can't remember her name?"

"Tallulah."

"Yes, of course. Tallulah. She thought there was something going on between Scarlett and Tallulah. Apparently, Scarlett was bisexual and she and Ruby had had a bit of a thing themselves when they were younger. The owner of a cake shop in Manton not far from the college said she'd seen Tallulah in there a few times earlier that year with a girl who matched Scarlett's description. But Scarlett denied it, said there were loads of girls who looked like her at the college." Jacinta rolls her eyes and lifts her glass to her mouth, putting it down again before having taken a sip to say, "And Scarlett's boyfriend. Liam. Have you met him?"

"Yes. Yes, I have." Sophie feels herself flush slightly at the mention of his name.

"Well, he was there that night and he claims that he'd never met Tallulah before then but . . ." She sighs. "I'm not so sure. I always thought he was holding something back. I always thought maybe he was protecting Scarlett, somehow, because he was so in love with that girl, so madly, crazily in love with her. And he had his heart well and truly broken when she ended things with him. Even as teachers at the school, we were all aware of it, and concerned—you know?"

"Oh," says Sophie. "When Liam told me about it, he said he was fine about it ending."

"Well, he was lying to you. I was there. We all saw him wandering around the college looking like a broken man."

Jacinta runs her finger around the base of her wineglass. "You know," she says, "that was probably the worst year of my life. So much stress. I found out my husband had been having an affair that year, we separated, and then he went for a walk one afternoon and never came back. To be fair, we were in utter crisis at the time. We were in the process of divorcing. He was only there at the weekends. So, when he didn't come back, at first I wasn't too worried. I assumed he'd just gone back to his flat without saying goodbye. But then when he didn't phone to speak to our son that night, or the night after, when he didn't reply to any of my son's text messages or ask about the dog, I reported him missing to the police. They sent dogs into the woods but they found nothing. And I had to accept, eventually, that he just didn't want to be part of our lives anymore. That he wanted to be gone. To this other woman. Exclusively." She sighs heavily, and then continues. "And then those teenagers went missing and it was all too much. My annus horribilis. The worst year of my life. I knew I had to leave."

Sophie gets back to the cottage a few minutes before eight. Shaun has only just returned from work and looks drained as he searches the still unfamiliar kitchen cupboards for a water glass. She comes up behind him and encircles his waist with her arm, burying a kiss into the creased cotton beneath his shoulder blade. "I'm back," she says.

"I can tell," he says, not turning to complete the hug. "How was town?"

"It was nice." She pulls away from him and says, "Look at my lovely hair."

He turns and touches the ends of it where it still kicks outward after her blow-dry. "Very pretty," he says distractedly. "I'm glad you had a nice day."

Sophie hasn't told him about the real content of her day. She wishes she could share it all with him, but feels very keenly that he will not approve.

"I did," she says. "It was lovely to get out and about."

He peers at her curiously. "Are you OK?" he asks.

"Yes. I'm fine."

"I mean, with this? With us? With the move? Are you getting on OK?"

"Yeah, I mean. It's not . . . I don't know. It's not—"

He cuts in. "Are you regretting it? Coming out here with me?"

"No," she says forcefully. "No. I'm not regretting it."

She sees his face soften with relief. "Good," he says.

"I knew what I was signing up for," she says. "I knew everything. And it's fine. Honestly. I just want you to concentrate on your job and not worry about me. Please."

He exhales and smiles and pulls her toward him in an embrace laced with regret and guilt and fear, because, despite the words that have just passed between them, they both know, deep down, that this is not going to work; that what brought them together in London, with the romance of separate homes and separate friends and jobs that they both knew how to do without thinking too hard about them, is not here anymore; that they rushed into this in a flurry of sex and summer and the romantic notion of the English countryside and manicured grounds and foreign princesses and now they are floundering.

Shaun's phone chirrups on the counter behind him and he goes to look at it. He never ignores his phone because he doesn't live with his children and Sophie entirely understands this. "It's Kerryanne," he says. "She wants me to come to her apartment. She says it's urgent."

"Shall I come too?"

She sees indecision pass across his features. He should say no. But in the light of the conversation they've just had, he nods and says, "Sure. Of course."

The sky is just growing dark as they crunch across the graveled path toward the accommodation block. It's the first cold evening of the autumn and Sophie shivers slightly in a thin cardigan and bare legs.

Kerryanne is waiting outside the door of her block, her arms folded across her chest. She looks relieved when she sees Shaun and Sophie approaching and says, "I'm so sorry to disturb you in your free time. I really am. But you need to see this."

She leads them around to the front of the block, where the balconies overlook the woods beyond and where her own large terrace overhangs the spot where they stand, and she points across the flower beds. "I didn't see it. It was Lexie. She just got back from Florida at lunchtime, she was vaping on the terrace, and there it was. She hasn't touched it. Thank goodness I'd already filled her in on all the shenanigans so she knew what it meant."

Behind the flower beds is a small straggly area of lawn, then a wide graveled pathway, and beyond that a second gateway into the woodlands. But there, tucked away but apparently visible from the balconies overhead, is a piece of cardboard nailed to the bottom of a tree, with the words "Dig Here" written on it in black marker pen and an arrow pointing to the soil underneath.

35

Noah falls asleep as soon as Kim puts him to bed. He'd been tetchy all evening. Kim can't quite remember what her two were like at this age. Her memory has recalibrated the detail. She knows that one of them used to have tantrums in the supermarket and she suspects it was Tallulah, but that suspicion has been subverted over the past fifteen months because Kim cannot remember anything bad about Tallulah. She cannot remember beyond Tallulah's upturned face in her bedroom as she painted black liquid wings onto her eyes before the Christmas party at college: the pale luminescence of her skin, the perfect upward slope of her nose, the pink of her rosebud lips, the fragile, barely noticeable beauty that had always felt like a secret just between the two of them. She can't square that calm, glorious girl with the two-year-old girl screaming in supermarkets. They cannot be the same person; therefore she tends to imagine that these things hadn't really happened or that it had been Ryan, in fact, or maybe somebody else's child. Not hers. Not Tallulah.

But she has no such ghostly veils across her opinion of her grandson. She loves him, but oh, she finds him so very, very difficult to live with. She had not wanted a third child. She had been offered the opportunity; there'd been a man a year or so after she and Jim split up, a man who said he'd give her a baby and she'd been in her early thirties and Ryan had been about to leave primary school and it had felt, for a moment, like the right time to do it. But she hadn't been able to face the prospect of the sleepless nights and the worry and

the adding of another eighteen years onto the journey of motherhood. She'd imagined herself the age she is now, just forty, with two
grown-up children, and she'd liked the idea of it. So she'd said no to
the nice man who'd offered her a baby and they'd gone the distance
as lovers, and then he'd left when he realized he wanted more and
that was that. She had specifically chosen not to have a third child
and now she has one and he is dark and angry and she is tired all the
time. All the time.

But for now he is asleep and they have crossed the bridge of
another day together and her love for him is as complete as the love
she has for the two children she gave birth to, especially now, when
he is close but not awake, when she has twelve hours to be herself.

She opens a bottle of wine and pours herself a small glass. The
cold kiss of it as it hits the bottom of her stomach is immediate and
pleasurable. She takes another sip and picks up her phone, about to
spend some time mindlessly scrolling through her Facebook feed.
But just as her thumb hits the blue icon on her screen, it is obliterated
by an incoming phone call.

Dom McCoy.

She clears her throat and presses answer.

"Kim. It's me. Dom. We've had a development. At Maypole
House. Are you able to come over?"

Kim's breath catches. "Erm. I just put the baby down. I'm alone. I
don't have anyone to ask to sit with him. Can you just tell me?"

There's a beat of silence; then he says, "OK, Kim, give me five.
Ten minutes. I'll come over. Just stay put."

The ten minutes turn to eighteen minutes before Dom's shadow
finally passes across the panes of glass in Kim's front door. She opens
the door before he's rung the bell and leads him into the living room.
While she's been waiting, she's tipped her wine back into the bottle

and put it in the fridge. She's plumped her cushions and put away some of Noah's toys. She's tied her hair back and put some socks on so that Dom won't see her unpolished toenails.

"How are you?" Dom begins, taking the blue denim armchair he always takes when he comes to see Kim with updates.

"I'm OK," she says. "Tired. You know."

"Yes," says Dom, "I completely empathize with that."

He doesn't wear a wedding ring anymore. Kim had first noticed this about six months ago. And he's lost weight. She stares at him eagerly, willing him to say something good.

"Kerryanne Mulligan called us about an hour ago. Her daughter saw something in the grounds of the college, from her balcony. She went to investigate and found this." He turns his phone toward her and shows her a photo of what looks like exactly the same cardboard sign that the head teacher's girlfriend had found nailed to her fence the week before.

"What?" she asks hoarsely. "What was it?"

He turns his phone back to himself and swipes left on the screen before turning it back to her. She stares at the image for a moment. It's a lumpy object in a clear bag with writing on it. It doesn't make any sense.

"What is it?" she asks.

"Well," says Dom, "I was hoping you might be able to tell us that."

She places her fingertips against the screen and pulls the image open. It's a strange metal tool, with a bent end with a U-shape cut out of it, almost like a very small garden spade. "I don't know what that is. I have no idea."

She sees a flash of disappointment pass across Dom's face. "Well," he says, "it's gone to forensics, so hopefully they might have some kind of idea what it is. And in the meantime, we're still waiting to hear back from the prints guys about the ring and the ring box, but

I have to be honest, Kim, it's not looking very optimistic there. And the handwriting analysis is back, apparently, so I'll be having a look at that first thing tomorrow. So, still lots to chew over."

He smiles at her and she knows he's trying to sound upbeat but she also knows that this isn't panning out as he'd hoped it might because as much as it's Kim whose daughter is missing, she also knows that not being able to solve this case has been deeply upsetting for Dom as well.

She musters a smile and says, "Thanks, Dom. Thank you for everything."

"I wish there was more for me to do," he replies. "There never seems to be enough for me to do. But this," he says, tucking his phone into his pocket, "is better than nothing. Someone knows something and someone wants us to know what they know. So keep your ear to the ground, Kim. Keep your wits about you. If you hear anything from anyone, if anyone tells you they've seen something strange, let me know immediately. OK?"

He glances at her seriously and she smiles and says, "Sure," and for a moment she feels as though she might just open her mouth and add, *I have wine. Do you have time?* but realizes immediately that of course he doesn't have time, that he's in the middle of doing a job, that he has a car to drive home and a life to live, children to put to bed, and that he has done what he came here to do, and of course he doesn't want to stay and drink wine with a tired, sad woman. So she gets to her feet and sees him to the door.

"I'll be in touch again, first thing tomorrow. Take care, Kim."

"Yes," she says, clutching the edge of the door, feeling the urgent pull of wanting to be close to another human being, wanting something more than just her and Noah and this house and all these unanswered questions, before closing the door behind him and immediately forcing her fist into her mouth to hold back her tears.

36

Spring wends its way toward summer in a haze of tedious college days and dull nights spent wedged next to Zach on the sofa, the baby monitor blinking on the table at their side. Noah gets to the stage where his head is too big for his body and they joke about how he looks like a bobblehead and have to prop his huge cranium up with cushions when he falls asleep in the back of the car.

The apartment on the Reigate ring road falls through when the bank refuses them a mortgage and Zach goes back to his spread-sheets and his bank statements with an air of dark resentment. It seems that buying a property is the only thing that matters to him now, that being a home owner at nineteen is some kind of badge of honor that will make him feel like a winner. They've taken to having sex on Wednesday afternoons when Zach gets home early, Kim is at work, Ryan is at school, and Noah is having his daily nap. It's the same every time, a practiced series of movements that ends, within roughly ten minutes, with Zach orgasming silently with his face pressed into a pillow and Tallulah running on tiptoe to the bathroom afterward and staring at herself in the mirror wondering who the naked, empty-eyed girl with blotchy breasts looking back at her is. But she also feels a sense of relief, a sense that it is done, that now she has a week in which her body is her own.

The weeks tick by and the days grow longer. Summer exams beckon and Tallulah spends more of her time at home revising and less sitting on the sofa with Zach, who stalks in and out of their bedroom when she's studying, finding stupid excuses to distract her.

At college, she sees Scarlett nearly every day and they have learned how to ignore each other to the point where Tallulah can sometimes believe that maybe none of it ever happened, that it was all a dream. Scarlett's friends had never accepted her as part of Scarlett's life in the first place and happily accept that she is no longer there. They wave at her if they pass on campus, they say, "Hi, Lules," and Tallulah says hi back. But in the canteen at lunchtime, Tallulah sits with the kids from her social care course, or on her own. She and Scarlett have not spoken a word to each other since the Sunday morning when Tallulah arrived to find her with her ex-boyfriend's teeth marks on her neck. Scarlett sent plaintive WhatsApps and Snaps for a few days, but Tallulah simply deleted them all immediately and then blocked her.

But it doesn't matter how much time passes or how efficiently they have been able to pretend that they don't know each other, the feeling of wanting Scarlett is still as raw, as red, as real as it was when they were together. Tallulah aches, physically, when she thinks about the feel of Scarlett's hand on hers under the table at their secret old-lady cake shop. About those Sunday mornings. When she closes her eyes, she gets flashbacks to the smell of the scented candle in Scarlett's bedroom, the heat of Scarlett's mouth on her skin, the flush of her flesh that stayed for hours after she got home. And she wants it all back. But she can't have it because Tallulah is a mother, she has a child and she has responsibilities and she cannot hand any of that over to the care of someone who doesn't see that it is wrong to let your ex give you love bites while your current love is on a bike coming to see you. She owes it to Noah to give him stable foundations, and Scarlett is lots of things, but she is not stable.

But then, one sunny Tuesday morning, as Tallulah pushes Noah to the pond in his buggy with a small plastic bag of dry bread slices tucked into the hood of the pram, she sees a familiar figure across the common. Scarlett is at college all day on Tuesdays. She shouldn't be here. She shouldn't be across the common, staring right at Tallulah.

Tallulah panics. For a moment she thinks she might just turn Noah's buggy 180 degrees and head home, but Scarlett's pace has picked up and she is heading straight toward her now, and Tallulah can see her brow is furrowed in confusion, her gaze oscillating between Tallulah and the buggy.

Tallulah lets her head drop into her chest, takes a deep breath, and walks to meet Scarlett in the middle of the common.

"Oh my God, is he yours?"

Tallulah nods. "Yes. This is Noah. He's mine."

Scarlett stares at her in disbelief. Then she crouches and reaches into the buggy and for a moment Tallulah's heart starts to race; she thinks maybe Scarlett is going to snatch him, pinch him, hurt him. She pulls the buggy toward herself, but Scarlett is merely greeting Noah.

"Hello, gorgeous," she says, rubbing the backs of her fingers against Noah's cheek. Noah stares at her, wide-eyed but not disturbed. Scarlett's gaze tips up to Tallulah. "Oh my God," she says. "He's so beautiful."

"Thanks."

Scarlett issues a nervous laugh. "God, Lules. You're a mummy."

Tallulah sighs and nods.

"Why didn't you fucking tell me?"

"Could you not," Tallulah begins, hating herself for saying it, but needing to say it because the words physically hurt when she's in front of her baby, "could you not swear? Do you mind?"

Scarlett muzzles herself with both her hands. "Shit," she says. "I'm sorry."

"It's fine. It's just, he's at that age, you know, when he's starting to try and talk. And I couldn't deal with it if that was his first word. You know."

Scarlett nods and smiles. "God. Yes. Of course." She brings herself back to standing and puts her hands in the pockets of a weird patchwork blouson jacket. Her hair is short and messy and she has an outbreak of zits around her mouth. But still she takes Tallulah's breath away.

"Why didn't you tell me?" she asks again.

Tallulah shrugs. "I don't really know."

"And so this is why you're stuck with that loser. I finally understand."

Tallulah feels her defenses rise. "He's not a loser."

Scarlett shrugs. "Whatever."

They stand and stare at each other for a moment. Noah starts to moan a little and kick his feet. "I'm taking him to the pond," Tallulah says. She doesn't add, *Do you want to come*, but Scarlett follows her anyway.

"I can't believe you, Lules. You binned me off because I kissed my ex, and all the while you've got a secret fucking baby."

Tallulah throws her a stern look and Scarlett says, "God. Sorry. Yes. But I just can't even . . . I mean, no one at college knows you've got a baby. I don't get it, why wouldn't you mention it?"

"That's not true actually. There are plenty of people at college who know I've got a baby, just not people you would ever think about talking to."

Scarlett tuts and says, "Oh, right, yeah, make me out to be the villain here. It's always me, isn't it? Never anyone else. And who cares, anyway, the deal here is that you kept this, like, huge secret from me and I never kept anything from you. Not ever. I was always totally honest with you. Even on that last Sunday. I could have kicked Liam out and made sure your paths didn't cross. But I didn't. Because even though what I did was a bit suspect, I didn't want to deceive you. I couldn't lie to you. I'm incapable of lying, basically. That's one of my biggest problems. So, wow, I mean, this . . ." She gestures at the buggy. "I mean, just wow."

Tallulah puts the brake on the buggy as they reach the edge of the pond and leans down to undo Noah's straps, before lifting him out. "It's not the same thing," she replies tersely. "Not the same at all." She takes a slice of the stale bread from the baggie and tears a bit off.

Noah grabs it from her hand and tries to throw it into the pond but it drops at Scarlett's feet. Scarlett picks it up and hands it back to him and says, "Try again, buddy."

She puts her hand over his and gently guides his arm into a proper throw and cheers when the bread hits the surface of the pond. "High five!" she says, touching her hand against his as he stares at her in wonder.

"You know I bloody love babies, Lula. I even told you that I love babies. I just don't get any of this."

Tallulah tears off another piece of bread and guides it into Noah's hand. "Yes," she says. "I should have told you. You're right. But I didn't because I wanted you . . ." She pauses to find words that won't make her sound as bad as she feels. "I wanted you to think I was like you. You know. A free spirit."

"But you've got a bloody boyfriend! How less free can you possibly be than that?"

"Yes, but a boyfriend isn't permanent. A child is permanent. Wherever I go, he goes. Whatever I'm doing, I'm his mother. Twenty-four-seven. For the rest of my life. And it's a lot, you know."

"Fuck, Lula. *Life* is a lot. All of it is a lot. You and me, we had this thing, this amazing, amazing thing that I thought was the most important thing that had ever happened to me. From minute one, that day on the bus, I saw you and I knew, I knew everything that was going to happen, that you and I were destined to be together. And then we were, and you made me so f—" She glances at Noah and pauses. "You made me so happy. And I know, I know what I did with Liam was wrong, but I suppose I just thought that as long as you had Zach in your life, as long as you made a secret out of you and me"—she gestures between them with her hand—"then we weren't real."

They both clap then, as Noah's next attempt to throw bread lands successfully and a group of ducks draws quickly toward it. Scarlett puts out her hand and cups the back of Noah's head. "God," she says. "He's so precious. He's so, so precious."

Tallulah feels something in her gut, a kick of pleasure, but also of fear. She pulls Noah slightly closer into her body and Scarlett lets her hand drop from his head.

"You know," she says, "we could do this. We could. I feel like you think I'm some kind of beautiful idiot, you know? And I know I do play up to that. I do. People are easier to deal with if they underestimate you. But I'm not an idiot, Lules. I've lived a life, things have happened, bad things. I've grown and learned and . . . and . . . matured. I could totally do the baby thing. With you. But the question is . . . are you ready to be honest about us?"

Tallulah glances at her questioningly. "You mean, tell people?"

Scarlett nods.

Tallulah turns her gaze back to the water, to the bowed heads of the ducks bobbing for the wet bread. She tries to picture herself telling various people in her life. Her mother would be fine. Ryan would be surprised but fine. Pretty much everyone she knows at college would be fine. There's only one person she can't ever imagine telling.

"I can never tell Zach," she says. "He'd kill me."

"Kill you?" Scarlett's eyes are wide.

"Yes. He'd kill me."

"Are you serious?"

Tallulah closes her eyes. She pictures his face, the way his jaw clenches together when he's displeased about something, the way his fist comes down upon inanimate objects when he's annoyed, the flare of his nostrils, the entitled tilt of his chin as he surveys the object of his displeasure. And she remembers the tightness of his hands around her arms when she told him that she didn't have time for him and imagines that amplified tenfold if she told him that she was leaving him for a girl. Zach isn't liberal. He has no time for political correctness. He is his mother's son: small-minded, self-absorbed, inward-thinking, a little bit racist, a little bit homophobic, a little bit misogynistic. All those things that don't matter when you're fourteen and in love, but start to sprout insidiously to the surface over the years it takes you to go from child to adult, and even now it's not blatant but she knows him well enough to know that it's there. And she knows him well enough to know that he would be humiliated if he found out about her affair with Scarlett and that that humiliation would spill over into anger and that he is strong and he is already only one flash away from hurting her, constantly.

"Yes," she replies, opening her eyes. "Yes. I think he would."

"Oh my God, Lula. Has he ever hit you?"

She shakes her head. "Not really."

"Not really?"

"No. No, he hasn't."

Scarlett laces her fingers into her short hair and tugs at it, takes a couple of paces away and then paces back again. "Lula. God. I mean, this is bad. Do you even love him?"

"I used to."

"But now?"

She shrugs and sniffs. "No," she says quietly. "Not anymore. Not really."

"And do you want to spend the rest of your life with him?"

She shakes her head, hard. She can feel tears coming and she doesn't want them. "No," she says, her voice cracking. "No. I don't."

"Then fuck, Tallulah, you need to sort this out. You need to get rid of him. Because you can't live your life like this. You can't live your life being scared."

"But how do I get rid of him?" Tallulah says. "How?"

PART THREE

37

The following afternoon, when she gets home from college, Tallulah takes Noah for a walk around the village at around the time that she would normally put him down for his afternoon nap and have sex with Zach. She turns her phone to silent and puts in her earbuds, the music turned up loud, refusing to allow the image of Zach getting back from work to an empty house to taint her thoughts.

She pushes the buggy into the co-op and scopes the shop for Keziah. She spies her in the bakery aisle, stacking the shelves with self-raising flour. "Hiya," she says.

Keziah turns around. She glances at Tallulah and then into the buggy. When she sees Noah she claps her hands to her mouth and makes a muffled squeaking noise. "Oh. My. God." She takes her hands from her mouth. "Oh my God. Lula. He is so beautiful."

Tallulah smiles and feels the swirl in her gut she always gets when someone tells her that her son is beautiful. "Thank you," she says. "Sorry he's not awake. But I said I'd bring him in to show you."

"How old is he now?"

"Eleven months."

"Oh my God. Where did the time go! Feels like it was only about five minutes ago you were just pregnant!"

Tallulah smiles again.

"How's Zach?"

"Oh, he's fine. You know."

"Still together?"

"Yeah. Just about." She laughs drily.

"It's tough, with a baby, isn't it?"

"Yeah," she replies. "It has its moments. Especially living together. Actually, I was going to say: remember you talked about getting together with the others? From school?"

"Yeah!" Keziah's face lights up. "Oh, definitely. We're going out tomorrow as it happens. Just to the Ducks. Want to come?"

"Yes, please," Tallulah says brightly, feeling the plan fall into place. "That'd be great. What time?"

"Sevenish? Or whenever you can get away, really. What with the bubba and everything." Keziah makes that pained face again, the face she makes every time she looks at Noah, almost as if his beauty is a terrible blight of some kind.

"Great," says Tallulah. "I'll see you then!"

She pushes the buggy back out of the shop and then walks for an hour, up to the other end of the village where the estate is, and to the common around the back lanes. She times her walk so that she gets back half an hour before her mother and Ryan return, long enough for the argument to play itself out. As she approaches the cul-de-sac her heart races with anticipation. She turns her key in the lock and pushes open the door. "Hello," she calls out.

Noah is still asleep and she leaves him in his buggy in the hallway and peers around the living room door.

Zach sits on the sofa, his phone in his hand. He looks up at her darkly. "Where the fuck have you been?"

She closes the door behind her.

"Took Noah out for a walk. It was too nice to stay in and I've done all my revision."

"I've called you, like, a hundred times. Why didn't you fucking answer?"

She pulls her phone from the pocket of her hoodie and glances at it. "Oh," she says. "Shit. Sorry. It was on silent."

"*Shit. Sorry. It was on silent,*" he mimics her. "What sort of mother goes out without telling anyone and leaves their phone on silent?"

"Er, me, I guess." Her tone is glib, but beneath her rib cage, her heart is hammering.

"I literally had no idea where you both were. You could have been dead for all I knew."

"Well, we're not. So it's fine."

He shakes his head. "Unbelievable," he says. "Totally unbelievable. And not only that but it's Wednesday. You know, *our* Wednesday."

"Oh shit," she says. "God. I forgot. I'm really sorry."

"No, you're not. You're not fucking sorry. I can tell."

"I am. Honestly. I just finished my revision and it was so gorgeous out and Noah was getting scratchy for his nap and I just thought how nice it would be to get out and about for a while and I totally forgot it was Wednesday."

"You *forgot it was Wednesday.*" He groans and rolls his eyes. "And here we go again. Just when I thought we were finally getting somewhere, that you were finally taking this seriously. I should have guessed. This is just like a joke to you, isn't it? This." He gestures between the two of them. "Me. You. Noah. Just a game. You know, I sometimes feel like if something better came along, you'd just walk away from Noah and me, you know, like you don't give a shit about anyone apart from yourself."

Tallulah swallows down a burst of rage. The idea of walking away from Noah is monstrous, unimaginable. She tips her head slightly and says, "Whatever."

"Whatever?"

"Yes. Whatever. You've clearly made your mind up about me and what sort of person I am and what I want and don't want. And I can't be bothered arguing with you." She sighs. "I'm going to get myself a cup of tea," she says, turning toward the kitchen. "Want anything?"

He shakes his head firmly and she sees a muscle in his cheek pulsing with anger.

"Oh," she calls back to him, "by the way. I bumped into Keziah just now. Remember Keziah, who I went to primary school with? She's invited me to a girls' night, a reunion thing, at the Ducks. Tomorrow night. You're all right staying in with Noah, aren't you?"

There's a dull silence from the living room and Tallulah holds her breath.

A moment later Zach is in the doorway of the kitchen, flexing and unflexing his fists. "Sorry," he says. "Keziah *who?*"

"Keziah Whitmore. I went to primary school with her. She works at the co-op now."

"Right. So. Let's get this straight. After knowing you for nearly five years, I've never heard of this person before and now you're just *going for drinks.*"

"Yes," she says, closing the fridge door. "Tomorrow night."

"And how are you going to pay for that?"

She shrugs. "I don't know. Mum will probably let me have some money."

"So here's me, working my-fucking-self to death, day in, day out, never spend a penny on anything, not a fucking penny. Single-handedly trying to get us a place to live, and you're just going to the pub with some slag called *Keziah* who I've never even fucking heard of."

"I don't ask you to work so hard," she replies evenly. "I don't expect you not to spend any money on anything. I don't tell you you can't go out. And, frankly, I don't even want us to buy a flat. I like living here with Mum."

She glances at him briefly. She can see the clenched jaw start to grind.

"I'm sorry?"

"I don't want to move out. I want to stay here, with Mum."

He grunts. "Christ, you are such a fucking child, Tallulah. You still haven't grown up, have you? You still think life is all swanning about, doing what you like, going to the pub, hanging out with Mummy. Well, it's not. We have a child. We have responsibilities. We're not kids anymore, Tallulah. It's time to grow the fuck up." He looms over her now and she can feel the heat of his breath on her face.

"I think you should move out," she says.

A taut silence follows.

"What?"

"I think we should split up. I don't want to be with you anymore."

Tallulah's gaze stays on the floor but she can feel Zach's rage coalescing in the air around her.

Another drawn-out silence follows and Tallulah waits. Waits to be hit, waits to be screamed at, waits for the anger that exists so close to the tight seams of Zach's psyche finally to burst through. But it doesn't. After a few seconds she feels his presence soften and shrink, sees his shoulders slope, and then he is gone. She follows him into the hallway. He is leaning over Noah's sleeping form in his buggy and whispering to him. Tallulah feels a terrible chill run through all of her. She moves closer and watches, her body primed and ready to do whatever it takes to protect Noah from Zach. She hears the click of the safety harness being unclipped and watches as Zach carefully plucks Noah from his buggy and lifts him toward his shoulder. Noah doesn't stir; he is heavy with sleep. His big head flops gently into the crook of Zach's neck and Zach kisses him softly on his crown.

His eyes meet Tallulah's over the top of their child's head and he says, in a voice hard with resolve, "I am not going anywhere, Tallulah, I am not going fucking anywhere."

38

Sophie sits at her desk in the hallway of the cottage by the front door. The weird burning-petrol smell in the hallway that's been there since they moved in has finally started to fade and she's moved her work area here where the window overlooks the college grounds so she can watch the comings and goings in the school. Shaun told her last night what the detectives had found buried in the flower bed outside the accommodation block; he said it was a lever of some kind, a piece of metal with a handle and a bent tip, very old, apparently. Nobody knows what it is or why it was buried there or by whom. It's a total mystery.

But there's another mystery preying on Sophie's mind.

The cardboard sign had been spotted by Lexie Mulligan, Kerryanne's daughter, just hours after she returned home from a trip to Florida. She claims to have seen it while standing on her mother's terrace, vaping. Earlier today, Sophie had gone for a walk around the accommodation block and stared upward to Kerryanne Mulligan's terrace and felt a jolt in the pit of her stomach at the stark realization that the terrace was far too low down to see across the flower bed to the spot where the cardboard sign had been left, and she'd known immediately that, for some reason, Lexie had been lying.

Sophie flips open the lid of her laptop now and googles Lexie Mulligan. She clicks the link to her Instagram account, which is called @lexiegoes. Lexie looks very different in her photos from how she looks in real life. In real life she is attractive but has a certain flatness to her features, a lack of delicacy, but in these shots she looks like a model. There she is in a black satin dressing gown printed with roses, cross-legged and sipping a cocktail on her Florida balcony with the backdrop of a heart-shaped swimming pool. The accompanying text is a thinly veiled promotion for the hotel and is full of hashtags relating to the hotel and its parent company. Sophie glances at the top of the page and sees that Lexie has 72,000 followers. She assumes that the hotel was a freebie as recompense for the publicity and she assumes that with that many followers (Sophie herself has 812) Lexie must get lots of freebies and lots of payouts from the businesses she promotes and she wonders why a grown woman with what looks like a great career is still living with her mum in a tiny flat in a boarding school in Surrey.

As she thinks this she glances again through the window and sees Lexie herself striding across the campus. She's wearing patterned leggings and a black hoodie and her hair is in two plaits. She has a carrier bag that looks like the ones they give you at the co-op and she looks a million miles from the girl in the Instagram posts. Sophie watches her as she heads toward the accommodation block. A few minutes later she sees the door open onto Kerryanne's terrace and Lexie appears with a mug of tea. She gazes out across the campus and into the woods beyond for a moment, before turning and heading back indoors.

For some reason there is something unsettling about the way she does this, something strangely forensic. Sophie glances down at Lexie's Instagram feed again and scrolls downward and downward, through Cuba, Colombia, Quebec, Saint Bart's, Copenhagen, Belfast, the Hebrides, Beijing, Nepal, Liverpool, Moscow. Her head spins with the breadth of Lexie's traveling. She keeps scrolling until she gets to something more familiar: it's Lexie in front of the beautiful main doors to the school. Behind her the light from the stained glass in the reception area falls into colored puddles on the tiled floor.

She's wearing an ankle-length fake-fur coat and a green woolen hat with a furry bobble. By her side is a pair of huge suitcases. The caption says, *Home sweet home.*

Sophie does a double take. She scrolls through the comments and sees that Lexie's followers are under the impression that these are the doors to her house. That this is her home. And Lexie does nothing to correct these misapprehensions. She lets her followers believe that yes, this is where she lives.

Sophie sees a comment from @kerryannemulligan:

And your mummy is so happy to have you back!

She blinks. Kerryanne appears to be supporting the illusion that Lexie lives in a Georgian mansion.

She's about to start scrolling deeper into Lexie's feed when she hears a knock at the back door. She closes her laptop and walks through the cottage. She calls out hello.

"Hi, Sophie, it's me, Liam."

Sophie's breath catches. "Oh," she says. "Hi. Just one minute."

She checks her reflection in the wall mirror and pulls her hair away from her face. Then she opens the door and greets Liam with a smile.

He stands before her clutching a novel in his hands.

She glances down and see that it is her book, the first of the series, the one she wrote when she was still a teaching assistant, the one she had no idea anyone would ever actually read. And now here it is, being held in the good, strong hands of a handsome boy called Liam, and her words, she realizes with a jolt, have been inside his head.

"I'm really sorry to disturb you," Liam says, breaking into her train of thought, "but I finished your book, last night. And I just—I loved it. I mean, I really, really loved it. And I just wondered, if you had a minute, I'd love to ask you a question about it. But I can come back another time if you're busy?"

She stares at him for a second; then she shakes her head a little and says, "Oh. Thank you. I wasn't expecting . . . I mean, yes, sorry. Please come in."

He follows her into the kitchen and pats the spine of her book against the palm of his free hand a couple of times. "I won't keep you. I just, er . . . But your book, there was something I wanted to ask you. Susie Beets. Is she you?"

Sophie blinks. It's not the question she was expecting.

"I mean," he continues, "you have the same initials. And she's blond and in her thirties and comes from South London and used to be a schoolteacher."

"No," she says. "No. She's not me. She's more like a really good friend. Or the sister I never had." It's a stock answer, but she continues: "If anything, Tiger has more of my personality traits and opinions in him."

"Really?" says Liam, his face lighting up. "Wow. That's so interesting. Because, I don't know, I felt like I was reading about you, when I pictured everything in my head; I just saw you doing everything that Susie does. Even down to your shoes."

"My shoes?"

They both glance down at her feet. She's wearing white trainers, as she nearly always does.

"I mean, you never describe her shoes, but I pictured her in white trainers. Because that's what you wear."

Sophie doesn't quite know how to respond. "Do I not describe her shoes?" she asks.

Liam shakes his head. "No. Never."

"Well," she says, slightly breathlessly. "Thank you for pointing that out. Next time I describe what she's wearing I will put in a description of her shoes, just for you."

"Seriously?" he says.

"Yes. Seriously."

"Wow. And which book would that be in? Are you writing one now?"

She glances behind her toward her laptop on the desk in the hallway. "Well, technically, yes. But I haven't written a word since I moved here, to be truthful. Despite my best intentions."

"Writer's block?"

"Well, no, not strictly. Writer's block is a serious psychological malaise. It can last for years. Forever in some particularly tragic cases."

"So why do you think you haven't been able to write?"

"Oh," she says. "Lots of reasons. But mainly, I think, because of finding that ring. And now all the other stuff going on."

Liam nods. "It's all a bit freaky, isn't it?" He taps her book against the palm of his other hand again and steps from one foot to another. He seems a little anxious. "I guess it'll all become clear eventually. I wonder what they'll uncover next. Maybe there's someone out there, as I'm talking to you, burying another little surprise for someone to uncover."

"Like Easter eggs."

"Yes," he says. "I suppose they are. I just . . ." He stops tapping the book and rubs the back of his neck with his free hand. "I just don't get it. I don't get any of it. If someone knows what happened to those kids, then why the hell don't they just go to the police and tell them?"

"Because maybe they had something to do with it?"

She sees him shudder slightly. "Freaks me out," he says. "Really freaks me out. Anyway . . ." He appears to reset himself. "I'd better let you get on. I just wanted to ask you that. About Susie Beets. About the shoes." He taps the book one more time against his hand and then turns and heads toward the back door.

After he's gone, Sophie goes back to her desk and sits for a while, imagining handsome Liam, alone in his room, reading her book.

She tries to remember the content of the book, but can't. She goes to her bedroom to find the packing box that has her P. J. Fox books in it. She slices through the tape and burrows through the contents until she finds the one she's looking for: the first in the series. Perched on the edge of the bed, she flicks through the pages, skimming them with her eyes. And that's when she sees it. The thing that's been hovering in her subconscious since the day she arrived. She flattens the two sides of the book and she reads:

> Susie opened the creaky gate and peered up and down the high street. It was just getting dark and the wet pavements were glowing warm amber in the streetlight. She pulled the sides of her furry coat together across her body and was about to head back out into the night when she saw something from the corner of her eye, in the flower bed to her left. It was a flap of cardboard, nailed to the wooden fence. In black marker, someone had scribbled the words "Dig Here," with an arrow pointing downward into the soil . . .

39

MAY 2017

Zach sits on the edge of the bed, watching Tallulah get ready to go to the pub.

"This is fucking ridiculous," he says.

"Can you stop watching me, please."

"I mean, for fuck's sake. It's not as if these people would even notice if you didn't show up. They wouldn't even care."

"How do you know?"

"Because people don't care. Everyone goes around thinking they're the center of the fucking universe and that people miss them when they don't come to things, but nobody gives a shit."

"So, if you didn't turn up for football one Sunday, you think nobody would notice?"

"That's different. That's a team. You need a certain number for a team. You don't need a certain number to sit in the fucking pub."

Tallulah doesn't reply. She focuses instead on rearranging her earrings, exchanging the plain silver studs and hoops she normally wears for a fancy set of earrings that loop together on chains from the top of her ear down to the lobes. They're similar to the sorts of earrings that Scarlett wears.

"What the hell is that?"

She glances at Zach's reflection in the mirror witheringly, but doesn't respond. "Aren't you going to give Noah his bath now?" she says. "It's getting late."

"I'm pretty sure that you don't get to dictate our schedule since you're not even going to be here."

Tallulah rolls her eyes. "I can't believe you're making such a fuss about me leaving the house."

"It's not you leaving the house that's the issue. You leave the house all the fucking time. It's you spending money. When we're trying to save up."

She turns and stares at him. "I told you," she says. "I don't want to move out. I don't want to buy a flat. I want to stay here."

"Yeah, well, I'm not particularly interested in what you want or don't want. This isn't about you. It's about Noah."

"Noah doesn't want to go and live in a box on the side of an A road either. He wants to stay here. It's lovely here. The countryside on our doorstep. There's the nursery just across the common. His nana. His uncle. Your mum."

There's a beat of silence. He narrows his eyes at her. "You know my mum doesn't even think Noah is mine."

Tallulah freezes.

"She reckons you're just using me for money. And you know what, when I think about it, she's got a point. I mean, all those months when you didn't want me anywhere near you. All those months where you just kept me at arm's length—"

"You *dumped me when I was pregnant*," she interjects through bared teeth.

"And why do you think that was?"

"I don't know," she says. "You tell me."

"Because I didn't believe you. Did I? I didn't believe you were really pregnant; I thought you were just trying to trap me. Because we were so careful and I knew we'd been careful and I couldn't see how it could have happened and then I started to think, all those times you said you were revising for your A levels, all those times you were too busy to see me. I just thought, you know, I wouldn't be surprised if you were off with someone else. And that that's how you got pregnant. Because it can't have been me."

"So you dumped me because you thought I was pregnant with somebody else's baby?"

"Yeah. Basically."

"Jesus Christ."

"But then I saw you out and about with the baby and you looked so happy and so beautiful and the baby was just, like, the most beautiful baby I'd ever seen and I thought—" His voice starts to crack. "I thought, well, I wouldn't be feeling that way if it weren't mine. I thought I'd know. *I'd know* if he were someone else's. And every time I saw him I just fell more and more in love with him, and even though he doesn't really look like me, I could just tell that he was mine. You know? Like, in here." He bangs his chest with his fist. "Mine. And I think my mum's wrong. I mean, I know she's wrong. Because he is. Isn't he? Noah is mine?"

Zach's eyes are filled with tears. He looks desperate and pathetic. For a moment Tallulah's heart fills with a kind of pitiful love for him and she finds herself moving toward where he sits on the edge of the bed and putting her arms around his neck and whispering into his ear, "God, of course he's yours, of course he is. He's yours. I promise he's yours."

And his arms reach around her and pull her tighter toward him and she feels the wetness of his tears against her cheek and he says, "Please, Lules, please don't go out tonight. Please stay home. I'll go out and get us a bottle of wine. And some Doritos. Just you and me. Please."

Tallulah thinks of Keziah and her weird little gang of local friends, all so alien to her with their barely begun lives and their safe little jobs, still waiting for boyfriends and babies as if that was all there was to life. She thinks of them all staring at her like an exhibit at a zoo, talking about motherhood and cohabitation as if it was an end goal, rather than a place you might find yourself by accident. She pictures them sitting primly on the velvet sofas at the Swan & Ducks, sipping cheap prosecco and laughing in high-pitched voices at things that aren't particularly funny, and then she thinks of drinking wine with Zach, of capitalizing on this rare moment of softness after all these weeks of hard edges and cutting comments, of pulling Zach back from the brink, persuading him that he could move back to his mum's, that they could just co-parent, amicably, just as they'd done before he moved in. She thinks, if they can be nice to each other tonight, maybe they can move on to a place where no one is angry and everyone gets what they want. And what they both want, more than anything, is Noah. And maybe Zach will learn to accept that this is enough, that he doesn't need Tallulah too, that he doesn't need a nuclear family, that there are other girls out there who will love him for what he is and not just put up with him for the sake of happy families, girls who would want a future with him, who would want to have sex with him more than once a week—girls who aren't into girls.

So she nods her head against his face and says, "Yes. Let's do that. It'll be good. I'll send Keziah a text now. We can stay in. We can stay in."

40

The following morning, Sophie stays in bed while Shaun gets up and ready for work. She has not slept well. She's nervous about the children coming tonight. Shaun's ex, Pippa, is bringing them, and there'll be an awkward handover to deal with. She knows the twins will be fine, they are robust and uncomplicated children, mainly, she suspects, because they are twins. But she's still stressed about having to play mother for two nights and two days, having to focus on someone else after all these days of having her head in the mysterious disappearance of Tallulah and Zach. It's forecast to rain for the entire weekend, which means that all the lovely things she thought they might do together are not going to happen and they'll be stuck indoors or having pub lunches across the common. But mainly she has not slept because of her chilling encounter with Liam the previous day and the revelation of the passage in her own book.

After he'd left she spent some time on Instagram searching for him and finally found his account twenty down; his profile photo was a picture of his face and his profile name was @BoobsBailey. He had very few posts, only about twenty or thirty. But one had jumped out at Sophie. A photo taken in June 2017. It appeared to have been taken in the small courtyard garden at the back of the Swan & Ducks; Sophie recognized the big wrought-iron clock that hangs on the wall out there. The photo was of Liam and Scarlett and Lexie. They all had their arms around one another and Scarlett had her tongue out, a flash of silver piercing as it caught the sun. Underneath Liam had written the word *Beauties*.

Liam and Lexie, it appeared, were friends.

The post had seven likes and Sophie clicked it to see if any were from people she knew. One was from Kerryanne Mulligan, another from someone called @AmeliaDisparue. She clicked on this and brought up a page for a young girl with fine blond hair and an elfin face. Her bio described her as *Skinny, Mini, Lost in the middle of f***ing nowhere.*

Her feed consisted of a few strangely abstract shots of landscapes and the last post was dated 16 June 2017. Sophie's heart had skipped a beat. A dark shimmer of underlit pool water, a hint of hot-pink flamingo, a hand just out of shot cupped around a lit cigarette, the blurred outlines of figures behind huddled together under a throw. She clicked on the image and zoomed in on it, but it was impossible to tell who the people in the background were. The photo had no caption and no likes and no comments. It hung suspended there, like an empty thought bubble, without context or meaning. But it was, Sophie was sure of it, a tantalizing fragment of the night Zach and Tallulah went missing.

She'd become distracted then by a flurry of activity in her inbox, always the way at that time of the day, as people who worked in offices tied up loose ends before leaving for home. And then Shaun had returned. That night in bed her head had spun with disparate pieces of information, dissonant feelings about the key players and unanswered questions. She dreamed about the pool, about inflatable flamingos and weird metal levers and Liam Bailey scribbling on her trainers with a pink highlighter pen and telling her that she needed to shave her legs.

Now she sits in bed, scrolling through her phone mindlessly. She has a food delivery coming at ten, lots of good healthy stuff for the twins, some wine, some treats—which the twins will look at in awe and wonder as if they had never seen chocolate rice cakes before—and extra milk for all the cereal. Apart from that, her day is free. She should pack for Denmark. She's leaving first thing on Monday morning; she has a car coming to take her to Gatwick at four thirty in the morning and the children will be here until early evening on Sunday. She should use the day wisely and sensibly to clear her email inbox, get ready for her trip, and be relaxed for the children's arrival.

But she can feel it inside her like a strange piece of music on repeat, the need to keep digging, both literally and metaphorically. She googles "Amelia Disparue." A girl called Mimi was the only other person at Dark Place that night, apart from Liam, Lexie, and Scarlett's mother. Like Scarlett and her family, Mimi has also erased her online presence. *Disparue* is French for "Disappeared," and Mimi, thinks Sophie, could be an abbreviation of Amelia.

The search results bring up a YouTube account for someone called Mimi Melia. She clicks on it.

Immediately she sits bolt upright in bed.

On-screen is the same young woman with the fine blond hair and elfin face. She appears to be in a bedroom. She adjusts the angle of the camera she's using to record herself and then says, "Hi, guys, welcome to my channel. My name is Amelia. Or Mimi. Or anything you like, really, at this point, who really cares. I was going to talk to you all today about my struggles with celiac disease. But as some of you know, I have had another struggle in my life for the past year, fifteen months. Post-traumatic stress caused by an incident last summer that I have hitherto not spoken about in order to protect someone very close to me. But I have recently discovered that that person is not the person I thought they were and . . ." She pauses then and her gaze leaves the camera and hovers somewhere toward the bottom of the screen. She's wearing a white vest top and her arms are very pale and thin.

Her eyes come back to the camera. "Well," she begins. "I can't say too much. In fact, I can't say anything. But . . ." She pauses for dramatic effect. ". . . the thing that cannot be named looks like it might finally, finally, finally"—she crosses two pairs of fingers—"be about to spill its guts. And just you wait, just you wait until it does." She makes her hands into two fists, side by side, and then explodes them. "Pyow," she says. "Pyow."

Then it ends and Sophie sits, dumbstruck, her jaw hanging slightly. She watches it again. The date on the video is yesterday's date.

Sophie has no idea if this is the girl called Mimi who was there the night that Zach and Tallulah disappeared. But this girl once liked a photo of Liam and Lexie and Scarlett taken at the Swan & Ducks and now she is discussing an event that happened over a year ago, that she has not been allowed to discuss but that has left her with PTSD.

Sophie turns off her phone, jumps out of bed, and gets in the shower.

Twenty minutes later she is outside Kim Knox's house.

Kim comes to the door holding a mascara tube in one hand and the wand in the other. Behind her, Sophie can hear Kim's grandson shouting about something. Kim closes her eyes, turns her head, and sighs before opening them again and staring straight at Sophie. "Oh," she says. "Sorry. I thought it was going to be an Amazon delivery."

"Sorry to disturb you so early, Kim. I can see you're busy, but I just wanted to show you something, quickly. If you've got a minute?"

"Yeah, sure. Come in. Sorry, it's all a bit chaotic; you know, mornings. Do you have kids?"

"No," Sophie replies. "No. Well, stepkids. Sort of. Not technically but just about. They're coming to stay this weekend so I guess I'll be the one in chaos then."

Kim's house is lovely, painted in soft shades of gray and teal and oyster-shell pink with splashes of mad wallpaper with birds of paradise printed on them and copper-shaded lights. But it's a mess. The floor is littered with shoes and toys and empty cardboard boxes. The TV blares from the living room and the boy is shouting ever louder. In the kitchen he sits on an aqua-blue chair at a white Formica-topped table eating cereal with a plastic spoon.

"Come on, Noah, you need to finish up now. We have to leave in ten minutes."

"No," he shouts. "No nursery." He throws his plastic spoon down onto the table, where it splatters milk everywhere. Kim grabs a damp cloth from the sink and wipes up the spills, before removing the boy's cereal bowl and carrying it toward the dishwasher.

"No!" the boy yells. "No. Give it back!"

"OK," says Kim. "But you have to promise to eat it up nice and fast. OK?"

He nods solemnly and she replaces the bowl in front of him, whereupon he slides it slowly and deliberately across the table until it is nearly hanging off the edge. Kim grabs it just before it falls, whisks it away from him, and says, "Sorry. That's your last chance. Now you need to finish your juice and we need to get ready to go."

"No," he shouts. "Not going."

"I can come back later, if you'd rather," says Sophie.

Kim sighs. "Can you just tell me what it is?"

"I was just looking through social media," Sophie begins hesitantly. "For all the kids who were at Dark Place that night. And I found a YouTube channel, for a girl. She's called Amelia, but she shortens it to Mimi. And I wondered if maybe it was her?"

"Mimi? Mimi Rhodes?"

"Yes. And this girl, she just posted something yesterday, something strange. I wanted you to see it so you could tell me if it's her or not? If it's Mimi?"

"Tell you what," says Kim. "Let me just corral this one and I'll meet you on the street. We can walk to the nursery together. If you have time?"

"Yes. Yes. I have time. I have loads of time. I'll see you in a minute."

She leaves the house, the sound of Kim's grandson's furious tantrum still ringing in her ears. She waits by the edge of the common for a few minutes and then finally Kim appears, her hair in a haphazard bun on top of her head, black-framed glasses on and no makeup, pushing the crying boy in his buggy.

He's quieting down now, and Sophie glances at him and then at Kim and says, "Everything OK?"

Kim nods. "Yes. We got there in the end. We have a reward chart. Don't we, Noah? And what do we get if we get up to the top level of the rainbow?"

"Legoland!"

"Yes. We get to go to Legoland. And how far up the ladder are we?"

"Half."

"Yes. We're halfway. So we just need to keep trying to be good, particularly in the mornings, so we're not late for nursery. Yes?"

"Yes." He nods. "Yes. And then . . . Legoland!"

They're halfway across the common, about to circle the duck pond. Sophie turns on her phone and sets the video to full screen, turns it on its side, and they watch it as they walk. "Is that her? Is that Mimi Rhodes?"

"God. I'm not a hundred percent sure. I only saw her a couple of times, at the police station. And she had red hair then, I think, not blond. But yes, it does sort of look like her."

"Me see?" asks Noah.

She sighs and says to Sophie, "Do you mind? He always has to see everything. Everything."

Sophie passes the phone to Noah. He grabs it and stares at the girl.

"Looks sad," says Noah, "like sad person."

"Yes. Probably," says Kim. "She probably is."

———————

A moment later they are outside the tiny primary school, which sits down a small lane around the back of the Swan & Ducks. Small children in gray and blue swarm past and into the gates and Sophie feels her senses twitch with echoes of her own time as a classroom assistant. Opposite the main gates is a small prefab building surrounded by its own picket fence. This is the nursery. They see Noah through the door into the care of a young girl with a bright smile and then they turn to each other.

"Shall we get a coffee?" asks Kim. "At the Ducks?"

"Sure."

Once seated they watch the video together in its entirety.

"Well," says Kim. "I can't see how this could not be her. Can you send me the link? So I can send it to the detective in charge of the case?"

"Sure, let me have your number."

She sends the link to Kim via WhatsApp and they wait for it to land in her inbox before putting down their phones.

"So, you're interested in the case, then?" says Kim, turning her coffee cup around and around in her saucer.

"Well, yeah. I mean, from the minute I saw that sign that said 'Dig Here,' my curiosity was piqued. I don't mean to sound mercenary, but I write detective novels, so I'm kind of hardwired to pick up on things like that. You know? And then when Kerryanne told me about people going missing—"

"Kerryanne? Kerryanne Mulligan?"

"Yes." She pauses, realizing that she's just betrayed Kerryanne's confidence. "It was probably a little indiscreet of her, but when I mentioned I wrote detective novels, she mentioned that there'd been a couple of police searches in those woods last summer. So I wondered if the sign I'd seen near the woods had anything to do with . . . with Tallulah. And then, well, you know the rest. But there is one thing . . . an odd thing."

Kim glances at her and stops turning her cup.

"You know that strange implement they found? In the flower bed? Outside the accommodation block?"

Kim nods.

"I mean, I could be wrong, but the cardboard sign—it doesn't look to me as if Kerryanne's daughter would have been able to see it from the edge of her own terrace. I can't help thinking that she was in somebody else's room when she saw it."

"Like who?"

"Like Liam Bailey? Maybe?" She shows her the photo of Liam and Lexie in the garden at the Ducks. "Look," she says. "They're friends. I didn't realize. So maybe she was in his apartment, not hers, when she saw it. I just think . . ." She pauses, because really, she doesn't know what she thinks. "I just thought maybe, if you were talking to the detective, maybe you could mention it to him? Just in case they haven't thought of it themselves. Which I'm sure they have. I mean, they must have."

Kim nods again. Then she says, "Why is someone doing this to me?"

Sophie flinches at the rawness of her voice.

"Why is someone not telling me what they know? Why are they being so cruel? And this girl, this Mimi. She's obviously been talking to someone in the village. It's the only way she could possibly have known about what's been happening here. So it must be the person who's been leaving the clues. And it doesn't make any sense. It just doesn't make any sense that half the people who were there that night have disappeared into thin air and the other half are still here and for some unknown reason are leading us all up the fucking garden path."

Her voice has grown louder and the woman behind the bar looks across at them. "You OK, Kim?" she calls.

Kim nods and sighs. "I'm fine," she says. "I'm fine." She takes her phone and puts it into her handbag. "I'll talk to Dom about the video. See what else he's got to tell me."

"Dom?"

"The detective."

"Ah." Sophie smiles. "The real detective."

Kim smiles too. "Yeah. The real detective." Then she says, "And I'm sorry, I don't really read. In fact I haven't read a book since I was about nineteen. Since before Tallulah was born. Otherwise I'd ask what your books are called. But I wouldn't have heard of them anyway."

Sophie thinks briefly of telling Kim about the passage in her own book that someone seems to be copycatting, the book that Liam Bailey brought into her home yesterday, tap-tapping its spine against the palm of his hand in a way that now feels vaguely sinister, but she decides against it. The revelation will take away from her impartiality, the impartiality, she feels, that is key to Kim trusting her.

"No," says Sophie, with a reassuring smile. "No. Probably not."

41

Scarlett is heading from the art block toward Tallulah. She has a small portfolio clutched against her chest and she looks like she's on a mission.

Tallulah turns and jumps into a shadow, but it's too late, Scarlett's seen her. She strides toward her, grabs her by her arm, and pulls her gently onto a pathway behind the art block.

"Well?" Scarlett asks, her eyes wide with desperation. "Did you do it? Did you finish it? What happened? Are you OK?"

Tallulah lowers her gaze toward her feet. It's dank and damp behind the block; the tarmac path is green with mildew and moss.

"I'm fine," she says. "I'm working on it. I know what I'm doing."

Scarlett peers down at her in disbelief. "Oh God," she says. "You chickened out, didn't you? Fuck, Tallulah. What happened?"

"I just . . . I don't know. I mean, I told him I wanted to split up. I told him I didn't want to live with him anymore, didn't want to move in with him, didn't want to be with him, and I thought he was going to shout, scream, you know, but he didn't. He . . ." She shudders at the memory. "He just picked the baby up and held him, like this, right next to his face, and said he wasn't going fucking anywhere. And it felt like—it felt like a threat. You know? Like he'd hurt Noah if I made him leave. And so I just left it, you know, I didn't want to push him. And then last night . . ." She draws in her breath. "I was meant to be going to the pub, and he started crying, saying how scared he'd been that Noah wasn't his and how much he loves him, and so I didn't go to the pub, I stayed in and we just talked, all night. You know? We had some wine and we just talked, like we haven't talked for so long. And I told him how I feel and how I don't want to be in a couple with him anymore, but that I do want to raise Noah with him, and he seemed to take it really well."

"So, he's moving out?"

Tallulah shifts awkwardly from one foot to the other. "No. Well, not yet, anyway. He says he's going to buy a flat, even if we don't live there, so he's got somewhere to have Noah on his own, you know. Because he really doesn't want to move back in with his mum, and to be fair, I don't blame him because his mum's not very nice and his dad's a total creep, so I said he can stay, just until he's got a place of his own."

"Stay—in your bed?"

"Well, yeah. But it's fine. We'll just put a cushion down the middle. You know, it's no big deal. I mean, we've been together since we were fourteen. Since we were, like, kids. And it won't be for long. He's already saved up so much money. It shouldn't be more than a few weeks."

"And what about your Wednesday afternoons? Will you still be, you know . . . ?"

"No," says Tallulah defiantly. "No. That's not going to happen anymore. Purely platonic. Purely co-parents. Just for a few more weeks. And then he'll go."

"And then?"

Tallulah looks at her questioningly.

"Then what? When he's gone? Will you and me, you know? Can we . . . ?"

Tallulah sighs. "I can't just jump into something. And you're still straight, or bi, or whatever it is that you are. Still mucking about with boys. I've got a baby to think about and if I was going to get into something with you, it would have to be serious. And I don't think you're capable of that. I really don't."

She sees Scarlett flinch at the words, but then rally. "You're right," she says. "You are. I'm a fucking moron. I've always been a moron. But I can change." She says this in a hammy, put-on voice, which makes Tallulah smile, but then she grows serious and puts her hand against Tallulah's arm. "I'm a knob, Lules, but I can try. Seriously. I mean, I'm nearly twenty. I'm not a kid anymore. I'm not a child. Will you give me another chance? Please?"

Tallulah pulls away from her touch at the sound of voices nearing the top of the path. When the voices pass she turns back to Scarlett. "I don't know," she says. "I can't think straight. I just need to deal with Zach for now. I need to get him out of my house and get my life back. Then I can get my head sorted. But I can't do this right now. I really can't. I'm sorry."

Scarlett nods. "Sure," she says. "I get it. It's fair. But I'm going to wait for you. I swear. I'm going to be like a nun for you. I'm going to be like ten nuns for you. Seriously, Lules, just don't let him manipulate you. OK? Don't let him trick you into staying with him. Because I reckon he totally will."

"He won't, I swear. I can tell. He means it."

Scarlett narrows her eyes at Tallulah and gazes at her skeptically.

"I swear."

Scarlett nods, just once, brushes Tallulah's cheek with the fingertips of her right hand, then turns and leaves her standing there, her touch on Tallulah's skin leaving behind a flush of nameless dread.

42

"Hi, Dom. It's me," says Kim. "I wondered if you'd had a chance to look at the link I sent you, to that girl on YouTube?"

"No," he says. "Not yet. I'm really sorry. I'll look at it now and get back to you. But we've had some good movement. We've finally tracked down Martin Jacques, Scarlett's father. Or at least, we've got hold of his PA, who keeps telling us that he'll get back to us but he's a bit tied up in Abu Dhabi. We're still trying to trace the rest of the family. They were in Guernsey but apparently nobody's seen them for a couple of weeks. But please believe me, Kim, we're doing everything we can. Things are happening. Painfully slowly, in some cases, I'll grant you that. But it just takes so long to get anything done these days, with all the government cuts, and when it's a cold case, it takes even longer . . ."

When the bones are already icy cold, Kim thinks. When the blood is dried hard. When it's too late to save anyone.

"I'm pushing against it all as hard as I can for you, Kim. It's all I'm doing. It's all I'm thinking about. I swear."

She hears a crack of emotion in his voice and feels it reverberate into her own psyche. She swallows it down and says, "Yes. Of course, Dom. I know you are. I know you are. I'm just so . . ."

"Yes," says Dom. "Yes. I know."

There's a heat contained within their exchange, created from the energy of desperation and loss and frustration and misguided hope, but also from the intimacy that's built up between the two of them as everything else has peeled away from them and the thing that unites them.

She sighs. "Thank you, Dom. Thank you for everything you're doing."

"It's my pleasure, Kim. Always."

He ends the call and Kim stands for a moment, staring through the kitchen window at the trees at the end of her garden. She thinks of the skinny, sad girl talking to a camera in a room somewhere, a girl who knows something about the things that are currently taking place at Maypole House. And then, clear as though it were actually happening, she remembers that hot June afternoon, walking up to Dark Place, the trickle of sweat down her back, Ryan rocking Noah in his pushchair, the drops of pool water on Scarlett's shoulder coalescing and collapsing, the handsome son with the beers in his hand, the brittle mother in the white sundress, the way Scarlett had been unable to make eye contact, but then the way she'd said her daughter's name. *Lula.* In every other respect she'd been so cold and distant, but when she said Tallulah's name, her voice had sounded thick and heavy, as though the name meant something to her. She thinks about the night that Tallulah said she'd spent at Chloe's because Chloe was feeling suicidal and wonders again where she'd been. She thinks of all those Sunday mornings when Zach was playing football and Tallulah took her bike and went for a ride in the countryside. She thinks of how she would return with a glow and a flush, looking engorged with secrets. She even remembers asking Tallulah once, "Where do you actually go when you go for your bike rides? You always look like you've just been somewhere magical when you get back."

And Tallulah had smiled and said, "Just around the back lanes, you know. Where there's no traffic. It's gorgeous."

"And do you stop?" she'd asked. "Stop and explore?"

"Yes," she'd replied, busying herself with removing Noah's bib. "I stop and explore."

And there'd been a richness in her tone, the same richness that she'd heard in Scarlett's voice when she said Tallulah's name. And as she thinks this, another memory jumps to the forefront of her mind, of Scarlett, in her towel, the pool water falling in rivulets from her wet hair and her fingers clasping her narrow feet, and then, just for the briefest of moments, a snatched view of a small tattoo just below her ankle, the letters *TM*, and Kim noticing it on some subliminal level but also not noticing it because, really, why would this girl she'd never heard of before have her daughter's initials tattooed onto her foot, and the hand had slipped down once again to cover the marks and Kim had both seen it and not seen it, but it was there all along, like a sunspot.

She grabs her phone and finds Sophie's number in her WhatsApp. She types her a message incredibly quickly.

It's me, Kim. Are you busy? Can I talk to you about something?

Immediately comes a reply.

Not busy at all. I can talk now.

43

For a few days after the night that Tallulah and Zach drink wine and talk, everything is fine between them. Zach is chilled and relaxed. He cooks dinner for them, he bathes Noah and keeps him entertained, he sits quietly at his spreadsheets playing around with his finances without constantly asking Tallulah to get involved. He gives Tallulah space to study and just to be. At night they sleep in her bed with the baby between them and he makes no attempt to be physically affectionate with her. He quietly gets ready for work every morning and quietly returns every night and all is well.

Then, at the beginning of June, just after Noah's first birthday, Scarlett messages Tallulah to ask her to wait for her after college so that they can get the bus home together. They meet on the pavement just outside college. Scarlett is halfway through her end-of-year exams. She's been doing a still life for two whole days.

"An artichoke and a bone," she says as they stride together toward the bus stop. "Seriously. I have spent two days staring at an artichoke and a bone."

"What do they symbolize?"

"Like, nothing. Just stuff I picked up as I left the house. The bone is Toby's. He's not impressed. But they look quite cool. I put them on black velvet and they look kind of, you know, Dutch master-y."

"When's your last exam?"

"Wednesday next week. Then I have to hand in my portfolio on

Thursday and then it'll be Friday and I am going to the pub to get absolutely shit-faced."

"Who are you going with?"

"The usuals. And maybe Liam." She looks at Tallulah sideways, to gauge her response.

But Tallulah just shrugs and says, "Whatever. It's not my business."

"No, but seriously. Just as friends. Because we are just good friends. Honestly. What happened that night, it was just stupid. Just a stupid, stupid thing, because I'm a stupid, stupid person."

"Scar, it's fine. You don't need to explain."

"Yeah, but I do. I do need to explain. I need to explain it to myself, if anything. I've always just been such a 'do it first, think about it later' kind of person. I never think through the consequences of anything I do. Look." She draws in her breath and turns hard to face her. "I know you think I've had this charmed life and that nothing bad has ever happened to me. But something bad has happened to me. Something really bad. Not long after you and me first met. It's why I dropped out of college. It's why I couldn't face anyone for so long."

Tallulah glances at her, quizzically, and waits for her to continue.

Scarlett sighs and says, "Come to the pub with me? When we get off the bus? I'll tell you everything."

They slide into a quiet corner of the Swan & Ducks with a Diet Coke for Tallulah and a hot chocolate with a shot of rum on the side for Scarlett. The pub is virtually empty at this time of the day, the summer sun bright through the windows. A man sits at the bar with a beagle spread out at his feet and Scarlett points at the dog and says, as she does about every dog she ever sees, "That's a good dog."

"OK, then," says Tallulah, "I'm ready to hear your dark confession."

Scarlett wriggles slightly. "I can't believe I'm going to tell you this. You're going to hate me more than you already do."

"I don't hate you."

"Whatever. Just promise me you will never, ever tell another soul what I'm about to tell you. Not ever."

"I swear."

"Seriously. Never."

"Never."

Scarlett blinks slowly and composes herself. "Early last summer," she begins, "at the beginning of the holidays, I was kind of alone a lot. Liam had gone back to his farm. Mum was back and forth from London. Everyone was away and I was really bored and really lonely. I mean, really, really lonely. And one day I went into school"—she points at the Maypole across the common—"just to go and say hi to Lexie Mulligan. Because I was so desperate for someone to talk to. I took the dog and we went through the woods. It was a really stunning day. I was wearing, like, a slip dress and boots and I was sweating hot, even in the shade of the trees. And then I realized there was a man coming the other way and I felt a bit scared, a bit like I wished I had a fucking Rottweiler instead of Lord Drool-a-lot, and that I was wearing more clothes. But then he got a bit closer and I realized I recognized him. He was familiar. And then I saw his dog and I knew that it was Mr. Croft."

"Mr. Croft?"

"Married to Jacinta Croft. The head teacher. You know, tiny weeny woman, looks like a Polly Pocket on HRT?"

Tallulah shakes her head. She's never paid any attention to anything that happens at Maypole House.

"You'd recognize her if you saw her. Anyway, she's married to Guy. He's kind of tall and bald and quiet. He's a web designer. Works from home. Looks after their kid. Keeps himself to himself. And I swear, I'd never even noticed him properly before that day. I only recognized him by his dog. A black Lab. Nelson. Literally, just the loveliest dog ever."

Tallulah glances at the time on her phone from the corner of her eye. It's nearly four. She'd normally be home about four fifteen. She can feel her window of freedom shrinking as Scarlett tells her about a dog called Nelson.

"Anyway, so of course Toby dragged me over to say hello to Nelson, and while Toby and Nelson were chatting, me and Mr. Croft started chatting too and he told me he was home alone, that Jacinta was at their London house with their son for a few weeks, he was going to join them later in the summer, that he had a project to finish, yada yada yada. And as he was talking I could see his eyes kept going to my boobs and I don't know why, because it should have been as creepy as fuck, but for some reason, it just really turned me on."

Tallulah bangs her glass of Coke down on the table and coughs as the liquid hits the back of her throat. "Oh my God," she gasps. "Please stop. I don't want to hear any more."

"I know, I'm sorry. It's gross. But bear with me. It gets worse."

"Oh Christ, Scarlett. I'm not sure I can."

"So yes, we were chatting about really boring shit and I was thinking, I want to fuck you, and I was probably ovulating or something, I dunno, but I looked at him and I thought: Now, do it to me now. And . . ."

Tallulah puts a hand between them and closes her eyes. "Honestly. I can't."

"Please," says Scarlett. "I have to purge. This is important."

Tallulah sighs. "Go on, then."

"I could tell he could feel it too. And seriously, he's, like, in his forties. And bald. And not even that good-looking. And I told him I was walking up to the school and he said he'd walk with me and we were chatting and the sexual tension was building and then we came out of the back of the woods and we were facing the back door of his cottage in the grounds and he said, 'Come in for a glass of water.' And that was that."

Tallulah throws her an appalled look. She has no idea how to respond.

Scarlett continues: "We spent the whole of that month fucking. Literally, that was all I did for a month. Walk the dog through the woods, knock on the back door of Mrs. Croft's house, he'd let me in, we'd fuck. I'd leave. And it was amazing. Kind of seedy, but amazing. It's like, you know, sex is such a weird stupid thing when you think about it, about the mechanics of it. About what a man does and what a woman does and what it's for. If you think about it for too long you'd never want to do it again because it's gross. But that was the thing. Neither of us was thinking. We were just bored and lonely and horny. I can't explain it any other way. When I look back on it, I don't even get it. I don't know what I was thinking. It was like this warped, twisted holiday romance. And anyway, after a few weeks he went up to London and I went off sailing with Rex and my mum and then it was September and Liam came back to college and I started at Manton and me and Guy both agreed to quit it and get on with our lives. And for a while it was fine. I didn't see him around and he didn't get in contact. But then, kind of around the time I first met you, that day on the bus, he was in the co-op and I was in the co-op and our eyes met and we made some kind of inane small talk and I scuttled off feeling really confused. Next thing he's sent me a fucking dick pic."

Tallulah gasps again and covers her mouth with her hands. "No," she whispers through her fingers.

"Yes. And I just immediately deleted it and typed back NO. In caps lock. And then it went quiet again for a while and then one night, I guess he must have been drunk, he started bombarding me with text messages and dick pics and declarations of love and hate and everything in between. He said Mrs. Croft was never at home and his son had gone to boarding school and he missed me and he couldn't live without me. And I just deleted everything and stopped replying and then the night of the Manton Christmas party, I just really, really couldn't think straight anymore. You'd just blown my mind and my inbox was full of all this crazy shit from Mr. Croft and I just didn't want to go anywhere near Maypole House or the village, I just wanted to stay away from everyone and everything, so I finished with Liam a couple of days later and then it was Christmas and I just hunkered down with my family, kept my head down. I was going to come back to college in January. Fresh start. Clear head.

"But then one day, in that weird bit between Christmas and New Year, I took Toby out in the woods and I had my AirPods in, it was kind of early afternoon, starting to get dark, darker still in the woods, and I was close to my house so I thought I was safe and then suddenly . . ." She pauses and her gaze drops to the table. "Someone came up behind me and put their hand over my mouth, like this, and pulled me back and I nearly died of a fucking heart attack. And it was him, of course, it was Mr. Croft, Guy. And he was smiling at me, like it was all a cute joke; he pointed at my AirPods, to take them out, tried to make out it was normal to put your hand over a teenage girl's mouth in the woods in the dark. So I took them out and said, 'What the fuck?' And he said, 'I'm leaving her.' I said, 'What?' He said, 'I'm leaving Jacinta. There's nothing left between us. It's over. I've got a flat. Come with me.' And I kind of laughed and said, 'I'm eighteen years old. I'm a student. I live with my mum. I can't go anywhere with anyone.' I might have sounded a bit flippant, I don't know. But seriously, it was just nuts. And then he started crying and Toby started whining because he always whines when people cry and that sort of made me laugh because, fuck's sake, a grown man crying and a Saint Bernard dog whining is funny. And then he threw me this look, this look that said 'Shut up,' and he started kissing me, and it was kind of rough and desperate. And I just went into this sort of trance. I can't explain it. I went into a trance and just did the movements. Just did the movements, like a preprogrammed doll. I just thought: Let it happen. Just let it happen. I think, in a way, that I was just stopping it from being rape because I couldn't fucking deal with it being rape. So I just turned it into sex in my head. And afterward—" She stops and pulls in her breath. Tallulah can hear tears catching at the back of her throat. "Afterward, he just sort of stared at me, breathlessly. He said, 'I'm going now.' And I just nodded and he went and I could tell he was really freaked-out because we'd just done this weird thing that was so gray, you know, so ambiguous, impossible to know where the consent was in it or even if there had been any consent. And he knew and I knew it but neither of us acknowledged it. And then he just went. And I never saw him again."

Tallulah doesn't know what to say. "God, that's horrible. Are you OK?"

Scarlett stirs her hot chocolate and shrugs. "I don't know. I felt, like, raw . . . exposed after. I didn't know who I was or what I was. I kept thinking I'd wake up the next morning and I'd feel normal but I never did. I couldn't tell my mum; I couldn't tell anyone. I finally snapped one day, thought I was having a nervous breakdown, called Liam, begged him to come over. I was going to tell him everything. But then he got there and all I wanted to do was just climb into his arms and hold on to him and let him rock me. But every time I closed my eyes I felt Guy's hand over my mouth; I felt him on me. Every time I looked at Toby I'd think, you were there. You were a witness. What did you see? What did you think? Did he rape me? Am I a victim? Or am I a whore . . . ?"

Scarlett rubs tears from her face with the backs of her hands. She sighs and drops the teaspoon, picks up her hot chocolate, and drinks it.

Tallulah puts her hand against her arm and says, "That sounds like a nightmare."

Scarlett nods forcefully. "Yes," she says. "Yes. That's exactly it. Exactly. The setting, the dusk. The unexpectedness of it. The way he disappeared afterward. No one ever talked about him; I never heard his name mentioned. Like maybe he'd never really existed; maybe he was just a figment of my imagination. It had that quality of a really unsettling dream, one of those ones that haunts you for days afterward, and I was lost, just totally lost, until that moment a few weeks later when the doorbell rang on a Sunday morning and there you were. Tallulah from the bus, come to save me."

She stops talking then, and Tallulah glances at her curiously. It feels, strangely, as though she has something else to share with her, as if she hasn't quite finished off-loading.

"And that was that?"

Scarlett nods forcefully. "Yes," she says. "And that was that."

It's nearly half past four when Tallulah leaves the pub. She feels warped and out of sorts. She glances at her phone briefly to check that nobody's been trying to get hold of her and then she puts it in her jeans pocket and starts across the common. As she does so she glances across at Maypole House. Somewhere in there, she ponders, is Jacinta Croft, the woman whose husband Scarlett had a tawdry affair with last summer. Somewhere in there is Liam Bailey, the man Scarlett cheated on with the head teacher's husband. And here she is, Tallulah Murray, a local teenage mum having her first gay love affair, and over there—she glances at her own home—is a boy called Zach Allister, who is the father of her child, and somewhere else is her own father, who loves his mother more than he loves his wife and children, and over there—she glances at the road out of the village— are Megs and Simon Allister, parents to five children, none of whom they know how to love properly. And over *there*, beyond the village, are the woods: the shadowy half-world where Scarlett may or may not have been raped by a man old enough to be her father. And there are no answers to anything, anywhere, no clear paths through. The only thing, she ponders as she walks, the only thing that is clear and plain and simple, is Noah.

She picks up her pace as she gets closer to home, desperate to hold him in her arms. As she nears the cul-de-sac she hears the familiar rumble of the bus pulling up at the stop outside the Maypole. The doors hiss open and she sees a familiar shape climb off the bus and turn left. It's Zach. He's late home from work; she thought he'd be back by now. That explains why she hasn't had any messages or missed calls from him. She picks up her pace and catches up with him. As he turns and looks at her, his face contorts slightly and she sees him stuff something into the pocket of his jacket, a small bag. She pretends not to have noticed and smiles as she approaches him. He seems so thrown by her having almost caught him with something that he didn't want her to see that he has not noticed she is returning home late and from the wrong direction.

"You're late back," she says.

"Yeah. I went into town after work. Needed a new phone charger."

They pause to cross the road to let a car pass by. It's Kerryanne Mulligan, the matron from the Maypole. She knows everyone and everyone knows her. She puts her hand up and waves at them from the window. They wave back. As they enter the house, Zach takes off his jacket, hangs it from a hook, and goes straight through to the living room, where she can hear him cooing at Noah. She quickly puts her hand inside the pocket of Zach's coat and pulls out the bag. It's a dark green plastic carrier bag with the words MASON & SON FINE JEWELLERY printed on it. She peers inside and sees a small black box with the same logo printed on it in gold. She's about to open the box when she feels someone appear in the hallway. She stuffs the bag back in the pocket and looks up. It's her mum.

"Are you OK, baby? You're late back."

She forces a smile. "I'm fine," she says. "Exam started late, overran a bit." She smiles again and moves away from Zach's jacket, which now feels as though it is sending out radioactive particles that could burn her flesh, and heads into the living room, where Noah is in Zach's arms and Zach is kissing his fingers and blowing raspberries into the palm of his hand, and even though she didn't open the box, she knows what's in it and she feels for a moment like she can't breathe, like someone is sitting on her chest, because she knows what it means and she knows that Zach will never ever leave her, that he is just pretending to be making plans to go. He's playing a game with her, she realizes, keeping her sweet, keeping her onside, biding his time.

Noah's face opens up into a huge gappy smile when he sees Tallulah and he puts his arms out to her. She grabs him from Zach and tries not to flinch when Zach encircles the two of them inside his arms, trying to make a family of them, trying to make them one.

44

The doorbell to Sophie's cottage rings; it's an old-fashioned doorbell, the type you don't hear very often in these days of apps and electric chimes. It's incredibly loud and it makes Sophie jump out of her skin every time she hears it.

Kim is standing at the front door.

"Sorry," says Sophie, clutching her heart as she opens the door, "that bell always make me jump. Sorry. Come in."

Kim follows Sophie into the kitchen and watches her fill the kettle at the tap. "I just spoke to Dom," she says. "He still hasn't looked at the clip of the Amelia girl. It's so frustrating. I know the police are doing everything they can, but the more time passes the slower things seem to move. I just thought, you seem to have a different view on things. I mean, you found that video of Mimi, and being a detective novelist . . ." She smiles wryly. "I don't know, there are just some bits and pieces that I've been trying to put together in my head. Flashes of stuff."

"Like what?"

"Oh, like, you know, the day after they went missing, I went to talk to Tallulah's college friend, her name's Chloe, she lives just over there on the road out of the village. Church Lane. I always thought she and Tallulah were really close friends. There was one night when Tallulah even slept over with her because she thought Chloe was feeling suicidal. So she was obviously the first person I'd think of to ask. Tallulah didn't have many friends, you know. She was so wrapped up with Noah—and with Zach too, to a certain extent. Anyway, I spoke to Chloe and she said not only were she and Tallulah not really friends anymore, she also told me that Tallulah had never spent the night at her house, and that Tallulah had gone off with Scarlett Jacques at the Christmas party the year before. Yet Scarlett was so adamant that she and Tallulah hadn't really known each other before that night. And then, just now, just before I messaged you, I remembered something. Something that didn't really hit me at the time. I'd been to see the Jacques family the day before and Scarlett had just got out of the pool and she was sitting in a towel and I noticed, just here"—Kim points at the side of her foot—"she had a tattoo and it was very clearly the initials *TM*."

Sophie looks at Kim questioningly.

"*TM*. Tallulah Murray. And now, you know, my head is spinning, replaying things, looking at everything from a different angle, because what if Tallulah and Scarlett were, you know, having an affair? And what if Zach had found out? And what if it all came out that night, at Scarlett's house. And what if—" She stops. "Anyway. Things are happening. I know things are happening. The lever they found in the flower bed. I'm certain it's got something to do with it. I know they're trying to trace the Jacques family and I know lots and lots of things are happening, but it just feels like we're getting so close now and I can't push Dom any harder and I just really need someone to bounce off. There isn't really anyone else, you know. I mean, don't get me wrong, I've got friends. I've got my son. But I haven't really got anyone else who might want to get sucked up into all of this with me. And I just wondered how you'd feel about maybe teaming up with me? I know that might sound a bit weird—"

"No," Sophie interjects forcefully. "No, it doesn't sound weird, not at all, it sounds great. To be honest, I've been wanting to help you but I didn't want you to think I was being morbid or ghoulish."

Kim smiles. "I would love for you to help me. I really would. And I thought it seems like you're quite up on social media, that kind of thing? And maybe we could see what else we can find? Maybe see if we can't get to the Jacques family before the police do?"

Sophie nods. "Yes," she says, her heart beginning to race slightly with excitement. "Yes." She goes to the front hallway and grabs her laptop, brings it to the kitchen table, and opens it wide. "Let's find these people."

Kim and Sophie sit side by side at the kitchen table, Sophie poised in front of the laptop. They look at Mimi's video again on YouTube and scroll down to see if there are any new messages in the comments section. There are three. They scan them quickly. The last one chills them. It's from someone called Cherry and it says, simply:

Take this down NOW.

45

Small gestures of physical affection start to proliferate over the next couple of days.

Zach tucks a strand of her hair behind her ear for her, runs his fingers across the back of her neck, slings an arm across the baby in bed at night that somehow encompasses Tallulah also. The gestures aren't sexual and they are so fleeting that she barely has time to register them and complain. She sees her mother's face sometimes, when she catches a glimpse of one of these encounters, the flash of a warm smile, no doubt thinking how lucky Tallulah is to have such a loving, attentive man in her life. But the gestures make Tallulah's flesh crawl. She wants to slap his hand away, hiss at him to *fuck off*. And all the while, the memory of the little black box in his jacket pocket pulses through her consciousness like an insistent, low-level alarm going off somewhere in the distance. She can feel it in the air, the buildup to it. Every time Zach clears his throat or calls her name she catches her breath, terrified that he is about to propose to her.

And then, one sunny June afternoon, he glances up at her from where's he's lying on the bed with his laptop and he says, "You know. I've been thinking. I've been too obsessed with this flat. Too obsessed with saving up. I'm thinking I might like to splash a bit of cash." He smiles at her. His tone is light and playful. "How about a night at the pub? You and me? My treat?"

"Well," she begins carefully, "I can't really at the moment. I've still got so much work to do for my exams."

He sits upright, eyes her eagerly. "When's your last exam?"

She shrugs. "Friday next week."

"Right, then," he says, "that Friday. We're going to the pub. I'll talk to your mum about sitting with Noah. And I'll book us a table."

Her heart sinks. This is it. "Oh," she says lightly. "Honestly. Don't waste your money on me. I'll be shattered that night; I'll be shit company. Why don't you go with your mates?"

He shakes his head. "No way! I'm not paying for my mates to get wankered. No, just you and me. It's a date."

Her gaze must have betrayed her thoughts as he moves across the bed toward her. "No pressure," he says, taking her hands inside his. "No big deal. Just a nice night out because we deserve it. OK?"

She doesn't have the energy to counter so she nods and forces a smile and she thinks that she will cross the bridge when she gets to it. And at least this way she won't be living on her nerves expecting the proposal any moment. At least this way she has some breathing space, some time to prepare. And then he kisses her hands before letting them go again. "I'll leave you to get on with it," he says. "I'll do Noah's dinner. Yeah?"

She nods. "Yes," she says. "Yes, please. Thank you."

He leaves the room, pulling the door closed quietly behind him, a gesture so incredibly unlike Zach, who usually engages inanimate objects forcefully and noisily, that it chills her to the bone.

The following day at college she finds Scarlett at lunchtime.

She takes her to the path at the back of the art block and says, "I think Zach is going to propose to me."

"What?"

"He bought a ring. I found it in his pocket. And now he wants to take me out on a date next week. And he's being just super nice and attentive and sweet."

"Oh fuck, Lula. What are you going to do? Please tell me you're going to say no."

"Of course I'm going to say no. Of course I am. But then what? He'll go mental. He'll threaten to take Noah away from me. He'll make my life hell. The only reason he's being so nice is so that I'll say yes. Or that if I say no, he'll be justified to go nuts."

"It doesn't matter," says Scarlett, clasping Tallulah's arm. "It does not matter what he says or what he thinks or how he reacts. You owe him nothing. That baby is yours. Your destiny is yours. He'll just need to accept that no means no and move on."

Tallulah nods. But she's not convinced. Noah is hers, but he's Zach's too. And Zach is the sort of father who a boy should grow up around: physically affectionate, loving, hard-working, loyal, reliable; a good role model. For a crazy moment she wishes Zach were more like the young deadbeat dads beloved of the tabloid press, the ones who spread their seed and move on, the ones who forget birthdays and don't turn up for access visits. She'd have no qualms about keeping Noah out of his life then. She wouldn't feel guilty about forcing them to live apart, for whittling Zach's relationship with his son down to rushed weekend visits in a lonely flat.

"But what if he can't move on?" she says. "What if he doesn't take no for an answer? What if he makes a scene? What if Noah never forgives me? What if I regret it?"

"Regret it?" Scarlett repeats incredulously. "How on earth would you regret not marrying a guy you don't love? Who wants to trap you in a box somewhere? Are you mad?"

Tallulah shakes her head. "No, but it's just . . . I don't know. Think how many women, girls, would love the chance to be a proper family. Would love a guy who's prepared to put his family before everything. And if I say no, that would be like saying no to some people's dream."

"Yes. But not your dream, FFS. Not your dream. Tallulah."

Scarlett looks hard at her. "What do you want? What's your goal in life? Once you've finished college? Once your baby's at nursery? Where do you picture yourself?"

Tallulah raises her gaze to the sky. She can feel herself starting to bubble up somehow, like treacle in a pan, just on the edge of burning. Overhead a fat white cloud passes slowly across the sun. She stares into the heart of it, where the sun burns a pale hole through it. She clenches her hands into fists and then relaxes them again. It's a question she's always been too scared to ask herself. All her life she's been passive. Her school reports always said she was a good student but that the teacher would love to see her contribute more to lessons, would love to hear her voice. At primary school she allowed herself to be subsumed into friendship groups with children she didn't really like. And then she'd met Zach at a difficult age, an age where her contemporaries were stressing about Saturday-night plans failing to materialize, about boys not replying to their messages quick enough or female friends talking shit about them behind their backs. Having a steady boyfriend had just allowed her to get on with studying, get on with life, get on with putting one foot in front of the other, mindlessly, unthinkingly, day after day after day. Until the day she'd realized she hadn't had a period for more than a month and she'd bought a test from the internet and taken it on a Tuesday morning just before school at the beginning of her second year in the sixth form and seen the two lines and immediately taken another test and thought: Well, there it is. I'm pregnant. She'd mentally calculated a due date that was well beyond the date of her last A-level exam and thought, Maybe I should just have it. Because that was the sort of girl that Tallulah was. Her mother might have blessed her with the name of a rebel and a river and a film star, but she had failed to live up to it. She had failed to do anything genuinely proactive until the moment she had leaped across Scarlett's kitchen that morning after their sleepover and kissed her. It was, she knew, the only moment in her entire life that she had made happen.

She takes her gaze from the sky and directs it back at Scarlett. "I don't know," she says, her voice an apologetic whisper.

"Do you want me?"

She nods, but she can't quite bring herself to say the word "yes."

"What else do you want?"

"Noah."

"And?"

"I don't know. I just want . . . I just want to be free."

"Yes," says Scarlett. "Yes. Exactly. That's exactly what you want. Of course it is. You're nineteen. You're beautiful. You're good. You want to be free. And having a baby shouldn't stop you being free. Being with me shouldn't stop you being free. Nothing should stop you being free. The last thing you want at this point in your life is a ring on your finger. You need to cut yourself away from him. And maybe this is the perfect opportunity. Let him propose. Say no. It's kind of un-come-back-from-able. It's a one-way exit. Seriously. Let him do it. Say no. Then your life can begin."

Tallulah has been nodding harder and harder as Scarlett talks. As she finishes Tallulah feels a surge of electric energy pass through every element of her being and she pushes herself toward Scarlett, presses her against the wall, and kisses her hard. After a minute she pulls back breathlessly. She stares at Scarlett, at the bright lights dancing behind her eyes, at the glazed wonder on her face, feels the heat of Scarlett's caught breath against her skin, feels dazzled, beyond anything, beyond words, beyond imagination, by the beauty of her and thinks, I love her. I love her. I love her.

"I wish," she says, tracing her fingers around the contours of Scarlett's face, "I wish that Zach didn't exist. I wish he would just, you know. Disappear."

46

Kim watches Sophie flying around the internet, her fingertips clicking lightly across the keyboard, chasing this person called Cherry.

"Cherry," Sophie is saying. "It's got to be Scarlett, hasn't it?"

Kim stares at her blankly.

"Red," says Sophie. "They're both red."

"Oh God," says Kim, realization dawning. "Of course. Shall we say something to Dom?"

Sophie sighs. "I don't know. The police are using their own techniques to locate Scarlett and her family. Maybe we should just stick with this for a while. Keep out of their way."

Kim nods. She feels instinctively that Sophie is right.

Sophie scrolls through the Instagram accounts of the main players again: Liam, Lexie, Mimi, Scarlett. Then she scrolls through the Instagram accounts of people who have commented on or liked anything in their Instagram accounts. She mutters the word "Cherry" repeatedly under her breath as she does so, and then suddenly she stops. "Look," she says. "Look!"

She angles the screen toward Kim and points.

"Whose account is this?" asks Kim.

"Ruby Reynolds. Roo. One of the Scarlett Jacques clique. She still lives in the area, according to the photos, look." She clicks on a photo of a dark-haired girl standing by a tree, wearing a battered leather jacket over a short dress. "That's just over there, isn't it?" Sophie gestures toward the village. "On the common?"

"Yes," says Kim, peering closer at the photo. "Yes. Just to the left of the duck pond."

"This was posted only ten days ago. And look." She jabs the screen with her finger. "Someone called Cherryjack has liked it. Cherryjack. *Scarlett Jacques.*"

The icon is a photograph of two red cherries hanging off a stalk and a tongue poking at them. The tongue is pierced. Sophie glances at Kim. "Scarlett has a pierced tongue," she says breathlessly. "I spotted it in another photo on Liam Bailey's account."

Sophie clicks on the profile picture and an account comes up. Amazingly, it's not private. "No followers," she says. "That's weird." She scroll down through the photos, faster and faster. The girl called Cherryjack appears to live on a boat. The shots are abstract: sunsets over endless ocean, the frothy tips of waves, the gleaming nub of a dolphin's beak held in the palm of the photographer's hand, tanned legs outstretched on cream leather with a dog's large paw resting on her calf.

Kim peers more closely at the photo of the legs. "Can you zoom in on that?" she asks.

Sophie enlarges the image and Kim stares at it. "There," she says. "There. On her foot, look, can you see it. That black smudge. Look."

Sophie nods. "Is that . . . ?"

"Yes, that's where the tattoo was. The *TM* tattoo. Oh my God," she says. "This is Scarlett. This is Scarlett Jacques! What dates are these photos from?"

Sophie scrolls quickly through them. The latest one is dated the previous day. The oldest one, just two weeks before.

Kim pulls back from the screen and exhales. Scarlett Jacques is on a boat. She's on a boat with her dog and her phone and her perfectly pedicured feet, posting pretty pictures to Instagram. She feels a wave of hot anger pass through her and she swallows it down.

They both turn back to the screen and Sophie clicks on all

Cherryjack's images in turn. Each has a handful of likes and Sophie clicks on the profile of every user. "Recognize any of these people?" she asks Kim.

"No," says Kim.

But then they both stop and draw in their breath hard when they scroll down to a name that is familiar to both of them.

@lexiegoes.

47

Tallulah sits at her dressing table. Zach isn't back from work yet; he's due in an hour. Noah is downstairs with her mum, who just sent her upstairs to get ready. "Go on," she said. "Take some time for a proper pamper. It's been so long since you went anywhere."

Her end-of-year exams are done. In a few weeks' time it will be the end of the summer term and there will be a long expanse of freedom ahead of her. And tonight Zach will propose to her and she will say no and that will hopefully, finally, draw a line underneath this teenage romance that has dragged on for far, far too long. She hears her mother singing songs to Noah downstairs and she smiles. She wants to have this house back to herself. She wants to have her room, her bed back to herself. Just her, her mother, her brother, her baby. And then somewhere, somehow, she wants to fit Scarlett into her life. She can't quite picture it. There are gay people in Upfield Common. The male teachers from Maypole House who share a tiny cottage just past the Swan & Ducks and walk their rescue greyhound together at the weekends. Gia, a girl Tallulah went to school with and always wanted to be friends with because she was so cool, who now walks around the village hand in hand with an older woman who runs mindfulness courses in the village hall once a week. It wouldn't be hugely controversial in the context of where Tallulah lives, but it would be hugely controversial in the context of Tallulah's own existence. She's not sure she could be open about it yet; she's not sure she could cope with the second glances and the dropped jaws and the sense that she was a news story of some description. If it happened, it would have to happen so slowly that no one would really notice.

But for now, she has a night at the pub to look forward to, a night, she now realizes, that her whole future hinges on, where her destiny will pivot from one outcome to another. She sighs and untwists the wand of her mascara. She wants to look pretty, not for Zach, but for Scarlett, who will also be in the pub tonight, who said she will keep an eye on her in case things go horribly wrong, in case Zach loses his shit, in case Tallulah needs her. She layers the mascara twice onto her eyelashes and then plays with her hair. Scarlett says she envies Tallulah's hair. Scarlett's hair is sparse and damaged by years of continual bleaching and coloring. She takes Tallulah's hair in her fist sometimes and runs her hand down it and says, "What is it like to have all of this? How can you bear being so beautiful?" And Tallulah just smiles and says, "Good genes, I guess. My mum's got lovely hair. And my dad."

"And your baby?"

"And my baby. Yes. There's lots of good hair in my family."

"You're so lucky," Scarlett will reply. "Imagine being me for just a minute and having to make do with this," and she'll tug at her damaged hair and make noises of disgust and Tallulah will say, "But it doesn't matter. It's just hair. You're still the most beautiful girl in any room you're in. And you know it."

"I'm not beautiful," she'll reply. "My mum is beautiful. But I, unfortunately, look just like my dad."

Tallulah once said, "Do you think I'll ever meet your parents?" and Scarlett had nodded and said, "Of course you will."

"Will they think I'm right for you? I mean, I guess they're used to you being with people more like you, you know? People with money."

"Look," Scarlett replied. "My parents are so wrapped up in themselves and their own pathetic lives that I could bring a fucking horse home and they wouldn't even notice. Seriously. They don't notice anything I do. Ever. What about your mum?" she countered. "Do you think I'll ever get to meet her?"

Tallulah nodded. "Yes," she said. "Yes. A hundred percent. My mum is so cool. And all she wants in the whole world is for me to be happy. So if you make me happy, she'll like you."

The conversation at the time had felt slightly fanciful. There seemed to be so much ground to conquer before they could reach the sunlit meadows of their happy ever after. But now it's here. The night where everything changes.

She combs her hair into two sections and plaits it.

She chooses a light and airy muslin top that falls flatteringly over her belly and she teams it with cutoff denim shorts.

She looks at the girl in the full-length mirror.

The girl looks back at her.

She is a strong woman. A gay woman. A mother. A future social worker. She is more than she always thought she was. So much more. It starts here, Tallulah thinks, holding in her stomach, patting at the fabric of the summer smock, imagining the new life she will have on the other side of tonight, when she is free and can do what she wants. All of it starts here.

She goes downstairs to sit with Noah and her mother while she waits for Zach to get home from work.

48

Kim and Sophie head across the school grounds toward the accommodation block. Sophie has the laptop pinned beneath her arm. Kim taps in Kerryanne Mulligan's apartment number and a female voice responds.

"Hi, Lexie. It's me, Kim. Can I come in, do you think, just for a minute?"

"Er, yeah. Sure."

The lock buzzes and they push open the gate and head toward the lift.

"Shall I do the talking?" Kim asks Sophie.

"Yes," says Sophie. "Definitely. Definitely you."

Lexie meets them at the door to her apartment. She's barefoot in patterned leggings and a hoodie. She looks from Kim to Sophie and then questioningly back at Kim. She says, "Oh. Hi," before holding the door open for them and leading them into the living area. The sofa is pulled out into a bed and her suitcase is on the floor by its side, with clothes spilling out of it. "Sorry," she says. "I haven't unpacked yet. I'm a bit of a nomad, I'm so used to living out of a suitcase, you know." She kicks some clothes away with her bare foot and says, "Let's sit at the breakfast bar."

They perch themselves on the bar stools lined up in front of the kitchenette and Lexie turns to Kim and says, "Everything OK?"

Sophie throws Kim an encouraging look that she hopes conveys the fact that she is here if Kim needs backup.

"Well, no," Kim replies, opening up her laptop. "Not really. It's all been a bit unsettling, all this business with the signs and the things being dug up. Got me raking everything up, all the stuff that's been racing around my head since Tallulah went, and then Sophie found a video online, posted by that girl who was there that night, Mimi. Remember Mimi?"

Lexie nods; then she says, "Yeah. Well, sort of. I mean, it all feels quite blurry now. But I do remember there was another girl there."

"Anyway, this girl, Mimi, in the video she made she seemed to know what was happening here at the school. Which is strange, as the only people who know what's happening here are the people who actually live here. So it looks like someone in the village has been in touch with Mimi. Or maybe even been in touch with her the whole time."

Kim pauses and Sophie sees something pass very quickly across Lexie's face, too fleeting for her to get a grip on it.

"Anyway," Kim continues. "That set me off thinking, so I came over to see Sophie and we've just been going through all the social media again, but this time from the starting point of this Mimi girl, and it led us to an Instagram account for a girl called Cherry-jack."

Kim pauses again and this time the startled look that crosses Lexie's face is more pronounced. But the expression passes quickly and she gives her head the tiniest of shakes before nodding and saying, "Right. OK."

"So, this appears to be Scarlett Jacques, on a boat. And look." Kim turns the screen slightly to face Lexie. "Here, on this post, from just last month, you've liked it, from your account."

Another pause follows and now the atmosphere is so thick with Lexie's discomfort that Sophie can almost touch it.

"That is you, isn't it? Lexiegoes? Yes?"

"Well, yes," says Lexie. "Yes, that's my account but I have no memory of ever liking that post. And I have no idea who this Cherry-jack is. I mean, how do you even know it's her?"

"Well," says Kim. "First there's the name. Cherry Jack. Scarlett Jacques. Then there's the dog—look—not many dogs have paws that huge. And the Jacqueses had that big dog, didn't they? And then there's this . . ." She zooms in on Scarlett's foot. "This tattoo. Which I saw with my own eyes the day after Tallulah disappeared."

"Honestly," Lexie cuts in. "Honestly. Kim. I don't even follow this account. Look . . ." She switches on her phone and starts scrolling and touching the screen. "Look." She turns her phone to face them. "Look, I hardly follow anyone. See? And there's no Cherryjack here. Seriously, I don't know why that photo was liked by my account."

Sophie gazes at Lexie. She seems incredibly genuine, highly believable. But then, this is the same Lexie who lets her Instagram followers believe that she lives in a huge Georgian manor house, the same Lexie who told the police that she saw the second "Dig Here" sign from her terrace when she couldn't possibly have.

"You don't have to follow an account to like someone's post," Sophie says measuredly. "You just have to know it's there."

"Does anyone else have your log-in?" asks Kim.

Lexie shrugs. "Well, my mum does. I sometimes ask her to reply to some of my comments when I'm traveling or can't get to them."

"Your mum?"

"Yes." She looks from Sophie to Kim and back again. "Well, obviously it's not my mum."

Sophie inhales sharply. "But your mum was friends with Scarlett, wasn't she?"

"I guess. But there's no way my mum would know where Scarlett is now. There's no way she'd have found her on Instagram."

"Why not?" Sophie asks simply.

"Because that's just weird. Why would she still be in touch with Scarlett?"

Sophie sighs. "I don't know," she says. "But from what I've heard about Scarlett, she was a charismatic young woman. She had a lot of admirers. There was her little clique of friends. Liam. Her ex-head, Jacinta Croft, said she had a way of managing people, manipulating them. And now it looks like maybe Tallulah and Scarlett weren't as unacquainted as Scarlett might have led everyone to believe. So it is possible that your mum's stayed in touch. Behind the scenes."

Lexie is already shaking her head, even before Sophie has finished talking. "Nope," she says. "No. You're barking up the wrong tree. Totally."

Sophie smiles at her sadly. "Lexie," she says. "You're not here very much. Your mum lives here alone nearly all the time. Who knows what she does when she's on her own? She's a very caring woman. It wouldn't surprise me in the least if she was still in touch with Scarlett Jacques."

Lexie doesn't reply this time. She says, "So, what are you going to do? Are you going to ask her?"

Sophie and Kim exchange a look. Kim nods and says, "Yes. We'll probably have a little chat with her."

"She won't know anything," Lexie says. "I promise you, she won't."

Sophie closes her laptop then and is about to pick it up and leave when her eye is caught by something poking out from the half-disgorged contents of Lexie's suitcase.

It's a copy of her book.

49

"You look gorgeous," says Zach, appearing in the kitchen a while later. "Look at you." He grins at Kim and says, "Your daughter is properly hot," and Kim laughs and looks at Tallulah indulgently and says, "Well, she's the prettiest thing I've ever seen."

Zach approaches Tallulah and kisses her gently on her cheek. Then he grabs Noah from his high chair and twirls him around the kitchen until Noah is helpless with laughter. Zach's energy is off the scale, high-octane, almost infectious. Almost, but not quite. Tallulah forces a smile as Zach passes Noah into her arms and says, "I'm off for a shower. I won't be long."

When he's gone, Tallulah's mum looks at her and says, "Well, someone's in a good mood."

"Yes," she replies. "He is a bit."

"Nice to see him so happy. He's seemed a bit, you know, pre-occupied lately. With the flat."

Tallulah nods but doesn't reply.

"So, tonight, any particular reason for it?"

"No," she replies airily. "No. I just think he was getting bogged down in saving up and wanted a break from it all."

"Well, you both deserve it," says her mum. "The two of you are incredible. So hard-working and selfless. It's about time you put yourselves first for a bit and went out and had some fun."

"Are you sure you'll be all right getting Noah down? He's been a nightmare lately."

"I'll be fine," her mum reassures her. "If the worst comes to the worst, we'll just stay up late. It's the first time I've babysat for ages; I don't care how challenging it is. I just want you to have a wonderful, relaxing, possibly exciting"—she throws Tallulah a mischievous look—"night out. I don't want you to think about Noah or me or anything that isn't fun-related. OK?"

Tallulah wonders about her mother's use of the words "possibly exciting" and the strange look she'd thrown her. Does her mother know? she wonders. Has Zach told her? Or, God, heaven forbid, maybe even asked her permission? The thought freaks her out.

But she smiles and says, "OK. I promise not to think about my mother or my child."

"Good girl." Her mother throws her another indulgent smile. "Good girl. And if you've got a hangover tomorrow, just stay in bed. I'll do the morning for you too, OK?"

Tallulah nods, then places Noah back in his high chair and holds out her arms toward her mother and says, "Hug?"

Her mother smiles and says, "Oh, yes please." And they hug there, in the kitchen, the midsummer sun shining on them from the garden, Zach singing in the shower overhead, Noah chewing thoughtfully on the corner of a book and watching them curiously, almost sagely, as if he knows that this is a night that will shape his destiny. At the very thought of it, Tallulah feels a tear roll down her cheek. She wipes it away quickly so that her mother doesn't notice.

50

It's four o'clock. Kim left Maypole House two hours ago to collect Noah from nursery and now Sophie pulls on a cardigan, grabs her phone, and heads out into the grounds. Classes are over for the day and the paths swarm with teenagers. She imagines these same paths swarming with Scarlett's cohort. She pictures tall, lean Scarlett as Liam described her back then, with her hair a natural dark brown, a minidress, opaque tights, and clumpy boots, followed by her adoring coterie.

And then she pictures Scarlett on a boat, her bleached hair burning blonder in the sun, sitting with her dog, posting abstract photos sporadically, possibly strategically, for a handful of people to see, so that they know that she is still alive. But what of Tallulah? What of Zach? And what, she wonders, of Jacinta Croft's husband?

Her thoughts spiral as she walks. A few students smile and say hello. She returns their greetings blankly; she has no idea who they are, but they know that she is Mr. Gray's girlfriend, and no doubt, by now, they know she is a published author too. She has an ephemeral, slightly elevated status here that she finds somewhat unsettling.

She sits on a bench in the cloisters and she googles "Cherryjack" on her phone. It brings up dozens of hits for a cherry-flavored rum from the Virgin Islands. It also brings up at least half a dozen social media accounts for other users calling themselves Cherryjack. She clicks the Google filter to "Images" and scrolls through them.

She finds endless photos of rum and rum-based cocktails and boys called Jack Cherry but nothing that looks anything like Scarlett Jacques.

She glances up as she feels someone approach. It's Liam. She smiles and says, "Just the man."

"Am I?" he says.

"Yes. I wondered, if you're not busy, could we have a chat?"

"Of course," he says, "sure. Here? Or . . . ?"

"I don't mind."

"I mean, you could come up to my room. I was on my way there. I have cold beers."

She nods and smiles. "Sure," she says. "That would be great."

Liam's room is nothing like Kerryanne's. It's a rectangular box with a bed on one side, a sofa on the other, sliding doors directly onto a small balcony, and a tiny kitchen tucked away inside an alcove.

"Snug," she says, running her eyes instinctively across his bookshelf as she walks past it.

"Yes," he says, pulling off his jacket and hanging it from a knob by the front door. "Small, but big enough. You know. Here." He moves some paperwork from the arm of the sofa and invites Sophie to take a seat.

The room is neat and fragrant, filled with the clutter of his life, but in a way that seems very organized.

"So," he says, going to his fridge. "How's your day been?"

"Kind of weird," she replies. "I've spent most of it with Kim Knox. You know, Tallulah's mum. We've been trying to find Scarlett Jacques online."

He takes two beers from the fridge and passes her one. She glances again around Liam's room. He has some interesting art on his walls, the most overpowering of which is a large canvas portrait. She narrows her eyes to make sense of it and sees that it is a rather jumbled painting of what appears to be a young woman sitting on a throne with a dog by her side, and then the pieces fall into place and she points at the painting and says, "Is that . . . ?"

"Yes. It's Scarlett. A self-portrait. She gave it to me."

"Is it OK if I have a look?"

"Of course," he says. "Be my guest."

She rests her beer on the coffee table and walks toward the painting. As she gets closer, more and more detail reveals itself. Both Scarlett and the dog are wearing crowns. Scarlett looks slightly imperious, her hands spread out upon her open knees, each finger sporting a huge golden ring, picked out in shiny metallic paint. There are various things on tables in the background, including a throbbing heart on a platter and a cake slice dripping with blood.

"Bloody hell," she says. "This is, erm . . . odd?"

"Yeah. It is." He shrugs.

"What does it all mean? The heart, for example. What do you think that represents?"

"She never really explained any of it to me, to be honest. She just turned up with it one day and asked if I wanted it and I said yeah, because I knew it would look really cool in here, and also because, you know, it was nice just to have a bit of her . . ." He trails off slightly.

"You know," she begins carefully, "I saw Jacinta Croft the other day and we were chatting about Scarlett and she told me how heart-broken you were after you split up."

He nods, just once, and then takes a swig of beer. "I guess I was," he says. "In a way. I mean, a girl like Scarlett doesn't come along very often, especially not for a guy like me. She made things feel kind of exciting. She made me feel like maybe I was special. Special because she chose me. You know. But . . ." He sighs and rallies: ". . . it is what it is. I'm over it now."

"Anyone else on the scene?" she asks.

"No," he says. "No. Not really. I mean, I'm on dating sites, so it's not as if I'm not actively looking, but I'm also not that bothered either. You know?"

"So, you and Lexie . . . ?"

He looks up at her smartly. He seems confused. "Lexie Mulligan? God. No. I mean, we're friends and everything. But no. Not in that way. You know, I'm pretty sure she's not even straight. She had a big crush on Scarlett for a while. But anyway. No. Not Lexie. Not anyone. Just me."

"You know the other night? When the police were here after they found the second 'Dig Here' sign?"

He nods.

"Had Lexie been up here that night?"

"Here? You mean, in my room?"

"Yes. In your room."

"No. Definitely not. I actually don't think Lexie's ever been in my room."

"Can I go out on your balcony?"

"Sure," he says. "It's not locked."

She slides the door open and goes to the edge of the balcony. She peers over and out toward the flower bed and she steps onto her tiptoes and leans out even farther and she realizes that even at this angle and at this height, she cannot see the spot where the "Dig Here" sign had been posted. She turns around and looks overhead, but there are no balconies above. Lexie had definitely been lying about seeing the "Dig Here" sign from her apartment. Or from anywhere, for that matter. She knew about it not because she'd seen it but because either she or her mother had put it there.

Sophie walks back toward the sofa, but as she does so, her eye is caught by another painting on Liam's wall; it's a smaller canvas than Scarlett's self-portrait, but painted using the same strokes and the same jolting, in-your-face color palette. It's a stone spiral staircase, with the steps painted in garish rainbow shades all blending and bleeding into one another almost like melted wax. A pole of bright golden light beams down from a circular window at the top of the tower that the steps are housed in and pierces the stone floor at the bottom, creating a plume of purply-gray smoke and sparks of glitter. Just to the side of the hole is another knife, again smeared with what looks like blood.

"What the hell is this one?"

Liam shrugs. "It's another one of Scarlett's. She painted it during her breakdown. She said she needed me to take care of it for her. For posterity."

"But what's it of?"

"I don't really know. I mean, I know what it looks like—there's a staircase in her house, in the really old part of the building. It goes up to a kind of turret with a tiny room at the top with little slit eyes for arrows. They never used the little room. It was too small to put any furniture in."

Sophie stares at the painting, hard, trying to divine some more meaning from it. "Did she ever say anything about the room?"

She stands closer and peers at the detail. There's a kind of rectangle of light around the bottom step. It bleeds through a small gap. The blood from the knife trickles toward this gap and then disappears. As she stares at the knife, she notices that it's not actually a knife at all, that it has a bent end with a U-shape cut into it. It's not a knife, it's a lever. She feels her heart stop beating for a split second, and then start again, twice as fast.

"Would you mind," she says, "if I take a picture of this?"

"Sure," he says casually. "Do you think it's a clue of some kind?"

She nods. "Yes," she says, her cool tone belying the electric instincts setting all her nerves on edge. "I think it might be."

51

The bright sun strobes through the willow hanks as Zach and Tallulah cross the common toward the pub. Zach takes her hand as they walk and keeps up a running commentary. He tells her about a guy at work who just got a rescue dog that can't bark and another guy at work whose kid was arrested last week for vandalism and he tells her about the possibility of a caravan in the New Forest that he might be able to borrow for a week off a friend of one of his sisters—they could go there for their summer holiday, maybe, and Tallulah nods and smiles and makes all the right noises because she has nothing to lose now by being nice to him. By the end of this evening they will never hold hands again, he will never chat to her like this again; by the end of tonight there will be a solid wall between them that will be, she knows, because it is how Zach works, absolutely unbreachable. So for now, while the sun shines and there is wine to be drunk and no more exams and a night out, why not be nice, why not pretend that everything is fine?

The garden at the front of the pub is packed. The Swan & Ducks is a destination pub, not just a local. People come from all the surrounding villages and hamlets, especially on a sunny Friday night in June.

It's quieter inside the pub. The barman points out their table to them and Tallulah catches her breath. There's a bottle of champagne chilling on the table in a chrome bucket, and two champagne flutes.

"Ta-da," says Zach, leading her to the table.

She goes to pull out her chair but Zach intervenes and says, "No, allow me," before pulling the chair out for her and then tucking her in on it.

Tallulah smiles and says, "Wow, thank you. This is amazing."

"The least you deserve," Zach replies, pulling out his own chair and seating himself.

Tallulah glances up at him. His face is soft, wreathed in smiles. He looks like the sweet lost boy who started secondary school half-way through and she feels her resolve start to diminish.

"We both deserve it," she says. "It's been quite a year."

His smile falters then and he says, "Yes. It really has been." He turns to grapple with the champagne bottle. "Right," he says, "please don't let me fuck this up." He eases the cork from the bottle and Tallulah brings her flute close to the bottle neck, just in case, but the cork leaves smoothly with a gentle pop and Zach pours her a glass and then himself and then he says, raising his glass to hers, "To us. Zach and Tallulah. And to Noah, the best little man in the world. Cheers."

Tallulah touches her glass against Zach's and is grateful when he doesn't hold her gaze or expect her to reciprocate his sentiments in any way and instead turns his attention to the paper menu in front of him. "Right," he says. "Literally order anything. Price is no object. Whatever you want."

She glances at the menu and sees a whole sea bass served with broccolini and pilau rice for thirty-five pounds. She gulps and says, "Well, I won't be having the sea bass."

"Have the sea bass," says Zach. "Seriously, have whatever you want."

"I don't even like sea bass."

He rolls his eyes at her affectionately and she sees his hand go to the pocket of his trousers as he's done a few times since they left the house and she knows that that's where the ring is and her mouth feels dry and she thinks: Why is she doing this? Why has she let it get this far? She is going to humiliate him and crush him and all of this, this golden midsummer night of champagne toasts and chivalry, will curdle into something unbearable and cruel. But no, she reminds herself, no, tonight is not real. Tonight is a mirage. She reminds herself of the night she slept over at Scarlett's, the barrage of increasingly abusive messages and videos, the way he pressed his face so close to Noah's, using him to get to her, to scare her, to bend her to his will. She thinks of the feel of his finger under her chin, poking hard and deep into the softness there, forcing her to look him in the eye. She thinks of how he wants her to give up her college course, give up her friends, stay at home, save money, be a good mother. She thinks of how he has manipulated his way into still living in her home, still sharing her bed, and she thinks of how she let him and she thinks no, no, this can't be a kind split, this can't be ambiguous, this can't leave any room for anything but animosity and pain. Because Zach is a controller and she has to show him that she cannot and will not be controlled and that all the champagne and big, soft eyes and compliments and expensive fish in the world is not going to change that.

She pulls in her breath to calm herself, and looks down at the menu.

As she does so, she hears a commotion at the door, the sounds of hooting laughter and loud chatter. She glances up and sees first Mimi, then Roo, then Jayden, then Rocky, with Scarlett and Liam bringing up the rear. Zach looks up and she sees displeasure register on his face. He hates the posh kids from the school across the common. He groans. "That's the end of the peace and quiet."

They head toward the bar, and Tallulah can feel Scarlett's eyes burning upon her, but she keeps her gaze fixed on the menu. The words swim before her, meaninglessly. Cannellini. Jus. Anchovy. Rigatoni. Chorizo. She doesn't know what any of it means. She just knows that Scarlett is at the bar and Scarlett is looking at her. She feels her phone vibrate and glances at the message.

Has it happened yet?

No, she replies.

I'm here if you need me.

K.

"Who's that?"

"Just Mum," she replies. "Wants to know which pajamas to put Noah in."

Zach smiles. Then he says, "Fancy sharing a seafood platter with me?"

"Oh," she says distractedly. "Maybe. What's it got on it?"

"King prawns. Smoked salmon. Clams. Potted shrimps. And caviar."

She glances at the price. "Are you sure?"

"Yes," he says. "I told you. We're fine dining tonight."

"OK, then." She nods. "I mean, it's up to you. I don't really like caviar . . ."

Zach laughs and says, "Don't worry. I'll eat your caviar."

She smiles and takes a large sip from her champagne glass. Scarlett and her mates are still at the bar putting in a long and very complicated order and asking for cash back and being generally loud and irritating. She glances up and catches Scarlett's eye very briefly. She can feel her face flush pink and she quickly looks away and says, "Shall we order some fries?"

"Hell yes," says Zach. "Triple-cooked chips. French fries. Or truffle chips. Shall we just have one of each?"

"Yes," she says, not really knowing what she's saying yes to. She has no idea what a truffle chip is.

"Excellent." He smiles and folds his arms.

Tallulah can hear Scarlett from here. "Have you got any rum from Barbados?" she asks. "It's called Mount Gay?"

"'Fraid not. We've got Bacardi. Kraken . . ."

"Kraken will do. But you should totally get some Mount Gay. It's, like, the best."

She sounds so posh, Tallulah thinks. So entitled. It's almost impossible to imagine her as she is when the two of them are alone together.

"Christ," says Zach. "Listen to them. Who do they think they are?" He impersonates Scarlett under his breath, *It's, like, the best.*"

Tallulah nods and says, "Yeah. I know. They're really annoying." Then she draws in her breath and says, "They go to my college. They're all studying art. I think some of them used to go to Maypole House."

"That figures," he says. Then he gets to his feet and says, "I'm going to order. Want anything else to drink?"

She taps her fingernails against her champagne flute and says, "I'm good with this, thank you."

He throws her an indulgent smile and then she holds her breath as he approaches the bar. He is standing inches from Scarlett, who has her back to him as she touches her debit card to the screen of a card reader. She waits for the receipt to roll out and then takes it from the barman. "Thank you," she says. Then she picks up her drink and turns, and now she is face-to-face with Zach, and Tallulah can barely breathe.

"Sorry," she hears him say, bobbing to his right to let her pass.

Tallulah sees her smile tightly at him and hears her say, "No worries."

As she passes Tallulah's table on her way back outside, Scarlett stares meaningfully at her. She touches her breastbone with a fist and blinks. Tallulah nods and then looks away. Adrenaline is pulsing through every part of her. She swallows down some champagne to distract herself from the horrible sensation of her heart pounding beneath her rib cage. Her phone buzzes. It's Scarlett.

You OK?

No, she replies. *I feel sick.*

You can do this. I'm here.

Tallulah types in a love heart and sends it, then places her phone under the menu so that she can't look at it.

Zach returns and takes his seat. "That's the girl, isn't it? From your selfie?"

She arranges her face into an expression of confusion, but she can tell it's unconvincing. "Which girl?"

"The one with scraggy hair. Who was going on about rum. The one I saw you at the bus stop with that time."

"Oh," she replies lightly. "Yes. That's Scarlett."

"How come she didn't come and say hello?"

She shrugs. "Maybe she didn't see me."

He takes the champagne bottle from the bucket and tops them both up. Tallulah can tell that the atmosphere has already soured slightly, that a cloud has drifted across Zach's burning sun of optimism.

"Yeah," he says. "Maybe."

They chat for a while about Noah, about Zach's sister who's just fallen pregnant with her first child and thinks she might be having twins, but it feels to Tallulah that she is doing all the work, that Zach is elsewhere, and she knows where he is. He's inside his head chewing over his brief exchange with Scarlett. Zach is very perceptive and he will have picked up on her energy, and now he will be picking up on Tallulah's energy and he will know that something is not quite right but he will have no idea what it is.

Their food arrives and it is quite a spectacle: a white platter laid upon a brass stand and strewn with shiny necklaces of samphire and ruby-red pomegranate seeds.

They both say wow and grab cutlery out of a pot on the table, and then begin to dismantle the platter, but Tallulah has no appetite and takes an inordinate amount of time to unpeel a prawn.

"Are you OK?" asks Zach.

"Yes," she says. "I'm fine."

"You're not really eating much."

"It's just a bit fiddly."

"Eat some chips." He tips a pot of massive, oily-looking chips toward her and she takes a few.

"More," he says. And that edge is back in his voice. It is not a suggestion, but a demand. She takes a couple more and he places the chips back on the table.

Her phone vibrates and she angles it toward her to look at it. It's Scarlett again. She sees the first few words of the message but doesn't open it: *Do you need me? I can . . .*

Zach throws her a questioning look.

"Mum again."

"Oh yes," he says. "What does she want?"

"Just asking if we were having a nice time?"

"And?" he says. "Are we?"

The question is loaded and she waits a beat to reply. "Yes," she says. "We're having a lovely time." And she puts out her champagne glass to his and says, "Cheers."

She can feel the night crumbling. She can tell that small talk has become impossible and that they will either sit here in silence or they will talk about *them* and either outcome will ruin the evening. So she hands him a prawn and says, "Go on. Peel it for me, will you? I'm too lazy," and she hits him with the best smile she can muster. He rolls his eyes affectionately and takes it from her and for a moment it feels as if the cordial atmosphere might have been restored. But then her phone buzzes again and he tuts and says, "Fuck's sake."

"Probably my mum, because I didn't reply to her last one."

"Well, go on, then," he says crossly, wrenching the head off the prawn.

She switches on her screen and clicks on Scarlett's message. Then she types in quickly: *He's in a bad mood. I don't think it's going to happen.*

Scarlett replies: *Plan B?*

Tallulah takes a deep breath and types back: *Yes. Plan B.*

PART FOUR

52

Scarlett strides into the bar, trying and failing to look natural and nonchalant. She stares hard at Tallulah, and Zach glances at her, then does a double take before looking at Tallulah, and she sees something fall into place.

He turns to her and says, "What's going on?"

"What?"

"You and that girl?"

"I don't know," she says. "Nothing."

Scarlett is heading toward them. She pulls across a chair from another table, sits down, sticks a chip into a dish of mayonnaise, and eats it. "Hi, Lula," she says. "How are you?"

Tallulah nods and says, "I'm fine. I'm sorry I didn't say hello earlier. You were with all your friends and I didn't want to interrupt."

"Oh, it's *fine*," Scarlett replies breezily, picking up another chip and sticking it back in the mayonnaise. "I understand. Anyway . . ." She waves her hand across the display of seafood and the champagne bucket. "Special occasion?"

"No," says Tallulah, "not really. We just haven't been out for a while."

"Ah, that's nice." She picks up a third chip and puts it to her nose. "Is this one truffled?" she asks. Zach nods stiffly and Scarlett says, "Nice," before eating it. "I didn't quite catch your name?" she says to Zach.

"It's Zach." His face is brittle with rage.

Scarlett is acting cool, but Tallulah can see the manic energy pumping through her.

"You know Tallulah from college?" Zach says.

"That is correct. Lovely, lovely Tallulah."

"She never talks about you."

"How rude!" Scarlett mocks affront and grabs another truffle chip.

"She's got a photo of you on her phone, though."

"Uh-oh," says Scarlett, widening her eyes. "Stalker alert."

"It's just that selfie, from the Christmas party. That's all."

"What selfie?"

"You don't remember taking it?" asks Zach.

"I can't say that I do, but then, I was off my face at the time. Anyway," she says, "I don't want to disturb you two while you're having such a gorgeous romantic evening. Lovely to see you, Lula. Lovely to meet you, Zach."

"No," says Tallulah. "Stay."

"Oh." She beams at Tallulah. "OK, then."

Zach looks as though he is about to say something, but then Mimi walks in, scanning the pub for Scarlett. "Oh," she says. "There you are. We were wondering where you'd got to."

"Sorry," says Scarlett, "I got sidetracked into eating all of Tallulah and her boyfriend's delicious chips. Why don't you join us?"

Within a few more minutes, Scarlett's whole crew is squashed around the table and all the chips are gone and all the prawns are gone and someone has gone to the bar and come back with a round of tequila shots, and Jayden and Liam have cornered Zach into an intense conversation about football, and Tallulah is talking to Scarlett and Ruby and Mimi about weird teachers at college. A waiter appears and reaches through them to collect the empty plates and bowls and asks them if they want anything else to eat and someone orders a sticky toffee pudding and someone else orders more chips and Tallulah has no idea who is paying for what or what exactly is happening, but it feels strangely like something, somewhere is on fire and it's already too late to put it out.

More tequila shots arrive as well as the extra chips and the sticky toffee pudding, which is served with six spoons, and Jayden gets a message on his phone and says, "He's outside. I'll be right back," and everyone seems to know what he's talking about and a couple of people pass him ten-pound notes from their wallets and a moment later he returns and passes pills to his friends under the table.

Tallulah watches Zach's reaction and is amazed to see him take a pill from Jayden and swallow it down with warm champagne. Zach has never taken drugs before, as far as she's aware, apart from smoking a little weed with his older sister in the back garden when she still lived at home. She gazes at him, trying to catch his eye, but he studiously ignores her, and Tallulah realizes that rather than trying to fight this situation that she and Scarlett have deliberately engineered, he is on some kind of mission. A mission to unnerve her, to undermine her, to catch her out somehow. He hates these kids, she knows he hates them, yet he's sucking up to them and laughing at their jokes and taking their drugs.

She feels something touch her hand under the table and looks up to find Scarlett looking at her. "I broke one in half for you," she says. "Want to share?"

Tallulah shakes her head.

"A quarter?"

Tallulah blinks and says, "Maybe later."

Scarlett passes her the tiny chunk and she clasps it inside her fist.

The night has transmogrified into something alien and electric. She is being played from both sides, by Zach and by Scarlett. Meanwhile, the muscles of her heart ache for Noah, lying now, she assumes, at nearly 10:00 p.m., sleeping in his cot, his hands furled into fists, his hair damp from the heat of his bedtime bath and warm milk and the hot summer night air through the open window.

Once again she feels Scarlett's hand under the table, cupping her bare leg, a finger sliding up toward the hem of her cutoff shorts, and she gasps and jumps very slightly.

She gets to her feet. "You know," she says, "it's getting late. I should probably get back." She doesn't want this to happen anymore. She's changed her mind. She wants to go home with Zach, tiptoe upstairs, and stand with him staring at their baby together, talking in almost silent whispers about how beautiful he is and how lucky they are to have him. They can split up another day. Not today. Not now.

"No," says Scarlett, pulling her down by her arm. She fixes her with a terrifying stare and says, "Stay, please stay. Just have one more drink. OK?"

Tallulah sighs and someone brings her another tequila, which she duly downs. She's about to try to leave again when someone else arrives at their table. It's a slightly older woman whom she vaguely recognizes from around the village, and upon her arrival Scarlett screeches, "Lexie!"; she hugs the woman to her and says to Tallulah, "Lexie is Kerryanne's daughter. You know, the matron at the Maypole. Not only has Lexie got the best mum in the world, she also has the best job in the world. Tell Tallulah what you do, Lex."

Lexie rolls her eyes good-naturedly and says, "I'm a travel blogger."

"Yeah," says Scarlett, "but not some fake-arse travel blogger who tries to blag freebies at hotels. Like a proper blogger. With thousands of followers on Instagram and a stupidly jet-set lifestyle. Where did you just get back from?"

"Peru."

"Peru. Fuck's sake. That is so cool it's ridiculous."

Stuck now in a conversation with Scarlett and Lexie, Tallulah gives in and has another shot of tequila when it's offered to her and uses it to swallow down the chunk of pill she still held in her hand. The bell is rung at the bar for last orders and Scarlett gets to her feet. "Anyone for a pool party?" she says loudly.

Tallulah looks at Zach and Zach looks at Tallulah, a look filled with bad intentions. He says, "Count me in." His pupils are dilated and he's smiling. "Come on, Tallulah," he says to her across the table, "we're going to a pool party."

53

Sophie stands at the front door of the cottage, her hands clasped in front of her, her hair neatly combed, her teeth freshly brushed to take away the scent of Liam's beer. Pippa crunches across the gravel pathway holding a twin's hand in each of hers, each twin towing a small wheely case behind them.

"Hello, hello, hello!" says Sophie. "Welcome!"

It's 6:00 p.m. and Shaun is running late at school and has called Sophie in a frazzle of anxious apologies to ask her to be there when they arrived. She'd held back a long, deep sigh and said, "Of course, of course, no problem."

"I'll try and be there as quickly as I can. I promise."

"It's fine," she'd said. "Just do what you have to do."

"Thank you, darling," he replied. And she'd started, because he'd never called her darling before. He always called her Sophes. Or baby. Darling seemed to her like something you called a wife you'd run out of genuine enthusiasm for. Darling was what her friends' parents called each other. Darling was old.

She moves toward Pippa and the children and leans down to hug them to her. They are both in Gap hoodies: Jack's is green, Lily's is baby pink. They hug her back hard and she feels a sense of relief because it's been so long since she's seen them and she'd been scared they might have forgotten that they like her.

"Come in," she says. "Come in."

"Is this really Daddy's house?" asks Jack.

"Well, sort of," Sophie says, holding the door for them to troop through. "It really belongs to the school. But they lend it to the head teacher for when they're working here."

"So does Daddy still have his other house in London?" asks Lily, wheeling her pink Trunki down the flagstones and toward the kitchen.

"Yes. Daddy still has his other house and I still have my flat. We're just borrowing this cottage for a while."

"It's nice," says Jack, who likes most things.

"It looks a bit spidery," says Lily, who always finds something to mention.

"I promise you," says Sophie, straightening their suitcases for them, "that I have cleaned every last inch of this cottage and there is not one solitary tiny weeny creature anywhere in it."

"I don't mind other creatures," says Lily. "I just don't like spiders. What's that smell?"

"What smell?"

"Like a burned smell."

"Oh God, I don't know. I thought I'd managed to get rid of it. I must have got used to it. Sorry. It's just an old house, I suppose." She turns to Pippa. "Can I get you a cup of tea?"

Pippa heaves a travel-weary sigh. "No," she says. "No. Very kind. But I'm expected for dinner in N5 at eight thirty. I'm only just going to make it as it is. I must say, I'm not sure how tenable this is going to be as an ongoing thing. I mean, if Shaun can't even make it back to a house that's actually in the same place as his school on time, how on earth is he going to get these children back and forth from N1 every other weekend? I can smell disaster already."

She angles her face slightly to the right, almost as if she is sniffing the air for the oncoming disaster, then checks her phone and says, "Jesus Christ, Google Maps is saying two hours and five minutes. Shaun swore blind this drive was only an hour and a half." She sighs and runs her fingers through her shiny chestnut hair. "So, children, be good for Sophie. And for Daddy. Make sure you do everything you're told."

"Do you want to see their room?" asks Sophie.

"No," she replies crisply. "I'm sure it's fine. Shaun said you'd made it lovely for them, and I'm sure it is."

Sophie feels a small flush of pleasure at Pippa's words, at the innate suggestion that she is to be trusted to do the right thing with regard to her precious children.

Pippa leans down and kisses her children. Then she kisses Sophie lightly on each cheek before heading up the path back toward the main building and the car park.

When she's gone, Sophie breathes a sigh of relief. She realizes immediately that Pippa's visit had been hanging over her for days without her even really being aware of it. And now it is done and the twins are here and she can cast the anxiety away from her like loosened chains.

"Right, kids," she says, coming back into the kitchen. "Who's hungry?"

Shaun returns half an hour later, and for an hour or so the cottage is alive with the energy of a joyful reunion. He loses his heavy demeanor the moment he removes his tie and lets the children crawl onto his lap. Sophie puts a chicken lasagna in the oven (Lily won't eat cows, sheep, or pigs, but says that chickens have scary faces so it's OK to eat them) and opens a bottle of wine, and afterward, Shaun pours the twins a bath and oversees them getting into their pajamas and they both run down the stairs bare-footed and damp-haired with pink cheeks and Sophie finds a movie on the TV and they all sit bunched together on the sofa watching something that swirls and twirls drunkenly through the pillars of Sophie's consciousness because she cannot focus on anything right now apart from the painting of the spiral staircase on Liam's wall.

She pulls her phone from the arm of the sofa and switches it on. She opens up the photo she took of the painting and zooms in on it with her fingertips, then moves around the image from corner to corner, trying to find the thing that makes sense of it. As happens when she's plotting a novel in her head, she mentally lines up the players and the timeline and the clues and tries to arrange them into a logical narrative.

And then she feels a shiver run through her as she realizes that she's got it. Or at least, she's got the key to it. The metaphorical monkey wrench to pull the whole thing open with. She gasps slightly, loud enough for Shaun and the twins to all turn to her as one and look at her questioningly.

"Are you OK?" asks Shaun.

"Yes," she says. "Yes. I just, er, I had a thought about the new book, a way to make it work. I think I might just, er . . ." She gets to her feet. "Do you mind?" she says. "If I do a bit of work? I won't be long."

She scurries from the living room and to her desk, where she flings open the lid of her laptop. She scrolls quickly through one of the articles she'd found after her meeting with Jacinta Croft about the history of secret tunnels in old houses and discovers, as she'd suspected, that many secret tunnels were accessed via "camouflaged doors hidden behind paintings or sliding bookcases, or even built into an architectural feature." She finds many pictures of stone spiral staircases in medieval buildings and castles, all of them spiraling upward, toward turrets like the one in Scarlett's painting. But what if the architect of Dark Place had designed a spiral staircase that went down as well as up? And what if you could access it through a secret slab of stone at the foot of the visible staircase? And what if that weird metal implement in Scarlett's painting was actually designed to lift up the secret slab of stone?

She screenshots the article and then WhatsApps the page and the photo of Scarlett's painting to Kim.

Is this what the tool looked like that the police found in the flower bed? she types, adding in an arrow pointing to the implement in the painting.

She presses send and waits for the ticks to turn blue. Almost immediately she sees that Kim is typing.

Yes, comes her response. *Nobody could work out what it was.*

A shiver runs through Sophie as she realizes what this might mean. *Look at the rectangle of light on the painting, at the bottom of the steps.*

Kim replies, *OK.*

This is a painting that Scarlett made. Apparently it's of a stone staircase in Dark Place.

Kim replies with an emoji with a slack jaw.

Then she says, *Can I send this to Dom?*

Yes, of course, Sophie types. *Be my guest.*

———————

Shaun and Sophie put the twins to bed at nine thirty, finish the dregs of the wine they'd had with dinner, and then head to bed themselves. Sophie watches Shaun remove his clothes and pull on the T-shirt and cotton trousers he wears in bed. The pulling on of the T-shirt and the cotton trousers is a silent signal that there will not be any sex tonight and that's fine with Sophie. The day has been inordinately long and intense. Her head is packed with things that have no correlation with sex: dusty tunnels and missing teenagers and grieving mothers and haunted-looking girls with PTSD on YouTube. She unties her hair from its ponytail and she slips into her own pajamas and then eases herself gratefully under the duvet.

"Did you manage to get some good work done?" Shaun asks.

She should tell him, she thinks. She should tell him what's been happening and whom she's been talking to, she should tell him about the paintings in Liam's room, about talking to Kim. But she can't. She just can't. This weekend is meant to be about the twins. He hasn't seen them for three weeks. It's the longest he's ever been without seeing his children. The only reason they ever came to this stupid school in the first place was so that Shaun could afford to educate his children the way their mother wanted them to be educated. This was never about Shaun's career. If this had been about his career, he'd be running a huge, sprawling state secondary school in inner London right now, not this glorified crammer college in a chocolate-box village. He sacrificed so much to do this and she did not have to come with him; it was her choice to be here. He didn't cajole or persuade her.

And now his children are finally here and this weekend needs to be perfect, absolutely perfect: two whole days unsullied by work or detectives. Just the four of them doing wholesome, countryside things as a family.

So she nods and she says, "Yes, I got a few words written."

He smiles at her and says, "Well, that's good. Maybe you've finally broken through your writer's block? Maybe it'll all start to flow now."

"Yes," she says. "Let's hope so."

As she says this her phone buzzes with a message. She picks it up and looks at it. It's Kim.

Dom says they'll definitely get a warrant to go into Dark Place now. Hopefully as soon as tomorrow morning. Thanks for everything. You're amazing.

She types a reply. *No worries. Glad I could help.*

"Who was that?" asks Shaun.

"Oh," she says, "just the family WhatsApp."

She turns her phone off, plugs it in to charge, and closes her eyes with her head full of staircases that spiral around and around and down into the dark soft sands of sleep.

54

Scarlett turns up the volume on the radio in Lexie's car and opens the window. Tallulah is sitting on Zach's lap, squashed in the back with Liam and Mimi. Her head is spinning. She hasn't drunk more than half a bottle of wine in months. She hasn't taken recreational drugs since she was fourteen. She can feel the outline of the ring box in Zach's pocket against the back of her leg. She sticks her head out of the window to suck in gulps of warm night air. Trees flash by in streaks of black and gold, lights race toward them coming the other way in blurred disks of white. The sky is still holding on to its last mouse-gray shreds of daylight.

Scarlett was meant to tell Zach about them. That was plan B. She was going to tell Zach that she and Tallulah were in love with each other, and Zach was going to look at Tallulah with wide eyes of disbelief and stifle a harsh laugh and say, *What?* And Tallulah was going to say, *It's true. I've been trying to tell you for weeks, but I couldn't find the right moment.* And then Zach would have stormed off or thrown up or started a fight or screamed or cried or raged or something. And it would have been over. It would have been dreadful, but it would have been a moment of no return.

But Scarlett has for some inexplicable reason extended the agony by dragging everyone back to her house for a pool party. Tallulah had messaged her earlier in the pub: *What r u doing???*

Scarlett had replied *ALL UNDER CONTROL* and then sent her a conspiratorial look across the table.

They pull through the gates of Dark Place and head down the long driveway to the house, the outline of which Tallulah can see in three separate and distinct versions. She blinks to try to bring the three images into alignment, but it doesn't work.

Lexie parks up and they all dismount, tumbling from the tightly packed car onto the graveled driveway. Scarlett leads them all through the metal gate at the side of the house and onto the pool terrace and heads straight into the pool house, where she switches on the garden lighting and the Sonos sound system and returns a moment later with a handful of cold beers from the fridge. Zach perches on the edge of a sun lounger and Tallulah sits behind him. Scarlett is singing along loudly to the music on the system and Liam is joining in. Lexie and Mimi are on their phones.

Scarlett passes Tallulah a beer and she takes it from her. "Cheers," says Scarlett, dancing as she holds her beer bottle out toward Tallulah's. "And cheers to you too, Zach. It's great to finally meet you."

Zach touches his bottle against hers and says, "Likewise," but even from here, sitting behind him, Tallulah can feel the dislike emanating from him.

Scarlett dances back toward Liam and Mimi and toasts them as well. Then she rests her beer on a table and pulls off her T-shirt. She's wearing a small vest top underneath. She unbuttons her shorts, steps out of them, revealing the unsexy black underpants that Tallulah is so familiar with, and then, in a flash, she's in the pool.

Tallulah stares as she soars across the bottom of the pool, the distorting lens of the pool water making her look even longer and leaner than she is. Then she emerges at the end and pulls herself up onto the pool edge, pulls her wet hair off her face, and says to Tallulah and Zach, "Are you coming in?"

Tallulah says, "No. I don't want to get my hair wet."

And Scarlett says, "Oh, come on, Lula, I know how much you like getting your hair wet."

And Tallulah sees Zach's shoulders flinch before he tips his beer bottle to his lips, briskly, and drinks hard from it.

She laughs nervously. "Seriously. I washed it this morning and blow-dried it and everything. I can't be bothered doing it all again tomorrow."

"Oh, Lula. You and your precious hair. Come on! Don't be moist. Get in!" She pulls two handfuls of water from the pool and throws them at Tallulah, splattering Zach in the process, who gets quickly to his feet, yells, "Fuck's sake! Watch it!"

"You may as well get properly wet now. Come on, Zach. Show your girlfriend how it's done."

Zach starts unbuttoning his shirt. He pulls it off and then he pulls off the white T-shirt he was wearing underneath and Tallulah can see the muscles in his back ripple and wriggle beneath his flesh. Then he unzips his trousers and pulls them off and he is naked apart from his fitted Lycra boxer shorts.

He turns to Tallulah and says, "Come on, then. Do as your friend tells you."

There is something in the atmosphere that is so sour and so swollen that Tallulah can barely breathe. It's formed directly in the space between Scarlett and Zach, and it's getting bigger and bigger. She nods and pulls off her shorts but not her floaty top, feeling self-conscious in front of Mimi and Liam and Lexie. She twists her hair into a knot and then jumps straight in, water rocketing into her ear canals, gushing over her skin, blowing her top up into a billowing cotton jellyfish. She bursts out again and finds herself face-to-face with Scarlett, who brushes her lips quickly against hers before going under again. Tallulah turns and sees Zach just as he emerges from the water and he makes the noise that people make when a swimming pool is colder than you expect it to be and he shakes his head, droplets of water catching the light as they fly from the tips of his hair like crystals. And now Tallulah is sitting between Zach and

Scarlett and the energy between the two of them is so toxic that you could choke on it.

Once again Tallulah finds herself thinking of her baby boy, the familiarity and warmth of his tiny body, the feel of him in her arms, against her body, the smell of his nighttime breath, and she feels, suddenly, that she doesn't want anyone. Not Scarlett, not Zach. She just wants to be alone.

She kicks her legs behind her to get her to the steps and climbs out. As she does so, Mimi and Liam both jump in. She goes to the pool house and grabs a big black towel from a perfectly arranged stack of rolled-up towels and she wraps herself in it and sits on a lounger and watches the others in the pool for a while. The loud music drowns out the sounds of screaming and squealing and Tallulah watches with discomfort as Zach puts Scarlett on his shoulders and enters into a battle with an inflatable hammer with Mimi, who sits atop Liam's shoulders.

She shakes her head a little, to dislodge some water, but also to try and right the wrongness of watching her lover and her partner entwined in wet underwear. She sees Zach turn slightly to acknowledge her; the look he gives her is like a shot of ice. She nods and forces a smile, shivering slightly as her body temperature starts to drop. "I'm going to get dressed," she says, collecting her shorts and Zach's shirt, her phone and her bag, and heading into the house.

There's a small room off the kitchen; Scarlett calls it the snug. It's lined with bookshelves and lit with low-level lighting, has two small red sofas facing each other across a big walnut coffee table covered with interesting objects, big glossy hardback books, and a fan of interiors magazines. She slides the door closed behind her and peels off her wet top, then puts on Zach's T-shirt, takes off her wet knickers, and pulls on her shorts. She turns her head upside down and twists the black towel into a turban over her wet hair. She wants to stay in here. It's warm and it's safe. She feels protected from the strangeness of the evening, from the terrible energy in the air. She taps on her phone and sees that it is nearly 1:00 a.m. She thinks about texting her mum, but then thinks that she is probably asleep by now and that she would be waking her up unnecessarily, so she turns it off again and sits down on the little red sofa and picks up one of the big glossy books and starts to flick through it, the words and images blurring in front of her eyes, reminding her that while she is less drunk than she was, she is still far from sober.

"There you are," says a deep voice at the door. It's Zach. He's back in his shirt and trousers, his wet hair slicked away from his face. "What's the matter with you?"

He slides the door closed behind him and stands framed by it, a halogen just above his head throwing sinister shadows down his face.

"Nothing," she says. "Just came in to get dry and warm."

"And left me out there like a dick?"

"Zach," she says. "It was your idea to come here. I wanted to go home two hours ago, remember?"

"Yes, I do remember. But then I thought, you know, maybe you were just saying you wanted to go home for my sake, and I didn't want your *friends* to think I was cramping your style."

"I didn't want to come. I wanted to go home. I still want to go home. I'm calling a cab now."

She gets to her feet, and as she does so, Zach strides toward her and says, "No. No, we're not going anywhere. Not yet."

He stands close enough for her to smell the chlorine on him, to feel the heat of his breath.

"I want to go home," she says again, a hint of defeat in her voice.

She goes to move past him, but he grabs her arms, hard. "Do you know what I was going to do tonight, Lula? Do you have any idea what I was going to do?" He releases one of her arms and dips his hand into the pocket of his trousers, pulls out the small black box, and shoves it against her breastbone so hard she can already feel a bruise start to form.

"Ow," she says, rubbing at her sternum. "That hurt."

"Open it," he snarls.

She inhales deeply and unclicks the fastening, then stares in numb horror at the tiny nub of diamond glittering at her under the low halogens. There it is, she thinks. There it is. The reason for every last dreadful minute of this evening.

She clicks the box shut again, hands it back to Zach, and says, "I would have said no."

The power of her own response leaves her feeling winded.

He rocks slightly. "Right," he says. "Right."

For a moment, Tallulah thinks maybe that's it. Maybe it's done. Maybe her journey with Zach is finally over and it really was simple as that. But she stares at Zach and sees his expression pass from numb acceptance through confusion and then, quickly, so quickly, into black rage.

"It's her, isn't it?" he says. "This is something to do with her."

"Who?"

"That girl. Scarlett. Ever since she walked into the pub tonight you've been on edge. That's why I came back here. I wanted to see what was going on. So. What's the deal?"

Tallulah feels something surge through her, like a stampede. "We're together," she says bluntly.

Zach's face contorts into an ugly mask of incomprehension. "What?"

"Me. And Scarlett. We've been seeing each other."

There. It's done. It's said. It's over. Tallulah breathes out heavily and waits.

"You mean, like . . ." He cannot find the words to describe something that he cannot countenance. "You and her? Like . . ."

"Having sex. Yes."

"Oh. Oh my God." He stumbles slightly and groans. "Oh my God. Oh Jesus. I knew it. Jesus fucking Christ, from the minute I saw that photo on your phone, I knew it. It was so obvious. So, were you *having sex* then? You and her?"

"No. God. No. That was only the second time I'd even spoken to her."

"But did it start that night?"

"No. No. Not for ages. Not until you and me started having problems."

"What problems? We haven't been having any problems."

She blinks at him. She has no idea if he's being deliberately obtuse or if he genuinely believes this rewriting of their history.

"Fuck's sake. Lula. I mean. Fuck's sake. With *her*? Of all the people. She's not even good-looking. She's literally ugly."

"She's not ugly. She's beautiful."

He clutches his head. "This is . . . this is insane, Lula. This isn't you. You're not fucking gay. This is her. She's done this to you. She's fucking groomed you. Can you not see that? She's groomed you."

He paces around for a moment and Tallulah has no idea whether he's on the edge of calming down and cajoling her into a state of submission, or whether he's about to kill her. But he does neither of these things. He draws himself up tall and straight, looks directly at her, and says, "You know that's it now, don't you? You know you can't be Noah's mother anymore. Not now. No court in the world would let a person like you raise a child. No court in the world. I'm going now, Tallulah. I'm going back to the house and I'm taking Noah, and you will never see him again. Do you hear me? You will never see him again."

He hurls the ring box at her again, and as he turns away, Tallulah feels her head fill with splintered shards of fear and rage. No, says every atom in her body; no, you do not get to take my baby; *no, you do not get to take my baby*. And she follows behind him, and she screams out, her arms outstretched, ready to pull him back, to stop him doing what he's doing, going where he's going. But as she leaves the room she sees that Scarlett is in the doorway in her wet underwear and that she is holding something in her hand, a bronze lump, carved into a shape that somehow resembles a group of people in a huddle, and that she is lifting it backward over her head and then swinging it forward again toward the crown of Zach's head. She sees the bronze lump hit the back of Zach's skull. She hears Scarlett's scream of anger, Zach's dull yell of pain. And she sees the blow fell him so that he lands in a perfect arc, face-first onto the white granite floor.

55

The following morning starts early, as is always the way when Shaun has the twins. Jack is first on their bed, trying to steal Shaun's phone off the bedside table and having a mock battle with him. Lily follows a minute later, her fine brown hair fuzzed up into a thick knot at the back of her head that Sophie knows she will have to spend twenty minutes brushing out before they can leave the house. Over Lily's shoulder, through a gap in the curtains, Sophie sees an inch of the gray damp day that the forecasters had predicted and she turns to Shaun and says, "Looks like it's the water park today." And Shaun peers through the gap in the curtains and sighs and says, "Looks like it."

The children are delighted and everyone runs downstairs to eat the special breakfasts that Sophie got in for them: fat American pancakes, Nutella, and Coco Pops. Sophie drinks coffee from a big mug, Shaun drinks an espresso from a tiny cup, the children chat and eat and drop Coco Pops on the floor and talk about how if they were at home their dog, Betty, would hoover up the spilled cereal. Rain splashes gently against the windowpanes and for a moment, Sophie feels at one, as though maybe this is how she's been waiting to feel ever since they first arrived. South London seems distant, and for a moment she thinks that maybe she can do this after all. All they needed was to see the children. Shaun has already lost some of the brittleness he's been displaying since he started his new job. The harsh haircut he had before they arrived has started to grow out and soften, and he can't stop smiling, even when the twins are being testy.

She picks up her phone to google the opening times of the leisure center in Manton, and as she does so, a message arrives from Kim.

They've got a warrant. They're going to Dark Place. I feel sick.

Sophie takes a sharp intake of breath, before typing her reply.

Oh my God. That was quick. When will they give you more developments?

They're just putting a team together. Maybe in a couple of hours? I can't breathe.

Is there anything I can do?

She knows it's the wrong thing to have said the minute she presses send.

Could you come over? Maybe. If you're not busy?

Sophie looks up from her phone. Lily and Jack are standing over the toaster waiting for their second round of pancakes to warm up, Shaun is loading the dishwasher, everyone is still in their pajamas and in varying degrees of unreadiness for the day, the day that was very much intended to be a day about the four of them. She sighs and types, *My partner's kids are here. We're going to the splash pool in Manton.*

She pauses. It sounds so harsh. This woman is possibly on the cusp of discovering that her daughter is dead. *Splash pool.* Really?

She adds another line, *But we're not going for a while, so I could come over for a little bit.*

Thank you so much, Kim replies. *I just can't face being on my own right now.*

———————————

Sophie gets to Kim's half an hour later. Shaun had looked a little confused when she'd tried to explain in as few words as possible where she was going, and why.

"I'll be back in an hour," she says as she leaves. "Probably less."

"But how do you know this woman?"

"From the ring," she says lightly. "The one I found in the woods. I guess I've got a little bit sucked into things with her, you know."

"Well, don't be too long, will you?"

"I promise I'll be back in time to go to swimming."

Kim looks gray when she opens the door to Sophie. She's not wearing makeup and her usually shiny hair is hanging in matte ropes over each shoulder.

The sound of children's TV blares from the living room, where Sophie can see the back of Noah's head as they pass by. Kim leads her into the kitchen and pulls out a chair for her.

"Tea?"

"Yes. Please."

Kim fills the kettle from the tap and Sophie hears her sigh.

"Any more word?" she asks.

"No, not yet. This is the worst feeling. I can't bear it."

Kim's shoulders look small and pointy through the cotton of her long-sleeved top and Sophie wants to touch her, comfort her, but she doesn't know her well enough.

"It's going to happen," says Kim. "They're going to open that slab in that tower, they're going to go down there, and they're going to find something. I know they are. And it could be something that breaks my world apart completely. And I'm not sure I'm ready for that. I'm not sure I'll ever, ever be ready for that. I want it to happen but I don't want it to happen. And I need to know, but I don't want to know. What if she's down there? My baby girl. What if she's down there? With spiders. You know, she suffers from arachnophobia. She's terrified of spiders. Literally to the point where she can't breathe if she sees one, where she would physically shake. And what if someone locked her down there, with spiders. In the dark. Alone. That's what I can't bear. The idea of her being down there, alone . . ."

And then Kim starts to cry and Sophie gets to her feet and encircles her in her arms and says, "Oh Kim. Oh Kim. I'm so sorry. This must be so tough. So tough." The kettle comes to a boil and clicks off but Kim does not make the tea; instead, she collapses onto a chair and stares at the clock on the kitchen wall as it turns from 10:01 a.m. to 10:02 a.m.

Then Kim's phone buzzes and Sophie can see from here the name *Dom* flash up on her screen.

Kim straps Noah into his car seat in the back of her car while Sophie gets into the passenger seat. She takes out her phone and messages Shaun.

Kim and I are going to Dark Place. Apparently they've found something.

Her message goes unread until they are almost out of the village, when Shaun replies with, *Oh God. I hope it's nothing too awful. We'll wait here till we hear from you.*

Kim drives hard through the country lanes outside the village and then rather too fast up the tiny lane that leads to Dark Place. There's a female police officer in high-vis standing at the gates to the house and Kim winds down her window and says, "DI McCoy told me to come. I'm Tallulah Murray's mother."

The officer lets her through the gates and they drive up the potholed driveway to the front of the house, which is circled with marked and unmarked police cars. Another police officer approaches them and Kim once again winds down her window and explains who she is and the police officer talks into a walkie-talkie and then asks her to wait in the car for a moment.

The front door of the house is wide-open. Inside Sophie can see an elegant marble hallway with a creamy stone staircase circling through the middle to a glass balustrade above, with a huge modernist chandelier hanging at its center. The walls are hung with abstract art and at the base of the staircase there is a pair of 1960s leather lounging chairs facing each other across a low coffee table. It's exquisitely tasteful, a perfect blend of old and new. But this beautiful house has been left abandoned for more than a year, and now, finally, everyone will know why.

Dom appears at the front door a moment later and Kim steps immediately out of her car and heads toward him. Sophie would like to follow but needs to stay in the car with Noah, so she opens her door and swivels around so that she is half in and half out of the car. She watches as Dom says something to Kim and then she sees Kim's body crumple at the knees and Dom and another man bring her back to standing with a hand under each elbow, before Dom takes her into his arms and holds on to her hard.

Sophie turns and looks at Noah. "I'm just going to check your nana's OK, all right? I won't be long. You just wait there, like a good, good boy. OK?"

Noah stares at her and then sticks out his tongue and blows her a raspberry, and she starts slightly. No child has ever blown a raspberry at her before and the classroom assistant inside her would like to react to it in some way. But instead she ignores it and strides toward the front door.

She rests a hand gently on the small of Kim's back and says, "Kim? What's happened?"

And Kim is breathing too hard to speak so Dom speaks for her and says, "We've just got into the tunnel. There are human remains down there."

Sophie feels a veil fall across her vision and wobbles slightly. "Is there any idea yet whose remains?"

"No. Not yet. But Kim," he says, turning to address her, "you should know that it is a male."

Kim sobs. A choking sound.

"And we found this, as well." He holds up a sealed clear plastic bag. "Are you able to identify it, Kim?"

Sophie looks at the object in the bag. It's a phone in a clear plastic case with some kind of design printed on it. She feels Kim's shoulders crumple under her hand and she hears a noise come from Kim that she has never heard before, half banshee wail, half feral growl, and Kim collapses onto her knees there on the graveled driveway and says, "No, no, no, no, no, no, not my baby. No, no, no, no, not my beautiful baby girl."

In the backseat of Kim's car Noah starts to scream and cry and soon the damp air is filled with the sounds of raw human agony being played out in stereo and everyone else falls completely silent.

56

"Zach?"

Tallulah shoves at his shoulder.

"*Zach?*"

His body seems oddly solid and resistant, she thinks, as though it has been emptied and refilled with ball bearings.

"Zach?" she hisses into his ear. "Oh. Fuck. Zach."

She puts her face to his face, which is turned at a strange angle, and feels for breath from his mouth and nose. But there is nothing. She tries to move him onto his back but he is too heavy. There is a small patch of blood on the tile beneath his cheeks and she sees a trickle coming from his ear canal.

"Oh my God. Scarlett. What have you done?"

Scarlett throws her a look of dismay. "He was going to take your baby, Lula! He was going to take your baby!"

"Yes. But you didn't need to . . . oh my God!" Tallulah gets to her feet and she stares from Scarlett to Zach and back again. "Scarlett. He's dead. Oh Jesus Christ. Scarlett."

"You told me you wanted him to disappear, Lula. *You* told me that. Remember? You said you wished he could just disappear. That it would easier. I heard what he said about the baby and I heard him threatening you and I just . . ."

They both look up at a clicking noise across the kitchen tiles and see that it is Toby. He looks at them inquisitively, and then pads toward Zach's body. He sniffs the toes of his bare foot and then sits down and looks at Tallulah. Behind him another figure appears: a middle-aged woman with a silken kimono wrapped around her small frame, a pale pink eye mask pushed halfway up her forehead.

The woman squints and grimaces at the tableau in front of her. Then she peels off the eye mask and says, "I just came down to ask you kids to turn down the pool music. What the hell is going on?"

Tallulah can't speak. She shakes her head.

"Oh Christ." The woman strides toward Zach's body. "Who is he? Who are you? Who *is* this, Scarlett?" The woman's eyes go to the object in Scarlett's hand. "Oh," she says, sadly and somewhat theatrically. "Not my Pipin."

Tallulah shakes her head again. *Pipin?*

The woman leans down toward Zach's face and says again, "Please can someone tell me who the hell this is?" She places two fingers to the underside of his neck and peers into his eyes.

"He's . . . Zach," says Tallulah. "He's, he's my boyfriend."

"And you are?"

"Tallulah. I'm Tallulah."

"Oh Christ. He's dead," says the woman. "Will one of you please tell me what's going on?"

"I don't know," says Scarlett, looking from the strange metal object in her hand that her mother called her "Pipin" to the lifeless form of Zach and back again. "I don't know. He was going—he was going to take Noah. And then—"

"Who's Noah?" asks the woman with a sigh.

Scarlett replies, "Noah is Lula's baby. He was going to take him away from her. And then . . ." Her eyes drop to the Pipin again and she stops talking.

There's a black square in Tallulah's head over the space where the memory of what just happened should be, like a redaction. She can remember chasing Zach into the kitchen. She can remember the dog walking into the kitchen and sniffing Zach's toes. In between a thing happened. A terrible thing. It flashes through her head like a lightning bolt. She starts to cry. "Oh," she says in a tiny, tiny voice. "Oh." She puts her hands over her mouth and starts to rock. "Oh."

"So, right. Let's think straight," says Scarlett's mother. "The time is . . ." She turns to look at the big metal clock on the wall. "Just after two a.m. Who else is here?"

"Just Mimi. Liam and Lexie have gone."

"And where's Mimi?"

"I don't know. She came inside a few minutes ago. To charge her phone, she said."

"So it's just us. And this boy, this Zach, was he trying to hurt you?"

Tallulah shakes her head. "No," she says. "He was leaving."

"Has he ever hurt you?"

"No," she says. "No, he's never hurt me."

"And you, Scarlett. Has he ever hurt you?"

Scarlett shakes her head sullenly.

"And did you think he was going to hurt you?"

She shakes her head again.

"So, you hit him on the head from behind because he said he was going to take your friend's baby?"

"Yes."

"And why was he going to take your baby?" she asks Tallulah.

"Because . . . I told him . . ." She looks at Scarlett, who nods, just once. "I told him that I was in love with Scarlett."

She waits to see what this pronouncement does to the perfect angles of Scarlett's mother's face, but it does nothing. Her face does not move in any way or register any kind of reaction. Instead, she simply sighs and says, "OK. So he was angry. And hurt. And maybe slightly disgusted. He said he was going to take your baby. He went to leave and then . . ." All three of them look again at the body on the floor.

For a moment, nobody says anything. Then Scarlett's mother sighs and says, "What a fucking mess. Right. Who knows you two were here?" she asks Tallulah.

Tallulah tries to arrange her thoughts. "Er, nobody. My mum knows I'm at someone's house, but I didn't tell her whose."

"And what about your friends, Scarlett?"

"Well, they all knew because we were all at the pub together. And Liam and Lexie, obviously, because they were here. And Mimi. And maybe some other people."

"Right, so eventually, people are going to realize that something's up when this boy doesn't come home."

Tallulah nods and thinks of her mother and thinks of her baby and thinks of her bed and thinks that all she wants is her baby and her mother and her bed.

"What time was your mother expecting you home?" Scarlett's mother asks Tallulah.

"I don't know, really. No particular time."

"Right, so we have a few hours at least before we need to make an account of ourselves."

"Aren't we going to call the police?" Tallulah asks.

"What? No. This is manslaughter. Scarlett will end up in prison. You too, probably. And you'll never see your baby grow up. No, this is a disaster, this is an absolute fucking disaster." She puts her hands on her hips and surveys the area. "So," she begins. "Mimi. What are we going to do about Mimi? Where is she?"

"I told you. I don't know. She came indoors to charge her phone."

"Go and find her," she says to Scarlett, without turning around. She goes to the sink, pours herself a glass of water, and knocks back two painkillers with it. "Urgh. My head."

Scarlett nods and disappears. Then for a moment or two, it is just Tallulah, Scarlett's mother, and the dog. "Well, life is never dull with Scarlett around, that's for sure," says her mother. "Jesus Christ.

One thing after another after another. From the moment she was born. I was so excited when I found out I was having a girl after the whirlwind of Rex. I thought it would be all calm afternoons doing crafts and playing with each other's hair. But no, Scarlett was even worse than Rex, if anything, always wanting to be outdoors, always wanting to run, to disobey, to talk. Oh my God, to talk." She rests a delicate hand against her cheekbone and then rubs it across her forehead. "Such a nightmare of a child. And then the teenage years. Oh my goodness. *The boys*—you know, she lost her virginity when she was thirteen. *Thirteen.* She was obsessed with boys. Then came the girls. Then more boys. More girls. Always being suspended from school after school. Never where she said she was going to be. Never cared, that was the thing. As much as I broke the rules when I was a teenager, I always cared about the consequences. But Scarlett never did. And what can you do with a child like that?"

Scarlett returns. "She's out cold on my bed," she says.

"Good," says Scarlett's mother. "Leave her there. OK. Now. First things first. We need to get rid of him."

Tallulah shakes her head. Although she is almost entirely numb, she also can't quite accept that Zach is now an object, that he is no different from the strange piece of bronze on the floor next to him, the Pipin, a thing to be got rid of. It feels wrong. She battles with these sickening, dizzying emotions for a short moment, trying to untwine them from one another, then feels weak with the realization that there is only one solution and it is the one that Scarlett's mother is suggesting.

She sees Scarlett and her mother exchange a look, an almost imperceptible nod. "The tunnel?" says her mother.

"Yes," says Scarlett. "The tunnel."

57

SEPTEMBER 2018

Kim and Sophie are sent away before the body bag is brought from the house. Noah has cried himself into a stupefied sleep and is snoring gently in the backseat as they turn onto the main road back to the village.

Kim's hands grip the steering wheel hard, her knuckles like nubs of ivory through her skin. "Those people," she says. "That woman. That girl. I knew. I knew when I was there. They were bad people. I could feel it in my gut. You know? That house, it had badness in it. Even on that perfect summer's day. And there they were! In the swimming pool! Laughing! Drinking beer! It sickens me. But why? Why, for God's sake? And then to carry on living there for weeks afterward. With that . . . down there . . ." Kim starts to cry again.

"Shall we pull over?" Sophie suggests softly. "Just for a minute."

Kim nods and signals and tucks the car into the curb. She flops her head onto the steering wheel and cries for a short while. After a minute or two she pulls herself together and moves the car back into the traffic and back toward the village.

At Kim's house, Sophie messages Shaun.

They found a body. A male. And Tallulah's mobile phone. I'm waiting with Kim until there's news. I'll stay in touch.

Shaun replies simply with *OK* and a kiss.

Kim sits in the kitchen with Noah and gives him something to eat while Sophie sits in the living room, looking around her at the photos in frames on shelves and on the walls, all of which show a family that was once unexceptional, in every way other than in their happiness. Tallulah is a pretty girl, but looks like the sort of girl who likes to blend into the background, who doesn't like compliments or fuss, the sort of girl who likes routine and normality and simple food, who doesn't experiment with clothes or makeup in case she gets it wrong. Yet somehow she found herself embroiled in a Bohemian, self-centered family like the Jacqueses. How did it happen? When did it happen? And why did it end the way it appears to have ended?

She checks her phone for messages, for updates. She goes to the link for Mimi's YouTube video again to see if she's uploaded anything new. But the video is gone. The whole account is gone. Mimi has been made to disappear by Scarlett Jacques, still somehow wielding her inexplicable power from a boat in the middle of an ocean.

58

The slab lands in place over the steps down to the tunnel and Scarlett locks it into place with the old lever. All three of them are sweaty and gray. They get to their feet and rub their hands down their legs. The air in this tiny damp turret is thick with the smell of old alcohol, sweat, and fear.

The dog is waiting anxiously outside the door to the anteroom, whining gently under his breath. He follows them into the kitchen, where the tiny puddle of blood sits in the middle of the floor like a splash of spilled Beaujolais. Scarlett's mum mops it up with kitchen paper and spray bleach and then burns the paper over the sink before swirling the ashes down the plug hole and cleaning the sink with more spray.

It is nearly 3:00 a.m. The glass of the sliding doors reflects the LED lights from the swimming pool, which swirl slowly from pale pink to hot pink to purple to blue.

Tallulah sits heavily on the edge of the big leather sofa and says, very quietly, "Can I go home now?"

"No," Scarlett's mother replies immediately and firmly. "No. You are in a state of shock. If you go home now, your mother will know. I can't let you go anywhere until we've fixed this. OK?"

Tallulah stares at her and a thousand objections jump to the surface of her consciousness. But she is so tired. So tired. And all she wants to do is sleep. She watches in a kind of blank fascination as Scarlett's mother makes them hot chocolate in a saucepan. "God," she is saying. "Just what we need with Rex coming home tomorrow. And Majorca next week. Life," she says, stirring the chocolate slowly with a wooden spoon. "Life."

She pours the hot chocolate into mugs and passes one to each of the girls.

"There," she says. "Drink that."

The hot chocolate is delicious, creamy, smooth, but with a strangely chemical taste to it.

"I've put a tot of rum in it," Scarlett's mother explains, "just to calm your stomachs. You must both be so, so exhausted. All that adrenaline. You know, adrenaline is terribly aging. It's a miracle hormone, but it's terrible for you. In the long run . . ."

Tallulah watches Scarlett's mother's mouth moving as she talks, and as she watches, a kind of disconnect occurs, the words no longer match the shapes her mouth is making, they start to sound weird, elongated, as though they're on a DJ's decks and they're being slowed right down and dragged out of shape, and Tallulah's eyes, her eyes are so heavy and she wants to close her eyes but she wants to keep them open because she needs to stay awake, but she can't stay awake and then all the lights in the room funnel inward toward the backs of her retinas and then . . .

When Tallulah opens her eyes, it is dark. And cold. Her body sings out with aches and pains and her mouth is so dry that at first she cannot remove her tongue from behind her teeth. As her eyes grow accustomed to the dark, she sees the flicker of a candle in a jar. She sees the outline of a large plastic bottle of water and she opens it and drinks from it greedily. She is wrapped in fur blankets and there is a pillow and there is chocolate and expensive-looking biscuits and a toilet roll and a bucket. Along the tunnel is a humped form and she knows that it is Zach and she knows that she is under the house, and that above her is solid stone, and that she is trapped down here with the dead body of her boyfriend.

There is a box of matches and more candles in a box. And there is her phone. She switches it on but there is no signal down here and she has only 16 percent of her charge left.

She puts the phone back down and as she does she feels something run across the skin of her bare ankle. She looks down and sees a spider, sitting on her flesh, all angles and legs and coiled energy, and she jumps to her feet and she screams and she screams and she screams.

59

The morning drifts slowly toward lunchtime and Kim says, "You can go now, Sophie. I'm OK here now. Ryan's on his way."

"Ryan?"

"My son. I've been trying to get hold of him all morning. Had his phone on silent." She rolls her eyes. "But he'll be here in a minute. You go. I'll be fine."

Sophie waits for Kim's son to arrive; when he does, a few minutes later, he immediately collapses into his mother's arms and starts to cry and Sophie closes the door quietly behind her and heads back toward the Maypole.

A figure across the common is also walking toward the school and it takes a moment for Sophie to realize that it is Lexie. She's carrying shopping bags, on her way back from the co-op. She slows down to wait for her to catch up and then greets her with a tight smile.

"They've found something," she says to Lexie. "In the secret tunnel at Dark Place."

Lexie's jaw drops and her eyes open wide. "Oh my God," she says. "Is it him?"

"Him? Who?"

"The boy. Zach."

"What makes you think that?" she asks carefully.

"Well, if the police have found something. And that was the last place they were seen . . . ?"

" 'They'? But you said 'him.' The boy. As if . . ." She stops and then pulls in her breath. "Lexie," she says, "I hope you won't take this the wrong way, and I'm not insinuating anything here, I promise, but . . . I saw you had a copy of my book in your suitcase yesterday and I think you know that there's a passage in the book about a detective finding a cardboard sign just like the ones here and it seems like such a weird coincidence. I mean, the 'Dig Here' signs? Did you have anything to do with them?"

Behind them the church bell rings, just once. The question sticks in the air between them, thick and raw, like a clamp holding open an incision.

Lexie doesn't answer at first. And then, almost imperceptibly, she nods.

60

Tallulah doesn't know how long she's been down here. The last time she switched on her phone before it finally ran out of charge, it was 10:48 on Saturday night. It feels as if another six hours at least have passed since then. It must be early on Sunday morning, more than twenty-four hours since she drank the drugged hot chocolate given to her by Scarlett's mother. Twenty-four hours since whatever happened, happened. The thing that happened when Zach threatened to take her baby away. The thing that means Zach is dead.

She closes her eyes again and then again, trying to bring that moment back into focus—and it never does. She's sure it was Scarlett who did it. She sees the metal lump in Scarlett's hands. She sees Zach on the floor. But then she feels the thrum of her own adrenaline around her own body, the thump of her own heart under her own rib cage, and she doesn't know what happened just before. Just before.

The fur blanket is wrapped high up her neck; she has made a spider-proof bag out of it, but still she feels the shiver of tiny feet on her flesh. She feels them in the places that the blanket doesn't cover: her eyes, her nostrils; climbing into her ear canals. She's needed to go to the toilet for hours now but is holding it, too scared to unwrap herself from her cocoon. She's thirsty but she doesn't want to drink the water because it will make her need to go more. She eats the biscuits instead. She hasn't moved for hours and all her joints ache.

She assumes, because she is alive, because she has been left with food and water and light and a blanket, that she is to be rescued, that she is down here temporarily. But she can't be sure. The thought of being wrong, the thought that she might die down here, is too much for her brain to process.

An hour goes by. Maybe longer. The need to go to the toilet has passed again. She imagines that her body has somehow absorbed the contents of her bladder, like a sponge. She braves sticking an arm out of the furry rug and lifts the candle up, lets the light it casts run down the tunnel, over the hump of Zach's body. There are lamps at intervals attached to the walls and she marvels briefly at the age of them, imagines them lit and guiding escapees toward safety. She wonders how far the tunnel goes. She wonders if there's an exit at the other end, an escape hatch. But in order to find out she'd have to take off the blanket and she does not want to take off the blanket. Because there are spiders.

A crack of light appears above Tallulah's head. She's been sitting on the steps, as close as possible to the opening in the room above, as far away as possible from the spiders on the tunnel floor and Zach's dead body. She doesn't know how long it's been. Long enough to burn through a second candle. To have finished the biscuits. To have finished the water. To have slept twice. She turns at the sound of the stone lid creaking open and peers up.

"Shh!"

It's Scarlett. It takes a few seconds for Tallulah's eyes to adjust enough to make out the slice of her face visible through the crack.

"Shh," she says again. Then she says, "Are you OK?"

Tallulah tries to talk but no words come. She shakes her head.

"Look," says Scarlett. "We're going to get you out of here. Just one more day, I think. Police everywhere still. But I'm pretty sure they're done with us. And then . . ."

"What about Noah?" she croaks.

"Noah's fine. I saw him. He's fine. Your mum's fine. Listen, Tallulah. It's going to be OK? Yes? Just hold on in there. And look what I got for you. It's a pecan Danish. Your favorite." She passes something wrapped in a kitchen towel through the gap and Tallulah takes it. "Do you need more water? Anything else?"

"I want to get out," she says, her voice still cracking, but growing stronger. "I want to get out now. I want to go home. I can't be down here, with Zach, with his . . . I just can't. And there's spiders. Please. Let me out. I can't . . . It's . . ."

She sees Scarlett put a finger to her mouth, her eyes track quickly back behind her. "Shh," she says again, before sliding the stone cover back into place.

And then it is dark again.

PART FIVE

61

**POLICE TRANSCRIPT OF INTERVIEW WITH
AMELIA BOO RHODES**
8 September 2018
Manton Police Station

In attendance:
DI Dominic McCoy
DCI Aisha Butt

DI McCoy: Amelia, or would you prefer Mimi?

Amelia Rhodes: Mimi. Please.

DM: OK, Mimi. Thank you for coming in, of your own volition.

AR: I've been wanting to say something for ages. For months. So long. But . . . I was too scared.

DM: Scared of what, Mimi?

AR: Scared of . . . It's hard. I don't know how to explain it. It's Scarlett. She's got this kind of . . . power?

DM: Can you explain a little what you mean by that?

AR: I just mean . . . I don't know. She just has this way of making you think that you'd be nothing without her. It's like, being with her is amazing and exciting, but there's always the threat that she would cut you out, just like that, if you displeased her. So you just never wanted to displease her.

DM: When did you first meet Scarlett Jacques?

AR: At Maypole House. When I was sixteen. We were both doing art A level. And textile design. So we were in a lot of the same lesson groups.

DM: And had you known her before that?

AR: [*doesn't reply*]

DM: Could you say yes or no, please? For the recording?

AR: No. I'd never met her before. But we hit it off, like, immediately. She was just, kind of, exciting to be around. Everyone wanted to be friends with her, and she chose me. And once Scarlett had chosen you, you were hers for life. Or that's what it felt like. I mean— all of us, me, Ruby, Jayden, Rocky—we all followed her to Manton. We could have gone to other colleges. Especially Jayden and Rocky—they were, like, geniuses, Jayden could have got into the Royal College and Rocky got a place at the London College of Fashion. They were so talented. But they went to Manton. Because that's where Scarlett went. It's kind of lame, really, when you think about it. When you look back on it. But she just had this way of making you feel as if your life would be meaningless without her. Not in anything she did. She never did anything bad. Just in the way she made you feel . . . I can't explain it. It's weird. Like she needed you. But also like you needed her more.

DM: And so, going back to the night of 16 June 2017. Please can you tell me, in your own words, exactly what happened?

AR: Erm, from, like, the pub?

DM: Yes. Start at the pub.

AR: It was a Friday. We all met up at the Swan & Ducks. In the village. Just a fun, normal night. The whole crew. Plus Scarlett's ex Liam. We all sat outside, had a few drinks. Then Scarlett went in to get a round and she didn't come back. So we went in to find her and she was sitting with them. With Tallulah and her boyfriend. Really weird atmosphere. Really tense.

DM: As far as you were aware, was there anything going on between Scarlett and Tallulah?

AR: Kind of. Yeah. We used to talk about it, their friendship. It seemed strange. Like, I don't want to sound horrible, but Tallulah just wasn't like . . . us. You know? She was very quiet, dressed very, like, ordinary. She was nice and everything, but I never really understood why Scarlett wanted to hang out with her. Then Ruby said she saw something, in the college grounds, the two of them holding hands when they thought no one was looking, and then after that we assumed that something was going on, or something had gone on. But she never told us and we never saw anything else. So, you know . . .

DM: And then, at the pub?

AR: Yes. So, we all ended up sitting with them and we all got quite drunk. Then Jayden, Rocky, and Roo all left; Roo's dad was coming to pick her up and Jayden and Rocky were lodging with Roo. So it was just us and Liam, and then Lexie came over too and she drove us over to Scar's house . . .

AR: [*pauses*]

DM: Carry on.

AR: Yeah. Sorry. So, erm . . . we went back to hers and we had beer and smoked some draw and played in the pool and then Zach and Tallulah went indoors and I went in a bit after, to go and charge my phone, and I could hear raised voices from the snug off the kitchen and I peered through a gap in the sliding door and I saw Zach kind of manhandling Tallulah. They were having a row. Zach was saying to Tallulah that he'd been going to ask her to marry him, I think. And then he threw the ring at her. I stopped watching then, backed away and then went to charge my phone, but there were no Android chargers in the kitchen and I had one in my bag upstairs in Scar's room, so I went up there to get it. It took me a while to find it. So then I came back down with the charger and I was still on the stairs . . . and I heard

AR: [*pauses*]

DM: Are you OK? Do you need a minute?

AR: No. It's OK. I heard Tallulah shouting, *What have you done?* And Scarlett saying something like, *You wanted this, you said you wanted him to disappear.* And I nearly went into the kitchen. But I didn't. I don't know why. But it was like—it was *Scarlett*. Something bad had happened and I was scared for Scarlett to know that I'd seen it. I was scared of Scarlett. You know? So I ran back up the stairs and was going to grab my clothes and my overnight bag and run. But then I heard her coming up the stairs so I flung myself under the covers on her bed and pretended to be asleep. I lay there like that for hours. I kept expecting to hear sirens or something, or for Scarlett to come up and tell me what was going on. I kept expecting something to happen. But it just didn't. It was silent. Like nothing had ever happened. I saw the sun come up, and then, at about six o'clock, I shoved all my stuff in my bag and came downstairs. I went into the kitchen. It was empty. I looked in the snug and Scarlett was out cold on the sofa in there. I tried to wake her, but it was like she was unconscious. I shook her so hard and she didn't wake up. And then I saw this little black box. It was a ring. On the floor. It was the one Zach had thrown at Tallulah. And I picked it up and shoved it in my bag. I don't know why. I just thought

AR: [*pauses*]

DM: It's OK. Carry on.

AR: I know I shouldn't have. But I wanted to protect Scarlett from whatever it was she'd done the night before. And I knew the ring was evidence—of something. Of some kind. I . . . I'm really, really sorry. I should have handed it to the police. I should have told them what I heard her saying in the kitchen. I know I should. It's so bad that I didn't. I know that. I really do know that.

DM: So what happened after you picked up the ring?

AR: I left. I walked down the driveway and my mum picked me up from the gates and drove me home. And that was that.

DM: Did you hear from Scarlett again? After you left her house?

AR: Yeah. She called about lunchtime, said she'd just woken up, asked where I was. I told her I was at home. Then she called again a few minutes later and said that Tallulah's mum wanted to talk to me because Tallulah hadn't come home. She gave me her number and asked me to call her. And I . . . I didn't ask Scarlett the right question. I didn't ask any questions. I just said yes. She said, Are you OK? And I said I was just tired. And that was that. That was basically the only conversation Scar and me ever had about it. About any of it. I didn't talk to her again really after that. I went to London to live with my dad for the summer. And by the time I got back to Manton that September, Scarlett and her family were gone.

DM: So you didn't talk to Scarlett at all over the whole of that summer?

AR: No. Not once. She didn't call me. I didn't call her.

DM: And what about the rest of your friendship group?

AR: Yeah, I mean, we messaged and stuff, but never about that night. We never talked about that night. Which is kind of weird, when you think about it.

DM: So, Mimi, earlier you told us that you gave the ring to Lexie a few weeks ago. Could you tell us about that please?

AR: Yes. Sure. So . . . I had the ring all this time and I've wanted to do something about it since forever. I've wanted to come forward and tell someone what I heard. Or what I thought I heard. Because, you know, I'd been drinking that night. I'd been taking drugs. What I saw, what I heard, it was all so fleeting. Just a glimmer of a thing. But I just kept thinking that the police would find some kind of evidence of whatever the hell happened that night, or that Scarlett would come back or Tallulah would come back, or even that Zach would come back . . . like, maybe I'd imagined the whole thing. I just thought the whole thing would sort itself out without me having to do anything or get involved, but then months and months and months went by and nothing happened and then the girl's mum did that candlelit vigil for the year anniversary and still nobody knew anything and I saw her mum once, in Manton, pushing Tallulah's baby in a pram, and she looked so sad and so broken and I felt so bad. And I've been . . . I've been in hell. In actual hell. So last month I went to see Lexie and I finally told her what I saw through the door of the snug that night, Zach and Tallulah fighting, Zach throwing the ring box at her. And then I told her what I heard afterward, Tallulah shouting *what have you done.* And Scarlett shouting *but you said you wanted him to disappear.* And then Lexie told me

AR: [*pauses*]

DM: Take your time. It's OK.

AR: [*crying*]

AR: Lexie told me . . . she told me that she'd heard from Scarlett, that Scarlett was on a boat, with her mum and her brother. She said that Scarlett's mum was making them go on a round-the-world trip for a year and that she wanted complete anonymity. Something to do with the father. Apparently, he'd been violent. I don't know. It didn't sound right to me. I mean, the father was never even with them. And they were still missing. Zach and Tallulah. And there was just this huge gaping hole in everything. And so I gave Lexie the ring last month, just before she went to Florida, and she said, I'll sort this out. OK. I'll sort this out.

62

Tallulah awakes from a sleep so deep that she can remember nothing about it. She awakes and there is light shining through the skin of her eyelids. She awakes and she is on a soft surface. She awakes to the sound of a gentle panting and a kind of lip-smacking noise and she slowly opens her eyes and she sees Toby's face. He is staring at her placidly. He licks his lips again and then pants some more. As her eyes grow accustomed to the light, she sees she is in the snug in Scarlett's house. The door is open just a crack and she can hear voices beyond. Gentle laughter.

She tries to sit up but stops when she realizes that she is tied down somehow. She glances at her feet—they are tied together with a plastic cord. Her hands are tied at the wrists.

"Hello!" she calls out, her voice a croak.

She hears it go quiet in the kitchen.

"Hello!"

She hears footsteps across the stone floor in the kitchen and then there is Scarlett. She's wearing black joggers and an oversize Levi's T-shirt.

"Oh," she says. "You're awake. Mum!" she calls out behind her. "Tallulah's awake."

She walks toward her and sits perched on the edge of the sofa between Toby and Tallulah's head. She puts out a hand to her face and strokes her cheek. "How are you doing?" she says.

"What's happening? Why am I tied up?"

"To keep you safe," says Scarlett's mother, appearing in the doorway. She's clutching a black mug, dressed in a jade-green cotton dress, which ties at the waist. Her hair is pulled back hard from her face.

"Safe from what?"

Scarlett's mother sighs. "We need to get you away from here. The police have gone for now. But they'll be back. They think you and Zach have both disappeared, together, and that's how it needs to stay."

"But . . ." Tallulah feels a kind of thrum pass through her head and her vision go gray around the edges. "No," she says. "I have to go home. I have to see my baby."

"Tallulah," says Scarlett, "if you go home now, you will never see your baby again. Do you understand? If you go home now, the police will ask you a million questions about Zach and you will somehow have to explain what happened to him. And what would you say?"

"I'd say that he . . . I'd say . . ." She stops, tries to pull the threads of her thoughts together and feels them unravel again almost immediately. "I'd say he left."

"Yes. And that would be an obvious lie. Do you want to lie to the police?"

"Yes. No. I don't care. I just want to go home."

"No," says Scarlett's mum. "I'm afraid that's not an option. A terrible thing happened here on Friday night. A really terrible thing. And I know you only acted out of passion, out of fear. I understand that mother's instinct. But the fact of the matter is that Zach is dead. And you killed him."

"No. No, I didn't. I—" Tallulah's mind fusses for a while over the detail of that moment as it has done nonstop for the past however many days it's been. And each time she sees it differently. But every time she sees it, she feels it, in her bile, in her gut, in her very essence, the knowledge that it wasn't her, that she didn't do it.

But how can she prove that to anybody?

"I didn't kill him," she says. "I didn't do it."

"Well, the whole thing was rather confused. Nobody was sober. Nobody was in a clear state of mind. But your fingerprints are on the sculpture. And clearly you were the only one with the motive to have wanted him dead. So, I think, or at least let's assume, that you are the prime suspect and that the safest place for you to be right now is far, far away from here."

"But for how long?" Tallulah asks.

"Well, until the police have come up with another theory about Zach's disappearance, I suppose."

"But what if they never do?"

"They will. Of course they will. We just need to get you away from here. Just for a while. So, the car is ready, Rex is waiting at the airfield for us with Martin's plane, and we are all off to Guernsey. But, Tallulah, we need you to be ever so careful. OK? You are flying as Rex's girlfriend, Seraphina. You look enough alike. Just play the role, play the part. We'll have you back here before you know it."

63

POLICE TRANSCRIPT OF INTERVIEW WITH
LIAM JOHN BAILEY
8 September 2018
Manton Police Station

In attendance:
DI Dominic McCoy
DCI Aisha Butt

DI McCoy: Thank you, Liam, for agreeing to talk to us again. I realize you probably think there can't be anything left to talk about. But there's been a considerable development today. Very considerable. And we think it would be good just to go over a few details again.

Liam Bailey: OK.

DM: So, your relationship with Scarlett, that was over by the time of the pool party on 16 June 2017.

LB: Yes, we were just friends.

DM: But you have lived at the Jacques residence on occasion over the past few years?

LB: Yes. The last time I lived there was February last year, just for a few weeks.

DM: And that was the time you were meant to be going home, back to your family?

LB: Yes. I was meant to be doing an A-level retake that summer but I changed my mind, decided to drop it and go home. And that was when Scarlett asked me to come to see her. She was having a kind of nervous breakdown and she needed my support. I ended up living there with her. And shortly afterward Jacinta Croft, the previous head teacher, told me about a job going at the school and I thought, well, maybe it'd be good for me to stick around a bit longer, for Scarlett's sake. So I took the job and moved back to the school.

DM: And when did Scarlett give you the painting, Liam?

LB: Which painting?

DM: Well, there was the self-portrait, I believe?

LB: Yeah, she gave me that when I moved into my room at Maypole House.

DM: And then there was one of a spiral staircase?

LB: Yup. She gave me that around the same time. They were housewarming gifts.

DM: And what did you know about the painting of the staircase?

LB: Nothing. It was just her favorite part of the house. She loved the sense of history there.

DM: And this—for the recording, I am showing Liam Bailey a detail of the painting in question—this item here in the painting. Do you know what it is?

LB: That metal thing?

DM: Yes.

LB: It's a knife, isn't it? Or, like, a cake slice?

DM: So you've never seen it in real life? At the Jacques residence?

LB: No. Never.

DM: For the sake of the recording I am now showing Liam Bailey item number DP7694, the metal lever found buried in the flower bed at Maypole House. Liam, have you ever seen this object before?

LB: No.

DM: Do you have any idea what it might be used for?

LB: None whatsoever.

DM: Thank you, Liam, that'll be all for now.

64

The house in Guernsey is like the house in Surrey. Tasteful. Pale. Comfortable. Elegant. More interesting lumps of sculpted metal arranged around piles of magazines on more low tables. More bronze sculptures on Perspex pedestals. More abstract art. More oversize chandeliers and light fittings. The main difference is the views from the windows: water, ink blue mostly, sometimes pastel aqua, sometimes topped with frothy peaks, sometimes still and flat as marble. Tallulah's room has walls painted with tumbling cherry blossom and shell-pink curtains lined with thick padding, a dressing table with a stool upholstered in baby pink astrakhan. Her room has its own bathroom, with a large slab-like basin that has a wide brass tap out of which water falls in a wide sheet from a slot. It has a tear-shaped bath with another flat-mouthed brass tap positioned above it and a large walk-in shower with golden mosaic tiles and a rainforest shower head. She is brought soft towels and organic food and glasses of champagne and bottles of water with orchids printed on the fronts. From the window she can see that this house is not near any other houses. They are on a cliff. Miles and miles and miles from anywhere.

Scarlett brings her nice things: products to make her hair and her skin feel nice, a cheese platter, a soft toy. She brings Toby in for cuddle time. She brings in her phone and they watch funny videos together on TikTok. She keeps promising Tallulah that she will buy her her own phone, but she never does.

Scarlett tells her things from the outside world. The police are hunting for Tallulah, apparently. They have found Zach's body and they have found her fingerprints on the statue and they have a witness, Mimi, who saw her doing it. Scarlett tells her that her father, Martin Jacques, is putting together a team of legal experts to try to counter the evidence. He knows people, says Scarlett, powerful people, who can tamper with police evidence, who can accidentally lose things. "Just give him a few more weeks, Lules," says Scarlett. "A few more weeks and we'll be able to go home. Just let us look after you for now. Just let us keep you safe."

After a few weeks the news from home dries up and Tallulah tells Scarlett that she doesn't care about the police, that she will face the music, go to court, go to prison, that she doesn't care anymore about whether she's guilty or not, she just wants to go home and see her baby. She tries to leave the house, and from nowhere, Joss and Rex appear and bundle her back to her room.

Tallulah has not left this room for days now, maybe longer. The edges of Tallulah's days feel ragged and unformed. Scarlett still comes and goes with food and drinks and treats but Tallulah no longer asks her about the outside world because she no longer cares, all she cares about is sleep. Scarlett holds her and tells her that she loves her and Tallulah squirms from her embrace, the way she once squirmed from Zach's. She has a foul taste in her mouth all the time. She can feel the roots of her hair wriggle and itch even though her hair is clean. She has scaly skin on her arms that she scratches at constantly. She sleeps most of the time, and when she's not sleeping, she's in a kind of netherworld where things happen but she forgets them almost immediately, her brain desperately trying to keep hold of the ends of them, drag them back, keep them, but it's always too late, they're always gone.

Sometimes she sees the cherry blossom on the walls twist and twirl.

In lucid moments, Tallulah replays the moments before the black square in her head that still obscures Zach's death, and she feels her own culpability in all of this. She had so many opportunities to do things differently. From the moment she had sex with Zach on New Year's Eve to the moment he landed facedown on Scarlett's kitchen floor, she had had opportunity after opportunity to do things differently, to make a good life for herself and for Noah, and she has blown each and every one of them.

And now she is here, in this pink room, with its cherry-blossom walls and its locked windows, and she knows that she is somehow being diminished, that the care she is being shown by Scarlett is warped and wrong, that Scarlett has been taught how to love by people who don't know how to love and that everything she thinks is good is actually bad, and Tallulah knows that she needs to keep just enough of herself floating across the top of the big black pool of weirdness, just enough to keep on breathing, just enough to bring her back to her mother and to her baby boy. Just enough.

65

SEPTEMBER 2018

**POLICE TRANSCRIPT OF INTERVIEW WITH
ALEXANDRA ROSE MULLIGAN**
8 September 2018
Manton Police Station

In attendance:
DI Dominic McCoy
DCI Aisha Butt

DI McCoy: Good afternoon, Lexie.

Lexie Mulligan: Good afternoon.

DM: So, we've just spoken with Mimi Rhodes and we're aware that Scarlett Jacques is currently, apparently, on a boat somewhere, with her mother.

LM: Yes. At least as far as I know. From what she's told me.

DM: And you were told to keep the details of this trip quiet because her mother was trying to escape from an abusive relationship with her husband?

LM: Yeah. That's what she told me. She gave me her secret Instagram account and I'd check in every now and then to see if she'd posted anything. But there was never much info. Never anything to show where they were. Just pictures of the sea, really, with little captions about her mood. And then, a few weeks ago, Mimi came over. She was really upset, really stressed. And she told me about what she heard at Scarlett's house, about Zach and Tallulah having a huge row, about Tallulah telling Zach she was in love with Scarlett and Zach losing the plot and throwing the ring at her.

DM: And what else did she tell you about that night?

LM: Nothing. Just that.

DM: She didn't tell you about what she heard through the kitchen door? What she heard Scarlett saying to Tallulah?

LM: [*pauses*]

LM: Well, yeah. Yes. She told me. Yes.

DM: And what did that make you think?

LM: It made me think that maybe Scarlett was involved somehow with what happened to those kids. To Zach and Tallulah. It made me think she was lying to me about them being on the boat to escape her father. And I know I should have brought the ring in to the police and told you what Mimi had told me. But I just . . . I had this big trip coming up to Florida, it was all booked and paid for and really complicated, five different hotels and all that, and I didn't want to risk getting involved in a police investigation and having to cancel it. I thought about giving the ring to my mum and asking her to bring it in after I'd gone. But I just thought it might have repercussions for her job? I didn't want to involve her; her job is her life, her world. But then I didn't want to wait until I got back, I wanted someone to work it all out without anyone ever having to tell anyone. And my mum had told me that the new head teacher's wife was a detective writer and I'm a big reader so I ordered one of her books, just out of curiosity, and there was this bit in it where someone hides a clue in a flower bed with a cardboard sign next to it saying "Dig Here." And I just thought, you know, that might work. So I took the ring the night before I flew to Florida, to bury it in the garden in the cottage, in a flower bed, like the clue had been buried in her book, but the back gate was padlocked, so I buried it just by the back gate, where I knew she would find it.

DM: And this boat, with Scarlett and her mother on it? Where is it exactly?

LM: I have no idea. But I can show you the photos on her Instagram. Maybe you can work it out from that?

DM: Yes. Please.

DM: For the recording, Lexie Mulligan is using her smartphone to locate the photographs.

LM: Here. This is the latest one. From a few days ago.

DM: For the recording, the photograph in question shows a foot against a cream vinyl surface, the prow of a boat or a yacht, a dog's paw.

DM: We need to get forensics to examine this account. Right now.

DM: So, Lexie. For the recording, I am showing Miss Mulligan item number DP7694, the metal lever found buried in the flower bed at Maypole House. Lexie, can you tell us what this object is?

LM: I have no idea.

DM: You've never seen this object before?

LM: No, never.

DM: Lexie, we've analyzed the second sign and compared it to a photograph of the first sign. They match exactly. It's the same handwriting. It seems unlikely, doesn't it, that two separate people with the same handwriting would have the idea to bury two objects in the school grounds within a few weeks of each other? So maybe you have a theory you might like to share with us about how this object ended up where it did?

LM: Honestly. I swear. It was definitely me who buried the ring. That was my handwriting; I made that sign. But the second one was nothing to do with me. I promise.

DM: Another thing that's bothering me, Lexie. You claim to have seen the sign in the flower bed from your mother's terrace. But there is no way that you would have been able to see the sign from, as you claimed at the time, the terrace of your apartment in the accommodation block. It's set far too low down the building. So would you please tell us how you really saw the sign that night, if, as you're telling us, you had nothing to do with placing it there?

LM: [*sighs*]

LM: I was in the garden.

DM: Near the flower bed?

LM: Yes. Near the flower bed.

DM: Planting the sign?

LM: No. Not planting the sign. I keep telling you. I did not put that sign there.

DM: So what were you doing in the garden?

LM: I was looking for someone.

DM: Who?

LM: Just one of the teachers. I saw her from the terrace and I came down to find her. And that's when I saw the sign.

DM: So why did you say that you'd seen it from the terrace? Why didn't you say you were in the garden at the time?

LM: I don't know. I didn't want to . . . I was protecting someone.

DM: Who?

LM: The teacher, she and I are . . . you know. We've been seeing each other. And she's married. So it's a bit . . . sensitive. I didn't want to bring her into it. It just seemed easier to pretend I hadn't been in the garden.

DM: Lexie. You should know that we found Zach Allister's body in a tunnel beneath the Jacques house this morning. And this lever was designed to open the secret tunnel where his body was found.

LM: [*audible intake of breath*].

DM: Tallulah Murray's mobile phone was also found in the tunnel.

LM: Oh my God.

DM: So, Lexie, really, if you know anything about this lever, if you have any idea how it ended up buried there, in the flower bed, so close to where you were meeting your friend, or if you saw anyone else in the vicinity of the flower bed, now would be the time to tell us.

LM: [*begins to cry*] I don't know. I swear. I didn't put that sign there. I don't know what that metal thing is and I don't know how it ended up being buried there. I don't know anything at all.

66

One day, Tallulah wakes up from another deep sleep, a sleep so deep it feels like death, the sleep she now knows is brought on by something from the well-stocked shelves of Scarlett's mother's bathroom cabinet, and she finds herself once again in a dark, silent space, all alone, the rhythm and roll of deep, cold water oscillating through her bones.

Through a circular window she sees the viscous cement wall of seawater. She feels her wrists bound. Her feet bound. And now she knows. She knows for sure that she is not being kept safe. That she is not being protected. She knows that everything Scarlett has told her about her father trying to corrupt the police investigation is lies and that this nightmare is about to come to the worst possible end. She knows that the only reason she is still alive is because Scarlett has made sure of it. But she also knows that Scarlett is losing control of her mother, losing control of the whole situation, and that now Tallulah is being taken to the farthest point from her own mother and her son and her home, to be dropped, dispatched, disappeared.

67

Kim sits in her back garden. She can't be indoors. Ryan is inside with Noah, distracting him.

It's nearly two o'clock. It's been four hours since they found the body in the tunnel in the Jacqueses' house. She stares at her phone, switches the screen on and off, checks and double-checks that she has a good connection, a good signal, that there is no impediment to a call from Dom.

And then there it is. The opening note of her ringtone. She swipes to reply before the second note has even begun. "Yes."

"Kim, listen. We think we've traced the current location of the Jacques family. We're working with Interpol on a maritime search. Because I didn't tell you before, but we found other things in the tunnel, Kim. We found the remains of a pastry that had been laced with large amounts of Zopiclone. We found some long dark hairs. We found empty water bottles, candles, a blanket as well as Tallulah's phone. And records from Manton airport show that the Jacqueses flew their private plane to Guernsey on June the thirtieth last year and on board were Jocelyn, Scarlett, and Rex Jacques. And Rex's girlfriend, Seraphina Goldberg. But Seraphina claims not to have flown to Guernsey at all that summer. So, Kim, we're looking at the possibility that the Jacques family may have taken Tallulah with them. And that they are now on board a boat, chartered by Jocelyn Jacques from Guernsey Yacht Club in late August. And that Tallulah may still be with them. Meanwhile, detectives in Guernsey are getting a warrant to enter the Jacques property there."

"OK," says Kim, managing her breathing. "OK. So, what do I do now?"

"Just sit tight, Kim. Just sit tight. We're moving everything as fast as we possibly can. The wheels are finally turning on this thing. At long bloody last. Just sit tight."

68

Days pass. The quality of the light that reaches through the ocean outside her window changes from gray to gold to white. It becomes warmer and warmer; at night an air-conditioning unit hums overhead. Scarlett comes and goes. She brings the dog with her sometimes and Tallulah curls around his neck and breathes in the salty scent of him.

"I'm doing things," says Scarlett. "I'm doing things, to get us home. To get you home. This will be over soon. This will be over soon."

Tallulah knows that every meal she eats, every drink she drinks, is laced with something that makes her sleep, but she doesn't care, she craves the sleep it brings, the sweet lull of it, the painlessness, the dreams. When Scarlett takes too long to bring her what she craves, she feels insane, torn into pieces, her gut sliced from side to side, her head shot through with shards of glass, and she snatches the drinks from Scarlett's hands, drinks them so fast she almost chokes.

And then one day, as she emerges from another dream made of lead, and forces her eyelids apart, she stares up at the honey-golden veneer of the wood above her head and she hears something she has not heard before. A steady, solid buzz, like an electric saw, like a man with a deep voice roaring, like a lorry revving its engine. It seems to circle her. She feels her eyes turning in circles, dry inside their sockets. She reaches for the water bottle that Scarlett always puts down for her at bedtime and takes a swig. The noise grows louder, more insistent. The boat starts to roil and rock; water slops over the neck of the bottle as she tries to screw the lid back into place. She hears something that sounds like a human voice, but strangely disembodied, as though it's shouting underwater.

"Scarlett!" she calls out, although she knows she cannot be heard down here in her little wood-lined casket. "Scarlett!"

She hears the painful metallic screech of the engine grinding to a halt. The boat falls silent and now she can hear what the voices outside are saying.

They're saying: *"This is the RAF. We are coming aboard your vessel. Please stand on the deck with your arms raised in the air."*

And then she hears the stamp of many feet overhead, the rush of voices, of shouting, the door to her cabin being kicked open, and there are men in navy, in hats, with guns, adrenaline-pumped bodies, like mannequins that cannot be real. And they come to her and she recoils and they say, "Are you Tallulah Murray?"

She nods.

———

Tallulah imagines that she will be able to walk after the police release her from her bindings. She imagines that the legs she hasn't used for days and days will somehow support her as she finally leaves this tiny wooden room. But they don't, of course. They buckle and flop like one of those little string-legged wooden puppets with a button at the base, and the policeman carries her in his arms.

"Where are we going?" she asks in a reedy voice.

"We're taking you to safety, Tallulah."

He has an accent. She doesn't know what it is.

"Where are we?" she asks.

"We're in the middle of the Atlantic Ocean."

"Am I going home?"

"Yes. Yes, you're going home. But first we need to get you to a hospital to be checked over. You're in a bad state."

On the deck of the boat, Tallulah sees the detritus of a meal. A bowl of salad, wineglasses, paper napkins being blown about in the violent wind of the helicopter blades. The idea that while she has been kept tied up in that tiny, dark wooden room, other people have been up here eating salad and drinking wine in the sunshine is unimaginable. She sees a huddle of people at the other side of the boat. It's Scarlett, Joss, and Rex. They turn and glance at her, then look away again quickly.

She sees another policeman approaching the Jacqueses, pushing their arms roughly behind their backs, clamping their wrists together with metal cuffs that glint in the bright sunlight. The dog sits at their feet, his thick fur being buffeted in every direction.

"What's going to happen to the dog?" she asks, suddenly overcome with concern that he might be left behind.

"He'll come too, don't worry about the dog."

She covers her eyes with her arm. The noise from the blades and the brightness of the sun are agonizing. "Where are we going?"

"Just relax, Tallulah. Just relax."

Soon she is being strapped into a hoist with the policeman who rescued her and then she is hovering over the gleaming white boat and she looks down and watches the Jacques family grow smaller and smaller in their huddle on the deck.

She sees Scarlett look up at her and mouth the words "I love you." But she knows that the person who once loved Scarlett Jacques has gone forever.

She closes her eyes and looks away.

69

As the plane comes to a standstill on the runway, Sophie clicks open the overhead locker and pulls down her small wheely case and her jacket. At the luggage carousel she is met by her Danish publisher, a woman her age with pale red hair held in a bun, wearing a long blue bouclé coat over a floral dress. They hug briefly—they have met twice before and even got drunk together last time Sophie was in Copenhagen and shared extraordinary intimacies including details of her publisher's extramarital affairs. But now a year on, it's like a fresh start; once again they are author and publisher, talent and manager, cordial, warm, but not friends.

Sophie is taken directly to a hotel with velvet chairs in sun-bleached colors and glass lifts that ascend and descend on metal poles, oversize cactus plants, and the Chainsmokers on the sound system. She opens up her suitcase on the footstool in her beautiful room and removes her toiletry bag, unzips it, and takes out her toothbrush and toothpaste.

In the bathroom she stares at her face as she brushes her teeth; she's been awake since 4:00 a.m., the alarm breaking into dark and worrying dreams. She's had two hours' sleep. She has the pallor of an early flight, but in twenty minutes she will be on her way to a conference at which she has a tight schedule of interviews and events detailed on a piece of paper handed to her by her publisher in a canvas gift bag that also includes energy bars, mineral water, and a copy of the Danish edition of her latest book.

Her phone buzzes in her bedroom and she wanders out of the bathroom and picks it up. It's a message from Kim.

They've found her, it says simply. *She's coming home.*

Sophie blinks. She sits heavily on the end of the bed and gasps, the phone clutched to her heart. Then she finds herself suddenly, dramatically, unexpectedly, weeping.

"Hello, Sophie. If I may?"

Sophie smiles encouragingly at the reader in the audience clutching the microphone that has just been passed to her by one of the team.

"Sophie. I am a big fan of your books. There have now been six of the books of the Little Hither Green Detective Agency. Do you have another one on the way? And if so, can you give us a clue about what to expect? And if not, what is next for P. J. Fox?"

At first she is wrong-footed by the question, but then she realizes exactly what to say. She smiles and lifts her own microphone to her mouth. "That is a very good question," she says. "And you know what, a few weeks ago I would have been able to give you a very straightforward answer to that question. A few weeks ago I was living in southeast London, very close to Hither Green, alone, in my nice little flat, which is not dissimilar to Susie Beets's flat, in fact. I had a boyfriend, a teacher, who I met through my job, just as Susie always meets her boyfriends. A few weeks ago I was, essentially, Susie Beets." The audience laughs. "And the funny thing is that I didn't even know it. Because two weeks ago I left London . . ." She pauses as she feels a rush of emotion pass through her. "I left London on a wing and a prayer and a sense of some invisible clock somewhere ticking away, to start a new life with my boyfriend in the countryside. I was to become the headmaster's wife in a very expensive boarding school in a picture-perfect English village." A murmur of laughter passes through the audience. "And I had no idea," she continues, "no idea at all how much this was going to change everything. Because I found myself not only stranded in the countryside, a million miles from my comfort zone, unable to get back into Susie, unable to write, but also in the middle of a real-life crime. Do you want me to tell you about it?"

A louder murmur passes through the audience. Sophie nods and recrosses her legs. She turns to her moderator and says, "Is it OK? Do we have time?" The moderator nods and says, "I am agog! Please take all the time you want."

"Well," says Sophie. "It all started on the first day, when I found a cardboard sign, nailed to a fence. It had the words 'Dig Here' scrawled on it."

She pauses and looks around the audience, waiting for someone to pick up on the significance of this. The girl who asked the question gets it first. "You mean," she says, "like in the first Hither Green book?"

"Yes," says Sophie. "Like in the first Hither Green book."

A gratifying ripple passes through the room, and Sophie carries on. "So I got a trowel," she says. "And I dug . . ."

As Sophie talks, she feels herself come together, as though she were a broken vase and now the pieces of her are being glued back into place. She knows that she cannot be in Upfield Common anymore. She knows that Shaun must leave Maypole House and get a job he loves. She knows that this was a mistake, for both of them, in so many ways, but that it was also fate, playing out in the most extraordinary way. The way it all happened, the steps in the dance. And now Tallulah Murray, found, alive. Sophie also knows that she does not want to write another Little Hither Green Detective Agency book after the one she's writing now, that it will be her last. That she needs to stop writing about herself and start writing about the wide world, not just one corner of it. That she is nearly thirty-five and it's time for her to move on.

With or without Shaun.

She gets to the end of the story and the woman in the audience says, "And so? What happens next? What will happen to the family? To the people who took her?"

Sophie says, "I guess I'll find out when I get home."

She rests her microphone on the table and smiles as the audience claps for her.

70

THE TIMES

14 September 2018

MISSING MOTHER FOUND CAPTIVE ON BOAT IN ATLANTIC

A young mother, Tallulah Murray, 20, who has been missing from home since attending a pool party with her boyfriend in June last year, has been found alive a hundred miles from land in the Atlantic on board a privately chartered yacht, where it is believed she was being held captive by Jocelyn Jacques, the 48-year-old wife of hedge-fund manager Martin Jacques, and her 23-year-old son, Rex Jacques, and 20-year-old daughter, Scarlett.

The family was traced after the remains of Murray's boyfriend, Zach Allister, were found in a tunnel that runs beneath the family's home in Upley Fold, near Manton in Surrey. It is believed that the boat was traced using identifying features from photographs posted by Scarlett Jacques onto an Instagram account. All three members of the Jacques family have been taken into custody, while Tallulah Murray is in a military hospital in Bermuda being treated for symptoms of severe dehydration and drug dependency.

Murray's family has been notified and it is believed she will be discharged later today from hospital and will be flown back to the UK immediately to be re-united with her family, including her two-year-old son, Noah.

No motive for either the killing of Zach Allister or for the abduction of Tallulah Murray has yet been provided.

71

Kim uses her expensive hair conditioner, the one that she has to scoop out of a pot with her fingertips. She smooths it down the length of her hair and she leaves it on for two minutes, as per the instructions, before rinsing it off.

Afterward she picks an outfit, leafing through clothes that she hasn't worn for months, clothes from another time that have looked so alien to her these past fifteen months: another woman's wardrobe of positive colors, optimistic prints. She pulls out a tea dress that buttons down the front. It's the same dress she wore at Tallulah's candlelight vigil on the anniversary of her disappearance. She teams it with a rose-pink cardigan and her army boots. She blow-dries her hair into a shiny sheet and she paints liquid wings onto her eyelids.

It's still five hours until Tallulah is flown into the army base. Five long hours. But five hours is nothing compared to the fifteen months she has lived without her.

Her ex is flying down. He'll be here any minute. Ryan is going to meet them there. Noah is at nursery, for the routine, for the normality, to give Kim this time to make herself ready. She'll collect him in a couple of hours.

"Mummy," he's been saying for days. "Mummy comin' home."

She wishes, in a selfish way, that it could just be her. Just her, on the tarmac, waiting with held breath, with flowers, with her heart pounding and her pulse racing, for those doors to open, for her girl to be there, on the steps, to take her in her arms. But she knows it can't be just her. She sits in the kitchen and waits for Jim to text that he's on his way.

––––––––

Megs. She cannot think of Megs. She cannot talk to Megs or see Megs or even say her name. She keeps expecting her to call or text or appear on her doorstep. But there's been no word from her. Kim feels the pain of Zach's death like a corset, tight around her gut; it stops her breathing sometimes when she thinks about it. That poor boy. Left down there. It was the girl. It was Scarlett. The mother had first told police that she had no idea where Zach was, that she and her children and Tallulah had just been enjoying an impromptu gap year together, "keeping a low profile." Kim had smashed her fist into her wall when Dom had relayed this nugget to her. When the police told Joss Jacques that they'd found Zach's body in a tunnel beneath her house she changed tack and told the police that actually it was Tallulah who'd killed Zach, that she'd hit him on the back of the head with a bronze statue and that they'd been trying to protect her. At first Scarlett had gone along with her mother's story, and for an endless day and a half Kim had felt nauseous at the prospect of her daughter spending the rest of her life in prison.

But then yesterday Scarlett had confessed, quite unexpectedly, quickly, as though the whole thing were a suit of armor that she wanted to rip off. She told police that Zach was a bully, that he'd controlled Tallulah, that he'd hurt her. She told them that she'd heard Zach threatening to take Tallulah's baby away, that she'd reacted instinctively to protect her, without aforethought. She told police that it was all because of her love for Tallulah. And Kim is sure that that is true and somewhere deep inside feels certain that she too would kill someone who threatened to take Noah away from Tallulah.

That is what she said happened. Who knows if it is true. And who knows what will become of Scarlett Jacques, this girl who has Kim's daughter's initials inked into her flesh. Kim doesn't know Scarlett Jacques. She has seen her only once, floating across a pool in a pink flamingo, dripping water in a black towel, answering questions about her missing daughter in a sulky, condescending tone. She doesn't know Scarlett Jacques. She doesn't need to know Scarlett Jacques. Kim cannot feel sorry for her or care about her fate, as young as she is, as much as Scarlett may claim to love her daughter. She simply cannot.

Tallulah was found to be in the grip of a profound opioid addiction when she was taken to hospital and Kim has been told that she will need to spend time in rehab to recover. She's been warned that Tallulah will not look like the fresh-faced girl she said goodbye to on that June night all those months and months ago. But she's also been told that Tallulah is desperate to get well and come home and be a mother to her son again.

And now they stand in a row on the gray tarmac. Kim, Ryan, Jim, Noah in his best shirt and trousers in Kim's arms. A warm wind whips around them and across them. It messes up Kim's shiny, flattened hair and she tucks it behind her ears repeatedly. A wheeled staircase is put into place below the door of the airplane. The door opens. A man appears, then another man. Kim sucks in her breath and breathes it out again into Noah's hair. She sucks in her stomach, tucks her hair behind her ear one last time, and then, there, with a huge brown dog standing at her side, is Tallulah.

Kim runs.

EPILOGUE

Liam takes off his sunglasses and puts them in the pocket of his shirt. He looks upward at the house where the sun shines blackly off the curtained windows, before crouching down to lift the edge of a large blue planter; a wood louse scuttles out of its hiding place. He grabs the object hidden there and takes it to the front door.

Inside, the house is cool and echoey. Everything is as the Jacqueses left it last summer, but there is the stillness, the held breath of an unlived-in home. He feels the echoes of the moments he has spent in this home: the ricochet of privileged laughter off the white walls, the anticipatory clank of a wine bottle being taken out of the fridge in the kitchen, the slap of the dog's heavy paws across stone flooring, the smell of Scarlett's perfume, the strange old-lady scent she always wears. It's all still here, but muted, dreamlike, a small ghost of a lost, enchanted world.

But there is also blood in the still air of the house: a heady, noxious undercurrent of death. As Liam passes from room to room, scenes flash through his head. Chilling memories of that night last year, at the end of January, when Scarlett had called him. The desperation in her voice.

"Boobs, I need you. Something's happened. Please come."

He left immediately, of course. He never wasted a beat when it came to Scarlett. She was his life force, his meaning. He was nothing before Scarlett and he would return to nothing after her. When she needed him, he came to life, like a marionette taken out of a box.

He found her on a lounger by the pool, her arms wrapped tight around her body, rocking gently.

"I think," she said, "I think I've been raped."

She wouldn't tell him who, when, how, where. Just that.

I think I've been raped.

Liam had felt his soft core go hard. Every element of his physical being had been primed to kill. With his bare hands if necessary.

He stayed that night, and the next and the next, waiting and waiting for Scarlett to tell him. His father called him constantly, demanding that he come back to the farm, that they needed him. But Scarlett needed him more, and nothing, not even the threat of familial excommunication, could make him leave her side. For weeks he stared at every man he crossed paths with, every student, every teacher, the man in the co-op, the vicar from the parish church. Who was it, he desperately needed to know, who did this to my girl? Which one of you dared hurt her, tried to break her. He lived those weeks inside a tightly furled paroxysm of violence, ready to burst.

In late February he took the job at Maypole House offered to him by Jacinta Croft and he moved into his room with its balcony and its views across the woods. And it was from there that he saw him, six weeks later: an old man from a distance, but on further inspection a forty-something man with a bald head.

Guy Croft, Jacinta's husband.

He'd moved away some time previously, amid talk of adultery, of them having split up. Once a familiar sight walking the grounds of the school with his Labrador, Guy Croft had not been seen for a while, but now he was back, walking from the rear of his cottage and into the woods with an urgency, almost an insanity, in his pace.

Liam immediately left his room and followed him through the woods. At the other side of the woods he saw him unlatch the back gate into the grounds of Dark Place, and then from a hiding place out of sight, he heard him talking to Scarlett.

"Let me in. Please, let me in. I've left her. OK? I've left her. For you."

"I didn't ask you to leave her. I told you. It's over."

"No. No. You said, you said you didn't want to be with a married man. Well, I'm not married anymore. OK? I'm free."

"Oh my God, Guy. Please, just fuck off."

"I'm not going anywhere, Scarlett. I've given up everything for you."

And then Liam saw Guy Croft lay his hands against Scarlett's shoulders, saw him push her, neither hard nor gently, but firmly, back into the house. "Everything," he said again. And then he took a step forward, his arms out again. Liam heard Scarlett say, "Get off me, Guy. Just fucking get your fucking hands off me."

Liam moved, fast enough to leave skid marks in the ground where he'd been standing, three, four, five bounds and into the door, his hands on Guy's arms, yanking him back, away from Scarlett, throwing him backward onto the ground, and then straddling him where he lay; then an awareness of his fist against the skin of Guy's head, his jaw, the rasp of his stubble against his knuckles, and then the hot stickiness of fresh blood, the slackness of flesh surrendering to trauma, the flop of a head no longer held proud by a neck, the realization that he was pounding away at something that held no resistance, like pounding at a pile of mince. And then, and only then, the awareness of a voice above his head, saying, *"Nonono, Liam, STOP,"* and hands against his clothing, tugging at the fabric of his shirt. A flock of swifts in a lazy formation passing through the cool blue of the sky overhead. His blood pumping through his ears. His breath hard in his chest. A dead body between his legs.

———

There was a time when Liam would have done anything Scarlett asked him to do. But that was before she abandoned him here, alone, estranged from his family, his plans in tatters because of all the sacrifices he'd made for her; before she left him without even saying goodbye.

Until a frantic phone call two days ago, over a terrible echoey line, Scarlett's voice in his ear for the first time in over a year.

"Boobs, the thing that happened at the pool party last summer, the thing. It was real. It happened and it was a bad thing. And Mimi knows about it and she's told Lex. Lex will tell Kerryanne. Kerryanne will tell Tallulah's mum. Everyone will know soon. I need you to sort it out. It's in the same place. The thing. The same place as the thing that you did. The lever is under the big blue pot by the front door. Please, Boobs. Get rid of both the things. Get rid of them. Completely. And then lock it and get rid of the lever. Take it into London or something, throw it in the Thames, put it in a bin, just get it away. Don't leave any trace of anything, Boobs. Please. I'm out here, in the middle of nowhere. Mum's losing the plot. She's gone mad and she's drugging me and I'm scared I'm going to die out here. I just want to come home. Please make it safe for me to come home. Please."

Now he wends his way through the kitchen, to the back hallway, and into the old wing of the house. He goes to the tiny anteroom outside the turret and pauses, just for a moment, before twisting the latch and entering. It is cold and dank in the turret. It does not feel like August. He pulls the ancient lever from his back pocket, the same one they used to open the tunnel that shocking day in April, and he prizes off the cover.

He steps over the body and then, using his phone as a flashlight, he walks down the tunnel for almost a mile, until it ends and there is no farther to go. Overhead a slab of stone in the ceiling lets in a trickle of gray light from whatever is above. He takes the bottle of petrol from his shoulder bag and he pours it over the shrunken form of Guy Croft's remains and then drops a match onto them. He watches the flames begin to lick around Guy Croft's crumbling bones and steps away when the heat starts to overwhelm him. As the flames subside he pokes at the ashes with the metal lever. He sees finger bones, still intact, a jawbone, large lumps of old rag and charred leather, and he pours another slug of petrol onto the pile, drops another match onto it.

He feels nothing for Guy Croft as he watches him turn to powder. All his feelings are held inside him like a fist and they are all for Scarlett. All of them. Scarlett, who uses people as mirrors, to better see herself. Scarlett, who picks people up and drops people as and when it suits her. Scarlett, who waited until Liam was over her, finally over her, ready to go home and get on with his life, before reeling him back in and using him again, as a comfort blanket, a lap to sit on, a person to see her as she wishes to be seen and not as what she really is. And what Scarlett Jacques really is, he now knows, is a vessel.

He'd allowed himself to be used by her as a plaything, a pet, no different from her precious dog. He'd even let her give him that terrible nickname—Boobs. He hated being called Boobs, but he'd let it happen. He'd allowed Scarlett and her hideous mother to use him as a handyman, a plumber, a chauffeur. He feels red-hot anger pass through him at the memory of Scarlett's mother passing him a spade and a plastic bag one hot summer's morning and asking him if he wouldn't mind clearing the dog's shit off the lawn because the gardener was off sick and it was starting to stink.

After he killed Guy Croft for her, they went to bed and had sex that was so raw and pure that he'd cried afterward.

"I love you, Boobs," she'd said, her body wrapped around his. "You know I'm going to love you forever, don't you?"

And then the doorbell had rung the next morning and she'd said, "Fuck, Boobs, quick, you have to go, you have to go now. It's Tallulah. She's early. Get dressed. Quickly!" And, being an obedient puppet, he'd done as she said, thrown on his clothes, and left. He'd killed a man for her and she'd thrown him out the next morning without even saying goodbye, then given herself over immediately and entirely to her pursuit of Tallulah. And now this. A year of radio silence and suddenly she needs him again.

Please, Boobs, please.

Angrily, he pokes again at the remains of Guy Croft. The lumps have burned down now to rubble and dust and he sweeps them with the small brush he'd brought down with him, onto sheets of tinfoil, which he wraps into warm parcels and puts into his shoulder bag. He will take them to the shady pond on the edge of the common when the sun has set tonight and empty them into the stagnant waters there for the ducks to pick over.

He passes the light of the phone across the floor of the tunnel, stooping to pick up what looks like a molar, which he slips quickly into his trouser pocket.

And then, as he turns to leave, he hears what sound like footsteps overhead, and then voices, thin, muted through the gap around the stone slab in the ceiling.

"So, what do you think, Sophie? Can you imagine it? Coming to live here with me? Being the head teacher's wife?"

Then a woman's voice in reply. *"Yes, yes, I really can. I think it'll be an adventure."*

Liam turns and heads back down the tunnel. As he nears the exit he glances down at Zach Allister's body, the body Scarlett thinks he's going to get rid of for her, and he steps over it.

Then he climbs the stone steps back to Dark Place, pulls the slab over the hole, and slides the lever back into his pocket, the lever that he won't be throwing in the Thames for Scarlett or disposing of in a far-flung bin, the lever he'll be keeping safe in his home until he decides exactly what he's going to do with it.

ACKNOWLEDGMENTS

This was my "lockdown novel." All annually published writers will have one of these in their list now. I started writing it in February 2020. I then got sidetracked by other things (signing six and a half thousand tip-in pages for the US being one of them!) and put it to one side for a while. By the time I came back to it, lockdown had started, I'd had COVID, and my children were at home all day. I typically write my books either at my kitchen table or in a coffee shop. Suddenly coffee shops were shut and my kitchen table was covered in my elder daughter's college work. The kitchen itself was used by my family as some kind of informal staff room, a place to hang out and take a breather from work and learning. Complex meals were prepared and cooked here at all hours of the day. People seemed to be milling about constantly and there were no coffee shops to escape to, and for eight long weeks I mooched about disconsolately saying that I COULD NOT WRITE. Not only were there people all over my work space but my book was set in 2018 and I couldn't get my head around the concept of writing about a world before COVID, a world of naive people going to pubs, sending their kids to school, and hugging one another. I spoke to my editor at intervals over this period and each time she would say, "Are you writing?" and each time I would explain that no, I wasn't, I couldn't, it was impossible, of course not. The first few times she was understanding, sympathetic. The fifth time she said, "You know you really do have to write this book, don't you?"

So thank you, Selina, for breaking me out of my paralysis and forcing me into problem-solving mode. This book was written in a rented writing space across the road from my house. My lockdown office. My godsend. Thank you so much, Lockdown Office, and thank you to Victoria and Rebecca at Swiss Quarters, who made me feel so welcome during my time renting the unit.

On a professional level, 2020 was an exceptional year for me. I hit the number one spot in both the *New York Times* bestseller and *Sunday Times* bestseller lists, I sold more than half a million copies of *The Family Upstairs* in the UK and more than a million copies of *Then She Was Gone* in the US. Whilst hunkered down in my tiny, shrunken lockdown world, it was joyful to think of so many new readers coming to my books, exploring my backlist, finding an escape from the scariness of the real world. So thank you to everyone who bought one of my books last year and welcome to all my new readers who have come back for more. I am so grateful to you all.

Thank you to booksellers across the globe who somehow found ways to keep selling books to people who wanted to read them; Jiffy bags must have experienced a sales boom over the past year! And thank you to librarians who also found ingenious ways to keep their lending programs going. Booksellers and librarians also kept up incredibly fast-moving and well-organized programs of events for writers and readers during COVID restrictions, so thank you to everyone who hosted me last year, from the comfort of my bedroom.

Thank you to amazing Jonny Geller, my agent at amazing Curtis Brown in the UK, and amazing Deborah Schneider, my agent at amazing Gelfman Schneider in the US. You have both been magnificent in maintaining incredibly high standards of service during such a challenging year.

Thank you to all my publishers, all over the world, with especial thanks to Selina and Najma and everyone at Cornerstone in the UK and to Lindsay Sagnette and Ariele Fredman and everyone at Atria in the US.

Thank you to my spectacular writer pals who have kept me sane on various social media platforms this year: Jenny Colgan, Maddy Wickham, Jojo Moyes, Amanda Jennings, Tammy Cohen, Serena Mackesy, Chris Manby, Tamsin Grey, Adele Parks, and a ton more.

And lastly, thank you to my family for being, on the whole, pretty decent company in a year when being decent company was about the most important thing to be.

Here's to the end of a weird footnote in history and to normal business soon being resumed. Bring on the coffee shops!